INFINITE DEVOTION

The Second Book of the Infinite Series

L.E. Waters

Rock Castle Publishing

Copyright © 2012 by L.E. Waters, 2012

Cover Art by Digital Donna

Layout and typesetting by Guido Henkel

ISBN: 978-0-983911-12-8

Printed in U.S.A.

*The heart can think of no devotion
Greater than being shore to ocean -
Holding the curve of one position,
Counting an endless repetition.*

~Robert Frost

I dedicate this book to the shores of my life

Foreword

I researched the time periods portrayed in my books and pulled many of my ideas from historic events. When I involve historical people in my books, I try to portray them accurately but take fictional liberty with conversations, timelines, and mysteries—filling in the details absent from written record. The reader must remember that this is, first and foremost, historical fantasy fiction. I maintained a sense of magical realism throughout and hope the reader will take such leaps of imagination with me, assured that there is fundamental support underneath this novel but keeping an open mind to enjoy the story envisioned.

If there are any doubts as to the accuracy or plausibility of story lines, please visit my website, www.infiniteseries.net, where I dedicated a whole section to a bibliography and more detailed research behind this fictional piece just for those who might enjoy reading further about these cultures, events, and people.

In regards to the spiritual/religious aspect of this book, it is not meant to come across as non-fiction. This is how I perceived heaven to be in an artistic sense and hope there are readers out there who will consider it enough for the simple enjoyment of storytelling.

If at any time, you should find yourself confused with so many intricate character histories, I have provided a helpful chart that tracks each character's traits and progression at the end of each life. It is there to use at any point to enhance the reader's experience. I would love to take this moment to thank you for reading this novel, and if you could take a moment to review my book where you purchased it, I would be extremely appreciative. Reviews are essential to independent authors like me and even one or two comments can do wonders for my series' exposure.

Fifth Life
The Pope's Pawn

Chapter 1

Pulling aside the burgundy velvet curtains, I peer down among the thick crowd surging below. The heavy August air creeps in through the open window, providing no relief for us inside. The Vatican square is in all its glory below, despite the heat, and I watch for the procession to come around under our balcony of the Palazzo Santa Maria.

"Lucrezia! Lucrezia! Over here! Your father is coming down this way!"

I fly to Adriana's side and stretch out over the railing to see his tall, massive form standing out among all others, with his hooked nose and full mouth beneath the heavy papal crown—his jeweled hand waving to his people.

"All of Italy has come to see your father elected!" Giulia squeals.

"There—the Borgia symbol!" Adriana points at the fountain.

A magnificent fountain, specially made for today, of a giant and powerful bull with one stream from its forehead that flows with red wine. Even though I'm sad to leave our happy place in Spain, I feel great things are going to come of our move to Rome.

The door to our chamber is thrown open, and my older brothers Cesare and Juan run to me.

"Lucrezia! You're here!" Juan shouts as he reaches me first.

Cesare practically pulls him off, trying to give me his hug next. The music starts up behind us, and Adriana opens the balcony doors wide to let the charming melody in. Juan pushes Cesare aside, takes me in his arms, and we giggle as we practice our courtly dances around the expansive tapestry-covered room. Cesare grabs Guilia up and follows us around the room. It's so nice to be together again, since I haven't seen them in months. Juan turns to Cesare, tapping his shoulder to cut in, and even though Juan doesn't want to yield, I let go and take Cesare's hands.

As we dance off, I have a hard time figuring out which brother is more handsome. Both are tall and well built, but Juan has a finer and more delicate face—Juan the poet. Cesare has more powerful facial features, high cheekbones, and a large but perfectly straight nose—Cesare the warrior. Peering into Juan's indigo eyes is like falling into a deep pool, and Cesare's amber eyes are the fire that warms you after. With only one year between them and both on the verge of manhood, it's hard to say whose look is more intriguing.

Out of breath, Juan decides to stop and falls down into a gold brocade chair near the fireplace. "Lucrezia and Giulia, how lovely you both are," Juan says with a sweet smile between catching his breath.

Giulia and I look at each other and blush. Little did they know we'd been standing in front of our dressing mirrors all day primping and trying on all of our dresses for the momentous occasion. I've stayed with the beautiful and good-natured Guilia the last few months, but I have everything I love dearest to me now in one place: Adriana, who is like a mother to me; Guilia the sister I never had; my exciting brothers; and most important of all, my father.

Shortly after the private door that leads directly to St. Peter's opens, my father's procession spills into the room. My father, still wearing the papal crown and gown, holds his arms out to me and embraces me tightly. He also looks to Giulia and gives her an equally warm hug.

He reaches to give Adriana a kiss. "Cousin, so nice to see you've arrived well."

She bows to him instead. "His Holiness, Alexander the Sixth, was very generous with our more than adequate quarters."

He smiles proudly at hearing his newly appointed name being said out loud. When she comes up, he still gives her the kiss he intended.

"Come with me to dine tonight. I want Giulia and Lucrezia at my side." He turns and looks us both up and down, hesitating a little longer on Guilia's fine form. "I have two angels dining with me tonight." He guides us both through the door into St. Peter's.

I'm seated in the huge and lavishly decorated dining room. My attention is drawn to the glistening of all the silver and gold pieces strategically placed around the long table. Besides our family all on one side, there are cardinals and noblemen dining with us.

During our first course, Father turns to me. "Lucrezia, given our new circumstances from my election, I feel it would be in our best interest to cancel yet another of your betrothals."

I'm relieved, hoping it will at least delay a few more months.

Cesare explains to me, "Now that we're here, it's more advantageous to choose someone who can be of more use to us in Rome."

"Giovanni Sforza, Lord of Pesaro," Father says more for Cesare to hear than me.

Cesare scoffs loudly. "Sforza? He's a minor prince. I'm sure you can find a greater alliance now from your new position."

"I think he'll be much help to us with his ties to Milan." Father pauses to chew and dabs his mouth with his napkin. "I may be pope, but we've still far to go."

Cesare nods, considering this. "What is the dowry?"

"Thirty-one thousand ducats. I talked Sforza down from fifty thousand." He smiles in delight and stuffs his mouth full. He rests one elbow on the table, and his silk sleeve slides down his arm, exposing a childhood scar running from his wrist to his elbow.

"Lucrezia, he will suit you well. Though he's already a widower, I hear he's quite handsome."

"I care not what he looks like, Father. I could marry a chair if it's most helpful for our family position." They nod happily. "That and the agreement that I'll have a year in Rome before I have to go live with him."

Twelve is a very early age to marry, and Father promised that he'll require me to stay in the Vatican one more year before the marriage is consummated.

"A Borgia through and through, always negotiating, just like I taught you." He smiles with his slate-blue eyes squinting.

Pushing away from his empty plate, Father points at me and says, "Lucrezia, get your brothers to dance with you and Giulia. It'll please me to see you all dance, but my Lucrezia dances on air."

After many dances and a rich dessert, Father takes us back through our private door. As he closes the door behind him, he pats it. Thick gold rings clank against the hard wood. "I had this put in so I can come and visit my most precious girls anytime, day"—and then he looks at Guilia—"and night."

Knowing my place, I give him another kiss and say, "Goodnight." Walking to my room, I hear Giulia scream in delight as they spin into her abode together and shut the door. I've grown accustomed to my father's lusty behavior and know Giulia is much adored by him. It's the reason he allows Giulia to come live with me, and I'm just as happy to have a good friend. I shut my door and try not to think on it any longer.

Chapter 2

"Lucrezia, you'll not believe it." Juan smiles and runs for the carriage I'm waiting in, basking in June sunshine. He's opulently dressed in gold cloth with embroidered pearls and a large chain of balas rubies and pearls around his neck. Juan always liked to indulge in luxuries of status.

"What is the delay?" I sent a few of my attendants inside St. Peter's to see what is holding up my entry into the church. My maids are busy fanning me with feathered fans to keep me from sweating.

"Procida, your last betrothed, came to Rome this morning upon hearing of your wedding to claim you as his bride. He made a huge stir inside the Vatican, saying that the King of Spain arranged the marriage, and he was promised."

"How is Father handling the situation?" I ask as I reach out to touch his alluring chain of jewels.

"Do you like it? It's worth one hundred fifty thousand ducats." He smiles with one side of his mouth and one eyebrow raised.

I gasp jealously but continue, "And Father?"

"He and Cesare are meeting with him as we speak. They're going to have to pay him a condotta so he'll leave."

"Can I go inside, then?"

"No, Father doesn't want Procida to see you like this because he might rather turn down the condotta." He laughs and points, as the attendants are coming back, waving me in. "Looks like Procida has given up on you after all."

He puts his arm out to help me down as my maids help lift the hems of my silk gown and robe off the ground. I'm ushered into a side room and wait yet again. I ask for a mirror and check that the golden brocade gown is free from dirt and wrinkles. I point for the maids to fix the jeweled headpiece and make sure it's straight.

Cesare enters and whistles. "Breathtaking in every way, dear sister. Sforza will fight to take you home tonight."

"What is the delay now? I saw the whole court was filled with guests!"

"You can't imagine. Sforza, your soon-to-be fool of a husband, is trying to delay the wedding. His astrologer has given him bad tiding to this day, and Sforza wanted to wait until tomorrow, since it would be happier among the stars." He takes his velvet hat off to fix his thick brown hair. "The pope is not pleased."

Cesare, although dressed handsomely in a red velvet jacket and gold chain, is much more subdued than the extravagant Juan.

Just as he says this, Guilia comes running. "It's time! Lucrezia, follow me."

Guilia, with her hazel eyes and long reddish hair down to her feet, dressed in my colors of mulberry and gold, leads me out and down the court where I see Giovanni Sforza waiting with my father and a few other cardinals. The room's filled with the smiling faces of Roman barons, bishops, and noble men and women. As I draw near, I see Sforza for the first time, and I'm slightly taken aback with how much older he looks. I immediately feel nervous in his presence but try to focus on the task ahead. He has thick brown hair, a full beard, and brown, slightly beady eyes. He is fashionably dressed in a long, Turkish-style robe of gold, adorned with the Gonzaga gold chain. Handsome enough.

We're asked to kneel at Father's feet, and he holds a naked sword above our bowed heads and pronounces us married.

Chapter 3

"The year went fast," I say to Guilia as I wipe away my tears. I'm packing the trousseau that Father bought.

"Oh, you shouldn't be crying with all these beautiful things to wear." Guilia picks up a purple velvet dress with gold threading.

"I wish you could come with me."

She picks up her handkerchief and dabs her eyes. "Your father wants me to stay in Rome," is all she has to say, and I know he'll never let her out of his sight. People in Rome are calling her Christ's Bride. My father makes no attempt to hide their relationship.

"I understand." And I did.

She nods sadly in agreement and then points to the most expensive dress my father purchased that is hanging on the door. "I've never seen a dress so rich!"

"It cost Father fifteen thousand ducats!"

She walks over and runs her hands down the embroidered pearls and jewels like it's an exotic animal. "I would go anywhere if I had a dress like this to go in."

Maybe she's right; maybe I should think myself blessed to have the things I have.

"I'll miss you and my family terribly."

"Well, at least Juan has already left for Granada, so it's only your father and Cesare to miss, and Cesare's in a terrible mood since your father gave Juan the dukedom over him."

Cesare has been reclusive and fuming for the last few months. Being the oldest, it is a slap in the face to be so overlooked.

"Guilia, so nice to see you noticed." Cesare snuck into the room behind her, and she looks worried. He picks up a cap off the gilded chair and sits.

"She was just trying to make me feel less distraught at leaving."

Guilia nods, embarrassed.

"It's fine." He doesn't seem convinced. "If I had been made Duke of Gandia, I certainly wouldn't have demanded such extravagant outfitting. Do you know the master goldsmith is still making his jewelry for the wedding, and it happened months ago?"

He's been talking like this since the dukedom was announced. I try to take his mind off Juan yet again.

"Tell me again about Giovanni Sforza." I say with a snide smile.

He lights up. "Oh, you're in for a thrill. Father has married you to one of the drabbest men I've ever met. Not only does he walk in like a shaking, nervous mouse, but he stands in front of you with nothing to say. He nods drolly at every word while his eyes are darting about the room looking for ghosts."

Even though he's described him so many times, we all still have a laugh.

"He came to court last week to speak with Father, and I'm convinced he's a spy for Milan. A poor spy, at that, but a spy nonetheless."

"Strange how Father married me because of Sforza's ties to Milan, and now he's at odds with them. It's only benefitting Sforza now."

Cesare smiles at this. "You're the only lady I know that can understand such things. Paring it right down to the bone."

Father comes in, and we stand up to bow at his entrance, but he gestures for us to sit as he always does. He comes and hugs me at once.

"I wish I could dissolve this useless marriage so you wouldn't have to leave." He smiles, and his eyes roll back as he remembers something. "Do you know what he wrote to me last week?" I know he's going to continue, even if we'd already known. "After hearing about my agreement with the King of Naples, enemy of the state of Milan, Giovanni asked me which he should stay devoted to: our contractual agreement or his illustrious state of Milan!" He's getting louder and laughing through his story. "I answered plainly, 'our agreement.'" He keeps laughing.

Cesare speaks. "Sforza's a total waste of Lucrezia's talents, with no political advantages."

"Yes, I know. It was a mistake," he says as he takes my shoulders and looks in my eyes. "I'll figure something out. A way to dissolve it without risking our future."

I know he will, and it makes it easier to leave knowing it won't be long before I can come back. No matter how bad Sforza is, I know I can put up a good front. The servants come in for the last of my bags. I throw my cloak on, and Adrianna and Guilia kiss me good-bye in my room as Father and Cesare walk me down to the envoy waiting outside. Father fixes a tight smile that holds back his tears, and Cesare gives me a strong hug and walks away before I even get in my coach.

Chapter 4

I'm only changing households in Rome, but it's the first time I've been away from everyone. Giovanni greets me at the door to the much smaller and less decorated palace, but I remember it won't be long before Father can figure some way out.

"So wonderful to finally have you here, my wife." He takes my hand and kisses it in a fumbling way. Cesare's right, he does always seem to be waiting for someone to sneak up on him.

I curtsy with head bowed to him. "It's time to take my rightful place in my wedding bed."

I seem to catch him off guard with this forward comment, and he begins to stutter.

"R-right, r-right. In your r-rightful place." The thought seems to overwhelm him so greatly that he can look upon me no longer and tries to busy himself with directing the servants bringing my trousseau in. He points to the room upstairs that leads to my suite.

"My lord, can you bring me to our room so my ladies can refresh me from my trip?"

"Yes"—he trips over a suitcase on the floor and hops back up, red-faced—"I will take you there myself."

I keep from laughing but note it to describe to Cesare and Juan the next time I see them.

Dinner's satisfactory, and Giovanni and I eat at the large table alone. He doesn't speak to me, and whenever I look up from my plate, I see him chewing his food like a cow. Even when I don't look, I can still hear him eat. He pushes his chair away from the table, and even though I'm only halfway through my meal, I realize he wants me to follow him.

Adriana's told me much of what's expected of women on their wedding night, and since I've attended many of my father's parties—rich with Rome's finest courtesans—sex is not something that intimidates me. Giovanni sits back on his bed and watches me undress by the fire. Even though he's the widower, he's the one who's shaking. He fumbles at every occasion for me that night, just as he fumbled to kiss my hand. I lie there playing my part, hoping Father will think of something soon.

∞∞∞∞∞∞∞∞∞∞∞∞∞∞∞∞∞∞

Six months later, Cesare and Father arrive for dinner, as they have every few weeks since I've been here. Giovanni's been away on a campaign for months, and I happily have the place to myself.

Cesare begins at dinner. "This isn't simply a visit tonight, dear sister." He swallows. "We have word Giovanni's on his way back tonight, and we think it's a good opportunity to speak to him about your annulment."

My heart leaps at the idea.

"I think the only way we can annul your marriage is via"— my father inhales a burp but continues—"non-consummation."

I'm dumbfounded; my expression makes them both laugh.

Father turns to me with a sudden, serious face. "You didn't consummate the marriage, did you?"

"You didn't tell me not to..." By the way they breakout in laughter, I know they're joking.

"Lucrezia, after Cesare gets through terrorizing him, he'll agree to anything." They're laughing so hard, Cesare's holding his sides.

"Impotence!" Cesare blurts out. "We'll get him to declare impotency!"

As much as I want a better marriage, I feel somewhat sorry for what Giovanni has ahead of him. Even though he's boring and unimportant, my stomach twists as I imagine what I'm going to have to publicly lie about at my father's demand.

Giovanni walks in, already angry from hearing Cesare and my father are here upon his return. He looks even more nervous than usual and doesn't even take his coat off when he enters the dining room.

I go to him at once and kiss him on his cheek.

"So glad you are home and well." But he doesn't hear me.

Cesare gives a fake smile and remains seated. "Yes, brother, so glad you are well."

My father extends his hand, and Giovanni, after an awkward moment of hesitation, kisses his ring. Giovanni then sits down stiffly next to Father, who's seated in Giovanni's seat at the head of the table.

"Giovanni, I sense you're unnerved at our unexpected visit, and I want to put all your concerns to rest by coming out with my proposition." As Father says this, Cesare gets up and moves his chair to the other side of Giovanni. Giovanni tenses in his seat.

My father laces the fingers of both hands, pushes back his large form, and sends a serious look to Giovanni. "Your pope *requests* you sign an annulment—"

"I will never sign an annulment!" He jumps up from his chair, spilling his glass. "You signed a contract with me. Lucrezia's *my wife.*"

Cesare and Father only become calmer with his outburst.

Cesare says, "Wouldn't you rather a wife that loves you?"

Giovanni looks at me. "I love her, and even if it isn't reciprocated, we're husband and wife under God."

My father raises one eyebrow and narrows the other eye. "Will you risk your life for it?"

"Are you threatening me?"

"No, I'm informing you," he replies with a strange smile.

Giovanni glares at me. "You say nothing, Lucrezia?"

I glance down and shake my head.

"The devil's wearing the papal crown." Giovanni turns and walks back out of the house.

"That went well." Cesare starts laughing.

My father exhales loudly. "This might be harder than I thought."

Chapter 5

Giovanni flees, and under the pretenses I now know, an annulment is going to be carried out. I don't feel right staying in the Sforza palace and decide to go back to where I always go in times of difficulty: the convent of San Sisto in Rome where I was raised. The peace of San Sisto, with all its fragrant herb gardens, nuns' ethereal songs, and serene church bells, puts my soul at ease like no other place. Something here reminds me of the time I wished I belonged to—something so different than the pretentious court in which I now am forced to live—something of a world I'd left behind.

It's three days before my father's messenger appears as I'm embroidering by the window in my room. He's a handsome youth close to my age. His hat falls off as he kneels to me and tries to hand me the letter, but I push it away.

"His Holiness has sent me everywhere to find you," he says, trying to catch his breath. "You didn't request his permission."

"His Holiness should've known I would come here," I say without looking down.

"If I had a daughter as lovely as you, I wouldn't let her out of my sight either."

Softening with his flattery, I gaze down onto sparkling grey-blue eyes and a glowing smile that breaks my defenses.

"Will you read me the letter?"

"Perotto is at your service."

He breaks the seal, opens it up, and reads:

> *My most cherished daughter,*
> *I am greatly displeased you left without notifying me of your destination. It has caused me much grief to send my messengers out to find you. I know you are facing a difficult time but if you keep with our plan, both you and Cesare will be in better position. Sforza is protected in Pesaro, and we cannot bring him to court to sign the annulment. We need you to go to Rome to bring him where we can influence him. I promise this will all be over soon. Lucrezia, please return with the messenger.*

> *Your devoted father*

Perotto folds the letter back up and puts it inside his satchel. "Shall I tell your ladies to start to gather your things?"

"I'm going nowhere."

He looks surprised. "But His Holiness has forgiven you; there's no need to fear coming back to Rome."

"I don't fear the Holy Father. I'm staying because this is where I choose to be."

The thought of walking into those papal courts and making false accusations causes my palms to sweat. Perotto sits down on the footstool in front of me, removes some paper from his satchel, and licks his quill.

"What message does your beatitude wish to send back to my master?"

"Dearest father,
I am staying and becoming a nun. I cannot do what is required of me and have failed you and Cesare both. Please forgive me and let me be.

Your Daughter,
Lucrezia"

Perotto tucks my letter away and gets up to leave. "It'll be a great shame to hide that golden hair under a habit."

I say nothing as he leaves. He comes back with yet another letter from Father a week later. I'm happy he sends Perotto back. I've dressed up every day for the week, expecting him to return. As he walks in, he bows at my feet and reaches to kiss my hand. He does so, so softly and slowly that blood rushes to my cheeks.

He stands. "Would the lady like me to read again?"

I nod and sit on the footstool as he kneels in front of me, very close.

Beloved Daughter,
Your letter caused me such stress that I fell ill and needed a bloodletting to bring me back to health. If you love me, you will return at once. The convent is not your calling. We have many other things ahead for you, and the unpleasantness that lies ahead is only temporary. I have spoken with the mother superior, and she is not in my favor as she is allowing you to stay. I hope you will come to your senses and do what is right for your family.

Pope Alexander VI

Perotto puts the letter away and stares at me. "Do you wish to write him a response?"

"No, it would be the same reply."

I walk to the window, and he moves with me.

"Do you get lonely here?"

"I have my ladies and the nuns. I'm not alone."

He comes closer to me than I thought he would and touches my hair. "I have heard men talk about the pope's beautiful daughter. I always imagined you lovely, but seeing you, I greatly underestimated your power."

I look up in his eyes that are so close, my stomach drops at this unexpected intensity he creates.

He bends in, kisses me softly, but pulls away too soon. He picks up his satchel, nods to me with a smile, and leaves. Even though I don't care to hear from Father, I wait every day for Perotto to return.

Five long days later, my maid notifies me of a messenger approaching, and my heart speeds as I wait to see if he'll run to me, but everything in me falls as I see it's Cesare's messenger. Completely disappointed, I hunch my shoulders and demand, "Read, messenger."

The messenger bows and begins:

Loveliest, Reclusive Sister,

I feel I have not seen the sun in months since you have run away. It is not like you to be so weak and guilty, and I am worried all the Borgias are becoming soft. I have received news that Juan is behaving badly in his misappointed dukedom. There has been much talk that he's not only been ignoring his wife, failing to sire an heir, but has been going about Barcelona at night making repeated visits to the city's whores and gambling for large fortunes and losing. He has been disrespectful to many of the alliances, and I fear he is on a course to great dishonor and embarrassment for the Borgia name. I seem to be the only Borgia who is striving for something better than that to which we were born. The only Borgia who is helping Father achieve his empiricist vision for us. Please pull yourself together and see what is the right thing to do. Sforza will be fine, Father will allow him to keep his large dowry, and we will leave him alone after he releases you. Please write to me, or I shall have to visit.

Your loving brother,
Cesare

I give no reply. I know he'll come anyway. Nothing can keep Cesare away if he wants something. I worry about Juan, though, how he won't live up to the men Father and Cesare are, and I love him the more for that.

Cesare comes a week later. He glides into the chapel as I'm finishing my morning prayers and claps his hands. "Enough of this strangeness, sister! Come away with me now to go welcome our youngest brother and his new wife, Sancia, to court."

He gets my attention. "Jofre was married? He's only fourteen." I rise up from my prayer bench.

"Yes, while you've been praying with the nuns, our awkward brother has consummated his marriage with a much older beauty, Sancia, to Father's great pride. Even though he's not one of Father's favorites, it seems he's already faring better than Juan."

I know I'll have to go. There'll be great talk if I'm not there to welcome them both to court. Cesare can tell I relent; he unwinds the rosary from my hand, and claps for my ladies to come at once to prepare me for court.

∞∞∞∞∞∞∞∞∞∞∞∞∞∞∞∞∞∞∞∞∞∞∞

When we arrive at the Vatican, I turn to Cesare and say, "I'm only staying for the week."

Cesare smiles. "You'll have so much fun dancing with me, you'll take that back." He helps me out of the coach. Juan's waiting upon my entrance. He grabs me up in his strong arms and spins me around in circles.

"Where have you been?" he exclaims.

"San Sisto."

"I know that, but I've missed you so much!" He gives me another hug.

I see something different in his eyes—the gleam's disappeared.

"You better go get all that gold you had Father make. I want a handsome accessory on my arm tonight to match my dress."

He gives me a wink and runs off. Cesare looks on jealously.

Hearing of Sancia's beauty, I dress in my finest dress, the one worth fifteen thousand ducats. Once I'm adorned, I know nothing could be more beautiful than what I see in the mirror. Feeling confident, I go out to the approaching envoy and everyone in court lines up to welcome them. Trumpets ring out as they approach on decorated mules, Jofre in front, looking young and gawky with reddish-tinged thin hair. I see why my father doubts his paternity, since Jofre doesn't have any of the beauty of the Borgia's. He's dark in complexion and rather greasy, with a prominent scar over his left eye from a fencing match. I see no features that improve him.

Sancia catches my attention with her long, shiny, black hair and poised stance in her saddle. She's not so fine-featured, but her aura is very enticing and charming. Jofre looks like a poor messenger boy next to her regal air. I sympathize with her at once, with how she's forced into such an odd marriage for family betterment. Father's at the front of the welcoming line. Juan and Cesare stand beside me, behind Father. Sancia gracefully dismounts, and Jofre awkwardly takes her arm. She dwarfs him by two inches. Sancia curtsies to my father, kisses the ring on his right hand, and as her eyes come up to see Juan and Cesare, she blushes. Juan and Cesare both reach for her arm, and in her graceful way, she smiles and holds both hands up to be kissed by the charmed brothers.

She turns to me and gives me a beautiful white-toothed smile. "I can tell you're Lucrezia, since you're the most dazzling woman at court."

I like her immediately. "Second only to you, Sancia."

"Oh, and a graceful liar too." I see a slight scar on her forehead between large honey-brown eyes as she smiles easily.

That night, Juan, Cesare, Sancia, and I perform a bassa dance. Jofre sits quietly next to Father. During the dance, Juan is forced to leave Sancia and switch partners with me. Yet his head remains turned toward her even while displaying his light-footed prancing for me. Cesare now beams as he is finally allowed to perform for her.

Juan glances back to me as it is my turn to dance for him and he asks, "Whom do you think Sancia favors?"

"Jofre?" I say between hops, and we both laugh.

He waits for me to answer honestly.

"Either she favors both or neither," I say, watching her laugh as Cesare takes her hand high to lead her in a glide around the circle, "or she may treat every man this way."

He says nothing back. After taking me around the circle as well, he stirs the air with a sweeping bow and moves on to the next partner. Cesare comes to me, still watching, glancing over his shoulder to Sancia, sizing up her new partner.

"I feel like Sancia's leftovers." I smirk.

"You're never leftover, not in a dress such as this." He looks at my gown with charitable admiration. "But I do wonder who will be in her bed tonight."

After the dance is over, we sit down to our first course. Sancia's seated that night next to Father, who never fails to seat all beauty nearest to him, and I'm on her left. Juan and Cesare are positioned out of hearing, and I see them leaning to catch occasional glimpses of Sancia.

Sancia turns to me during the main course and says, "You have three very distinguished brothers."

I know she's being kind, including Jofre.

"Yes, and they seem very enraptured with you."

She sparkles at the confirmation she's been fishing for. I know then, since she doesn't ask more, that she fancies both. This is yet another competition between Juan and Cesare.

When dinner ends, both brothers lurch out of their seats to help her leave the table. Juan reaches for her hand first and leads her away to her sleeping quarters. Cesare, fuming, comes back to help me up and motions for his henchman, Don Michelotto. He says to him as he comes close, "Follow them, and watch their door. When he leaves, come and find me."

Michelotto fixes his steel-grey eyes upon the flirting pair and nods.

Cesare turns to me with a grin. "The main course always follows the appetizer."

∞∞∞∞∞∞∞∞∞∞∞∞∞∞∞∞∞∞∞∞∞∞∞

I decide to leave in the morning while Cesare and Juan sleep in from their long night. I go again to San Sisto without permission. I know the first day will be focused on Sancia and Jofre, but it will not be long before Father and Cesare begin grooming me for the annulment proceedings.

A week later, Perotto comes. My heart jumps into my throat, so I can barely breathe when I see his slight but tall frame and youthful, happy face. I run to him while he's trying to take off his satchel, and he smiles as he sees the effect his absence had on me. My maid, Pantasilea, comes in to announce the messenger, but seeing us, she quickly looks to the floor and leaves. We're both wrestling to free each other of our clothes. Perotto, getting impatient, lifts me onto my bed, pulls up my skirts, and climbs on top of me in a sea of down pillows.

He reads his letter to me an hour later and says, "You'll have to write back to him this time, and for my sake, ask a question so I can be back in a matter of days."

He kisses me on the forehead. I start dictating as he grabs for ink and paper.

> "Most Holy Father,
> I am sorry my attempt for solitude has caused you such pain. I have run to San Sisto to calm my nerves exacerbated by the difficulty of what you and Cesare want for me. I am feeling better every day but am not quite ready to leave yet. What can I do for you from the convent?
>
> Ever your obedient daughter,
> Lucrezia."

"How is that?"

"Perfect, he'll have me run here in the night to instruct you, I'm sure." He puts the letter away, and then gives me a kiss as he leaves.

∞∞∞∞∞∞∞∞∞∞∞∞∞∞∞∞∞∞∞∞∞∞∞

He's back the next day and almost every other day after for two months. We keep writing letters with questions and talk of returning to keep Perotto coming back as soon as he can. Today is different, though; he enters, but as I run to him, he gives me a serious and foreboding look that causes my eagerness to halt.

"I bring you bad news, Princess."

He takes the letter out of his bag and reads:

> Sweet Daughter,
> Though I am very glad you have come around to move forward in our situation, I have only sad news to speak about. Juan disappeared on June 14. He had been hav-

ing dinner at your mother's vineyard in the country with Cesare. Cesare has reported that Juan said that he must leave. Cesare, knowing it was not safe for a Borgia to travel alone in the midst of such enemies in Gandia, tried to accompany him, but Juan would not have it. Cesare noticed a cloaked man follow closely behind Juan's mule as Juan left heading toward the Ghetto.

Cesare waited for Juan by the bridge by the Piazza Judea, but he did not return. Cesare decided to wait until the morning, thinking that Juan might be out on another one of his brothel visits. When he wasn't found the next morning, the word got out, and the whole city has closed up and armed in fear of a vendetta.

Lucrezia, dear, please sit down now — Perotto, make her sit.

Perotto guides me from my frozen position to sit on the bed. He sits and continues reading next to me.

A week later, a timber dealer notified officials that he had seen two wary men emerge from an alley to the place where refuse is thrown into the river. The men signaled back into the alley and a rider on a white horse appeared, carrying a body across the saddle. The two individuals on foot took either side of the body and flung it into the river. They then all disappeared into the alley whence they came.

I sent everyone I could, bought every fishing boat and fishermen to search for the body thrown in that night. First, they found a body of an unknown, but then we found Juan. He was still as beautiful as he was alive, fully clothed and gloved, even with the nine stab wounds. I am going to seek such revenge on whoever did this and fling him into the river like filth. I have closed myself away in my room without food or drink for four

days. I need you now, precious daughter. You must come
home now to grieve for Juan.

Your Tortured Father,
Pope Alexander VI

I'm in tears by the end of the letter and feel numb to the news of Juan being fished from the river. I feel guilty I've stayed here so long and not seen him for months. Feel guilty that I've been so selfish and run away from my family.

"Pantasilea!" I call.

She comes running in.

"A terrible thing has happened to the Duke of Gandia. I must have my things packed and leave at once for the Vatican."

∞∞∞∞∞∞∞∞∞∞∞∞∞∞∞∞∞∞∞∞

I go into my father's suite and see him sitting in a chair, staring out the open door to his balcony. Cesare gets up upon my arrival and gives me a kiss.

"Good to see you, sister. It has been too long."

Taking his jeer in stride, I go to hug Father, who sobs in my embrace.

"Juan was such a brilliant boy. Always full of such vitality. He was the spark in a room. I had such plans for him."

Cesare seems uncomfortable at his remembrance and tries to change the subject. He clears his throat. "I know this is the work of the Orsini family. It's in retaliation for imprisoning Virginio Orsini. He died only a few months ago during his imprisonment. I've heard they blame the pope."

I study Cesare. He seems to be telling the truth, but that can be hard to tell with Cesare, since he's learned deception from my father. The whole way home, I'd a terrible feeling that Juan's death is Cesare's attempt to control Juan's behavior, have Sancia to himself, and claim the dukedom that he feels was always his. I truly hope it is the Orsini. To think Cesare's capable of something like this is unnerving.

My father raises a hand weakly. "You're probably right, Cesare. Only the Orsini could retaliate like this. As soon as I bury Juan, I'll show them what a mistake they made."

It's true; Juan looks as handsome in death as he had in life. Father makes sure he's wearing his pearl-and-gold brocade jacket with the Duke of Gandia gold-and-ruby chain. I kiss his cold and hardened cheek for the last time, and as I'm walking away from him, I feel lightheaded and fall. I awake minutes later inside one of the Vatican rooms, and the papal doctor is attending to me. I feel hot and queasy still. When the doctor finishes examining me, he comes over as he wipes his hands.

"You are with child, my dear."

I can't speak.

"You seem to be two months along."

I turn to my lady in waiting. "Please bring my father at once."

The doctor turns to leave, but I say, "No, good doctor, you must stay. My father will need to speak to you."

My father comes in looking worried at my fall. He sits on the bed next to me and pats my head. "You're stressed over Juan's passing. It has been too much for you to bear."

"Father, the doctor has found that I'm two months pregnant."

My father's lips tense together, and then he raises his head up to stare at the ceiling, then back down at me.

"Perotto's?"

He has done the math.

"Yes."

He looks up again at the ceiling, and I hold my breath.

"I should've known better than to send the handsome Spaniard," he says out loud to himself.

He turns back to me. "This means you must go to Giovanni at once, before you show, and bring him back here. Do everything you can to get him to sign. Time is now of the essence."

"I'll bring him back as soon as I'm well, Father."

"Then you'll go back to San Sisto until the baby's born. Doctor?" Father calls.

The doctor comes near.

"I've always paid you well, haven't I?"

The doctor nods, wondering what my father is going to say next.

"You've now witnessed delicate information, information that must never go beyond these walls. I have many friends, friends that will do my bidding when I so much as whisper. If you're a friend of mine, you'll do far better than if you are not."

The doctor goes pale. "Yes, Your Holiness, I am a friend."

Father turns back to me. "Come, dear, let's get you ready for Sforza."

∞∞∞∞∞∞∞∞∞∞∞∞∞∞∞∞∞∞∞∞∞∞

By the time I reach Pesaro, I'm so queasy from the bumpy roads I have to open the door and get sick. My maids hold my hair back and assist me into the house. Giovanni's rushed down and, seeing my poor color, pulls a chair up for me to sit.

I push the fretting hands away, saying, "Leave me, I'm fine now."

Giovanni brings me a glass of water, and I say, "So nice to see you again."

He answers, "It's always nice to see you."

There's silence for a few moments as I drink the cool water. I try to think of what to say next, but he begins, "I know why you've come, and I'm not going to go with you to sign those papers. It's a lie, and you know it."

"Giovanni, I'm at the mercy of the pope and my brother. I do as they tell me. I've hidden myself in San Sisto for months, and they'll never relent in this. I'm sorry I've been such a disappointment, but I cannot change their minds. Can you understand that?"

He looks at me, and I can see he's absorbed it. His posture softens slightly. "Cesare's been sending messengers daily. Becoming increasingly threatening if I do not obey. He's even had his allies send letters showing me how many are against me."

"I know how Cesare is, and that's one of the reasons I've little choice or say in my life."

He nods in empathy.

"Will you please come back to Rome with me and free yourself once and for all?" I reach for his hand. "I will never be free of them but you can be."

He grasps my fingers within his warm hand. "I'll go with you but not for my freedom, only to appease your abusers."

Chapter 6

The Cardinal College assembles three months later. Giovanni stands with a few of his advisors at one table, and Cesare, Father, and I stand at another.

"Giovanni Sforza, do you agree to this annulment based on accusations of impotency?"

Giovanni's sideswiped by this new twist.

"That is not correct, Your Excellencies." He turns to Father. "We agreed to non-consummation, Your Holiness."

Father speaks, not to Giovanni, but to the papal court. "My son-in-law is embarrassed at the pronouncement of his impotency, but it most certainly is the reason for annulment."

This sends Giovanni into a tantrum. "This is a trick! You promised it would be non-consummation, but you're doing this to blame this on me so that your Lucrezia goes on unscathed. I will not have it! I will not sign!"

"Is it true that you are impotent?" one of the cardinals asks.

Giovanni turns to me and says, "I know the lady well."

"Lucrezia, is that true?" the cardinal asks.

I stand up and say, "I am still a virgin, sirs."

Giovanni laughs out loud in a hysterical way.

Another cardinal asks my father, "Is there a doctor that can testify to this?"

The papal doctor is brought in and stands before the court.

"Doctor, you have examined the lady?"

"Yes, Your Excellency."

"Do you proclaim her to be untouched?"

"Intact, Your Excellency," he lies.

"Thank you, you may leave."

Giovanni pleads, "Your Excellency, my last wife died in *child-birth*. How do you explain that if I'm impotent?"

"Is that verified, Your Holiness?" the cardinal asks of my father.

"It is true she died in childbirth, but there has been rumor he paid for another to sire it."

Giovanni punches the desk and kicks a chair. "I will not have such lies spoken!"

My father stays calm. "It's simple, then. Let Giovanni prove to the courts by consummating with his wife before us all so he can restore his reputation."

The court is quiet.

Giovanni states, "I will never!"

Father pushes. "A potent man would jump at the chance to prove his virility."

"I do not want to have to prove myself in front of a papal legate. But you and Cesare would surely enjoy watching Lucrezia, I'm sure."

This catches my father off guard and infuriates him.

"What do you imply with that comment?" Father says through his grinding teeth.

"Nothing, except that I've had to share Lucrezia our whole marriage. You and Cesare fight for her charms as only a husband would."

The court is unsettled by this accusation, and Giovanni begins to enjoy the stir he causes. I don't feel sorry for deceiving him any longer.

"My cardinals, this is slander."

"And my impotency is not?'

The cardinal proclaims, "Giovanni, since you will not demonstrate your potency in front of the court and the lady proclaims her virginity, which a papal doctor confirms, I can only rule that the marriage is annulled due to impotency."

The cardinal gives two papers for a servant of the court to bring to each of us. My father signs mine. Giovanni shakes his head as he begrudgingly signs his.

Giovanni looks up and says, "I will say a prayer for your next husband."

Father puts his arm around my shoulder, and I try to walk to hide the large bump that is getting bigger with each day.

∞∞∞∞∞∞∞∞∞∞∞∞∞∞∞∞∞∞∞∞∞

I'm delivered back to San Sisto. I'm sure the rumors of our humiliating annulment are buzzing throughout Rome and elsewhere. I'm glad to be secluded away from it all. Father has reassigned Perotto so that he won't be delivering any more messages to me, and I grow fat and lonely in my convent suite.

I'm tied up to a tree in the middle of a cropless field with fabric stuffed in my mouth. I squint up in the sunlight to see something floating down. When it floats nearer, I see it's a sealed letter. It's beautiful and mesmerizing as it flutters this way and that. As soon as it hits the ground, a brown wolf pounces on it and shreds it in pieces. I pull at my restraints to stop the wolf, but I can't get free, and my screams won't be heard.

I wake up sweating, alone with my enormous belly on the chilly moonless night.

There's a commotion at the door of the convent below my room the next morning, and I open the window to see what it's about.

"He can't keep me from her!" I hear Perotto's voice.

Three nuns push him back out the door, but he spins around and runs back through the open door. He tears down the corridor, and Pantasilea tries to hold the door shut, but he flings the door open with such force that Pantasilea falls on her backside.

"Lucrezia!" He rushes to me and wraps his arms around me but feels the swollen belly and pulls away, eyes wide.

"Is this mine?"

I shake my head without making eye contact.

"You lie to me! It is mine! That explains why His Holiness forbade me to see you. It's why he has allowed you to return here." He sits back in the chair, absorbing it all.

I say nothing; I have to be very careful. I'm supposed to speak to no one but my most trusted maids. Pantasilea looks out the window, worrying that Perotto knows now.

"You must go back and say nothing, or your life will be in danger."

"Say nothing? We should be wed. I'll talk to your father and make him understand it's the right thing to do."

What a fool. He actually thinks my father will allow me to wed a messenger! I clumsily kneel at his feet and grab his hand.

"Perotto, you must hear me. Father is hiding me so no one knows of this birth. I'll still be declared a virgin, and you *must not* say anything to the contrary."

Perotto throws his head back in anger.

"No, Perotto, you must be quiet, or you will be silenced!" Panicked tears stream.

"What will happen to my child?"

"It'll be raised as Cesare's illegitimate child and inherit rich papal lands. I'll watch over the child and make sure it has everything it wants. Our child will not suffer in the slightest."

He looks me in the eyes and takes me in for a prolonged hug. As he pulls away, he says, "I'm your father's favorite messenger. I'll speak to him and see if some other arrangement can be reached."

I open my mouth to protest, and he puts his finger up to my lips. "Shhh, calm yourself, I fear not your father or Cesare."

He gives me a sweet kiss and strides courageously out the door.

∞∞∞∞∞∞∞∞∞∞∞∞∞∞∞∞∞∞∞∞∞

One week later, one of my lesser maids comes running in with news. "Mistress, Mistress!"

"What has happened?" Many fears run through my head.

"Pantasilea! Don Michelotto came last night and took her away, and she hasn't shown up for work this morning."

Perotto must have met with Father.

"Fetch my messenger; I need to see to her whereabouts."

My messenger returns the next day and reads:

> *Dearest Sister,*
>
> *I regret to inform you that your maidservant, Pantasilea, has been found but under unhappy circumstance. She and the messenger boy, Perotto, must have been having a lover's stroll on Saint Valentine's day and fell into the Tiber and drowned. It is sad such young love was extinguished, but now all is right with the world. Your virtue is safe, and you have nothing to fear as long as your loving brother is keeping out a watchful eye.*
>
> *Your protector,*
> *Cesare, Duke of Gandia*

Chapter 7

One month later, I give birth. I name him Giovanni Borgia, after Juan, but due to his dubious parentage, he becomes better known as the Roman Infant. Father comes immediately to collect us to the Vatican, and the baby is kept away from me and raised by wet nurses.

I'm not allowed to love anything.

Cesare bursts into my room. "Sister, stop moping and come with me at once."

"Where are you going?" I look up from my embroidery.

"I have arranged something that will lift your spirits." He pulls me up from my chair.

Cesare has brought me everywhere with him since I returned. I can't be sure if he needs my company or is keeping a watchful eye on me. He helps me walk up the spiral stone stairway to the top of the Vatican walls. Don Michelotto is standing there on the balcony, and he gives me a cold steel stare that makes me shiver.

"My crossbow," Cesare barks.

Don Michelotto immediately obeys. Cesare holds up his bow and tests the tension on the bow.

He calls out, "Release the prisoners!"

Michelotto leans forward on the stone wall, picking his teeth. Two doors open up in the courtyard below, and a dozen haggard, starved men are herded out on the grounds below.

Cesare screams out, "Run you fools!" and he shoots one in the center of his chest. Before he falls, the other prisoners, grasping the situation, go clamoring and clawing their way back to the doors that the guards are closing. Two loud thuds tell the prisoners there's no escape, and with Cesare's terrifying laugh ringing out from above, the prisoners run for any cover they can find. Nevertheless, Cesare's arrows penetrate the topiaries and hedges they cower under. Two quick prisoners run along the courtyard wall, trying to find an open door or way out. I close my eyes at the horror, and I'm truly terrified by Cesare's inhumanity. After two guttural screams, I know he must've found the last prisoners, and I open my eyes to catch one falling from halfway up the wall.

He hands the crossbow back to Don Michelotto. "I never seem to tire of this." He turns to me. "Sister, did you enjoy my little surprise?"

I don't respond.

He laughs, opening his mouth wide. "You need to stop being so sensitive." His amber eyes are rolling. "You're either going to be the deer or the wolf. I choose to be the wolf."

We walk down to breakfast with Father. I can't think of eating after what I've just witnessed in the courtyard, but Cesare's already shoving food into his bearded mouth. Father hasn't even acknowledged my approach since he's so deep in conversation.

"Jews are fleeing from Spain in great numbers. They're flooding Rome, Holy Father," a cardinal stresses.

"Let them come." He shrugs as he tears off a piece of bread.

"Let them come? We are the center of the Church, and you want it populated with Jews?"

"I see nothing wrong with harboring the Jews. It's not my right to persecute them. They will serve Rome well as a great source of revenue."

The cardinal pauses. "I'm no longer hungry, Your Holiness."

He bows his head and leaves the table.

Father shrugs and turns to Cesare. "These ideological imbeciles try to pretend the Vatican is not a business."

Noticing me, he smiles. "Oh, hello! It's good to see you up so early. Cesare's been cheering you up, I see."

I give a pretend smile.

"Well, my spirits are up this morning also. I've received a promising response from Alfonso II, the former King of Naples. He's curious as to what our dowry would be should he give his illegitimate son, Alfonso of Aragon, in marriage to Lucrezia."

I grow weary of their talks about potential suitors, but this perks Cesare's interest.

"Nephew of the present King of Naples?"

"Correct, one step closer to marrying Carlotta, Princess of Naples."

"We should raise an attractive dowry to entice him," Cesare says, as his eyes roll back in calculation.

Father asks, "Do you think we can raise one hundred thousand ducats?"

"That's what he's asking?"

"I'll be auctioning off the next cardinal position in a few weeks. That can generate quite a fortune."

"We can always have Don Michelotto discreetly free up another cardinal position for bidding."

My father's eyes twinkle with pride at Cesare's ambition. "I know just the one." He chuckles to himself while looking where the last cardinal just sat. "I'll send a messenger to Alfonso II at once with the generous offer."

He pats Cesare on the back with a heavy hand.

∞∞∞∞∞∞∞∞∞∞∞∞∞∞∞∞∞∞∞

A week later, news circulates that the cardinal who had excused himself from breakfast had suddenly gone into fits and died within minutes while dining in the Vatican. The rumor is it was poison.

Father notifies me that Alfonso II has accepted their offer, and they're negotiating the marriage arrangement. The only thing I'm looking forward to is that Sancia is Alfonso's sister and will be sharing court with me.

I feel foolish walking down the aisle again, pretending to be a virgin. It's the exact same ceremony except I have a different dress, gold to pale blue. I wear a fine skirt of silken camel hair with jeweled sleeves. A belt of pearls and rubies adorns my waist, matching a heavy necklace of tiny pearls and embroidered cap with a band of enameled gold on top of my long braid of golden hair.

Also, sadly, Juan's not here to make me laugh in his childish way. I see my father standing sternly at the end of the aisle, but Alfonso catches my eye and holds it. He's the most beautiful man I've ever seen. I must have smiled involuntarily at the sight of him. He's young, tall, and muscularly lean. He has the most dazzling green eyes I've ever seen and shining brown hair with copper highlights. His cheekbones are high and he has a small goatee. My heavy heart suddenly lightens.

When our eyes meet, he glances down, slightly smiling but trying to control a serious face. Once I reach him, we're told to kneel, and I try to glance up at him whenever I get occasion to. My heart is racing. He picks up my left hand and pauses as he sees the mole I've had since birth. He bends down and softly kisses it, causing goose bumps to flash across my body.

Can I be so lucky?

Alfonso's dressed regally in black brocade lined with crimson velvet with a black velvet cap. Before the wedding, I've had my father's goldsmith create a brooch with something fitting for a wedding. My ladies delivered it to him to wear on his cap before the wedding, and I wasn't even interested enough to look at it. I study it now and see two joined circles flashing proudly over his dark brow.

After our vows, I hold on to Alfonso's strong arm as he brings me to the reception. Father claps for everyone's attention and makes a toast.

"May my daughter be cherished and adored by her worthy husband as much as I adore her. May you find riches in both gold and in love." Everyone raises their glasses and drinks. "Now let's have the young couple dance for us before we dine."

Alfonso sweeps me out onto the ballroom floor, and we perform the bassa dance. I feel for the first time that no one's watching me. The only person who seems important is holding me in his arms. Time flashes by; the night's a blur of clinking glasses, music, and laughter. I'm free and flying for the first time in my life. The forgotten sense of hope results in a perpetual smile, and I'm lit up from within.

Father gives another toast at sundown. "It's the twenty-fourth hour, and it's time to say good-bye to our newlyweds. Our night will go on drearily while they partake in virgin glory. Good luck to you, my new son!"

The drunks laugh heartily at this, but even his vulgarity can't penetrate the happiness I feel.

Alfonso escorts me up to our suite, and we walk out on the balcony together overlooking the same courtyard Cesare's tainted for me, but nothing can be ugly next to his beauty. The sun's red and low in the sky, basking us in a vibrant glow. He smiles at me, and I see a slight space between his front teeth that warms my heart.

He leans into me and asks, "How can it be that I've only known you for a day?" He picks up my long braid and brings it close to his mouth. "When I look in your eyes, I do not see a stranger."

I search his eyes, eyes that have known me much longer, and he bends down to kiss me, satisfying the waiting of what feels like a hundred years for such a kiss.

Chapter 8

Even with Perotto's passionate meetings, I'd always felt an emptiness inside that Alfonso seems to spill into and warm. One look, one touch, one laugh is enough to brighten any day, and every day with him is plain and wonderful. When we leave to Aragon, I don't even cry. He's all I want, and wherever he'll go, I'll follow. Sancia also becomes another great happiness to me. Whenever Alfonso's off hunting or traveling, she stays with me, and we stroll among the gardens and practice our courtly dances.

"Lucrezia, Cesare's messenger came yesterday while you and Alfonso were, how shall I say, indisposed."

I throw my cap at her.

"Isn't that when you were occupying Jofre?"

She snorts and glares over at Jofre climbing a tree on the far ground. "He's too busy occupied with his toys. So sad, really."

I feel badly for her being with such a child.

"Here is the letter. Read me the words of his magnificence." She rolls her eyes.

Your Beatitude,

It has been a month since your wedding, and neither Father nor I have heard from you. It is not like you to forget your family in such a way, and I may have to make a visit out to check on you if I don't get word within days. You seemed quite pleased with our choice of Alfonso for you, so much so you forgot to dance with me. However, I'll forgive you, sister, if you promise to write and visit us soon. No female pleases me in the way that you do, and I hope Alfonso's dashing looks do not keep you so entertained that you forget your brother.

Give Sancia a kiss for me.
Duke of Gandia

"Duke of Gandia! He writes that as if he didn't steal it!" Sancia grabs the letter out of my hand, tears it into a hundred pieces, and throws them up in the air, spinning around under the paper snow.

When she sits back down, she says, "Nothing pleased me more than watching Cesare watch you and Alfonso dance. The look of jealousy in his eyes, his pure contempt of your unexpected happiness, oh, it was a fine night! I think it was the first time Cesare didn't dance with anyone!"

"I didn't even notice what Cesare was doing. I was too busy staring at Alfonso."

"That's what angered Cesare the most. He wasn't the most amazing man in the room. Alfonso's light had outshone his, and he thought he had won that in ridding the world of my beautiful Juan."

She glances down at the grass she's splitting and then looks up. "How could you ever forgive him for that?"

I know she won't listen, but I try anyway. "My father investi-gated his death, and all leads pointed to the Orsini."

"Deep in my heart, I know it was Cesare, not only for the dukedom, but because I'd favored him."

"I know exactly why you loved him so." I try to soften her.

"Do you know there's a rumor that Juan had received a letter sent from me before he went to the country, telling him to meet me alone in Rome and to not tell Cesare?"

I straighten up with this news. "Did you send such a letter?"

"Of course not, and only a handful of people even knew of our meetings."

"Who did you hear that rumor from?"

"One of Juan's groomsmen was there when the messenger arrived."

"Why did he not tell my father?"

"He did, and your father said the matter was closed." Her eyes bat as if she's trying to keep them from rolling.

I lay back and stare up at the sky. I don't like to imagine it is possible.

Her playfulness returns as soon as she sees my despair. "You better write him back right away. We don't want a visit." She laughs.

∞∞∞∞∞∞∞∞∞∞∞∞∞∞∞∞∞∞∞∞

A month later, I'm running through the fields with Alfonso. Sancia shouts behind me, "You shouldn't be running in your condition!"

"I'm fine!" I yell back.

Alfonso's playfully tagging me and then running away. He's too fast for me to catch, so I give up and walk to the top of the vineyard. The light's glistening off the grapes, and the air smells sweet from the rotting grapes under the vines. Alfonso comes, gives me a tight hug, and then rolls all the way down the vineyard hill. I stand above with Sancia, laughing when Alfonso hits a tree at the bottom of the hill.

I carelessly start to run after him and begin picking up speed. Sancia runs behind me, telling me to slow down. My ankle turns on the uneven ground, and I know before I hit the ground that I've made a terrible mistake. Sancia's so close behind me that she careens into me on the ground. I feel the pain immediately, and Alfonso's to me in seconds. His face is white with fear. He picks me up and carries me all the way back into the palace to my bed. I bleed for days, and the doctor informs us that I lost the baby girl. Alfonso and Sancia stay with me for three days and keep my spirits high.

I'm pregnant again by the next month. Alfonso and Sancia are dancing after dinner one night as I look on, laughing every time Alfonso steps on Sancia's foot, when we hear trumpeting and drumming coming up the drive to the palace.

Alfonso's eyes dart to me. "Are we expecting an envoy?"

I shake my head curiously, and Sancia deduces, "Only one person I know would come unannounced with trumpet accompaniment."

She's right. As we stand on the balcony above the drawbridge, I see Cesare leading the procession gallantly on his black horse adorned and shod in silver. Four horsemen on his sides hold a large canopy of gold and scarlet above his head. The whole envoy's sparkling in silver, and I've never seen such fine horses.

Sancia turns to Alfonso rigidly. "Are you going to entertain Cesare's envoy?"

Alfonso watches at me and says, "Lucrezia's brother is welcome here as long as Lucrezia wills it."

"I've suddenly come down with something. I won't be joining you all tonight." She walks off the balcony.

∞∞∞∞∞∞∞∞∞∞∞∞∞∞∞∞∞∞

"Sister, you look as heavenly as ever." Cesare comes to kiss me in our dimly lit entrance hall, and I see as he draws near that he has horrible pits and scarring all over his once handsome face.

I put my arms up involuntarily, and he draws back, but he says rather flippantly, "It's only the French disease. I'm in its second stage, and this is what it does."

Besides the scarring, he seems to have changed. Usually wearing the brightest colors in the room to be seen, he's now all in black. He sits down at our grand banquet table, and Alfonso and I slowly settle beside him. The servants are rushing to light the candles and torches in the room and to accommodate the unexpected guests. The room slowly lights into a brilliant glow.

"You're now the handsomest in the room," he says to Alfonso. "So this is the little palace that has so captured the attention of my sister that she forgets to write and visit her family." He leans back in his chair and peers around the room. "Lucrezia, you take motherhood in stride so well, it's as if you've done this before," Cesare threatens.

He knows I never told Alfonso about Giovanni Borgia.

After an uncomfortable pause, I take a deep breath and begin, "Brother, what brings you here so unexpectedly?"

He smiles. "Well, I know how much you love my surprises." He then sits back up. "Where's Sancia? Her seat lies empty," he says in a sarcastic way.

"She's feeling poorly," Alfonso replies.

"Oooh, poor dear, you'll have to tell her I missed her company."

We are served our first course.

Cesare puts his spoon down beside his soup. "I'm actually on my way to France to marry the beautiful cousin of the French king, Charlotte d'Albret." This news catches us off guard, and Cesare continues, "Well, after two years of pursuing your frigid cousin Carlotta, Naples has fallen out of favor with the Borgias."

I start getting worried, and Alfonso stiffens at this new turn of events.

"Oh, you hadn't heard? I see, well, yes, France has now become our greatest ally and has happily promised his cousin to me as a sign of good will to come."

I know this means that my marriage has been to no advantage, and now Alfonso's an enemy instead of a benefit. I can tell the fear Cesare sees on our faces only provokes him to continue.

"Alfonso, do you know that the French king has asked if the Borgias had any beautiful maids to marry? He's been asking Father eagerly for a potential suitor for one of his cousins."

Sancia walks in at this moment and must have been listening at the door. Cesare looks up, and his eyes flash at her appearance.

"A miraculous recovery!" He gets up to kiss her cheek.

"Yet, you're still not recovered yourself," she spits as she pulls away from him. "I didn't even recognize you, you've changed so."

They both sit, glaring at each other.

"I've come here to warn you about the growing hostilities between Naples and France." He directs his gaze at me. "And my dear sister appears to be caught in the middle."

Alfonso stands up. "I think I've lost my appetite now too. Lucrezia, you'll have to excuse me."

Cesare turns to Sancia. "You seem to be contagious."

I kiss him and give him an apologetic look. He smiles sweetly and walks out of the room. Cesare watches with disdain.

"How manly of him, leaving you to discuss with me alone."

Sancia speaks. "She's not alone and will never be, as long as Alfonso and I am breathing."

"Well, that is all it will take, then?" He gives a scary smile.

I stand up, wishing I'd left when Alfonso did, and say, "Sancia, I think Cesare wants to be alone now. Will you follow me up to attend to Alfonso?"

Sancia says, "Yes, I think Cesare should get used to being alone."

Cesare laughs heartily and stands to kiss me. "I'll be leaving shortly. I don't trust closing my eyes in Naples."

I give him a cold kiss back. "Be careful, brother." More as a warning instead of a wish.

∞∞∞∞∞∞∞∞∞∞∞∞∞∞∞∞∞∞

A messenger from Cesare comes a week later.

Sister,

I so wish our visit had been longer, but with circumstances the way they are, it was best it was short. I was married two nights ago and disappointed you did not attend. Disappointed but not surprised, since you seem to have replaced me. Charlotte d'Albret is no doubt a beauty, but she seems to lack the grace and charm you possess.

Wanting to perform well on my wedding night, I was given a powerful aphrodisiac by a wedding guest and made Charlotte take double the dosage. It unfortunately had a laxative effect, and we were otherwise occupied throughout the night, but I managed to consummate it by dawn. Not the romantic wedding night I had planned but thought you would enjoy the story. My next visit may not be so pleasant, although you will always be safe while I still live.

Your neglected brother,
Cesare

That night, I have a bonfire lit in celebration of Cesare's marriage, hoping it will satisfy him so he'll leave us alone. I watch the bonfire spark and light up the night as Alfonso sleeps in our chamber within. Something catches my eye. A form emerges from the gardens and makes its way to the bonfire. The figure takes off its cape, and I see it's a well-shaped woman. The woman lifts up her arms to the fire and sings. She slowly begins to dance while chanting and keeps pushing and thrusting toward one direction: France. Her dancing is beautiful yet eerie. It's not a dance of joy or relaxation but has an air from another world, an ancient, forgotten world. When the woman puts back on her cape and makes her way back up the stairs to the palace, I lean over the balcony to catch her face—Sancia.

∞∞∞∞∞∞∞∞∞∞∞∞∞∞∞∞∞∞∞∞

I give Alfonso the letter, and a month later, we receive word that Cesare's attacking the provinces of Imola, Forli, and Pesaro. I know Alfonso has to flee to safety, and after sleeping tightly all night, he kisses me and then my belly and leaves for Genazzano with the Colona.

By the end of the next week, I'm back at the Vatican for protection. Sancia holds my hand as I weep the whole carriage ride back, and each day I don't receive a letter from Alfonso. When I stop eating entirely, Sancia panics so about the baby that she goes to urge Father to do something.

Father appears at my bedside. "Bring her a feast. She will eat tonight."

Three servants rush from the room.

"Father, I can't eat. Food has no taste for me." I keep sobbing.

"Is this because Alfonso is away?"

"Away and hasn't written." I sob hard, and the baby kicks at the assault.

He brings a stack of letters out from under his robe, and I immediately see Alfonso's handwriting and seal.

"I haven't read them but kept them because I thought it would help you adjust. But nothing is worth losing you."

He leaves, and I leap on the stack of letters and tear the first one open to read.

Sancia cries, "I knew he wrote to you."

Sweet Lucrezia,

I do not know why you have not replied to my letters, but I can only guess that you have not received them, since I have such faith in you. I have been begging you to come for weeks, and with no messengers arriving from you, I'm sick without you. I worry about you and the baby and wonder if you're safer in their protection or mine. I feel as though I've failed you, not having more power and riches to keep you safe by my side. I have decided I would rather risk great peril with you than safety without you. I am coming back as soon as I can gather a company. Give my love to Sancia and tell her I expect her to watch over you until I arrive.

Yours Forever,
Alfonso ∞

Chapter 9

I feel better instantly, knowing he's on his way to me. He arrives home a week before I give birth to a son. His eyes tear as he holds him out to the people gathered in the courtyard. Rodrigo's christened in gold with trumpets and oboes announcing the momentous occasion. For seven months, Alfonso, Sancia, and I stay secluded, doting on Rodrigo. Alfonso fears going out and stays close to his men he brought back with him for protection. I have the same nightmare repeatedly for a week:

A fawn walks down the steps of St. Peter's in the moonlight. A dark hunter appears at the top of the steps and shoots the fawn in the back. The poor thing runs back frantically to the courtyard for shelter. But as it reaches the illusion of safety, a brown wolf pounces and drags the fawn under the bushes.

One morning, there's a large commotion outside St. Peters. The triumphant son returns with horses, soldiers, and plunder of war. One of the pope's grooms comes knocking on our door for us to greet Cesare and celebrate. Alfonso stays behind as I hurry down the stairs to stand next to Father on his balcony. Cesare leads the way in his usual black attire but with the addition of a thick gold collar and gold and black cap. Father yells to circle the Vatican to show Rome how victorious he is, and I see Father's eyes well up with tears as he heartily laughs with joy. When Cesare goes around one side, Father runs to the next side to watch him go all around the palace, waving for me to follow him.

When the procession's over, we hurry out to greet him, and he jumps off his horse. He gives father a quick kiss on both cheeks and then his ring and gives me two kisses also.

"Guards! Bring Caterina to dine with us," Cesare yells back to his men, and two guards drag out a raging beauty: a dark-haired and brown-eyed slender woman with small faint freckles on her nose and under her eyes. She wears a crushed velvet dress with a pale blue robe, and she keeps struggling to free herself as she curses the guards.

Cesare motions for us to go in and not to wait for her, who I deduce is one of his prisoners. My stomach wrenches for what's going to play out at dinner with the poor woman seated with us.

Father sits first, and then we all take our seats. The woman is brought in and tied sitting in her chair so that her back and legs are tight to the chair, but her hands are free. The knots are tied out of her reach behind her back. She looks fierce and angry, which is impressive, since Cesare hadn't intimidated her yet. I sit across from her, and she stares at me while our course is served.

"You're the lying whore who's sleeping with her papal father and pig brother?"

I avert my eyes, completely caught off guard by her hatred.

Cesare starts laughing. "Isn't she charming?" He grabs her hair and holds her head back. "Now be nice if you want to be fed tonight."

"Lucrezia, this is Caterina Sforza, Ruler of Forli, relative of your impotent first husband," my father says.

Caterina guffaws at the word impotent.

My father continues, "This lovely duchess has been so kind as to have attempted to kill me twice in the last month. Trying to preempt the attack on Forli, she sent me letters steeped in poison that sickened two of my messengers and also tried wrapping her letters in clothes worn by plague victims."

She purses her lips and gives Father a burning stare.

Cesare speaks. "All other provinces gave way to me like cheap whores, but Caterina fought to the very end." She pulls at her ropes, and Cesare laughs. "She's still fighting!"

She shakes her head back and forth like she's gone mad and screams while doing so. "Why have you not killed me yet!"

Father and Cesare are enjoying the show.

"Why would I do something that could make me more enemies than I already have?" Father says with his eyes wide. "If you had only relented as the others had, then you'd still be in Forli."

"I will never sell my soul!"

"I'm sure Don Michelotto could find your price," Cesare says, but Father puts his hand up to keep him from going such places.

"Caterina, you're such a lovely young woman, and I respect your fight, but you must understand I've only two choices. Either I can accommodate you and your children very comfortably in St. Peter's—"

"What will you make me do, sleep with you and have your child as you forced your daughter to?" She looks back at me and enunciates the words. "The Roman Infant." She can see she strikes a sore spot with my father.

He pushes back slightly from the table and has a serious expression that I've learned to fear. "No, I would simply ask that you give up your rights and those of your children to Forli."

Caterina spits at him from two seats away and hits my father under his eye. He stands up and knocks his chair over and shouts through gritted teeth, "Take this ungrateful shrew and throw her in the dungeon!"

Some of Cesare's guards dining with us get up and take her away. As she's being dragged, she yells, "The Borgia will never see happiness long! Their murderous curse will follow close behind!"

After my father's cleaned, he tries to reclaim the evening by bringing out some of his best wine and having the string musicians play for us, but Caterina's words reverberate within.

Father lifts his wine as all follow. "To Cesare, Duke of Gandia and soon to be King of Romagna!"

Everyone cheers and clinks their glasses.

∞∞∞∞∞∞∞∞∞∞∞∞∞∞∞∞∞∞∞∞

The next day, there's a jousting match held outside the Vatican. Sancia and I decide to attend. We're sitting in our raised seats above the field, discussing yet another lover Sancia has snuck into her bed, when Cesare approaches. He comes and nods to both of us and stands up and yells across to the jousters getting ready to compete, "Yesterday, this noble Frenchman and this surly Burgundian had quarreled over a banner. The Burgundian has challenged this gallant Frenchman to a duel, which we're all so lucky to be attending this fine morning. I have total confidence that my Frenchman, who has fought so valiantly beside me, will be victorious. Let the joust begin!"

There are as many cheers as there are boos. While the men are getting their gear on for the match, Sancia and I see Cesare wave Don Michelotto over to him.

"Go to the Burgundian and offer him twenty ducats, clothes, and a new banner if he'll throw his match. Tell him I'll double the price if he does so in a humiliating way."

Sancia and I watch as Don Michelotto saunters his way over to the Burgundian getting his metal gloves on. The Burgundian pushes Don Michelotto back into a pile of manure and turns his back to finish dressing. Don Michelotto sucks his foot out of the pile, shakes his head at Cesare, and walks off. Sancia and I are trying our best to hold our laughter in, and Cesare says, "No matter, the Frenchman will win."

When the Burgundian throws the Frenchman off his horse on the second run, Cesare gets up and storms away.

Sancia says, "I think I'll see if our Burgundian is hungry after such a match."

She winks at me, then makes her way seductively to the sweaty handsome man removing his armor.

The next day, I watch from my balcony while holding Rodrigo as Cesare's running drills in the courtyard. Sancia dresses herself and twelve of her squires in livery in the colors of the Burgundian and parades them right by Cesare. Cesare holds his middle finger up to her forcefully. Sancia keeps her head held high and blows him a kiss. My worlds are colliding, and I don't want to see who will ultimately win.

After Alfonso and I dine one evening, he kisses my head. "I have to meet someone across St. Peter's Square for an hour about Cesare's push on Aragon."

"You aren't going alone, are you?"

"I'll have my best men with me." He points to two large men waiting by the door.

"I don't like you going out in the dark."

Alfonso laughs. "The moon is bright tonight, almost as light as day."

"Come home as soon as you can." I kiss him on the lips and start walking up the tower stairs, and every time I go around, I see a little higher up in the small window overlooking the steps below, waiting to see Alfonso and his men spilling down. A horrible feeling chokes me as I realize there is a full moon low in the sky, and it's shining down, illuminating St. Peter's steps. I freeze at the small window and watch as Alfonso's beautiful shape appears and cascades down the steps, and scream when I see four men on horseback gallop toward the bottom of the steps. I fly down the stairs and run to the dining room, where Father's still drinking with a few cardinals.

"Alfonso!" I scream, not being able to say any more words, and I point out the door. "Help him!"

I dash out the front door and see the four men, dismounted, dragging Alfonso from the steps toward the river. I scream again, and it pierces the night as my father's guards come streaming out behind me, causing the four men to jump on their horses and run to the protection of close to forty horsemen, and they charge off toward Porta Pertusa. I skip two or three steps, trying to get to him as fast as I can. He's bleeding heavily from one deep wound on his head and one gash across his shoulder. I hold his head up and call his name. He doesn't open his eyes or make a sound.

My father stands at the top of the steps and calls, "Guards, carry him in to my personal doctor."

The men carry him up all thirty steps to his apartments as I lie rocking on the stone ground, crying his name again and again.

My father finally heaves his large body down the steps. "Lucrezia, stop this now. Your husband is still alive and needs your protection."

I immediately stop. He's right. If he has any hope to live, I will have to stay by his side and keep whoever committed this from doing it again. I get up quickly, pulling my skirts high so I won't trip, not caring my legs are showing. The doctors rush into the room and cut off his clothes to examine the wounds. I go to hold a towel to his head, and a doctor pushes me away.

"Let us handle this. Why don't you wait outside?"

"I'm not leaving his side."

"Well, go stand over there out of the way, then."

I obey and watch from the door and see Sancia running down the hall frantically. "Alfonso!" she searches for him.

"Sancia! Alfonso is in here." I begin crying again at the sight of her.

She takes one look at his condition and grabs for me. We hold each other, crying, for what seems hours. Once we're alone with the attending doctor, she cries, "This is all my fault."

"How is this your fault?"

"I said a... prayer for Cesare to leave us alone once and for all. It has come back on us threefold!"

I know she is referring to her strange behavior by the bonfire, and I don't want her divulging more. There are serious crimes for what she is speaking about.

"I'm sure it had nothing to do with this."

My father comes in looking forlorn, and he asks, "Will he live?"

The doctor's finishing stitching the small wound on his arm; Alfonso's head's wrapped in cloths dipped in healing herbs.

"Only God knows. We have done our best. Now he needs to rest."

My father nods.

"Father, I will need only our most trusted guards to guard him."

"Don Michelotto?"

"No, none of Cesare's guards."

He stays quiet at my accusation and stares at his feet.

"I want only Alfonso's men. Will you please see to it that they are sent to the Borgia tower?"

He looks up. "Why the Borgia tower?"

"That is where I'm having him moved. It has only one stairway and entrance so that it can be watched night and day."

He nods again. "I'll do anything to help you."

He leaves to fetch his guards.

"It could kill him to be moved," the doctor protests.

"Better than staying here where he'll surely die," I say as I point to the four guards. "Carry him as gently and carefully as you can up to the tower."

I look to Sancia, and she gives me a nod in agreement.

The doctor begins to follow us up into the tower when I turn to him and say, "Thank you for your help. You may take your leave now."

"He needs a doctor by his side at all times."

"I'm the pope's daughter, and I say you are relieved!" I command.

As he walks away, I instruct Sancia, "Go at once with your fastest messenger to your cousin, the King of Naples, and request his best doctor to be sent on his fastest horse."

"Yes." She runs off down the stone corridor.

I sit beside Alfonso on my knees, holding his hand and praying for him to live. Sancia comes back an hour later, and we stay up all night. The doctor arrives in the early morning and goes to work on aiding Alfonso, who's sweating through a fever all night.

"He made it through his first day. That is most encouraging," the doctor says.

Sancia and I cry in hope that it may be true.

Two days later, he opens his eyes and rasps, "Lucrezia."

"I'm here, my love." I squeeze his hand.

"I still breathe?"

"Yes, and as soon as you're better, we're leaving for Naples."

A servant brings a tray of broth and water in for Alfonso.

"Take that back; we'll not be needing your services."

The servant backs out of the room. Sancia looks puzzled.

"We'll have to take turns cooking him food and fetching water. I don't trust anything while we stay in the holy city."

"I will go first, then. You stay with Alfonso."

He slowly recuperates, and as he's sleeping one morning, I peer out and see that the whole city is closed down.

I turn to Sancia. "What's happening? All of the houses are shut up."

"News of Alfonso's attack has caused the people of Rome to stay home for fear of a vendetta." Sancia continues as she makes a stitch in her embroidery. "They say whoever killed Juan has tried to kill Alfonso."

I know what she's thinking, and I haven't left Alfonso's side to confront him yet.

"Cesare has even issued an edict forbidding the carrying of arms!" She laughs. "I wonder why he has so much to fear?"

There's a great commotion outside the door, and our guards try to block the door from opening. Sancia throws down her sewing, and we both stand on either side of Alfonso, ready for what's trying to penetrate. The door pushes open, and six men, Don Michelotto, and Cesare burst in.

"You're not allowed in here!" I shout at him.

His guards begin fighting our guards, as Don Michelotto and Cesare come to the foot of Alfonso's bed.

"I have business with your husband!" He throws down three arrows on the bed.

Sancia yells, "I think you've done enough, Cesare, leave now!"

"Oh, you think I've landed him in this sick bed?"

"There's no doubt it was you," Sancia spits.

"I did not attack your weakling husband, but if I had, it would have been no more deserved!"

"What has Alfonso done to you?" I scream.

"Everything!" he screams back. "What hasn't he taken from me?"

Alfonso stirs and tries to talk. "Lucrezia, I will handle this." He attempts to sit up, wincing and holding his head.

"It is I who have been wronged," Cesare says. "Your guards shot these arrows at me while I was walking in the courtyard. One nearly hit my head."

"That is not true," I state.

"It is true," Alfonso replies. "I instructed them to kill him."

Sancia looks proud, and I realize quickly that she must have delivered his order for him.

"Listen, you imp, you're lucky it was Orsini and not Don Michelotto that met you on those steps. If he had, you would already be rotting in your Naples mausoleum!"

Cesare bends over Alfonso on the bed, and Sancia and I try to push him back, but he says slowly, "What has begun at breakfast will be finished by supper."

He walks back out with Don Michelotto and his guards.

"I hate lying here like a useless child." Alfonso throws his head back on the pillow but then winces in pain.

"Sancia, go to your cousin again and plead for him to come with an envoy to bring Alfonso to safety. I fear every night he's still within these walls. I know the doctor says he can't be moved yet, but tell him he's in great peril."

As she runs off, Alfonso studies me. "You're so beautiful, my guardian angel."

I lie across his chest and hold on tight. I feel fear running through me every moment; I can't sleep unless Sancia is there. She's the only one I can truly trust. I'll send her with Alfonso to Naples and leave with Rodrigo as soon as Father will grant me permission. I hate the thought of leaving him.

Sancia quickly returns and breathless from running up the tower stairs, she says, "King Frederico replied he'll send his men at once." Smiling in triumph, she sits beside Alfonso on his bed.

"My *two* angels." He takes her hand.

The next day, we hear the trumpets and peer out to see the beautiful sight of the small envoy with the colors and flags of Naples.

"They've made it!" I cry. "Sancia come look."

Sancia runs over. "It's a miracle! God is on our side!"

I tell his groomsmen, "Please, pack up the duke's things. He'll be leaving shortly."

"Do you need to get your things as well, sister?" Alfonso asks.

"I have been ready for a week!" She smiles.

"Sancia, help me dress him."

"Whoa, whoa, whoa! It's been a month and as much as I'd enjoy you dressing me, I think I'll draw the line at my sister. Turn away, Sancia."

"Fine." She turns. "It hasn't dawned on you that I've changed your bed sheets for a month, but I'll let you salvage whatever dignity you have left."

We all laugh.

"Easy, Lucrezia, easy!" He squeals as I try to get him into his pants too fast.

Once he's dressed, Sancia's hitting the bottom of his boots, trying to get them on. "Did they stab your foot too? It has swollen double the size!" She chuckles as she pinches both sides of his foot and tries in one motion to squish it into the stiff leather.

"Ouch! I think Cesare would be kinder to me!"

Sancia drops the boot and grabs her sides in laughter. We've been stressed for so long, it's such a relief to feel everything will be okay. The door opens, and in walks a handsome white-haired man with at least twelve strong men behind him.

Sancia runs to him. "Uncle!"

She hugs him, and he gives her two kisses. "Lucrezia." He bows. "Alfonso." Another bow.

"Uncle, thank you for coming for me."

"We had better hurry. At our entrance we saw three times our men rush to the opposite side of St. Peter's in arms."

He motions four men to go and lift Alfonso to carry him down. As they're picking him up, Don Michelotto bursts through with two dozen men at the ready. "I'm under the orders of Cesare to keep the prisoner in the tower."

"Prisoner?" I yell.

"Yes, he's held until healed for the attempted murder of the Duke of Gandia."

Sancia recoils. "The Duke of Gandia is already dead, murdered, and drowned by your master."

"Seize them and bring them to the gaol. They've plotted to free the prisoner without the pope's permission."

"Why are you doing this, Michelotto?" I cry.

"I'm at the will of others, Duchess." He bows his head and leaves, motioning his men to follow.

The soldiers lower Alfonso back down and let Michelotto's men tie their hands and walk them out of the tower.

I run out of the room without thinking and hear Sancia close behind. I dash down the winding steps and head toward the pope's apartments. When I throw the door open, Sancia has caught up, and Father sits straight up in his chair at our frantic interruption.

"Father! Father!" I can barely talk; I can't catch my breath.

"What is it, child? Calm down!"

"They've imprisoned my uncle and the men from Alfonso's envoy!" Sancia gets out.

"What envoy?"

"The envoy my king has sent to move Alfonso."

"Who's with Alfonso now?"

I see Sancia's face lose all color, and I'm sure it mirrors mine. Without words, we both rush back up to the tower.

"Stupid women!" I cry as we clamor up the stairs.

"How could we fall into his trap!" Sancia cries.

Seeing the door, we know our worst fears have come true. Don Michelotto's huge guards are blocking the door. Sancia and I throw ourselves at them, beating our fists on their armored chests.

"Let us by!"

"By order of the pope, I command you to step aside!" I scream.

They don't budge.

"Alfonso!" Sancia shrieks.

The door opens, and Don Michelotto walks out, putting his gloves on. "He's dead."

"Aaaahhahhh!" I rip at him.

His guards pull me off him as Sancia runs into the room.

Her high-pitched scream makes my heart bleed as I realize what undoubtedly has just taken place.

I drop to the floor, and Michelotto says, "Leave her."

I sob on the ground and then pull myself up to see Sancia draped across Alfonso's still body. I sweep the covers up to hide the purple marks around his neck and fall on top of him, both lamenting at our great mistake.

"Brother!" she weeps over and over again.

"Husband!" I wail, as if we can undo time.

Chapter 10

As soon as the prisoners are released, Sancia readies to take Alfonso's body with her uncle.

"I hate to leave you here, Lucrezia."

"I can't leave. I'm now the property of my father again. He's forbidden me to go to his enemy."

"I have to leave. I can't stay one more day here, or I'll kill Cesare myself."

She gives me a kiss. "You must write me every day and visit when you can break away."

"Leave a rose for me on his tomb."

I start sobbing again and keep crying for hours in the dark room after she leaves. Knowing his body's taken from me where I can't go rips me in two. I know Father will look to marry me again, and that will mean I can't be laid to rest beside Alfonso, ever.

I don't eat for three weeks and only sleep or weep. I won't get dressed or see Rodrigo. I pray for death to come every night, but every morning, my eyes open yet again.

Father comes in and draws the curtains.

I protest, "Leave them closed."

"It's time for you to get out of bed, Lucrezia."

He sits beside me, making the mattress sag toward his weight.

"I'll come out when I hear Cesare and Michelotto have been convicted of murder."

"I too was furious and surprised at Cesare's aggressive action, but he's spoken to me and told me of how Alfonso sent his men to kill him in the courtyard. It's only fair if he should seek revenge."

I begin crying again. "Leave me."

"Everyone's talking about your absence from court since Alfonso's death, and it taints the Borgia name—"

"I taint the Borgia name!" I sit up furiously in bed. "You and Cesare have destroyed the Borgia name! Everyone fears it, shakes at its mention, and you dare say I'm responsible for that!"

"It's outbursts such as this that make me worry about your sanity. I'll forgive you in this instance for your dishonor, but if you proceed to spew such venom for your brother and me, I'll be forced to send you away so that no one can witness it."

With that, he gets up to leave, and in a week, I'm sent off to grieve in the town of Nepi with Rodrigo. I dress head to toe in black and dress my whole envoy in black to show my grief to all who pass. Cesare comes daily to try to talk to me. I turn him away every day. I laugh, though, when I see him come armed with a hundred guards in full armor like he's in jeopardy in my presence. I isolate myself and go for walks alone. Any time I can gather the energy, I have Rodrigo come in to see how fast he's growing. He looks more and more like Alfonso every day. I'll hold him back in my arms, gaze into his sparkling black eyes, and tickle him up to the two little moles on his jaw as he laughs so deeply he turns red. Only Rodrigo can make me laugh, but I feel unwell so frequently that it can be days before I see him again. I fear I will never function again.

I live for Rodrigo and for Sancia's letters. Only she knows what a life without Alfonso feels like.

> *Sweet Sister,*
> *I too am still mourning Alfonso's loss. Every day I think of him and cry inside. The tragedy of his last moments still sends chills through me, and I will never have a light heart again. When you tell me you wish you were dead too, I understand how you must feel. Being a puppet in such careless hands. You must fear what your future will be, and that must extinguish all hope for any happiness. But when I hear you say that, Alfonso's voice rings in my ear and tells me that he would never want you to be so unhappy without him, and he would want you to still shine for your son in his absence.*
> *Even though I am away from you, know that you are always in my thoughts and prayers. It will be a joyful day when I get to kiss you and Rodrigo again.*
>
> *Your sister always,*
> *Sancia*

∞∞∞∞∞∞∞∞∞∞∞∞∞∞∞∞∞∞∞∞

A year passes and I still wear black, when a servant comes saying Cesare's here again but without his guards.

"Bring him to me."

Cesare walks in and kneels before me. Something takes over me, and I knock him in the head and don't stop until my hands hurt. I fall over on him, and he holds me, saying, "I'm sorry," again and again.

I pull myself together and sit across from him at the table in my room, where I take all my meals, not wanting to be social.

"You look beautiful even in black," he flatters.

"I want to die."

"What a waste that would be." He puts his feet up on my table. "I bring you great news of potential riches beyond your wildest dreams."

Only Cesare comes in and speaks this way after he sees how withdrawn I've become.

"Besides coming here to beg your forgiveness, I've been ransacking the Italian countryside, working my way toward Romagna. The only thing that stands in my way is the Duchy of Ferrara. The duke and his son Alfonso—"

I wince at the mention of his name.

"—are ammunition experts and present great challenge with their military prowess. Ferrara lies strategically between me and Romagna."

I'm wondering how this concerns me.

"We need an alliance with Ferrara."

"You'll never get the Duke of Ferrara to consider me for marriage."

Cesare laughs at how fast I catch on.

"Never say never, sister." He pulls his legs back down to lean toward me. "Father and I have been working on this for months."

I feel a twinge of anger that they've been advertising me in my anguish.

"First it was quite entertaining when Father offered you. Ercole d'Este wrote back that never would he give his son in marriage to a Borgia, with their frightful reputation. His son would never agree to such an unequal match with such upstart foreigners!" He laughs. "If Father and I didn't have the sense of humor that we do, one would have been extremely insulted!" He gets up to continue his story from a more comfortable chair in front of the fire. "We persisted, and after an offer of two hundred thousand ducats in dowry and the threat of me and my allies' attack, they started to come around. Ercole agreed as long as he received three things: a reduction of his annual contribution to the Church, the position of archpriest for his other son, and control of the cities of Cento and Pieve in addition to the Cesenatico harbor."

I can't believe he's now telling me I'm betrothed again.

"Did you not hear what I just said?" He sits up. "Have you grown deaf in your mourning? This is wonderful news!"

"I have heard what you said and can hardly believe it. The Dukedom of Ferrara is far beyond our reach."

"Not anymore. Your wedding is in a month. That's as long as Father can generate the dowry."

"And they're letting me bring Rodrigo?"

"Oh, yes, that's the fourth circumstance. Rodrigo will not go to Ferrara. In light of the... uh, um... scandal, Ercole thinks it's best not to remind the people by his presence. He wants you to appear as a virgin bride."

I feel sick again. *How much is God going to ask me to bear?*

I stand up. "Cesare, thank you for informing me, but I have a headache now and want to rest."

"I understand. Father will be bringing an envoy within the week to bring you back to St. Peters to prepare for the joyous event." He gives me a kiss on the lips and leaves.

Chapter 11

I write to Sancia immediately and beg her to come at once to Rome. It's so nice having her with me again, but I know not to get too attached, since it's only temporary. A month later, advisors sent from Ferrara come to have a marriage by proxy. Sancia stays away from wherever Cesare will be, so she declines coming to the wedding dinner. The whole capital is celebrating the much-talked-about union, and bells ring and beacons are lit as far as the eye can reach. Cesare and Father sit next to me and rejoice that night, but it's bittersweet, since we all know Ferrara is quite a distance away.

"Lucrezia, you will enjoy this."

Father pulls out from beside his chair a genealogy chart.

"What is this?"

"This is the Borgia family tree." He starts smirking. "Ercole sent a request for our pedigree to be displayed for all at the wedding in Ferrara to see, so here it is."

Cesare examines it closely. "I didn't know that Don Pedro de Atares, lord of Borgia and pretender to the throne of Aragon, was directly related to us."

Father begins to shake with laughter. "That's because he's not! He died childless, but not many know that."

"Why lie?" I ask.

"Because Ercole is a smug son of a bitch and asked for this just to look better than us, so I spiced it up a bit." He smiles proudly.

∞∞∞∞∞∞∞∞∞∞∞∞∞∞∞∞∞∞∞

I can't sleep at all that night, knowing tomorrow will be the day I have to leave Rodrigo. I meet Sancia in the garden, and she holds my hand and pats my back.

"Lucrezia, you have no choice."

Her eyes steady me. We both look on as nearly two-year-old Rodrigo runs around the garden, throwing rocks.

"I can only leave knowing he'll have you."

"I'll take the best care of him and write to you about everything he does."

I begin crying again.

"Will you tell him of me so he won't forget?"

"I'll talk of you so much he'll feel as though you're there."

She gives me a long hug, and Rodrigo comes running into my arms, his cheeks rosy from the winter cold.

"Give Mama a kiss! I'll be leaving, but Auntie Sancia will take good care of you."

He puckers his tiny lips, gives me a kiss, and I watch them walk away with Sancia holding his little arm. When they're out of sight, I break down.

∞∞∞∞∞∞∞∞∞∞∞∞∞∞∞∞∞∞∞

Downtrodden from the sadness of the morning, I go to Father's apartment. He's there discussing with some advisors, and I sit at his feet with my head rested on his knee.

As soon as the advisors leave and we're alone, he says, "Lucrezia, don't look so distraught. This is the beginning of greatness for you."

I say nothing.

"Cesare and I have worked very hard to achieve the unimaginable, something far beyond your birthright. You'll someday be the Duchess of Ferrara!"

"I only wish Rodrigo could have come with me."

"That's a shame, but boys grow up fine without their mothers. He'll have the best nurses to care for him and will want for nothing."

He turns my head toward him with his hand under my chin. "You look lovely today."

I'm dressed in a robe of curled cloth of gold cut with crimson thread, with a cloak of gold lined with ermine.

"I'll be frantic while you're en route to Ferrara. These are dangerous times to be traveling. I'll send my best men to ride with you, but you must promise me something."

He pauses to see I will agree. I nod.

"You must promise to send messengers every hour to let me know you're safe. Make sure to write in your own hand so I know it's you."

"I promise."

I get up and look out the window to the large envoy waiting below.

"There must be a hundred fifty mules gathered there!"

"That's how many we need to carry all your previous wedding presents to Ferrara." He jokes, but it's very true. "Plus all the dresses, underskirts, robes, tabards, capes, shoes, fans, jewelry, and tapestries you've made me buy for you."

"If I'm going to be the future Duchess of Ferrara, then I have to dress like her."

Father gives me a kiss on the cheek. "That's the girl I love!" He gives me one final hug. "You better go. The envoy will be leaving shortly."

"Now make sure," he reminds me, "Alfonso sleeps in your bed every night. I heard a rumor that he failed to do so with his first wife, and I wouldn't want Ercole using that the way we did with Sforza to escape the marriage later. Bed him and bed him well."

We say our good-byes, and I walk down to my very fine and heavily decorated mule. As I ride away, I see Father move from window to window, waving at me, and I've a terrible feeling it's the last time I'll see him.

∞∞∞∞∞∞∞∞∞∞∞∞∞∞∞∞∞∞∞

As at every other time in my life, I've no choice but to bottle my feelings. We stop at every city along the way so that my company of one thousand can be fed and lodged. There's much rejoicing as we make our way through towns, and children dressed in my colors of yellow and mulberry are waving olive branches at our passing. When we draw nearer to Ferrara, I worry about the duke seeing me for the first time. I bring a mirror up and see that I need to stop to color my hair.

I call out the window of my carriage to my lady riding her mule beside me, "Please go at once to ask if we can stop the envoy immediately to attend to my beauty ritual."

She kicks her heels on the mule's side to ride ahead and comes back quickly, saying, "He wants me to implore you that we don't stop here. We have reached Imola, and he says it's a very dangerous place for us."

I breathe out to show my annoyance. "If we're in Imola, then we're nearing Ferrara, and I cannot delay my beauty regimen! Tell him he'll stop!"

A man yells out, and the envoy stops. Pleased with my stubbornness, I step out of the carriage as the leader is coming up, red-faced.

"I've only stopped to come back myself to tell you what a mistake you're making."

I ignore him and keep walking. I call back to my lady, "Fetch me the dye man."

They bring a chair out in a clearing in the woods next to a river. The dye man is busy pouring, crushing, boiling, and chopping for about an hour. Finally, he brushes his solution on close to my scalp and leaves it to dry for another hour.

"Your hair will glitter and shine like golden threads for the duke!" he promises.

"While this dries, will you mix your skin-whitening treatment to apply also?"

"Anything for the duchess."

He bows and goes away. These are the things that are expected of noblewomen and can be achieved only through tedious illusion.

The leader looks disappointed that no harm befalls us and throws his gloves on the ground as I get back into the carriage, shouting, "Women!"

Ten miles from the end of our two hundred twenty mile journey, a rider comes up on his horse and paces beside my passing carriage.

"Is this the envoy delivering the future Duchess of Ferrara?"

The coachman confirms it.

"I'm from the house Este, and I've brought Dona Lucrezia a message from Alfonso d'Este."

The coach comes to a halt. He maneuvers his horse skillfully and brings him around in front of my window.

"Alfonso instructed me to bring this kiss for his lady." He puts his hand out for me to fill. I extend my arm, and he brings my gloved hand up but pauses. "He told me to only deliver this kiss if she was of astounding and divine beauty."

His brownish-green eyes search me up and down, and with a smile, he bends down to kiss my hand, but I withdraw before his lips can touch. He's of excellent form and has one dimple on his cheek that shows when he smiles through a trimmed moustache and beard.

"Please tell my lord that I'm eager to have him kiss my hand himself."

The messenger gives a wide grin and pulls his horse in a circle and gallops away.

We arrive in Ferrara at dusk, and I see the walled city glowing in the yellow and pink sunset. The palace is glorious, even more beautiful than the Vatican. There are towers, turrets, balconies, and great stained windows. The Este flags fly on the tops of every tower. When the drawbridge is lowered for our envoy to enter, trumpets and oboes sound. We stop in the square inside the entrance, and someone has gone to great lengths to make two large wreaths that hang on the great wooden door to the castle. One is the Este crest: a majestic white eagle combined with the French fleur-de-lis granted by Charles VII of France and the black-crowned, double-headed imperial eagle granted by Emperor Frederick III. Next to it is the Borgia crest: a humble grazing bull.

The doors are opened, and my ladies and I enter into a lavishly decorated front hall. An older, slender man comes down the stairs with two younger men and one young female. I notice the messenger at once among them.

The older man bows to me and takes my hand. "I am Ercole, the Duke of Este." He kisses it. "It is so nice to finally meet you. We have heard so much about you."

I'm sure this is tongue-in-cheek, but my relentless charm persists.

"It's a great pleasure, my lord." I curtsy.

"I will only have you call me Father." He turns to his right, to the men, and says, "Lucrezia, meet your husband, Alfonso d'Este."

I naturally deduce that the man standing next to the messenger is Alfonso and hold my hand out to him, but the messenger takes my hand. "You promised me this kiss."

My eyes widen in surprise, and he laughs as he explains to his father, "I got too anxious waiting here for the envoy and decided to go out and see her for myself."

Ercole looks embarrassed by his rash behavior. "I take it since you returned, Lucrezia was to your liking then?"

"Far exceeded my expectations." He kisses my hand again.

Ercole interrupts. "This is my daughter, Isabella d'Este."

She stares at me like I'm her servant and gives a frigid curtsy, then glares at her father.

I try, "The generous patroness of the arts and antiques. Your reputation precedes you."

She nods, chin held up. "As does yours."

I know this is another attack.

Isabella's of normal height, slightly plump, with ice blue eyes and an abundance of light brown hair.

"Let us go show you to your rooms, where you can dress for our ceremony and celebration," Ercole interrupts.

Isabella looks all too happy to walk away. Alfonso's groomsmen motion for me and my servants to follow them.

Chapter 12

My ladies change me into a black velvet dress with a cape of gold brocade trimmed with ermine, a necklace of rubies and pearls, and a net of gold and diamonds in my golden hair. Alfonso's waiting for me outside of the celebration, wearing red velvet. He holds his arm up for me to hold, and I enter yet another wedding celebration on the arm of a stranger.

After Alfonso's stiff dancing, we're seated across from each other with Ercole at the head of the banquet table. Isabella and the other noblemen and women are talking amongst themselves.

Ercole speaks to me. "Your father has been extremely tenacious about getting your yearly allowance of ten thousand ducats raised."

I feel uncomfortable with him talking about this in front of everyone. "My father is persistent."

"Yes, but you must let it be clear to him that I am already paying you two thousand ducats more than my daughter Isabella."

Isabella glares at me with immense disdain. This explained things.

"I am more than happy to have what you are granting me, Father." I'm going to let my father haggle with him and stay out of it.

He appears happy at my giving in and attacks further. "Another matter we must speak of is your new household."

"My new household? I do not need a *new* household."

"Your household is comprised of Spaniards. I think it would look better to the people if you had a household comprised of people from Ferrara."

I sit up straight in my chair and look him squarely in the eyes and say, "My household has been with me since I was twelve. I have given up my son at your request. Please leave me my household."

"Well, I had no idea you were so attached. Fine, have it your way, but maybe as you get more comfortable here, you will make improvements."

He begins sipping his soup, and I take that to mean his negotiations are over. As I'm waiting between dances, Isabella comes to me directly, out of earshot of Alfonso.

"You, lowly Borgia, will never fulfill the shoes of my mother. She's turning in her grave right now at this fraud." She walks off as quickly as she attacked.

The trumpets rise to send Alfonso and me off to our wedding bed, and it reminds me of Sforza all over again. After he leaves in the morning to proclaim his success of three times to his father, I cry in my pillow, remembering Aragon.

I come to learn what kind of man Alfonso is, and it only takes a few days. He's a very simple man, interested—actually obsessed—with seven things: artillery, tournaments, dogs, horses, pottery, the viol, and whores. Anything outside of these categories he doesn't have time for.

Ercole one morning at breakfast says to me, "I am very pleased. You seem to be the only woman Alfonso can bear."

I reply lightly, "If that is so, then why the need for the secret tunnel into the brothels of Ferrara?"

He's surprised I learned of that so soon. "I said the only woman he can *bear*, not the only one he rides."

It's fine. I don't care how he spends his time. I know I don't love him, and we both are playing a part. One morning, he awakes and asks me if I'd like to come hunting with him. Shocked by this request, I agree. After dressing for the occasion, I'm helped onto my fastest horse, and we ride off in the chilly spring air toward his hunting grounds.

He proudly shows me his modern musket and shouts down the hill to his men, "Release the rabbits and leopards!"

"Wait until you see these amazing animal's speed."

I watch as one man walks out in the center of the field and empties three lean rabbits out of a basket. The rabbits go scattering, and the man releases two leopards that flash out across the field, one grabbing an unlucky rabbit instantly, and the other running this way and that until the rabbit loses. The last rabbit finds safety under the brush on the edge of the field. Alfonso turns to catch my reaction with an expression that he showed me something rare.

"Oh, fantastic!" I pretend. Little did he know Cesare had shown me every type of hunter and prey, from hawks to prisoners. "Miraculous animals!" I clap.

When they recover the leopards, Alfonso shouts, "Release the wolf!"

A skittish black and grey wolf is set free in the clearing, and Alfonso follows, "Release the dogs!"

I look away as five large and fierce hunting dogs are let out, and hear the struggle. When the cries die down, I open my eyes again and see the wolf lying dead in the grass and the dogs running back to their grinning master. Even though the dogs' faces are covered in blood, Alfonso lets them all jump on him and lick his face. It's so hard to keep smiling.

Men and their sadistic pleasures.

∞∞∞∞∞∞∞∞∞∞∞∞∞∞∞∞∞∞∞

When we return, I walk into my dressing room and collapse on the chair, thankful I'm alone, until disrupted by a timid knock.

I open the door quickly to a young man, all in tawny leather with a flapping hooded falcon on his thick-gloved hand.

"Lady d'Este." He bows awkwardly. "This falcon's still jumpy yet." He tries to calm her with a thinner-gloved hand and steps in without my offer to enter, but bows his head respectfully again. "Lady, the Master d'Este sent for me to train this peregrine as your personal gaming bird."

I blink at the beautiful statuesque creature held high on his strong arm.

He mistakes my hesitation, and with a flush, removes his light cap and takes it in a hasty bunch to his chest. "I beg your pardon, lady, I should have introduced myself. Niccolo, at your service." His pointed ears protrude from his scraggly hair, giving him an elfish look.

"Thank you, Niccolo. I'm just overwhelmed with this gracious gift. He's a magnificent specimen."

Niccolo beams. "She. I climbed and took her from the nest myself."

"What do I do with her, though?" I try to walk toward her, but she senses my approach and begins flapping again frantically.

"Why don't we start out on the balcony?" He heads toward the open narrow doors and leans on the stone wall.

I stand at a distance as he grips her tethers tight and removes the hood. She cries meekly as she futilely flaps and tries to pull her steel claws free. I gasp when I see that her large eyes are half-sewn shut.

"What has happened to her eyes?"

"That is part of her training—was fully sealed up until a week ago. I've had her in the dark for months. She's just getting used to her sight again."

"Why would you restrict her sight?"

"She would never relax enough to get used to my handling. I seal her up and carry her in a nice quiet place until she calms. Then I remove half the stitches and calm her all over again. She's ready now to begin to get used to you." He pulls out a glove from the pouch at his side.

My small hand disappears inside the stiffest leather I'd ever put on—like putting on a giant's petrified hand. Niccolo makes a motion for me to lift my arm, a challenge due to the heaviness.

He gathers the tethers in one hand. "Hold on tight to these or else we'd never get Fia back."

"Fia," I repeat softly to her.

I grab the tethers as tight as I can in the unyielding glove, and the bird's weight makes me drop my hand on top of the wall for support. Niccolo steadies the bird immediately, and the bird blinks its already squinted eyes. Once he feels I've secured her, he brings out a small pair of shears and slowly cuts the last stitches and pulls each one out. She stretches her eyes wide with forgotten freedom, and I drift into her golden bright eyes, eyes that seem to see far more than humans give them credit for.

"Now let her feel your control, and show her that you're her mistress."

I nod partially and stare at the buckles on her tethers, the supple leather suffocating her mighty talons; stone-like talons hurting my forearm even through the hardened glove. The sleek curves of her beak lead to a glorious dagger, which opens with a sweet little peep. Her feathers all lay silken like a fur painted by a master.

"Will we be letting her fly today?"

He shakes his head and leans his elbows on the ledge. "No, she won't fly for some time. I'll come daily and let you carry her out here until she adjusts to you. Only when she's completely accepted your control will we let her out on a long leash."

I don't want to be anyone's captor.

"Niccolo, I feel a chill in the air. Will you be so kind to fetch my maid to bring me my favorite cape?"

He bows his head immediately and reaches his arm out to take the falcon back, but I put my free hand up to stop him. "I have a secure hold."

He nods again and leaves the balcony on light feet. I watch her beak carefully as I slowly reach my other hand to release the buckle. She doesn't even notice the freedom, allowing me to quickly undo the other one. Fia studies me and turns her head so that each eye can look through me. Each one has the faintest spark, the dwindling soul-fire yet to be extinguished.

"Go!" I flip my free hand slightly, but she only hops up my arm.

"Go!" I shout. "Be free!"

This time the bird hops into the air, reaches up its suddenly powerful wings, and flies off to the lush forest surrounding the palace. A tight smile brings with it tears, as I wish it could always be this easy. Niccolo closes the door to my suite, and I quickly wipe the shallow tears away. His face falls once he sees the flaccid tethers hanging in my glove.

"How—" But he can't find any respectful words, so he chews on his lower lip and turns to search the sky behind him.

"I saw that the tethers seemed too tight, and I only went to loosen them—"

He spins around again and stares out to a small spot disappearing by the seconds.

"Won't she come back?" I pretend.

"She is gone completely." He lets out a hot breath and pulls all his restraint to force a humble bow. "You must excuse me, lady."

I hold back a smile and nod, then look back into the spotless sky. My maid rushes out with my cloak, and I shake off the glove with the tethers.

"What shall I do with these?" she asks.

I drape the cloak on and brush the whole last hour away with my arm.

"I'm so sick of tethered things."

∞∞∞∞∞∞∞∞∞∞∞∞∞∞∞∞∞∞∞

My maid informs me that I have to dress for a ball that night—the last thing I want to do. I know from the signs I'm at least two months pregnant, and I feel like sleeping all day. I have to wear one of my finest dresses. It's become an unspoken competition between Isabella and me to be told we're the most beautiful in the room. I dress in the blue gown I married Alfonso of Aragon in, and I go down late, after most of the guests are already in the ballroom. I peer in from behind the lush gold velvet curtains with red silk pom-pom trim and see Isabella in a new purple silk dress. She looks heavenly, and I know she has found a more beautiful dress than mine. I have an idea. I take the silver-jeweled lit candelabrum and sweep into the room at the end of the song. All eyes gaze upon me, and I can tell I'm illuminated in the dim room. Everyone turns and gasps at my glowing golden hair and sparkling pearls and rubies in the crown in my hair.

I see Isabella's face as a horde of men make their way to me, trying to engage me in conversation, and it's priceless. After a dozen dances with the many handsome poets and painters invited to Isabella's event, we sit down to dinner. Alfonso's nowhere to be seen, and I'm just as glad not to have to witness him sitting there in pain all night. Isabella's two seats away from me, but she speaks loudly for my benefit.

"Cesare Borgia is a snake. He has crawled in on his belly to sink his teeth into the Duke of Urbino and taken his dukedom."

I say nothing, which provokes her further.

"Lady Lucrezia Borgia"—she never calls me Lucrezia d'Este—"you stayed with my kind cousin in Urbino on your way to us, didn't you?"

"Yes, and the duke and his family were very kind to me and my envoy."

She turns back to her guests. "And her brother, Valentino, repays him with such brutality."

A man states, "Valentino's on his way to conquering Romagna. Everyone is vulnerable to his grasp. Whatever he sets his sights on, he conquers."

A twinge of pride runs through me that Cesare has the country shaking under his thumb.

"I guess we should find some benefit to keeping Dona Borgia in Ferrara," she throws at me.

The gentleman next to me, with whom I've been pleasantly conversing, snaps back, "I can count many, many more reasons to benefit," and he kisses my hand.

"Oh, if you're referring to her beauty, you should see how long it takes her to get that way. I grow tired of waiting for her each morning. I, on the other hand, practically wake up this way."

The man next to her brings us back to Cesare. "I heard that the duke took the right hand and part of a man's tongue off for spreading scandalous rumors about him!"

"I can just imagine what *scandalous rumors* he was spreading." Her eyes flash at me.

"Imagine what he'd do if he heard someone spreading rumors about me?" I flash back.

She gets the message and changes the subject immediately. I'm glad to have such protection.

Once back to my room, my maids are quickly removing all my articles, when one of them gasps while closing the balcony doors.

"What is it?" I ask as I step out of my gown.

"It's a large bird, lady!"

I rush over in my underclothes, and there Fia is, standing resolute on the stone wall. I shoo the maids back and slowly open the doors, expecting her to fly away at any moment. But she stays, and I tiptoe to the other side of the balcony and pretend not to notice her. Slowly, she hops into my peripheral vision, and my heart races when she stands right beside my arm. We stand there together until the cold becomes unbearable, and once I move, she hops back to the other wall.

The next morning, and every morning after, she is there. I save some of the meat from my breakfast, and she slowly begins to take it from my hand. By the end of the week, she even lets me touch her. After our morning hellos, she flies off again into her forest and returns again faithfully at dusk.

∞∞∞∞∞∞∞∞∞∞∞∞∞∞∞∞∞∞∞∞∞

I awake one morning drenched in sweat and wake Alfonso from his snoring to fetch the doctor. There's a fever epidemic spreading through Ferrara, and I fear I have come down with it in my seventh month of pregnancy. I'm burning and shivering and start having severe spasms by nightfall. Alfonso never leaves my side. He sleeps near me and feeds me when my fever lowers. I'm surprised by his attachment and worry. Father and Cesare both send their best doctors when they receive word of my condition. Father takes this opportunity to guilt Ercole into granting two thousand more in my allowance, saying it's the stress from not paying my debts that caused my fever. It works. I'm immediately brought up to the price my father originally fought for. Although my fever continues. Cesare sneaks in to see me on his way to visit the French king in secret, and he wears a disguise of a knight of St. John. He walks in and immediately kneels at my bed and throws his arms around me. I don't even recognize him until he takes his armor off.

"Sister, it's Cesare, be calm. I'm frantic to see you, and I'm glad you don't seem as ill as I've been told."

"I think I may be improving." I try to sit up straighter. "I haven't had a fit all day."

"Well, that's good news, and I brought some cheer of my own to lift your spirits." He starts removing his gloves. "Camerino is yielding," he says with a smile.

"I hope I live to see you King of Romagna."

"You must, for certain. I love you more than I love myself."

I wonder if that's true. He stays for hours, and by the time we kiss our good-byes, I feel I've rebounded. But again by nightfall, my fever rises, causing me great convulsions. One particularly terrible convulsion sends my back arching, and a great pain tears down my abdomen. I scream, sure that I'm dying, but something warm and large slips out between my legs. I begin crying and motion for the doctor to see to what is born far too early. I clench my eyes, hoping to hear a cry, but none comes. I go quickly into delirium, where I have no memory.

Cesare comes rushing back to my side, cutting short his meeting with the king, and is there when I open my eyes again.

"They told me you were dying," he says, holding my hand.

"I still might yet." I laugh but feel it could be true.

The doctor comes in and says, "She needs to be bled, sir."

I panic. "No I don't want to be bled." I remember doctors who performed it on me before.

He speaks to Cesare. "We fear she will perish without a bleeding."

Cesare rubs my hand. "I'll help you through it. You are strong."

The doctor readies to slash across my forearm, and Cesare grabs my foot and pinches it hard. While I'm yelling at Cesare for doing so, the doctor makes his cut, and thanks to Cesare, I hardly register it.

He then rubs my swollen foot soothingly as the blood runs out of my arm and into the bowl it's resting on.

"Do you know that Isabella wrote to me a few days ago?"

"If you are trying to distract me, it's working." I laugh.

"The plump shrew sent me a glowing letter of great praise of my bravery and the valor of my troops at Camerino. She sent with her messenger one hundred carnival masks for us to enjoy ourselves at carnival time."

"Why do you think she's doing that? A month ago, she was spitting venom with your name."

"Well, now that I'm seizing all of these kingdoms, suddenly my two-year-old daughter Luisa is very attractive to her two-year-old son."

"Never do so. Any spawn of hers will be torture for sweet little Luisa."

The next day, I'm much improved, and Cesare comes in to say good-bye.

"You come in and out of my life like a bird in a nest. It would be so nice to stay with you longer."

"Illustrious but sickly sister, I have to go and conquer the world." He puts his hat back on, laughing. We say our good-byes and give our kisses, and I watch him walk out regally. Even though he's done me great harm indirectly, he always shows me great love. I miss him like I've never missed him before.

After I recuperate, I'm told it was a girl. She was buried when I was still delirious. Father sends a messenger, saying:

> *Lucrezia dear,*
> *I am so ecstatic to hear you are better and making a full recovery. If I had not been so sick myself, I would have made my way to be at your side through it all. I'm sure Cesare gave you much comfort, and I heard much of your doting husband who barely left your side. It was a great loss to hear of your premature delivery and of the little angel's passing. The only condolence that can be offered is that at least it was not male.*
>
> *Always,*
> *Your father*

He always has a way of almost making me feel better but then says the wrong thing, leaving me with a bad taste in my mouth.

Alfonso made a promise to God that if I lived, he'll make a pilgrimage by foot to the Madonna di Loreto shrine, but as soon as I'm well, he decides to take a comfortable boat there instead.

My vow to God is that I'll only wear grey. I do so faithfully for two months, but once Christmas arrives, I give in to indulge in my red velvet dress. I know Isabella's getting far too much enjoyment out of my dreary attire.

Christmas morning, the news comes to Ferrara of how the former governor of Romagna is found decapitated and displayed in the piazza, his head impaled on a lance. Cesare proclaims that he carried this act out due to the improper treatment of the people of Romagna, but he writes to me another story:

> *Dearest Sister,*
> *You have probably heard by now about my generous present to Romagna. Though disliked by the people, I have done away with him for personal reasons. I have found that he was plotting against me along with others, including the Orsini that plagues our lives.*
> *I enticed the conspirators to me, closed up all ways out of my city, and locked the gates behind them. I brought the Orsini into a house where Michelotto seized and tied them up and killed them one by one, the Spanish way. I spit in each of their faces as they were turning blue, and said, "This is for Juan."*
>
> *Your faithful and devoted brother,*
> *Duke Valentino*

I try hard to believe him.

Chapter 13

Light emerges red over the dingy city as stiffened corpses float sleep-ily down the putrid river, mouths frozen agape with death. A gasping rattle escapes my lungs as warm little arms furiously try to keep hold of me, their terrified cries fade into the background. A ribbon-tied braid spills out of a man's hand and falls slowly like a feather to the stone floor.

I awake with beads of sweat upon my brow and fumble for my pearl rosary in the dark. The only thing that squelches the persistent nightmares is saying a Hail Mary for each bead, and then I can return to slumber. These nightmares have cropped up just as the plague reached Ferrara, along with the knowledge of many people dying in the streets. There's little I'm afraid of, but the Black Death makes my heart race at the very mention of it.

The only way I can sleep uninterrupted is to flee to the coun-tryside to the Este Villa of Medelana. I bring only my household and forbid them to see anyone from outside the villa. I miss Fia, but I know she will take care of herself. One morning, my maid comes in and says that although they tried to explain to a messenger from the Vatican that we aren't taking messages in this dreadful time of plague, he persists that he has dire news. Immediately, my thoughts go to Father.

"Let him up," I say quickly. It feels like hours until he comes to my room.

Lady Lucrezia d'Este,

I am sorry to have sent this news out so late, but the Vatican was sealed for days due to the delicacy of the pope's illness. Malaria has been consuming Rome this hot summer, and even though his advisors all warned His Holiness to leave to the cool hills of Alban, he dutifully said he had pressing matters to attend to in Rome. Even your corpulent nephew, Juan Borgia, died of malaria, and at the funeral, your father commented rather prophetically, "This month is fatal for fat men."

That night, Cesare and your father dined with the Cardinal Adriano da Corneto. Late that night, your father had fits of vomiting and a high fever. At the very same time, your brother Cesare also fell extremely ill, and the two of them were in separate rooms, both fighting for their lives. His Excellency's stomach became swollen and turned to liquid, while his face became wine-colored. Finally his stomach and bowels bled profusely. After six days of suffering, his last rites were given, and he expired on August 18th. He uttered his last words, "Wait a minute," before expiring.

Thankfully the Duke Valentino recovered, and I am happy to deliver some good news.

Your father was entered in the crypts of St. Peters, but after Pope Pius III was sworn in, he had your father removed after his short stay and forbade the saying of mass

for him, telling the public it was blasphemous to pray for the damned. Your father now lies in Santa Maria in Monse.
I know this is terrible news, and I regret to tell you in such a way, but your father requested that I inform you of all the details.

Your friend,
The Cardinal Cosenza

I wave the messenger away and fall to the floor. To know that the last two weeks he was dying a horrible death without me there ripped my heart. I hadn't seen him in so long, and I should've tried to go to him more. I sit in the dark for two days, turning away all food and drink. On the third day, I bring out my black dress again and ready myself to go to Rome to fight to put Father back in St. Peter's, where he belongs. But another messenger interrupts my packing.

Dear Sister,
I know you must be heartbroken and grieving as I am. Cardinal Cosenza has informed me that he has sent you a messenger with the news, and knowing you, I bet you are packing to come to Rome. Do not come here; it is not safe. While I was struggling to live, I got word Father was passing and his servants were already robbing his dying body. May they all go to Hell.
Too ill to go myself, I sent Don Michelotto to salvage whatever he could of Father's treasured possessions. There was a wild scene of disorder that ensued. I scrambled to save anything I could and had to flee the Vatican to the protection of the cardinals at the Castel Sant'Angelo. Promise me you will not come to pay respects to Father. You will be in jeopardy if you do so.

Your brother,

Cesare

I send back a message.

> *Dearest Brother,*
> *I am so glad that you are well, but I am distraught at the suddenness and brutality of Father's death and burial. I will not go to Rome, but promise me you will be careful. I have raised as many ducats as I can in such short notice and will be sending you my cavalry to aid you. I will send more money as I can procure it when I get back to Ferrara.*
>
> *Love and prayers for you,*
> *Lucrezia*

Alfonso is on his way home from a campaign when he hears the news. I decide to return to Ferrara, and my only solace is that Fia hasn't given up in my absence. She's there, preening her feathers, and peeps happily as I offer her some rabbit. I run my hand down her scale-like back and say, "Thank God I have you, my little flame."

After declining to go to a dinner party that night with the Estes, I creep to the balcony above the dining room to hear what news people have from Rome. After some small idle chatter, my name is mentioned, and my ears perk up.

"Where is Lady Lucrezia tonight? I hear she has returned."

"She is grieving in her room," Ercole answers.

"I understand she must be beside herself with all of the horrors she must have gotten wind of."

"Do tell, what kinds of horrors are you referring to?" Isabella inquires.

"Well, Pope Alexander VI's terrible death, to start. People who went to his viewing said they had never seen such a terrible state of decomposition only days after death."

"Some have said his face was a ghastly color of over-ripened mulberry, and his tongue was doubled its size and not able to fit within his also swollen lips," another chimes in.

I fight back the bile rising in my throat in order to continue listening to what everyone's talking about behind my back.

"That's nothing compared to unusual swelling of his already opulent belly. They say he swelled as wide as he was long!"

"Yes, I'd heard that the swelling caused great trouble for the undertakers, since they couldn't fit him into the largest coffin. They had to jump on the bloated body to jam it into the coffin, which made it spew sulfurous gasses out of every orifice!"

Isabella as well as a few of the others speaking laugh at this part, and I turn to leave, not wanting to hear any more about my father's end.

Yet Ercole changes the subject slightly. "I have heard a rumor that they thought, due to the strange decomposition and parallel illness of Cesare, it might have been poison."

Whomever he had been speaking to laughs. "Indeed, there has been discussion of poison since they got ill after dining, but many are suspecting that Duke Valentino and Alexander mistakenly poisoned each other while attempting to poison the cardinal!"

Some gasp at this idea, and I know it's lies, and I walk back to the comfortable isolation of my room. When news comes of Pius's death, I know things will worsen for Cesare when I hear who has replaced him.

A messenger comes from Sancia.

Dearest Lucrezia,
I wish this was another letter about how Rodrigo is growing and becoming handsomer by the day, but unfortunately I have more bad news to deliver. Pope Julius II's army captured Michelotto and Cesare's cavalry on December 1st. He wrote to Cesare that he couldn't wait to torture his infamous henchman to derive such

"political skills" to gain for his own personal use. Cesare, enraged by his threat, promised that he would negotiate, but once his messenger arrived, he had him beaten and dangled from one of the fortresses' turrets. Furious, Julius had Cesare locked in the same tower Cesare had my poor brother murdered in. A week later, he was sent to a prison in Spain.

Even though I will always harbor a deep hatred for Cesare and feel that this is what he is due for all of the harm he has done to so many, I know you love him and would want to hear of his imprisonment.

Rodrigo is thriving and wants me to tell you he loves you as do I. Please write me back. I have written five letters without word of how you are faring and will only be able to rest when I receive word that you are well.

Your sister,
Sancia

I decide I'll be of no help to Cesare if I wallow in my room, and I know I need to try to get him freed. Alfonso makes it clear he will not support me when it comes to Cesare, so I write to everyone I can, begging for help. In the meantime, I've yet another failed pregnancy and worry that if I don't provide Alfonso with an heir, I can be removed and replaced. I know now, with no protection from Father or Cesare, I'm extremely vulnerable, and know I have to keep trying to carry a baby to full term. I get pregnant right away, and I'm happy to see Alfonso never showing any signs of dissatisfaction with me.

Ercole reveals signs of illness around Christmas, and by January twenty-fifth, he passes on, making Alfonso and me Duke and Duchess of Ferrara. I dress in crimson velvet with gold fringes with matching headdress and go down to hundreds of Ferrarians gathered outside our palace in the frigid cold. I watch as Alfonso rides his adorned horse through the crowd, waving, and as he comes up to the palace plaza, I go down to meet him.

It's a powerful moment as I look down on all of the happy faces in the crowd calling out our names, and I realize all that Father and Cesare had hoped for me. With Father buried in an unknown grave and Cesare imprisoned, here I am standing as the Duchess of Ferrara. Alfonso, looking the handsomest I've ever seen him, smiles with dimple showing and holds his hand out to me. As I bend to kiss it, he shakes his head, pulls me into him, and kisses my forehead instead. The people cheer.

I try to keep my mind off of my pregnancy by throwing myself into patronizing the arts. I enjoy dining with the poets, artists, and courtiers of Ferrara and hearing of the world in their fresh and observant eyes. Everything I lack with Alfonso I find at these dinners. Ferrara quickly begins a thriving center for the arts, thanks to my attention.

September nineteenth, I give birth finally to a son that we name Alexandro. I know something is wrong, though, when I hear a weak and low cry, not the strong cries I remember hearing from Giovanni and Rodrigo. Not only is the child not well, but my legs feel ice cold. The doctors attending me try to warm them with hot towels, and a fever comes and burns for five hours. I pull the fragile Alexandro to my breast, and he will not nurse, only sleeps in my arms. I send for the best doctors, and I'm angered when Isabella, who was having a sickly pregnancy, requests me to send my doctors to her.

I write back:

No, Alexandro is still in need of their care.

He holds on for a month and three days but dies anyway. Isabella gives birth to her second son.

Finally, some good news comes through a messenger to raise my spirits.

Dear Sister,

I am writing to you from the safety of Navarre. I escaped from La Mota by throwing a rope out of the window in the tower where they held me. The rope was smuggled in by allies you had begged to assist me. While I was hanging from the rope, guards, seeing my escape in progress, cut the rope, and I fell half the way down into their putrid moat. Though badly injured and limping, I crawled out and ran for the safe harbor of my in-law Jean d'Albret. While I was imprisoned, His Evilness Julius II robbed all of my bank accounts and took away my titles. I am still loved greatly by my soldiers, who are already swarming to my cause and have some faithful allies prepared to regain my titles. I would appreciate anything you can send to aid me, although I am grateful enough for all that you have done for me.

Yours,
Duke of Romagna

I send everything I can and feel that the tide may be turning back in our benefit. I'm pregnant again, and carnival celebrations are to begin. I throw myself into the festivities. I dance, ride carriages all over Ferrara, climb stairs to various parties, and have a joyous night. During the night, though, my body protests to all of the activities by aborting yet another small piece of me— God's punishment for leaving others to raise my two healthy sons.

Alfonso blames me at once. "You're a fool thinking you can enjoy carnival when you are carrying a child! You know you have such difficulties, but you still are so careless."

I keep crying in guilt.

"You must not want this as much as I do, or you would be more careful."

He's right, and when I get pregnant, again I barely leave my bed. Isabella has her third son.

∞∞∞∞∞∞∞∞∞∞∞∞∞∞∞∞∞∞∞∞

It's the same brown wolf I've seen in so many dreams. Its coat shining in the sunlight, with head bowed, sniffing out its next prey. Suddenly, five large dogs surround him with teeth bared. The wolf lunges at the closest dog, and the dogs take him down with great yelping. The dogs disappear, and the bleeding wolf limps feebly over to me and dies at my feet.

Alfonso comes in to see me like he usually does after a day of testing grenades, but this time he has a somber look on his face.

"What has happened?"

"I hate to bring you more bad news, especially when this pregnancy is faring so well."

He sits on the edge of my bed as I hold my breath.

"Cesare's dead."

I throw my head in my pillow and can hear only parts of what Alfonso's saying between my sobs.

"Cesare was fighting for the King of Navarre when he was ambushed, stripped of armor, and left bleeding on the ground."

I pull myself up and yell to God, "The more I try to please you, the more you try me!"

Alfonso tries to console me, even though he hated Cesare so. "It may please you to know that he died triumphant against my brother-in-law's enemies."

He walks out to let me grieve yet again. I decide to pretend fortitude when I'm among the public, although I feel so much of me has died inside, not even being able to share grief with anyone else who loved Cesare.

A happy day comes to me when I need it most, as Ercole is born healthy, handsome, and full of life. I never saw Alfonso so happy. I relax at finally having done my part.

After another successful birth of a son a year later, Ferrara is at war. The despicable Pope Julius II sets his sights on attaining Ferrara and lays siege to our city. It is the first time Fia stays away from the palace, and I hope she doesn't attempt to return amidst all the warfare. I try to flee with my children to Milan, but as I'm getting into my carriage, a mob of villagers comes rushing at me frantically, screaming, "The duchess is leaving us!"

They get in front of the horses, grab hold of their bridles, and circle around us. A young man pleads, "Our lady, you cannot leave us now!"

"I must protect the heirs to Ferrara," I try to explain, but they start shaking the carriage.

Their leader shouts, "If you leave, then we will all abandon Ferrara!"

A desperate uproar rings in our ears and grows with fisted encouragement. I bow my head and take Ercole's and Ippolito's little hands and walk back into the palace.

For three years, the wars rage, and we're held hostage in the palace. I've completely given up that Fia will ever return. Alfonso shows amazing fortitude and resistance against the powerful pope. Only his exceptional knowledge of ammunition keeps the pope at bay. One day, as Alfonso is instructing the defense of one of the palace walls, a ricocheting piece of masonry hits his head. They carry him to our bedroom with his head and nose bleeding profusely, and I'm sure he's dead.

"Alfonso!" I scream as the doctors are wiping off the blood.

A doctor begins pressing around on his forehead. "It's a miracle; it did not damage the bone."

I lie with him all night as the explosions ring out outside the palace walls, and he wakes up early that morning.

"My head aches terribly." He winces as he holds his swollen head.

"The doctors need you to rest."

"Rest? How can I rest when Julius's men are storming the castle!"

He starts trying to take off his bandages, and I call for the doctor outside.

The doctor runs in, saying, "Duke d'Este you must rest and leave your bandages still. They are keeping you from bleeding."

"I have to go to my men. I will leave the bandages, but I must go."

No one can keep him, and he leaves. His soldiers were so proud that he returned that they all bandaged their heads in fraternal support.

Trumpets ring out a week later, and a herald calls out, "Julius is retreating! Duke d'Este is victorious!"

Everyone in the palace runs out on the balconies around the palace and watches as the soldiers of Ferrara parade around the city with Alfonso cantering his noble horse in the lead. Bells ring out from every church, children are throwing flowers, and guns are going off in celebration as the sun sets, while chills run up and down my body in sheer joy.

The joy is effervescent, as all the joy in my life seems to be. Sancia's letter arrives a week later.

> *Dearest Sister,*
> *My hand shakes so as I write this letter; please excuse the effect that it has upon my penmanship. I would rather this be our usual letter of courtly gossip and fashion, but I fear I need to deliver you terrible news. Rodrigo became ill suddenly only days ago and quickly succumbed to death in a quiet sleep of fever. The best doctors ministered to him, and I never left his side. He left this world knowing you loved him dearly, and I find such relief knowing he's gone to be with Alfonso in heaven. Please, sister, do not despair and be sure to write me immediately so I am assured you are well.*
>
> *Always yours,*
> *Sancia*

I would not let this in. There is only so much grief one can absorb. I asked Alfonso every year if I could bring him to court, and every year he said there would be talk. I kept planning a trip to visit him, but my pregnancies always kept me from traveling. Now it was too late. I'll never get to hold him again. The last time I kissed him was that day in the garden; now he's gone at thirteen. I feel nothing and lose all interest in anything I loved before. I can only devote myself to the nearby convent; I think that if I'm more pious and charitable, God will stop testing me so. Even though I have so little to lose now, I sell all of my fine dresses and give the money to the church. I stop caring about my appearance as my body thickens, and I seem to age ten years overnight.

Even though I've lost my youthful looks, Alfonso still sleeps in my bed, and another boy is born, Alexandro. He suffers with fever and sores all over his head. One of my doctors says, "I have seen babies born with this condition when parents are syphilitic."

Syphilis seemed a benign condition to me. Cesare, my father, and Alfonso d'Este all had it.

"Syphilis can cause infant deaths?"

"Yes, that and miscarriage. It's a wonder you've had healthy children at all."

I'm relieved that this whole time it was not something I should feel guilty about but actually something given to me by Alfonso.

Alexandro dies at four months old, and I decide never to give another child the doomed name Alexandro.

I get pregnant again immediately and see that I grow weaker and weaker with each pregnancy. I have a daughter named Leonora prematurely, but she survives, and a year later I have a healthy boy I named Francesco. Each pregnancy, I've complete bed rest, leaving only for church, and each one takes me longer and longer to recuperate from.

Pregnant for the eighth time, I'm so weak I can't get out of bed. I feel faint upon standing.

Alfonso grows extremely worried. "You're wasting away, Lucrezia. You must have lost ten pounds in a month."

"I will lie in bed until the baby comes, and I'll be fine."

"I'm demanding that there will be no more dieting or fasting for Lent!"

"I promise no fasting."

"This is the last time you'll be with child. I fear it's killing you and feel responsible. We will have separate rooms after this baby is born."

Two months later, I become so listless that I'm drifting in and out of consciousness and cannot eat. I awake to overhearing a doctor talking to Alfonso.

"We have all come to the agreement that we must purge her of the bad material in her womb. It is killing her and needs to be emptied, or she may not live another day."

Alfonso gives permission, and the doctors prepare me for the procedure, when I feel a rush of hot liquid spill between my thighs and onto the sheets under me.

"Her water has just broke. The procedure is useless now. She's giving birth."

Alfonso leaves the room as my ladies come and hold my hand. Too tired to keep my eyes open, I hear everything that's happening, and only when something confuses me will I exert the energy to open my eyes for a moment. I feel another rush of warm liquid and can tell by the quiet that the baby has been born. I open my eyes to see a tiny weak baby girl.

Closing my eyes again, I say with all my energy, "Name her Isabella Maria and have her christened right away."

Six days becomes a blur of infrequent short moments of lucidity, a fever rages within me, and my nose keeps bleeding. Even when I try to open my eyes, I see darkness, and only slurred words fall out of my cracked lips. The seventh day, I regain both speech and sight, and even though everyone thinks I'm recovering, I can feel it's my moment to atone before I die.

I dictate a letter immediately.

Your Holiness, Pope Leo X,
I beg God's forgiveness as I feel my life is fading from
me. Though I have always tried to live chaste and pious,
my life is not free from sin. Please say a prayer for my
soul, as I fear I must yield to nature soon; I am tired and
welcome the rest.

Your humble servant,
Lucrezia d'Este

Alfonso opens the balcony doors to let in fresh air, and he ducks as something wonderful flies through the doors and lands like a baby's kiss on the top of my canopy.

"Oh, Fia, you've come back."

She chirps away in long-awaited greeting, but all those present know the omen of a bird in the house. Alfonso hands me pieces of chicken he needlessly brought for me to eat, and Fia hops down to take the pieces gently from my thin fingers.

I cling to life for a few more days, I hold on to Alfonso, who never leaves to eat or sleep. The doctors try to purge my womb of infection one last time, but I have a few great convulsions and close my eyes to the night.

Beacons	Life 1 Ancient Egypt	Life 2 Ancient Sparta	Life 3 Viking Denmark	Life 4 Medieval England	Life 5 Renaissance Italy
Mole on left hand—Prophetic dreams	Sokaris	Alcina	Liam	Elizabeth	Lucrezia
Scar on forehead—Large, honey-brown eyes—Magic	Bastet	Ophira	Erna	Rowan	Sancia
Space between teeth—Green sparkling eyes	Nun	Theodon	Thora	Simon	Alfonso of Aragon
Mole by wide-set, dark eyes	Nebu	Mother	Ansgar	Malkyn	Adriana
Freckles—Brown eyes	Khons	Arcen	Keelin-Mother	Emeline	Caterina
Birthmark above knee—Amber eyes	Edjo	Kali	Dalla	Lady Jacquelyn	Cesare
Two moles on jaw—Black eyes	Apep	Leander	Ragnar	Brom—Children's Father	Rodrigio
Picks teeth—Steel-grey eyes	Vizier	Magistrate	Seamus-Father	Ulric	Michelotto
Golden eyes—Animal	Sehket-Cat	Proauga-Horse	Borga-Goose	Mousie-kitten	Fia-Falcon
Scar on forearm—Slate-blue eyes	*	Nereus	Chief Toke	Daniel	Pope Alexander VI
Big Smile—Grey-blue eyes	*	Demetrius	Una	*	Perotto
Dimpled cheek—Brown-green eyes	*	*	Rolf	Hadrian	Alfonso d'Este Duke of Ferrara
Indigo eyes—Musician / Dancer	*	*	Gunhilda	Oliver	Juan
Orange Hair—Hazel eyes	*	*	Inga	Maid Helena	Guilia
Widow's peak—Ice blue eyes	*	*	Konr	Fendel	Isabella
Bray laugh	*	*	Orm	Gussalen	*
Pointed ears	*	*	Hela	*	Niccolo

Scar above eye	*	*	*	*	Jofre
Beady eyes—Cleft Chin	*	*	*	*	Sforza
Breaks out in nervous hives	*	*	*	*	*
Fish-lips—Empty, dull eyes	*	*	*	*	*
Very rosy cheeks	*	*	*	*	*

* = Not present in that life

Sixth Life
The Spanish Crusade

Chapter 1

"Clean up, you little pig!" Hector shouts as he grabs the back of my shirt.

"Let me go!" I scream.

He puts my head in a chokehold and drags me back into the house. I can barely breathe with how tight his arm is pressing against my throat.

"I didn't make that mess!"

"Of course, you did. Your mother makes your food and works all day to provide for you, so this is your mess to clean."

I look around. There are plates left in the sink from our breakfast this morning. My mother is working so much since Hector is now worthless, and she doesn't have much time to sweep and clean. She always asks Hector to clean while she's gone, and this is how Hector cleaned.

"Clean or I'm going to get the crop."

"Fine!" I have to relent. "Let go of me!"

He gives me a hard shove that sends me headfirst into the wall, and I go to work while rubbing my head.

I scrub the dishes, dry, and put them away. I sweep up all of the dirt in the three rooms to our small house and take the rugs outside to beat. The whole time under his watchful eye, so I don't escape like I have so many times before.

He inspects everything I do. He tells me to keep scrubbing a dish even though it's clean; he keeps making me sweep even though there's no end to the dust you can pick up; he keeps making me beat and beat the rugs for an hour. He relishes these moments of control and sits with his feet up on the wall, drinking his wine, watching me.

At the end, when he can't possibly find more for me to clean, I ask, "Can I go now?"

He searches around, not finding anything, but then slowly, and with a treacherous smile, takes off his mud-crusted boots and rubs the bottoms together, making a filthy mess on the immaculate floor. "Look at how dirty my boots are. Make them shine, and clean up that mess."

I take them outside and see him now sitting in the window, ready to pounce in case I run. I sit on the doorstep as a boy rides down the street on the shoulders of his father.

My mother comes home early, looking very tired, with her hair falling out of her braid like frazzled wings. She kisses me on the head weakly and goes inside.

"Why is Luis polishing your boots?"

"The boy asked me if he could polish them."

"Everything is perfect, thank you."

"All this cleaning's made my back worse." He grimaces as he rubs his back.

"Oh, I'm sorry, you didn't need to do all this," she says and rubs his back for him.

He makes me sick.

"I have some bad news," my mother says.

"What news?"

"Lady de Strozzi is leaving with her household to her country estate next week for the whole summer."

"Well, wouldn't we go too?"

"She is only bringing those without families." She nervously tucks her disheveled hair behind both of her pointed ears.

"Can't we leave Luis with someone?"

"I have no family here, and his father's family lives three days away."

He breathes out a heavy, prolonged sigh.

"You will have to get a job, Hector."

"You know I can't work with my bad back."

He threw his back out lifting baskets of fish months ago and still enjoys pretending to be sore whenever Mother is home but gets up with great speed and agility when catching me for a beating.

"The armada ships have come to harbor here, fleeing the storms. They're restocking supplies and looking for volunteers." Her voice lifts up optimistically at the end.

He clears his throat. "Are you telling me I should sign on?"

She gets nervous and begins picking lint from her muslin skirt. "I was only thinking you might want to ask what the pay would be?"

"I am broken, but if you want me to suffer, I will do anything for you."

I hear my mother walk over to him, and I gather they're embracing, and my lip involuntarily pulls up in one corner.

"No, I'll speak to the lady of the house tomorrow and plead to have her bring us."

∞∞∞∞∞∞∞∞∞∞∞∞∞∞∞∞∞∞∞∞∞∞

That night, I go to bed only to wake up hearing the noises I've grown so used to coming from the bed my stepfather and mother share. I know all too well what is occurring right behind me. I try to go back to bed as fast as I can, but I can't fall back asleep until his unashamed grunting ends.

As soon as the sun comes up, I run out of the house. I skip breakfast, even though my stomach is aching from hunger, just to avoid having Hector catch me. Once I'm out on the streets, I feel safe. I waste the day by making my usual rounds to all of my favorite places. I go to the house in the market where an old man always gives me an apple if I roll his cart from his shed and push it to his spot down the street.

Then I sit on the docks and eat every bit I can chew off the apple, only spitting out the seeds. I watch the ships come in and unload their goods and ship back out of port. I stay there for hours. The water is clear and a deep blue, especially against the rocky coast. The bay is large and sheltered, with our small, walled city on the peninsula out in the center. Today I see the ships my mother spoke about. It looks as if the whole horizon is filled with ships. I've never seen so many in my life.

There are many children running wild in the streets. I never have the courage to go up and talk to them, but I sit and watch them play from afar. When my stomach starts gnawing again, I have to distract myself by running up to the graveyard. The cemetery is right beside the stone cathedral up a small, gradual hill from the water. There's a worn pathway up the center with the most beautiful statuaries on top of the wealthy people's graves. One of my favorites is a beautiful angel with her wings spread over a child's grave—Don Tomas, 1580-1587—and I always wish I had his parents. My other favorite is one with the Virgin Mary carved from stone. She has her head down and her hand covering her face, weeping.

I wish Papa's stone was fancy like that. His is at the very top in the pauper's graves, which are unmarked except for a small stone embedded in the ground with a number on it. Number seventy-seven. At least he had lucky numbers. I spend the time wiping away the dirt and moss that would creep over his stone, and gather any sort of free beauty I can find in the woods and fields near it. If there are no wild flowers to gather, I find shiny sticks or smooth rocks. I remember when he took me down to the water to skip stones I found for him. Every time I tried, my father laughed as mine sank after hitting the water, and I watched in awe as he threw his, and the stone seemed to skip off into the horizon like it had wings.

I bring him a nice flat and smooth stone, place it on his grave, and imagine him saying, "This is perfect; let's watch it fly."

He died before he could ever teach me how to skip.

When I see the sun starting to go down, I race off to the market again to bring the old man's cart back in for another apple I start salivating for before I even reach for it from his spotted hand. Then I get nervous that it's time to go back home and pray my mother doesn't have to stay late for her Lady. I creep up to the window and try to see if my mother is cooking dinner, when I'm grabbed by my collar.

"What do we have here?" His breath makes my eyes water. "You ran away again without doing your chores," he says with his voice going up and down in a singsong way.

This means my mother still isn't home.

"You know what your punishment will be, and I don't understand why you make me do this to you."

He drags me back into the house into our bedroom. He closes the door and walks to his trunk to get the too familiar crop. I make a dash for the door, but I'm stopped by a kick to the side of my thigh, sending me crashing into the door. He's on top of me quickly and hits every unexposed area, any area that can be concealed from my mother. After he's finished, and I stop screaming and give in to crying, he sits back on his bed. I don't attempt to get up but try to rub away the sting from my thighs and back, curled up on the floor.

He's still holding his whip in his hand, scratching the two moles on the side of his jaw where hair won't grow.

He stares at me with his black eyes. "It's your fault your mother won't have a job. They don't want any misbehaving bastards at their country villa."

I wonder if this is true and keep sniffling.

"You know you'd be doing us all a favor if you went out tomorrow and never came back." He keeps laughing. "Your mother has practically said that to me, that she wished she didn't have to worry about you or care for you anymore."

I wish it wasn't true.

"I'm going to keep beating you and beating you until you get tired of it and leave. Or I might get lucky one of these days and hit you hard enough that you never get back up."

"I'm going to tell her this time." I start getting up, and he stands over me.

"This time!" His voice rises up to a squeal. "You've done it before, and how'd that work out? She always believes me. You see she loves me more than you."

I hate that he's right.

"Just go, go right now. Don't come back; we'll all be better off." He opens the door wide.

I want to get away from him and away from his words. I wish I could believe my mother would pick me over him, but I'm not sure. She's taken his side in everything, and even when I showed her my bruises, he would make up some story of something terrible I did, and then she sends me to bed without dinner, with him laughing silently behind her back. I can't trust her, and part of me feels he's right, she does wish I'd leave. Leave her to start a new life with Hector.

I run, and when I turn around to close the front door, I see triumph in his cold eyes, and the last words I hear are, "Don't come back."

I don't know where to go. These streets are dangerous at night, and my mother always makes me come in when the sun goes down. I keep running along the stone road cupping the harbor, but I'm running without any destination in mind. I keep searching my memory for any place I might go, and the only one I think I can go to.

Chapter 2

I knock on the door. It takes a long time, and by how slow he's shuffling, I realize that is why it's taking so long. He smiles when he sees me, but then concern creeps over his face.

"What brings you here so late, boy?"

"I have no place to go tonight. Can I stay with you?"

His eyes widen and then he runs his hand over his wiry beard. "You have no home?"

"No, sir."

He glances back into his apartment as an old woman calls for him.

"It's nothing. I'll be right back!" he yells to her, rubbing a large mole by his eye worriedly.

He whispers now, "You can't stay with me, but you can sleep in the shed. For one night!"

He points to the shed where his fruit cart is. "Go out to the shed, and I'll come out to unlock it when I get a chance."

I go to the shed, but it's almost an hour before I see his hunched form shuffle out and darkness has already fallen.

"Boy?" he calls out into the darkness.

"Here, sir."

His hand shakes as he pulls his long key from his coat pocket. It's excruciating watching him fumble over and over again trying to get the key into the lock hole.

"Tricky little thing." He finally gets it in, and it pops open. A little white terrier runs out happily around his master's legs. I'm surprised he keeps his dog in the shed.

The old man pats the dog on the head. "Bella, good girl." Then looks at me and says, "She keeps the rats away from my apples." He puts his hand on my shoulder. "Now, boy, I have my whole cart filled with fruit. I'm trusting you to take only one apple for your supper and leave the rest, since it's all I have to make my living." He pulls a piece of bread out of his pocket and puts it in my hand. "This is all I can give you." He points in the shed. "There's a cart cover in there made of burlap you can sleep on."

"Thank you, sir."

"Just one night."

I bow my head to him and walk into the shed as he closes it behind me. I hear him fumble once again with the lock, and I realize I should have relieved myself before I went in. I'm locked in for the night. If he dies in his sleep, no one will know I'm here. As soon as I make a bed out of the scratchy burlap, I take the bread and stuff it into my mouth, barely chewing it before I hurry it down to my impatient stomach. Bella watches me eagerly with her golden eyes, and I feel so bad, I give her a small piece, even though my stomach moans in protest. I take the fattest apple I can find, and it disappears too fast. I lie back and look up at the mountain of red shining apples and can't sleep with the terrible temptation of devouring the pile. Bella, happy to have someone in her shed, curls up in the crook between my shoulder and head and lays her head in the dip of my neck. We're glad to have each other.

In the morning, the keys jingle, and I'm relieved he didn't die overnight. Bella gets up and wags her tail at his approach. His wife opens up the back door and croaks out, "Bella," but the dog stays right by my feet.

The old man laughs. "I think she likes you. She never passes up sausage in the morning."

I help him move his cart to market, and Bella runs beside me the whole way. He reaches for the usual apple but puts his finger up for me to wait, and my mouth waters as he withdraws a greasy parcel from his pocket and hands it to me. I can smell what it is—sausages! I take them quickly, and I'm so happy I hug him and nearly knock him over. He smiles and coughs as he regains his balance. I run off as Bella follows.

"Don't forget to help me at sunset!" he calls out between cupped hands. "And take care of Bella!"

I'm so happy to have a friend that I share my sausages with her. She is the whitest white and has a look to her eyes that makes her different from any dog I've known: a spark of human understanding. She follows me to the docks and even snatches a fish from a basket left by some fishermen. The look on their faces as she pulls a herring out of the basket that is half the size of her and runs back to me is priceless. As soon as I see what she did, I start running, trying to find a good place for us to escape to.

When she drops the fish for me, I say, "You can eat it like that, but I can't."

I try to think about how I can find a fire to cook it on. I pick up the fish and walk along the dirt road until I catch the smell of an open fire. I follow it around some houses and see a small lean-to made out of sailcloth and a small fire with an empty spit over it. I approach slowly, but Bella runs right into the tent.

"Bella!" I whisper, but nothing seems to happen, and I peer in and see Bella sitting down on someone's tattered quilt.

With no one in sight, I risk using the fire for a few minutes and take my shirt off to take the skewer off and pierce the already gutted fish. My mouth waters as the smell emerges from the fish, but it seems to draw the attention of someone else.

"Get out of my house!"

I hear a voice behind me and turn to see a boy who is either slightly older than me or simply taller. He is dirty, unkempt, and carries a large stick in his hands that he holds over me threateningly. Bella barks and grabs on to his pant leg and begins thrashing.

"Get him off!"

"Bella!" I shout, and she runs back over to me.

"Look, I was just using your fire for a minute. If you let me finish cooking this fish, I'll give you some."

He thinks about it for a moment and gives a stiff nod. He sits across from me with his thumbnail between the small space in his teeth and watches the fish turn in the fire.

"I think it's done," he says only a minute after waiting.

"You must be starving."

He holds his stomach. "I couldn't find anything all day."

I take the fish off the spit as he pulls out a knife. I straighten away from him, but he reaches for the fish and fillets it, giving me the bigger half. He gives the skin to Bella.

It's the best fish I've ever had, and after it's gone, I get up to leave and say, "Thanks for the fire."

"Where are you going?"

"Don't you want me to leave?'

"Well," he says as he dribbles his stick, making an eight on its side over and over again in the dirt, "there's nothing else to do."

I sit again, and Bella crawls into my lap and lies down.

"My name's Pepe. What's yours?"

"Luis."

"Do you live in a house?"

"No."

"Do you have parents?"

"Not anymore."

He looks happy about this.

"I live here and can move whenever I want to. If I feel like being by the water, I move. If I feel like being in the woods, I go."

"That sounds really good."

I envy his little lean-to, studying it to see if I can find material to do the same.

"All I need, I have right here." He pats his pocket proudly and slowly pulls out each item. "This here's my knife. Used to be my father's before he died fighting the Dutch. Here's Auradona; she's my flint rock. If I lost her, I'd be done for. Last, I have my sewing kit."

He unwraps a piece of cloth with a needle made of bone and one spool of black thread.

"It was my mother's. I use it to fix all of the holes in my clothes and the quilt I found." He carefully wraps everything back up. "She gave it to me before she dumped me at Saint Mary's." He points back up the hill.

"St. Mary's?"

"The orphanage." He begins making his eights again incessantly. "You don't ever want to end up there." His eyes light up. "That place was so full of kids, the nuns would try to control them, but they were so wild, one of the nuns went crazy. She started running up and down the hall with her hands up by her head saying 'Baah-dah-da-da-da-da-da-da-da!'"

I start laughing, and he gets up to show me.

"Baah-dah-da-da-da-da-da-da-da!" he screams and runs around the fire.

I keep laughing until Bella begins barking, and as I look up, I see dark clouds moving in.

"Pepe, I have to go. A storm is coming."

"Where do you sleep?"

"I have to go!" I start running. "Come, Bella!"

"I might have room for you if you need a place to stay!" he screams out over the distance, but I only wave him off, trying to get to the market before the sky opens up.

The old man's already put the burlap cover on and is trying to move the cart but is having trouble. I run right up and start helping him push. He releases the cart and pats his head with his handkerchief as he sighs. "Thank the Lord."

I push as fast as I can without toppling the apples, but the rain begins pouring down as we round the corner to his house.

We're getting soaked as he stands with the lock and once he opens it, he gives me an apple. He asks as I turn to go, "Where are you going?"

"I thought you didn't want me to stay another night?"

"It's pouring. God would strike me dead if I sent you out in this rain after helping me. Now get in quick."

He smiles and leaves but comes back ten minutes later with a few things under his arms. He hands them to me. "Bella will be happy to have you again. She hates storms."

After pulling the door closed, he locks the shed. There's no light in the shed, but I can feel he gave me a whole loaf of bread with a pat of butter and what feels like an old nightshirt. It smells a little of him, but I'm soaked to the bone and start to get a chill. It feels wonderful to put on the soft, old shirt, and I make my bed of burlap and share my dinner. When the cracking thunder rattles the shed, Bella won't stop shaking. I try to fold her ears over so she can't hear it, but she doesn't relax until it's passed. I think of Pepe and wonder how it must be sleeping on the ground tonight.

Chapter 3

The morning routine is the same, and Bella and I run off with our sausages. I decide to save one, even though my stomach wants it, and run off to find Pepe. His camp is empty. I wander back in the brushy area above the large rocks by the water and hear a strange call.

"Chick-a-bow!"

I look up and see Pepe standing on a huge rock, calling to me. I run up quickly and see he was smart in making his lean-to under a boulder that sticks out like a ledge.

"Were you dry last night?"

"As a biscuit," he says proudly. "What about you? Where'd you go?"

"I know a good place." Not wanting to admit someone has to help me.

"I smell something good." He puts his nose up to the air, and his light green eyes sparkle as I bring out the sausage I saved for him.

"You owe me," I say as he throws the sausage into his mouth and smiles after. Why does that space in his teeth always draw my eyes so?

"I'm still starving." He rubs his bony ribs. "Let's go and see what we can find at the docks."

"Bella got that fish yesterday." I laugh.

"Maybe she'll do it again."

We hide behind some crates by a pier as the fishermen are bringing in their baskets. Once Bella sees them put one on the dock, she runs for it, but this time, the fishermen shout at her as she nears. She tries to bite their ankles, and once they shake her loose, she runs in circles as they try to kick her. One of the fishermen knocks into the basket, spilling the fish in the whole chaotic scene. Bella quickly grabs a large fish and takes off with two fishermen after her. Pepe looks at me, and we both know she's heading right for us. We run off back into the street, and Pepe just misses getting hit by a carriage. He's much faster than me, but I see a small woodshed by a house and whistle. Pepe comes running back, and we hide, along with Bella and her huge fish.

We hear the men come running by, panting. One curses, and then it sounds like they left. After waiting a little longer, we look at each other and start laughing. We laugh so hard that we realized they must not be around, and we start pulling ourselves out, when we hear crying. It's coming from under the wood. As we pull a few pieces away, we see a younger, smaller boy curled up in a space between the wood stack and the shed wall.

"Go away!" he yells as he feels the wood pulled off his back.

"We're not going to hurt you. We were only hiding in here."

"I found this place first," he snaps.

"Whoa, easy there, tough guy," Pepe says.

"We're leaving with our fish." I start to move out.

At the mention of fish, his brown-haired head pops up, he searches our hands, and upon seeing the big fish, he suddenly sits up.

"How old are you?" Pepe asks.

"Twelve."

"Yeah, right!" Pepe says.

"Okay, I'm ten."

Even that seems old for his small stature.

"How did you get that?" I ask, seeing a large wound on his forehead, not yet healed.

"A group of boys around the block beat me with sticks, telling me this was their street."

I suddenly feel bad for him.

"Why don't you come with us and share our fish?" Pepe says as he pulls Auradona out of his pocket. "I can start a fire to cook it."

The small boy's eyes flash at the mention of a cooked dinner. We help him out and run off with Bella in front spinning this way and that to figure out which direction we are headed.

After we eat our fish, I pull out my apple, and the new boy and Pepe both cheer. I feel like a hero. I put my hand out, and Pepe realizes I want his knife. I cut the apple into equal pieces. We lay back after our bellies are full. Full is such an unfamiliar feeling to us all.

"What's your name?" I ask.

"Andres."

"This is Pepe, and I'm Luis."

"We make a pretty good team," Pepe says to me.

"I can help too!" Andres tries. "I can run really fast, you know."

"What's your story?"

Andres looks down. "My mother died, and no one came for me."

We both nod and feel sad for ourselves for a moment.

"It doesn't matter, though. We can take care of ourselves," Pepe says.

"I can't go back to my woodshed, because if those boys find me again, they said they'd shove their sticks up my ass." His eyes widen like plates as he says this.

Pepe and I can't help laughing.

"Really, they are! I can't go back there. I want to stay with you guys. I'll help you."

Pepe cocks his head. "Fine, you can stay with me. I think you'll fit. Just don't stink it up." He goes back under the rock but starts throwing leaves in the air, saying, "I left it here! Someone stole it!"

"Stole what?" Andres asks me.

"His tent."

"Oh, that's not good." Andres frowns.

"Of course it's not good! Where am I going to find a piece of canvas like that? I had to sneak on a galleon to get it!"

I squint up at the sky. "It looks like it's going to rain again tonight too."

"Great!" Pepe throws a large pebble.

"Well, you can come sleep with me, maybe?" I venture, thinking the old man probably won't allow it.

"Where do you sleep?"

"In an old man's shed, where he keeps his apple cart. I bring his cart back and forth from market for him, and he gives me some food and lets me sleep in his shed. Bella's his dog."

"You let me sleep in the rain when you had a nice warm shed to sleep in?" Pepe says half-jokingly.

"Well, let's go help the old man!" Andres starts for the market.

The old man is leaning back on the wall having a coughing fit when his eyes widen as he sees who I brought with me.

"Oh, no. Oh, no! What do you think I am, St. Mary's?"

Andres tries to look as cute as he can while Pepe avoids making eye contact.

"They don't have anywhere to sleep either and"—he's shaking his head back and forth, still coughing as I speak—"you don't have to give me more food. I've been sharing mine."

He takes a deep breath once his fit is over and looks up to the sky. "Anna Maria will skin me alive if she finds out."

Andres cleverly says with a sad face, "We understand. Don't worry about us; we'll find a rock we can sleep under."

He starts walking away, and Bella barks at him.

"Oh, I'm going to die soon anyway. What do I care?" He pulls his old body from the wall. "Come help me put this cover on and get my cart back for me."

When the cart is in, he pulls one apple out for each of us and brings back another loaf of bread and butter for us and a bone for Bella.

"Thank you," we say, and I spread the burlap around for us all to lie on.

The old man's eyes soften. "It breaks my heart to see this. Saint Nicholas, please help them."

He closes and locks the door.

∞∞∞∞∞∞∞∞∞∞∞∞∞∞∞∞∞∞

I'm back inside my house, and it's unusually quiet in the purple dark right before dawn.

"Mama?" I cry out.

No answer, just a wind blowing the white muslin curtain slightly at the open window.

"Hector?" I whisper, not really wanting to hear him answer as I poke my head into the bedroom.

Empty.

There's a strange roar outside the house, and an orange glow shines in around the window edges. I pull the curtain away from the window and jump back at the wall of flames beside the house. I turn and run out the front door, away from the fire, but I'm horrified to see the fire burning in every direction down each alley. No one can be seen. The fire keeps changing in my direction until I'm forced to the docks with the heat of the fire pushing after me. I step to the very edge of the landing just above the dark lapping water and face the fire. I have no choice. I turn and leap into the water and swear I see a flapping, giant ship right before I break through the surface.

A faraway voice says as I'm swimming back to air, "Fire or water—choose."

We all wake up, and I tell them my dream as we wait for the old man to come and unlock us, but morning passes, and no one comes. Pepe tries to grab for an apple, and I slap his hand.

"I promised him we wouldn't steal from him!"

"Where is he, then?" Pepe rubs his stinging hand.

I stare at the door. "Maybe he's sick today. He never misses a day."

"Maybe he's a crazy man and likes locking children up in his shed until they die, and then he eats them," Andres says, wide-eyed.

"That's not true."

"Well, I have to pee." Pepe shifts his feet.

"Go in that corner, over there."

We hear a carriage come up to the house, and an old woman calls, "Doctor, he's not going to last long. I don't even know why he called for you."

Pepe turns to me. "You see, he's dying, and we're locked in this shed!"

"You don't know he's going to die. The doctor's only arrived. Maybe he'll get better, and he'll come and get us. Someone's going to remember the dog's in here."

"I'm not staying to find out." Pepe starts kicking the wood slats.

"Don't wreck his shed!" I yell.

"What about cutting a hole so we could pull ourselves out?" Andres offers.

I shake my head. "That would have to be a big hole, and then all the rats will come in."

"Luis, we have to get out of here. If someone opens this and finds us, they'll take us to St. Mary's," Pepe warns.

He's right.

"All right, if we get out, I think the best way would be to kick out one or two slats so he can repair it easily if he gets better."

"Okay on three! One, two, three!"

We all kick at different points on the wood slat, and it pulls out. One more kick and it flies down. We do it for one more slat, and we shimmy through. It's late afternoon when we get out as the front door of his house opens; we all duck behind the shed.

I peek out when I see the doctor leave, and the old woman comes out and shouts, "Don't bother sending the bill. I told you he was almost dead."

I feel sad he's gone. He had always been kind to me. I turn back to see Pepe with his arms full of apples.

"What?" He shrugs. "She's a nasty old lady, right? She doesn't deserve his apples."

He's right. Andres and I both fill our arms, and we run off as Bella chooses to follow us.

Chapter 4

"All of the carts at the market are starting to pack up for the day, so we'll have to work fast," Andres says.

"You and Pepe try to distract the baker so I can sneak up behind him and grab a loaf. Try to get him to turn around."

Andres and Pepe nod, and I creep along the street behind the vendors as they walk right to him.

"Sir," Andres starts, "I'm looking for St. Mary's. My brother and I have nowhere to go."

The baker glances up sympathetically to Andre's very sincere face as Pepe looks awkward and nervous, and I realize I should have only sent Andres.

"Poor things." He stands up and turns to point up the hill to St. Mary's, giving him directions, and I dash for his cart.

I see out of the corner of my eye that Pepe is watching me, which makes the baker turn quickly. He lunges for me as I grab a large white loaf.

"Street wretch!" he fumes. "Dirty little thief!"

I run for my life as all of the vendors unite to impede my escape. I break through two women who try to keep me from entering the street and run out into the road right in front of a horse that rears at my interruption. I dart and jump over baskets and carts that lead into an alley to a quieter part of the docks. I didn't even notice until after I'm breathing easier that Bella has been running with me the whole time. I realize too late that I should've told Andres and Pepe where we should meet and worry I wouldn't find them for days now. The sun goes down as I eat my share of the loaf.

I hear a familiar voice. "Luis!" It is Andres.

I stand up and see two happy faces at my appearance.

Pepe starts laughing. "You should have seen how close you were to being caught!"

"Yeah, no thanks to you!"

Andres keeps back his laughter as he attempts to chide. "Yeah, Pepe's so smooth, staring right at Luis as I was doing all the work!"

Pepe has to bend over, he's laughing so hard. "I couldn't help it, he just jumped out, and I watched him! How was I supposed to know I shouldn't have watched him?"

"Next time it's me and Andres." I can't keep from laughing with them.

Andres looks proud that he has been complimented. I give them their share, and they turn around to the harbor while eating.

They both gaze out on the water, and Andres says, "Whoa! What are all those ships doing here?"

The harbor's full of hundreds of large ships of every size, all flying red-and-yellow and red-and-white flags. Andres and Pepe have their mouths agape and marvel at the ship's majesty.

Andres asks, "Are those pirates?"

Pepe spurts out laughing at his comment.

I say, "My mother talked many times about this. King Philip had been planning his attack on England since Queen Elizabeth had her cousin Mary's head cut off."

Andres pulls up his lip. "Her cousin?"

"Yeah and now Philip's sending his navy to teach her a lesson."

"Wow!" Pepe exclaims. "Look at all their cannons!"

There must have been twenty-eight warships in the harbor, most with oars and cannons. We stare at the huge ships that are four times the size of the biggest merchant vessel we had seen in the harbor. There are many more ships, both heavy vessels and light sailing vessels, all too many to count.

"Why are they here?" Pepe asks.

"I think they're gathering replacements and more volunteers before they leave for England."

"Spain has the greatest navy in the world, and it's all here gathered in our port!" Pepe's eyes are sparkling as he studies each beautiful ship.

"Luis! I think this is your dream! Was it a ship like that?" Pepe points toward one of the largest vessels closest to shore.

"Yeah, it was just like that," I say, thinking about it more.

"I think your dream was telling you to join the armada!" Pepe is excited by this.

"He also dreamed the city was on fire, but it's not," Andres says. "It was only the apples he ate before he went to bed."

"Do you think they'd take me?" Pepe asks.

I snort and say, "How old are you?"

"Thirteen and a half."

Andres and I break out in laughter.

"Well, I think they'd take me." Pepe looks toward the ship, and he kicks a rock. He turns and marches off toward the docks defiantly now, to prove a point.

"Pepe! Come back!" Andres yells.

Andres and I get worried as he stealthily darts in and out behind the pillars lining the docks, so we follow him. A group of mariners are filling up an old rowboat with supplies. They have half the boat filled and go back into a storeroom as we see Pepe climb on and sink under the stores. I panic at the thought of not having him with me. I hear the voice again in my mind: *"Fire or water, choose."*

In a moment, I jump on too and find a space to sink into. I can hear Andres also climbing on, and even Bella jumps in and curls up under me. The men bring a few more things and throw them next to us, and I think how lucky it is they didn't throw it on top of us. It's a rocky trip over the harbor waves to the larger ship, and the men shout up for the men on the boat to pull them in. They crank the boat up into the air beside the ship, and the men start pulling off the stores.

My heart races as I try to think of a way to keep from being discovered, when Andres screams, "Get off me!"

"Oh, look at what we got here."

I peek through to see Andres dangling upside down by his foot at the end of a giant man's grasp.

"A little mangy sea beggar!" The man laughs.

Bella jumps out growling at the man, and he drops Andres on his head. He bounces up quickly. "Luis! He's after Bella!"

I pull myself out to see the skinny-looking sailor swatting at Bella, while the other sailor leans back, enjoying the crazy scene.

I grab up Bella, who's still barking in my arms, and see Pepe also surfaces in defense of Bella and Andres.

"We're infested!" one of the sailors cracks.

"What we do with 'em?" says the skinny one with the cleft chin.

"Go ask the captain, Philippe," says a tall, dark-haired man with indigo eyes. He's dressed fancy in white jerkin over a loose linen shirt, and golden hose with a leather codpiece. He has a red velvet hat that matches his short velvet cape. He holds a silver jewel-adorned sword in his right hand, and I wonder if I've ever seen a more handsome man.

We stand together with the sailors leering at us.

"If we get to keep 'em, the little one's mine," a filthy, rough sailor jeers as he points to Andres. Andres moves closer to me.

The sailors part as the captain walks through to see what's causing the commotion. He's large framed and younger than I expected. I hear his expensive, loud, leather-soled boots first as he slowly makes his way through the men. A blue velvet hat with a large, blue plume bobs high over the sailor's heads. When he comes into the circle in front of us, he pauses a moment and stands looking at us. He wears a blue velvet cape over an ivory-and-gold doublet tied to puffy linen sleeves with large white ruffs that match the one around his neck, looking like it's choking him.

"Alvaro, what is all this noise?"

The man with indigo eyes steps forward. "We have three puny stowaways and a dog."

The captain stares at the partially unpacked rowboat. "They got on while you were watching the provisions closely like I asked?" he asks with one eye narrowed.

Alvaro, realizing what the captain has figured out, bows his head. "Sorry, Captain, it will never happen again."

He steps up to us and looks us over with his small slate-blue eyes. "You want to join up with us to cripple England?"

Pepe steps forward and nods proudly as Andres and I stay still.

The sailors snicker.

The captain smirks. "So at least two of you have a brain."

There is a roar of laughter at this as Pepe realizes the insult and his shoulders drop.

"Any of you ever sailed before?"

None of us say anything.

"Any of you fired a gun?"

Say nothing again.

"So you're as qualified as most of the English navy!"

Again everyone laughs around us.

He turns and starts walking away.

Alvaro asks, "What will we do with them, Captain?"

"Hand the brainless one a mop to swab the poop deck and bring the dog and the other two to serve me in my quarters."

Chapter 5

Philippe takes Andres and me by the arm and pushes us into the captain's quarters, located at the very back of the ship. His large room smells of pipe smoke and cologne. He has a trunk, a chair, a small desk, and a low bed. He sits in his chair and thumps his boots on the footstool.

He points at Andres. "Remove my boots, boy."

Andres pulls off the boots that are so tight, a sweaty suction sound can be heard when they're coming off.

He wriggles his toes in his woolen stockings. "Now fetch the powder and rub my feet."

Andres sneers at the command, begrudgingly reaches for the powder, and begins peeling of the sweat-dampened stocking. By the way he pushes himself back and scrunches up his nose, I know it must be fragrant.

He turns to me and points. "My back."

Happy to have the top end, I put down Bella, who goes to the captain's side and reaches up for a biscuit he's offering her. He starts talking to her in strange high-pitched sounds. "Oh, nice, oh, good girl, so nice." A very different captain than what I'd just seen on the deck. After we're rubbing for more than thirty minutes and our hands are beginning to ache, he says, "Now help me get ready to retire."

I panic at the thought he wants assistance getting undressed, but he points for Andres to turn down his bed and gives me his clothes to hang up. As he takes his linen undershirt off, I noticed the scar running down from his wrist down to his elbow. Thankfully, he leaves his hose on but removes the codpiece and gets in bed, motioning us to turn the candle off.

As I pick Bella up, he says, "No, leave the dog. There's a rat problem on the ship."

We walk out on the deck and see Pepe still cleaning, with Alvaro watching over him.

Alvaro says to us, "I think your boyfriend's about done. Dump your bucket overboard and go find a hole to sleep in."

He walks away, and Andres and I exchange glances, wondering where that would be.

Pepe returns, and Andres says, "Good one, Pepe, now we're stuck on this ship, and they just expect us to take care of ourselves."

"I didn't tell you guys you had to come. They probably would've treated me better if I came alone."

Andres and I look at each other, disgusted with Pepe turning this on us. I start to try to find a way belowdecks as Andres follows behind me. There's a hatch open, and we venture down. We're met with a rancid, musty smell of bad food and sweat. The hold is filled with men lying in hammocks or sitting on the floor on filthy blankets in a circle playing a game of some sort. Some stare at us, and we look away, trying to find a spot we can disappear into. I see there's a spot right under the stairs that has some old rope coiled up, and I quickly go to it. When I turn around, Andres is there like my shadow. I curl myself up in one coil of rope, and Andres finds the other. When I wake up in the night from the chill I felt from not having a blanket, I see Pepe's in the coil next to us. He's sleeping soundly, and I smile, thinking he must've searched all over the ship for us. I try to pull some of the coils up around me for warmth and fall back asleep.

Something hits me in the forehead, and I open my eyes to see Alvaro throwing trash at our heads.

"Wake up, little kittens! Captain wants everyone on deck." He gets up and sticks his head through the ladder steps. "Follow me, and don't get in my way."

As I get up I feel the assault sleeping on ropes did to my body and rub the sore spots. Andres and Pepe start climbing up on deck.

The captain bellows, "Take all the salt pork, cheese, and fish and throw them overboard!"

Sailors walk past me down into the hold and come back, arms full, and the same terrible smell down below wafts past me.

"That was the food?" Andres puts his hand over his nose.

Alvaro says to the captain, busy swinging back and forth something hanging from a red silk ribbon with his nose pinched, "The wood's too green. Old wood's the only kind you can use. The new wood has too much moisture, rots all the food."

The captain nods. "Well, the king thinks we'll be scavenging in England in a few days' time, so he feels ninety days of biscuits is more than enough." The captain seemed weary, though, as he looks at the grey sky and churning sea. "Let's hope he's right."

He hands me the thing on the silk ribbon, and a strong smell of spices comes from it, sweetening the air.

BOOM-BOOM!

Andres, Pepe, and I all jump and duck at a cannon firing from one of the ships nearby.

The captain grins. "You heard them, my boys of the *San Pedro*! Weigh anchor!"

The deck's a fury of men running to different positions all over the ship. I stare out to a line of ships gathering to leave the bay. A good wind's blowing, and it looks like we're leaving the only home I'd ever known. Men call to each other, sails flap and catch the wind, as Andres' and Pepe's excited voices fall silent as the rocky peninsula drifts away. The church and the graveyard I know so well disappear—and I know somehow I will never see this bay again.

Chapter 6

"Ship boys!" Alvaro calls out. We turn to attention after watching the waves under us for about an hour. "Captain wants you to tend to the horses below."

"Horses?" Pepe asks. "On a ship?"

"Haven't you ever heard of seahorses?" He starts laughing and gestures for us to follow him.

"The horseman's fallen ill, so this hold's horses need tending." We walk to a part of the ship we hadn't ventured to yet, and as soon as he lifts the hatch, I smell them. Corunna had a lot of farms, and on warm days, you would get wafts of foul air.

"The shovels and buckets are all down there. It's a good idea to have one shovel, the other pass up the buckets, and the last one dump it overboard. Give each horse half a bale, fresh water, and a cup of oats." Alvaro asks, "Who's the lucky one doing the shoveling?"

Both Andres and Pepe point at me.

"Well, that was easy. Down you go. Let the little one stay up here and do the dumping."

I take a fresh breath of air and start down. An earthy waft of manure and pungent horse urine saturate the air. There are twelve stalls, each with a horse hung in its comfort sling, sticking its head out and snorting for oats and fresh hay. Most are grey, with a few bays. Strange to imagine there are three other holds like this on the ship. Pepe comes down next to me.

"Have you ever done this before?"

He shakes his head. "No, never even touched a horse."

"Do you think I get in there with them?"

"No, I think you just lift them up and clean under them." He laughs.

"No, I was thinking maybe I'm supposed to move them somewhere first."

We look around and see two ropes hanging from either side of two stalls.

"See, that's what I was thinking."

I take down the netting across one of the horse stalls and try to walk slowly toward the large animal as it steps back, clearly sensing how I've never done this before. She's a beauty—a marbled grey mare with a mane of white hair all the way down to her knees. I remove one side of the sling and let it drop on the floor. She snorts and turns in her stall. I see her tail is equally as thick and long. She flips it in the air as she comes around again. She's solid muscle, with a thick curving neck, and as she moves, her muscles tense and ripple as if she's transparent. I grab hold of her halter and pretend I feel comfortable as I pull her into the cross ties and latch each rope to either ring on the sides of the halter.

She falls under my command with ease, and it makes me feel that much more confident. Pepe flees to the ladder when the animal is brought out, and now, when it is safe, he gets brave again. "I would've figured it out if you gave me a moment."

"Right." I take up the shovel, begin to scoop up the soiled hay, and put it in the buckets.

Pepe makes a disgusted face as he picks each one up and lifts it up the hatch, and Andres yells down, "Do you mind not getting it all over the edge! I don't have anywhere to put my hands!"

Pepe laughs so hard he almost drops his bucket. It took us hours to move each horse, clean, feed them, and put each one back. We're tired, and when we get back up on deck, we're anxious to show Alvaro the great job we did. When he sees us looking for him, he comes over and glances down the hatch. He closes the hatch, turns, and walks away.

"That was it?" Andres raises his hands, open palms to the air.

A few minutes later, Alvaro emerges again with the steward, who brings three rations of biscuits, salted meat, and dried peas in three wooden bowls and a wine-filled goatskin bag with a wooden mouthpiece and stopper.

Our mouths drool at the sight.

"Those Andalusians are yours now," he says, and he walks away to work.

We eat our supper up near the bow as Alvaro takes over the helm and studies a wooden box in front of him. Andres grabs his share and skips over to Alvaro, who doesn't even acknowledge his presence. Curious, Pepe and I both carry our vittles and walk over too.

"What are you looking at in that box?" Andres asks.

"The compass," Alvaro answers. "Now, step out of my light."

Andres moves.

"That's how you know where we're going?" Pepe ventures.

"No, I have a little pigeon I send out to chat with Queen Elizabeth, and he comes back and whispers directions in my ear."

Pepe looks out to see if he can see a bird in the sky, and I shake my head, embarrassed for him.

Alvaro laughs, noticing it. "Don't you boys realize where we're going?" he scoffs. "We're going to war and you three act like you've joined up here for a parade."

He stands there, shaking his head, watching the horizon.

"What are the horses for?" I ask, trying to keep him from scaring us.

"Well, the plan is to sink England's navy immediately, then land and wage a land war on horseback." He sighs. "We have twenty more horses on the other side of the ship."

We look back across the huge expanse of the ship and take in the magnitude of the situation we jumped in. To the front, sides, and back, the horizon's scattered with ships. We seem to be centered in the middle of the convoy.

"Why don't you three find yourselves a spot out of everyone's way? Don't go poking around the ship, the galley's full of convicts, and keep out of the soldiers' way. Oh, and make sure to relieve yourself over the side of the ship, and if you can't reach"—he eyes Andres—"then you go in a bucket and spill it overboard. No relieving yourself in the bilge!"

Pepe pulls me and Andres back, and we decide to take his advice and find a quiet place by the center hatch where we watch the sailors' synchronicity. That night, we go back to our ropes under the stairs, and we're surprised to see wool blankets spread out for us. We check around to see who'd left them for us, but no one's looking our way. We fall asleep quickly, and I awake in a tangled mass of the arms and legs of Pepe and Andres. Bella also found us in the middle of the night, and I smile, wondering how she escaped the captain.

∞∞∞∞∞∞∞∞∞∞∞∞∞∞∞∞∞∞∞

Three days of wonderful sailing weather pass, and as I'm handing the last manure bucket up to Pepe, the captain comes by and approaches Alvaro within earshot.

"I think we're approaching the English coast. Get your lead out and report your findings to me in my cabin."

"Captain, if you don't mind me asking, why are we sailing in sight of England? Why not sail the other side of the Channel so we can surprise them?"

"The king has instructed us to stay away from the French and the Flemish coast because of the shoals and banks."

"But they'll see us coming."

"I think that is his other intention."

The captain walks away.

Alvaro takes out a long, slender coil of rope and what looks to be a scoop at the end. He reaches into a pouch at his hip as he walks to the prow, places something in the hollow of the scoop, and casts the line into the depths as the ship's moving. He lets his line out slowly until he quickly pulls it back up. He reaches down, cradles the scoop, and walks back over to the helm, pulling out an old tattered book.

He speaks to the sailor next to him. "We still haven't hit the shelf yet, but we're nearing. Put up the short sails and send the lookouts up on alert."

He sends the sailor to the captain's cabin. News travels fast, and soon most of the men are assembled on deck, solemnly watching for the coast in enemy waters through a hazy horizon.

"Why don't you three climb up into the crow's nest to see the shape the ships are in?" Alvaro says with a proud smile.

"Shape?" Andres asks, one eye squinting trying to see up to the great height of the mast.

"It's something no one's ever seen before. You should take a look."

Pepe starts up first, and Andres only makes it halfway up.

"Climb up here with us, Andres!" Pepe shouts down.

"No, I can see fine from here," he says, high-pitched, red-and-white fingers clutched around the ropes.

Pepe and I both reach the top at the same time, even though he started first, and he whistles as he takes in the view. It seems as though we're riding on the back of a large flying bird. The ships in front of us make up the head, the merchant and galas on our sides stretch out like powerful wings, and the ships behind us spread out like tail feathers.

"Hey, you guys, come down!" Andres calls from the deck now, and Pepe and I are hesitant to leave. It's a view we would never see again in our lives. One of those instances you know you've witnessed something extraordinary. Pepe smiles at me and starts down.

We inch for hours at a leisurely sail, watching as Alvaro takes a reading with his line every hour or so.

"Where are all the ships?" one sailor next to us asks.

"Yeah, not one fishing boat within sight." Alvaro squints with one side of his mouth drawn.

Suddenly, a lookout shouts, "Land on the port bow!"

The captain's amongst us at once, and the other ships around us come to life, all hoisting their crucifix and the Virgin flags.

Three guns shoot, and the captain calls out, "Thanks be to God and the king, who have allowed us to get this far, and Lord have mercy on England."

As we approach closer to shore, the darkness sets in as every beacon upon every hilltop along the coast ignites, announcing our arrival—lighting our way up the channel—ironically, welcoming.

That night, it's hard to fall asleep, and after lying still and quiet for many minutes out of the silence, Andres says, "I'm glad I came with you, Luis."

"Hey, what about me? I'm the reason we're here."

We both throw wood shavings that littered the floor at Pepe.

"Yeah, great idea," I say.

"I meant I'm glad we're all together." Andres's eyes fill with water.

"Me too," I say, hoping not to cry too.

"Me too," Pepe quietly states.

∞∞∞∞∞∞∞∞∞∞∞∞∞∞∞∞∞∞∞∞∞

The next day, at dawn, we awake to shouting which found its way down under the ladder where we slept. We go up right away.

"They beat us to windward!" yells the captain, grinding his teeth and hitting his fancy blue velvet on the railing of the ship.

Standing up on deck, I can barely see through the squall of rain. Squinting, I faintly see the sails lined up upwind of us. The English navy has made it out of their harbors.

"How did they do it in this wind? I thought we had them trapped." He kicks a bucket over. "Now they've gotten upwind!"

Alvaro turns to us. "Go water and feed the horses. Skip the mucking and make sure they're tied in the stalls. After, go below. There's going to be fighting soon."

He pushes Andres in the direction of the horses, and we obey. As we're filling up the water buckets, gunfire rings out, and we quickly throw hay and scamper down under the ladder. Every time the cannons shoot, Bella runs out under the ladder and barks fiercely. Our own ship doesn't fire any cannons off, but we hear ships around us, battling. After a few hours without damage, we sneak on deck. The sailors are hastily running back and forth on deck, untying and tying the rigging to change course and maneuver as the soldiers on our ship come out with their swords, muskets, and arquebuses. The smaller English ships are navigating more quickly, darting out of range, but with their cannon fire falling short also. A few ships have some rigging damage, but the majority of the ships seem without a scratch. By afternoon, the fighting ends, and the waves lap against the boat as our captain's called to the duke's ship for war council. We stand next to Alvaro as he blows a happy melody on a small whistle he carried in his pocket.

When the captain returns, Alvaro asks, "What are our orders from the duke?"

"We're waiting for Parma to join the tea party as they promised... Cowards." He spits off the deck. "But if bad weather comes, we'll have no harbor big enough for us all."

He stares off to grey clouds in the distance.

"So we have to keep to the helm and sails to keep this formation until Parma decides to join us?" Alvaro asks.

"If we break this formation, even one ship, we're back to Philip with an English boot up our britches." He starts off to his cabin again. "Oh, that and the proclamation has gone out that the king will hang any captain of the ship that breaks formation. And I'll be taking my leadsman and commander with me." He laughs all the way back.

Two terrible things happen that night. The flagship, the *Don Pedro*, collides with two other ships in the night due to the close proximity of the ships. The *Don Pedro's* bowsprit and forestay were carried away, causing great distress on our own ship of impending collision. A few hours later, just when we drift back to sleep, our eyes open at the sound of a great explosion. All hands run to deck, and Andres is almost trampled in the chaos. About five ships away, the *San Salvador*, a vice-flagship, is up in flames. All night, a rescue attempt is underway to put out the ship and rescue survivors, but in the chaos, the crippled *Don Pedro* drifts away, out of range of the fleet.

Orders are given to gradually move in formation up the channel. We move so slowly that we can see the thatched roofs and church steeples of the quaint English villages on our way across Lyme Bay. We spend a calm night drifting in formation in the bay, but by morning, the wind and the sea begin churning.

"A beautiful northeast wind, Alvaro!"

"Yes, Captain, it will be in our favor!"

Alvaro turns around, points for us to go to the horses, and then points belowdecks. We get the message and obey. This fight is different. The cannon fire and the guns won't cease. Our ship shudders every time the cannons are fired, and we expect to see massive casualties when we come on deck that night but see none.

"Alvaro, no one was hurt?"

"Oh, Juan had a nasty kickback of the cannon and was sent below, but other than that, not a scratch."

He lights his pipe and turns to us. "You see, the English are faster than us, but as long as our longer-range cannons stay in the positions we're in, it's at a standstill." He looks concerned, suddenly. "Either Parma shows or we'll have to last as long as our supplies do."

Fighting begins again, but this time, we stay above deck. Alvaro notices us but doesn't point us belowdecks. Andres, Pepe, and I all hang over the starboard side as the British ship's sides flash at the gunports, and we each point to where it will land in the water. Every once in a while, the cannonball will hit with a weak thud against one of the closer ship's strong hulls. But what we really enjoy is when one hits and crashes through the upper deck, sending splinters flying through the air. We're sorry when the fighting stops that night and can't wait for it to continue the next day, but the winds change.

The armada begins to move up the channel again, with the English trailing behind, provoking skirmishes, testing our borders. Finally, reaching the Flemish coast, we all anchor. Parma never came.

∞∞∞∞∞∞∞∞∞∞∞∞∞∞∞∞∞∞∞∞

At midnight, an English signal gun goes off, and it summons all the sailors to deck.

"What is it?" I ask Pepe, who is the first up the ladder.

"It looks like the English are up to something," he says as we hand Bella up.

Alvaro's at the bow with a leg up on an overturned bucket, and we immediately go to him. He's watching the commotion of boats taking sailors off some of the English ships. He directs Pepe. "Go get the captain right away."

Pepe's off running as eight ships' masts in the distance catch fire, the sails still open and flapping in the pitch dark. From this distance, it appears like eight burning crosses.

Immediately, the sailors go running around the ship like a disturbed beehive. Everyone shouts, everyone runs; all the while, my eyes are fixed on the mesmerizing fires coming toward us. Halfway across the bay, they burst out in flames across the deck and down below, with fire spurting out from their gunports.

Alvaro shouts, "Don't cut the anchors! Leave the anchor buoys as the duke instructed!"

But no one's listening.

One sailor screams, "Giambelli's infernal machines! They'll kill us all as soon as they explode!"

"Cut the cables!" another sailor yells as he runs and hits the anchor lines with an ax.

The captain fires off his gun. Pepe's heaving from the running he just did, with his hands on his knees.

"Attention or I'll shoot!"

All on deck regain their composure as ships collide around us.

"Hear that, boys? That's the result of idiot sailors who all cut anchor just to collide with the one hundred thirty ships ass-to-ass in this shallow harbor!" He scans his loaded gun around the deck at every sailor. "Now do as I say, or I will shoot every last poltroon here."

Behind the captain, small pinnace ships tow two fire ships away, but the remaining six are still advancing, threatening to explode any minute.

He turns and barks to a group of sailors, "Heave the anchor buoys overboard and up mainsail!" He points to another group who goes off dutifully.

"Bring the ship's head round!" he screams up to the sailors climbing the riggings. "Then reset the sails for a safe course!"

He then turns and says to Alvaro, "Get to the helm and steer clear of the fire ships, but keep up off those damned shoals!"

Everyone ducks at the sound of the explosion, even the captain, but after a moment, we realize it's English cannons going off. Though it wasn't the explosion we expected, the cannons severely damage the ships that are trying to tow the fire ships away and cause the pinnaces to give up towing the remaining ships coming at us.

We gasp as we barely miss other Spanish ships racing for safety. Pepe, Andres, and I watch the six remaining ships float, blazing, past the spots our ship had just rested. We wait for the explosion, but our hearts sink as they uneventfully burn themselves down.

"Eight ships can scatter one hundred thirty ships!" the captain says, shaking his head. "What a trick."

"Captain, where should we go?" Alvaro asks.

"The duke wants us to drop anchor immediately, then go back to the anchor buoys in the morning."

"But, Captain, the crew cut both our anchors. All we have is a kedge on board, and that'll be useless with this tide."

"Well, then, we must go with the tide and see where we are at dawn." The captain stares out across the water. "There must be three hundred anchors at the bottom of that harbor now." He looks at Alvaro. "I'm beginning to wonder which side God is on."

With that, he makes the sign of the cross up to the Virgin flapping on the flag above us in the wind.

Chapter 7

I awake alone in the morning. I must have slept through Andres and Pepe leaving. As I hurry out under the stairs, a strange panic of being forgotten hits me. Images of Pepe and Andres plotting to leave me behind and going off together happily flood my brain and only make me climb up on deck faster. My heart slows as I come upon the sight of Pepe leaning against the mast, washing his face, alone.

"Where's Andres?" I ask.

He points as the water's streaming into his squinted eyes between splashing. I look where his finger leads and see Andres sitting on a bucket with his pants down around his knees. As he spies me, he gives an unabashed and lazy wave, and I laugh inside about my paranoia. Not wanting to go to Andres in his activity, I turn back to Pepe, who's feverishly throwing water, not

only on his face, but splashing out around him, getting everything wet.

"Hey, what about the water shortage?" I say with a smile.

"Eh," he says as he's wiping his face now. "This is the only
way I can do it without touching my face."

"Everyone touches their face when they wash."

"Not me."

The deck's busy for this hour of the morning. The sailors
carry a look of worry and a task on their minds. I should've been
more concerned with what's happening around us, but I still feel
unsettled.

I venture, "Why did you guys leave me down there when you
woke up?"

He shrugs. "We tried to wake you but you were dead to the
world."

That makes me feel even better, and I realize there's nothing
to worry about.

"How are you doing over there, Andres?" Pepe yells down
deck.

"My rear's sick," Andres says, and we both laugh and roll in
the folded canvas under us.

"Seriously, I might need some more rags over here," Andres
pleads.

Pepe checks around and finds some ripped-up cotton and
goes over to give it to him. He reaches out with his head away
and drops them just within Andres's reach and runs back like a
cannon went off.

"Hey, I can't reach it!" he says as his white rump pulls out of
the bucket, exposing the red indentation the bucket was causing.
Once he has them in his hands, he yells, "They're dirty!"

We're having so much fun that we forget all the commotion.
Suddenly, Alvaro's voice comes within earshot. "We're trapped
on a lee shore!" He hits his hand on the mast.

Philippe says, "We all got back into formation as best we could without anchors"—he points to Alvaro—"and that was quite a feat."

Alvaro scans the water. "We're still stuck with this wind, and the English have the upper hand again."

A shot of cannon fire rings out, and Pepe and I stand up to see where it's coming from. I catch Andres standing, pantsless, with his mouth open in surprise and worry, looking for the direction of fire.

"The English are firing on the duke's ship. It's begun again." Alvaro commands the sailors out of the path to the captain's quarters.

Pepe and I turn to see Andres rushing around, pulling his pants up and emptying his bucket over the side. In his rush, he doesn't tie his pants tight, and every time he reaches to dump the bucket, his pants fall to his knees again. Then he pulls them half up with one hand, grabbing the bucket, he comes back running to us. He trips on his droopy pants and goes rolling to starboard with the dirty bucket. Pepe and I drop to our knees, laughing at the sight as Andres curses, "Stupid pants!"

We're still laughing by the time we get belowdecks and hear the most cannon fire we've heard yet. Within a few hours, our ship's taking fire, and Philippe comes down in search of us.

"Boys!"

Pepe pokes his head out. "No boys here!"

"Whatever you are, get down in the galleys and help pump!"

Unsure what that means, we go farther down into the ship and see the ship's taking on water through small holes in the hull. A filthy man is sweating profusely at the pump, and I guess he must have been doing this for hours. Bella, who followed us down, puts one paw in the water and decides to go back up the ship.

"You boys better take this seriously. You stop for a minute, and we're at the bottom of the ocean."

He throws down the pump and walks away, and I quickly pick it up and continue. Pepe and Andres watch, and every time one gets tired, we switch. Every once in a while, something crashes against the hull with such force it sends the pumper to the floor. When we get back up, a new fresh leak appears. Even though there are four pumpers continuously pumping in our section alone, the water keeps rising.

"Can the cannons break the hull?" Andres asks as he's pumping and staring at the hull.

Another pumper answers him, "Sure as the wind changes." He spits, and I watch as the frothy spittle makes its way over to us in the putrid tide under our feet—obviously some are using the bilge to relieve themselves.

"This hull may take a few beatings, but it gets enough beatings and it'll pop like a pimple." He laughs at our worried looks. "But don't you worry your pretty faces. You won't know what even hit you."

We don't talk for hours after that. We don't even know what time it is and if it's still light out. No one has come down to relieve us or bring us water or food. Our stomachs are growling constantly, and surprisingly, it's Alvaro who comes to our rescue.

"I hate to break you girls' hearts, but your time's up."

I drop the pump gladly, and we run back up on deck. I hadn't realized how stagnant and wet the air in the hull was, and the fresh rain-misted breeze that hits me is very welcome. It's dusk, and in the faint light, I see we're clearly losing the battle. The skies are grey and filled with the promise of much more rain, and the strong wind's distressing the ocean. The English appear to have pulled back outside the pathetic formation that seems to have gone from the bird shape to a loose, hole-filled crescent shape, a sea of floundering sinking ships with split masts and broken riggings. As Alvaro hands us three wine bags and our rations, I watch as divers are sent overboard to try to repair some of the damage. Pepe, Andres, and I quietly sit to eat, and we look at each other in surprise, since Alvaro stays with us as we're eating.

First, he stares out over our heads, but then he starts talking. "You missed quite a fight, ladies."

We nod, and Andres asks, "Do you think they won?"

Alvaro lets out a puff of laughter. "I am sure they won."

"How do you know?" Pepe asks.

"Look around you." He puts his hands out, and his eyes flash with emotion. "The English haven't had one ship damaged, yet every ship of ours has been cracked." He shakes his head. "I don't understand it. We have longer range, better gunpowder, and we've been hitting their ships with greater accuracy. Yet their hulls are not breaking, and ours seem made out of paper!"

"Tell us about the fight." Pepe's curious eyes open fully to absorb his tale.

"The English broadsided us within full range. Both our ships let loose with the cannons. All of the sailors took command and maneuvered as best as we could. I shouted to the English with our grappling hooks at the ready to 'Come to close quarters!'"

Then he realizes we don't know what that means, and he explains, "So we could board their ship *Spanish style*." He stretches his legs out and begins chuckling at the memory. "So then an Englishman replies from the top of the mast with his sword in the air, 'Good soldiers! Surrender on fair terms!'" He laughs. "And our musketeer gave him his answer with a bullet in the side of his head!" He can barely finish his story through his laughter. "And we all cheered as he fell from his great height."

Pepe crushes a balled fist. "I wish I was there for that."

Andres and I exchange looks, unsure how we feel about the story.

"Well, the English retreated after, and we called them 'Protestant hens' and clucked and strutted around the deck."

"It sounded like we won, then," Andres says, confused.

"They left, all right, but it seems we're worse for the wear now." Alvaro cleans his fingernails.

We hear an uproar on the ships near us and get up to watch as a vessel nine ships away begins to go under.

Alvaro gasps. "It's the *Maria Juan.*"

The flagship sends out a rescue boat, but they save only one boatful before the whole deck slips under the darkening water. No one has to tell us there were more than two hundred men on that ship that sank below with the Virgin flag.

∞∞∞∞∞∞∞∞∞∞∞∞∞∞∞∞∞∞∞∞∞∞

No one feels like talking after seeing that, and everyone either goes to work repairing the ship or sleeps. After a whole day of pumping, I can't tell you who fell asleep first that night, but the groaning and moaning of those injured during battle found us in our deep sleep. A sailor awakens us halfway through sleep that night, sending us to go back to the galleys.

"I never wished I was shoveling poop so much," Andres says as we stagger back down into the ship.

The water is disturbingly higher. When we left, it was past our ankles, but now it's mid-calf. We pump and pray until dawn.

"Captain calls all hands on deck!" someone calls down to us.

Everyone except the wounded and a few pumpers are present. There is a sea of defeated faces, even before the captain speaks. The crowd parts as the captain walks through. He looks like he hasn't slept in days, with his swollen eyes and disheveled hair. He makes no eye contact and paces in a hypnotic trance for longer than is comfortable. Suddenly he glances up, almost surprised we are all still there.

He squints up at the sky and begins, "I'm not going to blow smoke up your asses and tell you we have a chance in hell here." He brings his wise gaze around and looks in every sailor's eyes before continuing, "You have all fought too bravely and sailed too skillfully for me to let you down like that." He stares at his shoes for a moment. "I will tell you thanks to our talented leadsman here that we are a deadly six fathoms away from shore." The sailors tense as I gather that must be far too close. "We have no choice here; the wind hasn't changed and is forcing us on the shoals." He pauses again uncomfortably long. "Goddamn Parma never showed, and with that, the leadsmen that know these waters. We're like a blind man sailing right now, with the English waiting upwind, ready to attack at any moment, and we're completely out of shot."

I feel sick and watch as every sailor's face falls even further than I thought possible.

He again scans the faces. "My courageous men, we're awaiting either quick death or a miracle. Get out your rosaries, my Catholic sinners, and pray for whichever one you prefer."

And with that, he walks back to his quarters in a solemn stride as sailors nod respectfully at his honesty. After he leaves, despair comes over like a heavy mist, and everyone retreats within to pray for deliverance. Pepe, Andres, Bella, and I curl in to sleep especially close that night.

"I don't know how to swim," Andres worries right as I close my eyes.

Pepe's eyes open wide. "How can you not know how to swim, living right on a bay?"

"My mother never taught me."

"Don't worry, we're not going to sink," I try.

Pepe says, "If we do sink, you just have to grab on to anything that will float."

That makes him feel better than my lie, and I catch him glancing around the ship, probably looking for things that will float.

No one could sleep, though, since the feeling that at any moment you might hear the scraping sound of the hull tearing against the rocky coast and will have only seconds to escape keeps you awake.

By morning, we're all exhausted. The winds haven't changed but at least have weakened to some small relief. As we're tiredly mucking the stalls, we hear a cracking of sails and a cheer across the deck.

Andres calls down, "Pepe! Luis!"

We bolt up the ladder and see the sails are flapping in the southwest direction, and the boat's already turning toward the ocean.

"A miracle!" someone shouts, and everyone claps, not only on our ship, but celebrations ring out on every ship. The captain's door opens, and he gives two brisk steps out to see what has occurred. Several tears trickle down his tense face, which cracks into a tight smile as he turns to go back into his room.

Not a single ship has grounded.

Chapter 8

The captain leaves the next day to meet with the war council on the flagship. When he returns, he gives orders to, "Obey the wind."

Alvaro questions him. "Take a northerly course through unknown waters?"

"We have no choice. We can't go back the way we came. Unless the wind changes, which we don't have the patience for. Around the Irish coast is our only option." The captain pauses and rubs his tired eyes, then looks at Alvaro. "Good Commander, raise the main sails, make north, and by God, get some rest."

He heads straight to his cabin.

Alvaro goes to the ship's master, Philippe, and says, "Raise the sails and follow the winds north. I'm going to rest, and you're in charge." He walks away slowly down ship.

A few hours later, a three-gun signal goes off. We clamber to the railing and try to see where it came from.

"That's the signal to shorten sail." Pepe's proud he's learned this.

"Is it from the duke's ship?" Andres asks.

"Yes," I answer, seeing the smoke still wisping from the cannon on the side of the flagship.

"It looks like the English are catching up to him, getting too close."

"Why does he want us to slow down?" I ask, amazed I'm actually asking Pepe about this.

"I bet he needs every ship to slow down so that the English will back off."

We wait for the orders to shorten sail to be made but hear none.

Philippe instead yells, "Do not shorten sail. We need to go ahead so we can heave to for repairs!"

"But the duke has signaled?" one sailor questions.

"We're taking on far too much water. We need to make repairs up ahead, or we'll be done for." He points out to an Urca that's far ahead still and has not shortened sail. "You see, others are doing the same thing. We must do what's best for our ship."

Everyone nods, and no one touches the sails. The rest of the armada shortens, and all others fall back. We must be miles ahead by the time we see the pinnace pull up with our ship. Shots ring out for us to slow down, and we're boarded by armed soldiers.

"Where is Captain de Cuellar?" One haughty, over-embellished officer steps forward between his soldiers and demands.

Philippe points for me to go and fetch the captain. I run as fast as I can and hear Andres and Pepe in tow. I knock twice on his door and decide to open it after no reply. In the darkened cabin, there he lies with his broken snoring, eyes closed sleepily, and his mouth open in exhaustion.

"Captain!" I say too loudly.

He sits up and looks around wildly at the disruption, clearly reacting to what must be a matter of great importance, since no one would dare disturb him otherwise.

"What is it?" He grabs for his boots.

"A pinnace has boarded our ship, and a general wants to speak to you."

His eyes drop down as his mouth purses. He must have realized what occurred for this to happen. He stumbles out of the cabin, and it seems all of the ship is on deck by now.

I watch as the captain straightens and walks more assuredly as he proceeds down the ship to the prow where the general stands. When he meets him, the captain regains all composure. He attempts to shake the general's hand, but the general stares at him in disgust and only stands taller. "I am Senior Army General Bovadillo, and you, Captain de Cuellar, are under violation of the duke's orders to stay in formation and not to advance. You are condemned to death by hanging, and you will need to go with us to the Judge Advocate's ship immediately."

We all watch as the captain rather nonchalantly turns slightly toward Philippe, and he glares at him with one eye narrowed. The group's disrupted by Alvaro rushing into the fray with his hair all in disarray from sleep.

"General, this is a mistake! The captain's not responsible!" he screams.

The captain calmly puts one hand up to stay him. "This is all a misunderstanding. I'll go with the good general, and I'll be back by nightfall."

He turns to the general and asks, "Can I bring along my cabin boys to assist me?"

We gape at each other in surprise and wonder what this will mean for us. But he motions with a finger for us to follow him after he receives a curt nod from the general.

"What about your first mate and commander, sir?" Alvaro asks as he steps forward hopefully.

"No need for that; the boys will do."

The captain steps onto the boards they laid across to connect the ships. Pepe crosses first, I follow, and Andres cautiously takes up the rear. As the captain stiffly leaps off onto the frigate, he glances back to Philippe. "It's going to be either you or me by nightfall," he says with a wink, then gives a salute and says loudly for all to hear, "You all report to the commander in my absence."

Pepe, Andres, and I stand close together, and we watch as the captain turns to the soldier next to him. "So, soldier, where do you hail from?"

"Galicia," the haggard soldier tersely answers.

"Oh, Galicia! I knew a certain captain's wife from Galicia. Beautiful in the extreme! I never saw a more pleasing shape. Far too beautiful not to share with such a handsome man as myself, especially with her troll of a husband."

That makes them laugh, except for Bovadillo, of course, who sits like he has a bad taste in his mouth the entire ride.

How can he be so jovial with what lays before him?

We reach the smaller ship all too soon. My stomach tenses as the judge stands there with a stern and unyielding look to him. There is another captain in the process of questioning. The captain strides forward, wanting to watch the interrogation.

Pepe, Andres, and I disappear behind those gathered to watch and speak to each other for the first time.

"Why would he bring us?" Pepe asks.

"I don't want to see him hanged," Andres says.

"If he's hanged, what will happen to us? Do we get to go back to the *San Pedro*, or will we stay here?" I worry.

We glance around at the strange faces, and this ship seems much different than the *San Pedro*. I already miss our little bed under the ladder and Alvaro, who watches out for us.

"Bella!" I cry, realizing too late she is back on the ship.

Pepe and Andres appear sick at this, and we all involuntarily check back to where the *San Pedro* rocks low in the water in the background, one mile away.

Suddenly, the crowd roars, and we move around to see what's happening. A group of men are dragging the other captain back toward the main mast as he protests and tries to pull away from his captors.

"This is a vendetta against sea captains, I tell you!" He spits on the deck. "You army generals blame us for your defeat. You think this is all our fault!" His voice rises to a scream. "You want to get a scapegoat, and here we are. Blame us for your bad judgment and poor timing. God will have my revenge!" And with that, they slip the noose over his neck, and three sailors pull his weight up with a terrible gurgling and choking sound. I close my eyes but can still hear the heaving of the rope, the kicking and banging of his feet against the mast, and then the quiet stillness two minutes later. When I reopen my eyes, the other captain hangs lifeless, his mouth and eyes open as he turns back and forth gracefully in the wind.

General Bovadillo yells, "Make sure to sail 'round to every ship and show our other captains why they should heed the duke's signals!"

The pinnace leaves with the dead captain swinging to and fro with the rigging.

Pepe, who must not have closed his eyes, rushes to the railing and gets sick. The captain's looking at his shoes when the judge calls him forward. The judge is an imposing figure, not of great height but of extra width. He wears all black velvet except for the white fluffy ruffs around his neck and hands. Thick gold chains and a large jeweled cross rest heavily on his black doublet. His eyes appear worn from too much reading, and his frown seems permanent. His hair is white and wispy, giving away his great age.

"Captain de Cuellar, you have been brought before me, accused of failing to obey the duke's orders issued in Lisbon, which is a technical offense and punishable by death. What say you?"

We hold our breath as the captain steps forward with his head bowed. "Your Honor, I am falsely accused of this crime." He looks deep into the judge's ice-blue eyes. "I am the captain of the galleon *San Pedro*, one of the squadron of Seville, that fought courageously and bravely beside the duke throughout the fight. I had stayed up for ten days straight to be sure I could command my ship through the greatest perils of the battle and did everything I could to bring success for Spain. I kept my eyes open for ten days, watching the wind and the Flemish shoals trying to keep my sinking ship afloat in the leeward wind." He pauses here and gives an exhausted look. "After the good God changed the winds and the duke decided to go north around the Irish coast, homeward bound, the human frailty in me gave way to much needed sleep, and I left my faith in my second mate, which I deeply regret."

He stops talking and, to my horror, makes his way over to Pepe, Andres, and me. We move, hoping he's going somewhere else, but he puts his hand on Andres's shoulder and mine and continues, "I have brought these three cabin boys who came aboard my ship in Corunna to serve as my witness to the events which occurred while I was exhausted in my cabin bunk. I have brought these destitute boys because of their innocence and open eyes, which the court can trust. Will the court hear their account?"

The judge looks surprised and taken off guard with this and nods hesitantly to proceed.

The captain nudges me forward. "Speak loudly and clearly."

I'm pushed out into the middle of the circle and instantly feel naked. I glance back over my shoulder at Pepe, who looks behind him, embarrassed, and then to Andres, whose eyes are full of pity for me that I've been picked.

I try to speak, but my voice cracks. The silence makes me sweat much more. I clear my throat and begin, "Your Honor," and I look at the captain who appears pleased with that touch. "What do you want to know?"

This breaks the tension, and some even laugh before the judge gives them a reproachful stare.

"Tell us what happened on your ship after you heard the signal to shorten sail. Was the captain in command?"

"No, we"—I turn around to point—"Pepe, Andres, and I were sitting on deck and watched as the captain came up to the leadsmen and commander, Alvaro, and told him to get some rest. The captain said he was going to get some sleep also, and that Alvaro should give the command to the ship's master, Philippe." I pause a moment, mindful of every word. "I watched as the captain made his way to his cabin, and Alvaro spoke to Philippe and went to his bunk." I check with the captain now to see if I'm doing a good job, and he gives me an encouraging nod. "A few hours later, we heard the signal for shorten sail given by the flagship and overheard a sailor asking the second mate to give orders. The second mate replied he was not going to shorten sail since he needed to get ahead to heave to for much needed repairs because we were taking on so much water still." I stop, and some seem like they're waiting for me to continue, but I keep still.

The judge speaks. "When did the captain wake up?"

"Not until the general boarded our frigate and I was sent to wake him. I found him out cold."

I look to the captain, who can barely contain his contentment with my answer and purses his lips to control his smile, but his eyes still glisten.

"Do the other two boys back up this story?" The judge looks to Pepe and Andres, who both nod strongly. "You may step back. Captain Cuellar, a last plea?"

The captain steps forward with his hands clasped below his belly. "I testify that I have fought stoically for the duke and the king, following every command and pushing the limits of my constitution. I ask you, if you do not believe me, go back to my ship and ask any one of the three hundred fifty men that I have been in charge of and fought with. If I have done anything wrong, and if even one testifies that I have, then put away your rope"—and his whole face tenses as he narrows one eye at the judge—"you can hack me to pieces!"

Everyone on ship is quiet, and their bloodthirsty look seen before while hanging the last captain now turns to a solemn respect. The judge looks to the captain, then to us boys, and back to the general.

"Write to the duke," he instructs his page. "Say that I will not condemn Captain de Cuellar, who I do believe was not in command at the time of offense, unless I get a written order signed in his name. We will await his reply."

The general turns and takes the letter begrudgingly and steps back onto his frigate to go to the duke.

"Thank you, Judge Advocate, for hearing my defense," the captain says with his head bowed.

"We shall see what the duke replies." And he walks back to his cabin.

We sit with the captain, who is busy making friends with the sailors on deck. He's right in the middle of the story of his trips to the southern Irish coast, which make me wonder if he's telling strategically to show his importance onboard, when the frigate comes back. It's a promising sign that only the general's page returns with a letter and goes right to the judge's quarters. The captain winks at me and heads to where the page went. He doesn't come back for hours, and when he emerges, he has his arm around the judge's neck, and they're both laughing like old buddies. Pepe, Andres, and I smile at each other in relief, and we hope this will mean we're on our way back to Bella.

When the captain returns to us and tells us the news of the duke annulling the death sentence, Pepe asks, "So when will they take us back?"

The Captain replies with a confused look, "They won't be taking us back. I've been stripped of my command, and I'm in-

structed to stay on the advocate's ship until we return home."
He strains to get up. "No, this is our ship-home now."

"Is this ship in better shape to make it home?" Andres asks
hopefully.

"Oh, no, this one's sinking too," he says nonchalantly, "but
thank you, boys. You did a fine job."

As he walks away, the three of us look to the light we can see
coming from the *San Pedro* in the distance, and I can hear Bella
barking.

Chapter 9

We awake to the purple light of dawn. Pepe stretches with his hair sticking up and, with a pained expression, says, "I miss our spot under the stairs."

Andres opens his eyes begrudgingly. "Every muscle hurts, and it didn't help to have Luis kicking me all night."

We tried to find a place under the stairs on this ship but found our clever spot was already occupied at every stair.

"We can go farther down into the ship, but the farther we go, the wetter it gets," I say.

Pepe holds his nose and says in a hush to us, "I can't stand the stink down here. They smell so bad."

I look to the sick and wounded all sprawled about in every free space and know all too well the smell Pepe's referring to: rot of many different kinds.

"I stopped breathing through my nose as soon as we came down last night, but I can taste it now," Andres says with a grimace.

"Well, let's go on deck, then." I say as I hoist myself out from behind some of the barrels of water with a grunt.

"Hopefully we can find a better place to sleep outside the hold. The rats were especially terrible this close to the stores. I can still feel them crawling over me," Pepe complains with a shiver.

Andres and I look at each other, knowing how Pepe always exaggerates.

"Right, Pepe, they crawled all over you but didn't touch us." Andres smirks.

He laughs. "I can't help it if the rats only want me."

Many of the ship's healthier mates are on deck by now. No one with any strength left stays below longer than they have to. We find a place to stand on the crowded deck where we can hold the railing, since the ship's constantly rolling on the heavy seas. We take in the surroundings, trying to see if anything has changed while we were asleep.

"I wish Alvaro was here so he could tell us what's happening." Andres squints his eyes at the fine mist of rain that's plagued us for the last three days.

"Well," Pepe says, trying to fill Alvaro's much larger shoes, "the English are still following us."

"Do you really think so?" I scoff, and Andres laughs.

The captain surprises us by putting his large arms on Andres's and my shoulders, squeezing the three of us together tightly and awkwardly.

"Beautiful morning, boys!" he says, far too happy, and makes me think of his nice dry bunk in the officer's quarters he was given.

"What are we going to do, Captain?" Andres asks.

"Well, the greatest fleet that has ever sailed to conquer will limp away like a beaten dog with its tail between its legs."

"You think we'll make it home before the English get us?" I ask.

"Oh, them, no, they're just making sure we leave. They won't attack again." He looks toward the north with his eyes squinted at the dark clouds gathering. "Let's see, our ships are taking on water faster than we can pump, our water is dangerously low, and most of our stores are rotted, a gale is gathering, and we're being pushed into unknown, uncharted waters." He let out a long breath. "It will be another miracle if we see Corunna's coast again." He pats our backs and walks away.

We hear him bellow almost immediately and happily, "The good judge! Shall we have tea in your cabin and discuss our plan?"

"No need to discuss, my good man. I have the orders right here." We watch as he clears his throat with a gurgling sound. "Crew, listen now, for these are the orders for our wayward journey home. 'Hold north-northeast until you reach sixty-one point half degrees. After that point, there is much peril of being driven onto the coast of Ireland, so take great care to run west-southwest until fifty-eight degrees, then southwest to fifty-three degrees; keep heading round the Cape of Finisterre south-southeast, and there you will be safe to land on Spanish soil at any port on the Galician coast.'"

He rolls up the note for safekeeping and grabs for the deck railing as the ship rolls unexpectedly.

As soon as he braces himself, he commands, "These are vague instructions, we all know, so we will have to do our very best to tirelessly keep this sinking ship afloat and off the pitiless Irish rocks. As dangerous as this route will be, we will never make it with the stores of water and food we have left. I hate to do this to my already starving crew, but if we have any hope of touching Spanish soil again, I must put everyone, at every rank including myself, on starvation ration immediately. Every person shall receive half a pound of biscuit, a pint of water, and a half pint of wine a day." Everyone looks down at their already wasting stomachs. "My greatest concern is that of water. The horses and mules must be thrown overboard at once, since we cannot afford a drop to them. See to it!"

The horror of this hits me, and I can't believe they're going to throw the animals overboard.

The captain yells out, "The wind's too strong to drop them in with the boom hoist! We're going to have to take each one up on its own to be sure we don't tear up the deck with their steel shoes!"

A sailor shouts, "We're starving, Captain. We should butcher them instead!"

"These are the duke's orders, my mates. Besides, our ship's taking on water, it'll do us good to lighten the load."

The sailors split into groups and march to the different areas where the beasts are kept. I can hardly watch as the first beautiful and shining stallion, with dark chestnut hair comes prancing out up the plank from the stables. The horse takes in the much-needed fresh air and whinnies happily to be out of the darkness it was kept confined in for months. It steps stiffly with lean muscles as the swarthy sailor pulls begrudgingly at its reins to the stern of the ship.

I turn back around to the protests of the horseman responsible for the horse they just brought up. He's struggling between the strong arms of two sailors. He yells out, "These are cavalry-trained Andalusians! You can't just throw them overboard!"

The sailors look to the captain as they lift him up to keep him from running toward the horse. "Take him below, and don't let him up until the last horse is dealt with."

The man lets loose one final defeated scream before fading belowdecks. The railing's unfastened and swung away, and the sailor brings the willing horse up to the edge. Men light and swing blazing torches behind and to the side of the horse, keeping it from turning around. When the poor horse sees the drop below into churning white water, it squeals and rears back, but before the horse can pull away, two thick sailors both push the horse's hindquarters with such force that the graceful horse goes leaping off the ship.

It's like some strange dream to see this wondrous sight—this shining beauty flying through the air, mane and tail wisping in the wind of the sea—delicate black hooves kicking to stop the fall. The shrill fearful whinny cracks the surreal fantastic slow motion and brings the horror to a climax as the dark horse breaks the even darker, angry water with a painful slap. I stop breathing, as does everyone perched over the rail staring into the ship's wake behind. We all take in a deep breath of relief as the dark head surfaces. The frightened horse fights to stay afloat in the current of the ship and spins out in every direction frantically. Its once-calm eyes are now so wide the whites show and its nostrils flare, sucking in and snorting wet air.

As we're watching to see if the horse will swim in the direction of the nearest coast, a voice barks out, "Out of the way!" and Pepe pulls me back just in time as another disagreeable sailor pulls up a grey mare, almost identical to the first mare I touched on the *San Pedro*. A tear streams down my cheek against my permission with a burn as I see my faint reflection in its dark shiny almond eye. I disappear as the animal flutters its long white eyelashes. She gives me a knowing snort and accepts her fate as she jumps off into the air with only a hind slap. She surfaces also and goes paddling off in the same direction as the bay.

We watch in horror as mythical horse after horse goes flying off the ship. Some go easy while others go rearing and kicking, but each one ends up in the wake, paddling for their lives. Ships all around us are following the bitter order, and the concert of the frightening, primitive whinnies of the struggling horses echoes over the churning sea to us.

I hope never again to see such a horrific and strange sight. After the last one goes over, I take Pepe's and Andres's hands as we bow our heads, and I say, "Pray that each horse makes it to shore."

At this, Andres lets go of our hands and takes out his wooden cross around his neck and begins chanting under his breath something foreign-sounding to us. A strange haze comes over his eyes as he focuses on the French coast. Without a word, Pepe points in the direction of the horses, and I watch in awe as each one turns and starts toward land. Pepe and I exchange looks as we realize we don't know much about Andres after all.

Chapter 10

I'm riding the flying grey mare through the sea. The damp salty air is soaking my hair, and it whips my face with great stinging force. I hear Pepe to my right and Andres to my left and see up ahead the captain on the bay. He's far ahead, and I worry I'll lose him. I give a kick to the mare's flank, and she speeds up and dives closer to the water. I lose my focus as my eyes are hypnotized by the flashing surface right below. A crack of thunder lashes out, and I look up to see a dark, menacing cloud in front of us. The captain is bravely screaming at the clouds as the winds pick up and large waves reach for him on his flying horse. A crack of lightning strikes out right between Pepe and me, and when I open my eyes again, he's gone. Suddenly, Andres is no longer on his horse but is clinging to me on my horse, but the weight makes the horse drop like a pebble into the black ocean, and when we come up, we're clinging to a door. There's no sign of Pepe or the horses. The captain

calls to us, and a light shines around him on a green and shining shore
as a wave comes over our heads.

I wake to Pepe's groan as I come to the realization that I had
kicked his back, trying to stay afloat in my quickly disappearing
nightmare.

"Easy!" Pepe mumbles. "What's wrong with you?" He swats
tiredly at my foot.

"You keep doing that, we're going to make you sleep near the
moldy cheese barrels over there," Andres says without moving
under his arms wrapped around his head.

"I had a terrible dream."

"So keep it to yourself and let us sleep," Pepe says.

I think about the dream for a while in the humid, smelly dark
of the hold. It wasn't just a dream. I can tell it's a warning. My
eyes focus on the glistening drops of water that are seeping
through the ship's walls, like beads of sweat on a horse's hide.
My eyes begin closing again as the sounds of snoring, farting,
and rolling cabin mates continue in the background.

"Shetland straight ahead!" the lookout bellows.

The deck's packed, since the storms of the last few days have
weakened and allowed us all a reprieve.

"Well, at least we're staying on course," Pepe says.

"I'm just glad the English stopped following us." Andres
checks back. "Seeing them in the shadows of our sails was terrible."

Pepe squints up at the sails. "Even though the wind's been
strong we seem to be only moving two or three knots." He leans
over the rail and peers into the ocean. "I bet the whole hull's full
of barnacles by now, slowing us down."

"How very right you are." The captain saunters up with a
smile. "We usually careen them every summer, but we didn't get
the chance. But look on the bright side, those barnacles are
probably the only thing keeping this ship together."

He walks away, laughing, with his hands clasped behind his back.

We hear some hollering on the starboard side and rush over to look. There are some small fishing boats huddled in the waters. The crew slows the ship, and the small boat is dropped with a few sailors holding a purse. My stomach begins to growl as we watch the sailors purchase every last bag they had of dried fish. The whole deck cheers as the men swing the bags onto the deck, and we all grab for the fish that spill out. My hands come up empty as I watch the sailors take the bags to the judge's quarters for rationing. I turn back to see Pepe's managed to get one and is hiding behind the mast so no one will fight him for it. We run over to him, and he sighs as he fights the urge to stuff the whole thing in his mouth. He hands us each our share. "You better remember this."

Even though the next few days are fair, it seems fewer and fewer of the crew are on deck. Every night we go to bed, we see the men are falling ill at a frightening rate, crowding the holds. As quickly as the good weather comes, the bad weather rolls in, and we awake in the night to hail hitting the deck with such force that it sounds like it will go through wood.

"Every able man either on deck or to the pumps!" Captain de Cuellar shouts down belowdecks.

Given the dreadful sound of the hail, I go straight for the pumps. We haven't been at the pumps all week, and we're surprised at the level of the water. All of the pumps are being manned but we wait; we didn't want someone forcing us on deck. I try to squat but find the water so high, it reaches my rear. So we stand there awkwardly, watching the tired, wet, and dirty men work. I notice there are not only the soldiers present pumping, but there are caulkers tiredly filling in all the increasing cracks in the hull.

Andres gasps. "The ship *is* coming apart."

This gets the attention of one of the caulkers, who turns and shouts, "She's been spewing her oakum all week. Treenails have begun to loosen. I give it a week before the bolts pop!"

A rush of dread flashes through me.

The man continues, "So I've been plugging holes and seams for a week, but once those bolts go, no amount of caulk will keep this ship together."

A dripping wet man comes from another part of the ship with a long plank of wood. Another man stops pumping to assist him to hold up the plank over the biggest seam. I pick up the pump, and the soldier gives me a nod of thanks as the sledge hammer clangs the plank into place.

We work the pumps all night, and by morning, we're soaked. It doesn't matter if we go out into the rain, since we can't get any wetter. The ship's rolling in the turbulent seas, and there is only dark grey all around us—the sea to horizon, the land to the sky. Everything grey. The rain is coming down slanted, just so it hits me right in the face. We huddle together at the railing and look out. There isn't another ship visible in this fog. What a desperately alone feeling. If we went down here, there would be no chance of rescue, although no ship would take any more men on in such similar hopeless condition.

Either we're going to sink or make it back somehow. Suddenly an especially large wave rolls the ship, and I lose my hold and start to go with the momentum, when Pepe quickly grabs my arm and pulls me back to the railing. I nod in quick thanks, barely seeing him through the rain, and even though I'm cold and wet, I feel warm knowing I'll always have Andres and Pepe watching out for me.

"I don't feel so good," Andres says, pale with purple chattering lips.

"Yeah, you don't look so good either." Pepe laughs, but he nods to me to help him get his head clear over the railing just in time as he vomits.

He wipes his mouth with the back of his hand. "Okay, pull me back down," he gets out between chattering teeth. He slumps down against the ship.

"I want to go up to the crow's nest!" Pepe shouts right next to us, but we can barely hear him through the wind.

Andres shakes his head in disbelief, and I shout back, "Why?"

"I want to see the storm from up there!" He points.

I shake my head also, but he turns and starts to walk against the roll which slowed him, but then the roll changes, and he stumbles double-time, careening against the main mast. He turns back, embarrassed but smiling at us, as Andres and I now cling to each other for balance while we watch him kill himself. Once he begins climbing, he looks like he'd done it a hundred times before, with an ease that laughs in the face of the tempest. He's beaming with pride as he drops into the nest, and he stays there for hours, watching the clouds roar by and dump their burden on us. The mast rocks twenty degrees back and forth, and he rides it like a giant horse on a frolic. Andres and I decide to go down to sleep and wonder if he's planning to sleep up there, but I feel him squeeze beside us as wet and sloppy as a sponge. Once he's with us, I can finally drift off to sleep.

oooooooooooooooooooooooo

"Boys, to your feet and on deck!" We jump at the sound of the captain's voice.

We get up quickly and pull our still-soaked selves up the ladder while the ship's listing dangerously. We come up to much commotion. The judge and second officers throw out commands left and right.

"We are embayed, boys!" The captain's brow is deeply furrowed. "Our ship and two others cannot beat out again round that head." He points to a misty black jut of foreboding jagged rocks. "We're going to try to anchor off this sandy strip of land

and pray our puny kedge holds and we don't wind up on that shore or those rocks."

We stare off toward the sand he's talking about and can barely see the faint whiteness of the sands through the thick grey fog on shore. The three of us stay quiet, and the captain gives Andres a fatherly pat. "Stay above deck for as long as you can. I don't like the looks of the gale that's blowing in." He nods off to shore, and we see a large dark mass even darker than the dark skies already smothering us.

"What a storm!" Pepe actually appears excited upon seeing this and turns to exclaim to the captain, but he's already walked away.

Andres turns dead pale at the thing that's headed toward us.

Pepe's already running for the crow's nest, and Andres and I try to find a drier spot to wait out the approaching storm. The westerly wind rages, and tremendous breakers start reaching us far off the shore.

The captain comes up in a huff, and Andres and I pull out of our huddle to see the captain holding Pepe from the back of his shirt like a naughty kitten. "I found this idiot headed up to the crow's nest." He turns to Pepe and says, "If you want to kill yourself, you're doing a great job." He pushes him toward us. "Even if you don't have any good sense these boys do, stay with them."

I shout, but he shakes his head like he can't hear me. He takes another bumbling step as the ship creaks and rocks with the rising waves, practically falling on top of us.

"What's happening, Captain?" I scream as loud as I can.

He screams as loud back, "We're being dragged into the shallow sands. As soon as we beach, those hellish waves will break our ship to pieces!"

With that, a huge wave crashes over the deck and sends all the sailors and the captain grabbing for anything in reach. One sailor's swept over with a bloodcurdling scream. Pepe grabs for us, and we brace ourselves between the mast and the cabin of the ship. Waves keep crashing on the deck. Every man with any life left in his body straggles up to find something to hold, but at least one man's carried away with every wave. Suddenly, we feel the ship buck violently during a roll, and the whole ship seems to moan and groan and crack. Pepe, Andres, and I look up at each other, silently speaking the same thing—*we're beached.*

Andres's mouth opens in panic, and he cries, "I can't swim! I can't swim!"

Men all over the ship shout, "Save yourselves!" as one man takes a running leap over the side.

Another large wave crashes on us, and the worst sound I've heard ricochets across the desperate scene—*Rrrrr-reeeeaaaaaggghhhhhh*—CRACK! The ship lurches to starboard, and Andres holds me tighter. Many more men stand on the railing, make the sign of the cross, and jump into the surging waves. Part of me thinks if I stay in this exact spot that everything will be fine. The gale will blow out, and I can wait for a ship to come save us.

The noblemen on ship heave bags of gold out from their cabins and load them on the only lifeboat we had. The finest nobleman shouts something to a caulker he drags out. He puts his precious items in first and steps into the hold of the small boat with two other well-dressed men. They put the hatch on the hold, and next the caulker caulks in the hatch so they're completely sealed in. An officer starts to lower the boat over the side, when a gang of desperate sailors and soldiers all clamor and shove each other to jump on top. The officers try to keep them off, but it's no use as the boat's going over the side with as many as thirty men already on it.

Pepe gets up to watch the spectacle and, upon returning a few minutes later, says, "Once it hit the water, drowning men also tried to get on the boat and capsized it!"

I realize that now those noblemen were upside down in the waves—trapped.

I start to get up from our spot to see the situation below. There are men floating in the water, struggling to stay afloat, as every wave washes over them, pulling them down just to clamor back to the surface for half a desperate breath before the next wave hits again. Any man given a slight reprieve from the berating waves screams, "God help me!"

Two other larger ships are also floundering and breaking up on the sands. Three identical scenes of horror. No hope for rescue.

I cling to the railing as a wave washes over again, and Andres slides away back to the spot where we were just hiding. He stays there, clutching the mast alone. Pepe and I study how each man jumps. One man jumps too close to the ship and never resurfaces. Another man jumps as a wave is coming, and he's slapped against the ship's hull. It seems the only ones who resurface time it perfectly between waves and swim immediately away from the ship. Even though more and more men keep plunging into the water, it seems less and less were bobbing in the churning sea.

Suddenly the captain's beside us along with the judge.

"Judge, it's time to go in!" the captain yells.

"It's no use!" he says back, his eyes fixed on the drowning below. "We have no hope in these waters."

"The ship can't last much longer!" the captain screams. "If we stay here any longer, we'll surely die. In the water, we have a chance!"

The judge is quiet, and I imagine him measuring how far the fall.

Then it hits me—my dream of the storm—*I held on to a door.* A door just like a hatch! I look at the large hatch cover next to us and grab the captain's arm.

"Captain! I think this will float!"

They all turn, and the captain's eyes light up when he realizes what I mean.

"Boys! Help me throw this over!"

Pepe, the captain, and I all heave the hatch up to waist level and carry it to the bow. The judge and Andres follow behind quietly.

"On three! One, two, three!" the captain cries.

We throw it the farthest we can, but it still lands pretty close to the bow of the ship.

The captain says, "We'll need another one!"

We run to another hatch and throw that in.

The captain gets on the railing and puts his hand down to the judge. The judge looks back at the beaten, hopeless ship and despairingly takes the captain's hand, which pulls the plumper, older man up on the railing.

The captain says, "Jump as far as you can when I tell you!"

Then, after a wave comes, he jumps and yanks the hesitating judge with him. Pepe, Andres, and I watch eagerly as the captain surfaces and searches for the door. We yell and point where it bobs. He reaches it and shouts for the judge, who finally resurfaces, spitting water and having spasms to stay afloat.

I notice the other door's drifting farther away, and I yell, "We have to go too!"

Pepe nods and jumps up on the railing. He tries to give me a hand, but I leap up without needing his help. I stand next to him and leave a space for Andres to stand. When we glance back, he's stepping away backwards.

"I can't! I really can't! I can't swim! I can't go in! I'll be okay here. You two go!" he sputters, hyperventilating.

"Andres, get up here right now! We'll help you, and you can float on that door! But if we don't go now, you'll surely die here or in the water—ALONE!"

Andres halts and stares back up to us, and we both put our hands out. He slowly comes to take them, and we pull him up with us. I make the mistake of looking down off the railing into the surging, angry water. It no longer is beautiful but primal, with its dark black water and frothy white rage reaching for us at every crisscrossing wave. Nothing except the fear of death can make me go into that water. My stomach feels like it rose into my throat, making it hard to breathe.

Now I'm the flying horse.

We three boys—the tallest, smallest, and middle—all holding hands on a sinking ship, all say together, gathering strength, "ONE, TWO, THREE!" and we both pull Andres off with us, and I hear his scream the whole way down until we hit the dark, hostile water.

I'm unprepared for how painful the cold is. The water is like ice and feels like I fell on knives. I have to push the pain away from my mind and resist the urge to gasp out of sheer shock and fight my way back to air. I break away from Andres as soon as we hit the water, and I look all over for him.

"Andres! Pepe! Captain!" I scream, but hear and see no one. I search for the door and am relieved to see the captain holding Andres on his door a few feet away from me. But every time I try to reach them, the current and waves keep pulling me under. I'm struggling to avoid getting sucked back to hit against the ship. Suddenly, a monstrous wave breaks across the ship and sends broken planks and barrels flying. I come up in time to see a large piece of ship on top of a wave crash right down on top of the captain and Andres. I realize I have to give up trying to get to them and instead swim with the waves away from the ship.

"Pepe!" I yell when I can get a breath, but the salty water invades my throat, and I cough and sputter as it burns up my nasal passages.

I haven't seen him anywhere. I wonder if he ever resurfaced. About a wave away, I see something dark in the water. It's the size of a boy, and I start to swim as hard as I possibly can toward it. When I get nearer, my heart drops when I see it's only a barrel. But then I realize it's floating after all and grab on to it. I don't know how long I'm in the waves or how I even managed to keep holding the barrel as my body shuts down to the cold. A strange primal scream brings me out of my stupor, and I pull my aching head up out of the waves to see what's making that sound.

"Póg mo thóin!" The thing gurgles as he looks up to the sky, both arms beating his drumlike chest.

There, on the center of the beach ahead, about two feet deep in the water, stands a naked giant. With the constant disruption on the choppy waves closer to shore, this hairy beast of a man with muscles bulging obscenely and covered in vibrant blood shakes his ax and large mallet to the sky. I freeze at the sight of him and know he is not from our ship. I instantly let go of my barrel and try to swim backwards. I watch in horror as a sailor makes it to shore about thirty feet away from him. With the scariest sound I've ever heard a human make, the giant runs right at the poor man and swings his mallet round in a circle mid-flight, making contact with the petrified man's head. A cloud of blood and matter explodes from where his head had been.

Panic shoots through me, and I swim against the waves the best I can. I try to swim westward to land among the reeds on the side of the shore. The savage yells over and over again and I count at least forty-three yells before I reach the safety of the marsh. As I lie there, panting and completely exhausted, I fight the urge to noisily cough up the water I had swallowed. I think about the chances that the captain, Pepe, or Andres made it to shore. My stomach lurches at the thought that maybe one of those yells has been the end of one of them. Blackness comes quickly and without warning.

Chapter 11

Before I open my eyes, a rustling sound is coming closer to me. The image of the naked warrior swinging his ax down on my head keeps me from opening my eyes. The noise stops, but I feel the thing right beside me. I open my eyes one at a time, and I'm relieved to see a naked and shivering Spaniard clutching his knees to his chest, trying to generate some warmth on the cold night.

"Which... sh-sh-ship... are you from?" I ask, but I'm shivering almost as much and can barely get the words out. A convulsion of cold rolls through me and locks my jaw. I hold my body closer also.

The man turns a haunted face to me, and his eyes don't even find mine. He seems in a fog.

"What... is... your name?" I try again.

This time he just folds into himself once again, and I realize he must not be well.

We sit quietly shivering in the wind howling off the sea until I hear many footsteps coming toward us in the reeds. I look up to see three foreign faces and can't understand a word they speak to each other. They all hold sacks in one hand and a club in the other, but as soon as they see me, a boy, and the already stripped, shivering man, clinging to our lives, they put down their clubs and instead grab at the reeds around us and start to cover the naked man in them. Then they do the same for me. Dusk falls.

∞∞∞∞∞∞∞∞∞∞∞∞∞∞∞∞∞∞

The reeds and ferns might have been the thing that kept me alive that night, but they didn't help my new friend at all. I find him in the dawn completely frozen, with his arms and legs pulled close to him, eyes fixed and his jaw hanging open. From far away, I hear the sound of many horses. Peeking up through the reeds, I see as many as two hundred men on horseback flood the beach, each man circling around the wreckage washed ashore before continuing on. After the whole strand is looked over, they leave to the next strand. Not being able to stay a moment longer next to the corpse, I stand up in the reeds and survey the scene, mostly looking for the warrior.

The beach is terribly quiet with the soft lapping of the now calming seas in the morning light. The sands are covered with items washed up from the wreck, and as I draw closer, I realize they're all bodies. I couldn't have imagined such a sight. Ravens and wild dogs are taking advantage of the bounty. I run and throw rocks, trying to shoo the animals away, turning each body over, searching their faces. Most are badly disfigured due to blows from mallets and clubs, and I realize that many of these men had made it to shore alive. All were stripped of their clothing and robbed of everything they tried to save on them. Every crate and barrel was pried open and emptied. Body after body all strewn on the sands like fish after the tide's gone out. There are hundreds upon hundreds, and still, bodies are floating up in the sleepy waves.

"Luis!" something croaks downwind.

I turn and see Andres clutching his soaked self and running toward me, shivering so hard he can barely run. Limping in the background, I see the captain, smiling. I run to Andres. I grab him and spin him around.

"I told you you'd be fine!" I give him another hug.

He laughs. "Yeah, I held onto the captain and never let go," he says between shivers.

I see the large blood stain down the captain's pants.

"What happened, Captain?"

He winces as he takes another step forward. "Oh, a wave carrying a piece of floating timber came right down on my legs."

"Where's Pepe?" Andres asks, searching the shoreline behind me.

"He's not with you?"

"No," Andres answers, and his eyes fill.

"Did you see him after we hit the water?'

"No," Andres says.

"Is the judge with you too?" I ask the captain.

He shakes his head. "No, sunk right to the bottom. I'm guessing his whole coat must have been sewn with gold."

We stand and look at what lies all around us.

The captain proclaims, "Well, we must get out of here before that warrior-thing comes back. There must be someone who'll take a fellow Catholic in." He takes his cross from underneath his shirt and kisses it.

We make our way slowly, with the captain grimacing with every other step.

"Luis! Stay off the path," he shouts from behind as he puts his arm out for Andres, "and help me here." He stumbles over the rocks on the edge of the path.

We travel for less than an hour when we come upon a smoking stone church at the top of a knoll. Andres and I make to run up to the church, but the captain grabs hold of our wet shirts and pulls us back and whispers in our ears, "*Never* run up to a smoking church."

We inch up to the small and charred holy place. The thatched roof is completely gone, and we see shapes hanging from the iron bars of the windows. Once inside, we see that twelve Spaniards were slaughtered within. Each youthful face blue, each one struggled out of the water and escaped the warrior to come to this place of refuge to be hanged.

Was there no escape?

Everything's hypnotically still—a silence that only follows a tragedy.

Evil swallows all sound.

We leave the desecrated ground, walking backwards, attempting to undo a curse. Behind the church, the captain notices a faint path through the thick woods and nods toward it. No one talks for half an hour. We keep looking for death in every direction. Andres sees her first, crouches down instinctively, and we follow. An old lady pulls five cows down the path but halts as soon as she sees us and tries to push her cows back down the path to no avail.

The captain jumps forward, which causes her ancient eyes to open wide. He says, "Spain! We are from Spain! We mean you no harm." But she doesn't seem to understand a word and keeps trying to move back down the path, her cheeks flaming pink from the hard work.

The captain smiles his friendliest smile and holds his hands to his chest over his heart. The women watches this movement with curiosity. The captain points to his bloody leg, and she winces in sympathy. Then the captain mocks shivering and rubs his stomach to show hunger. The old woman looks at us sadly, shrugs, and put her hands up empty. She points to the woods behind her and puts her hands out like a musket and points to us. She raises her fingers up in a cross and points to us and then shakes her head at what was back in the woods. She points at her cows and then covers one of her hands over the other and points forward. The captain seems to understand it all and nods in thanks for her assistance. She smiles as she pulls her cows past us, hunched over with age.

"What did she say?" I ask.

"She warned us the English were that way, and we should go back from where we came."

"Back to the church?" Andres fumes.

"Never doubt an old woman hiding her cows." And he steps forward, even more sore than before, and we follow tiredly behind.

We pass the church again in silence, and we stare at our feet. The sound of Spanish words make us glance up at once as two naked figures run toward us.

Chapter 12

"Forget all about me!" one yells as they near, his arms bent at the elbows and swinging as he runs awkwardly.

My heart jumps as I see a familiar form. Andres must have recognized him also, since he goes running to him.

"Pepe!" I say, and the captain looks up, pursing his thin lips, trying to keep from smiling but his eyes well up.

"You're all alive!" Pepe says as he hugs Andres. "I was sure you all drowned!" He reaches to hug me and engulfs me in his arms.

He goes to hug the captain, but the captain draws back. "I never hugged a naked man and don't want to say I did now." We laugh, and Pepe suddenly looks self-conscious and tries to cover himself with his hands.

"How did you all keep your clothes?" Pepe points to his companion. "As soon as we came up to that beach"—he points to the strand next to ours—"the natives were all dancing with their sticks above their heads, just waiting for us to make it to shore." He grabs the man next to him. "They took every stitch we had off us, and Carlos, here, took a bad blow to the head." He turns the skinny man to the side, showing a river of blood down to his neck.

Pepe's brow knits. "I could care less about my clothes, but they took Auradona, my father's knife, and my sewing kit my mother left me."

I immediately take my top layer off and hand it to Pepe. "It's still wet, but it's something."

He gives me a grateful look and happily throws it over his head. Andres eyes Carlos's shivering form and begrudgingly removes his top layer. He throws it to Carlos, who thanks him eagerly.

"Are the beaches clear?" the captain asks.

"We had to wait until the scavengers were gone, and we don't know when the horses will come back. I think we should stay off the beach. There's a church there."

The captain shakes his head. "Nothing holy that way." He starts to hobble toward the beach. "We need to find some biscuits or wine that wash up if we're going to make it anywhere."

From the knoll, I can see two strands of beach, the one we came in from and the one where Pepe had landed. I'm surprised to see an equal number of bodies on both beaches. Coming closer, I can see more had washed up since we'd been there. Andres runs to an opened crate nearest to us, and the captain yells, "Now, why would you go to an *opened* crate?"

Embarrassed, he runs farther down the shore to the crates that have recently washed up, and Pepe and Andres kick away at one, trying to open it. Finally, it pops open, and soggy biscuits glob out on the lid. I never tasted such delicious mush in my life. We were starving and all too quickly finished the crate; then we ran off for another. After we filled our bellies with the contents of three crates, the captain points to a group of natives coming toward us. Three short savages come up with foreign tongues wagging and spears high. We all put our hands up as they begin to pull off our clothes, but the captain screams, "Please, we are friends of Ireland!" to no avail.

Luckily, a larger savage comes down and pulls them away from us. He picks up my shirt and throws it back to us apologetically. After his stern command, the others back away and go off looking through the wreckage. The leader turns and sees us all in our misfortune and points up to another dirt road that disappears through a different patch of woods. He thumps his fist against his chest and points up the path, and we all think he's saying it is his village.

We bow and make our way to the path. The captain pants as he hobbles. "Quickly, before they change their minds."

After trudging over sharp stones and rocky paths, the captain commands wearily, "Give me pause here."

We stand watching him, anxious to get through the eerie wood to some shelter. He arches his back and looks to the sky through the short, wind-hindered treetops.

"It's hard to tell when dusk is falling due to how grey and dismal the weather is here," the captain says with his mouth opened, panting slightly.

Suddenly, we all turn to the noise coming from the path ahead of us. It's too late to jump into the underbrush to hide. The group sees us and are hurrying straight at us.

Two men lead the way, and the captain quickly pushes us behind him as he brings the stick he's walking with out in front of him. One of the men draws out a knife and quickly stabs at the captain's already wounded leg. The captain catches the blow with his stick, but the knifepoint breaks flesh. The captain grunts and lunges at the men out of range. The other man swings at his head and knocks the captain over easily. Carlos jumps forward, only to put his hands up as soon as he sees the man brandish the knife with a grin of intent. Out of nowhere, a very beautiful girl with orange, shining hair jumps in front of them and says something feverishly to the young man with the knife, causing him to lower it to his side. An old man pulls the other young man back and says something in a calming tone.

The man steps around the girl and old man, toward Carlos. He lifts Carlos's already too short tunic Andres loaned him and pushes him away in disgust, seeing he's completely naked underneath. The man looks at me, Andres, and half-naked Pepe and realizes we carry no worth and focuses on the captain lying on the ground, still.

The two men step over him and pull off his clothes. One removes his doublet and the other pulls off his pants. They rip open every seam, from which drop coin after coin. Our mouths fall open at the sight of so much gold as the savage's eyes sparkle. While pulling off his undershirt, they gasp as they unveil the thick gold chain and a thinner gold chain with a red jeweled cross around his neck. In seconds, they remove them from him. They pull off his hose and leave the captain in an unflattering position on the ground.

The men start stuffing the captain's clothing into the satchels they have on their sides, but the girl again stays their hands with a touch and pleading look, and the young men throw the captain's clothing back to the ground. The man with the knife puts his hand up to the girl's face gently and dangles the chain with the cross in front of her. She smiles sweetly and takes the chain as the man turns and motions for the young man and the older man to continue on the path toward the shore. They leave the girl behind with us.

She picks up the clothes and hands them to the captain. As he pulls back on the ripped hose and cut doublet, she puts his cross around her neck and smiles. She pulls up the cross and kisses it, obviously trying to show she's a Catholic and wants to keep it.

The captain scoffs and turns to us. "A savage Catholic," he says, and he groans as he gets back on his feet. "Are there no good Catholics in this wretched place?"

The beautiful girl motions for us to follow her back up the path. We watch her graceful form dance between the large stones on the path ahead of us. As the light's fading, all we can see is her shiny orange hair, and she keeps spinning and smiling at us like some strange nymph or fairy. Just when we can barely see right in front of us, the path opens up to a small village on top of a hill. There are small wooden houses with thatched roofs, all with smoke coming out of their centers. She points to one in the center, and as we open the door, a small boy runs to the girl. I try to figure out if this is her son, but she looks too young to be a mother. She speaks to him, and he runs off. We all happily sit next to the fire, but the captain has trouble getting to the floor, and beads of sweat appear on his brow.

The boy returns carrying a pitcher of milk, loaves of oaten bread, and butter. My mouth opens, and drool spills out on the dirt floor. Pepe, seeing this, pulls away to his side and laughs.

The girl points to herself and says, "Carra," and we all point and say our names, which pleases her. After giving us generous helpings, she sits very close beside the captain and motions for the boy, who brings a small jar to her from a basket in the corner.

She pulls at the captain's trousers, and the captain balks once at the request, but Carra pulls even harder on them with an angry look. The captain turns red in the face and tries to pull off his pants and hose as discreetly as possible as we all look away. He bundles up his pants and covers himself with them as Carra spreads some herbal concoction over his wounds. When the fire begins to warm the concoction, a pungent smell fills the cottage, opening my sinuses, and makes my eyes sting. I'm forced to close them and soon fall asleep, happy, with the warm fire and full belly. We just might make it home.

∞∞∞∞∞∞∞∞∞∞∞∞∞∞∞∞∞∞

I awake with a stick hitting my head and open my eyes to the boy tending the fire. *Did he just hit me with a stick on purpose?* I couldn't tell by how he seems to be ignoring me now. I look over to Andres holding back his laughter, and I see he's dangling a stick over my head. He and Pepe spurt out in laughter as soon as I realize it had been them.

I sit up and rub my eyes. "Where's the captain and Carlos?"

"They're outside trying to talk to some of the savages, trying to get directions where we can go next," Pepe says.

The captain walks back in much stronger than he had been yesterday and proclaims, "All my boys up!" and he throws Pepe a pair of pants that have seen better days. "This boy here's going to walk us in the right direction." He points a new, carved walking stick—some villager must have given him—at the boy, who seems unaware he has been nominated. Carra walks in and speaks to the boy, who hops up immediately and looks back for us to follow.

Pepe pulls the pants on like he's afraid they'll burn him, and we scoff at his ungratefulness.

"What?" he says. "These look like someone died, got buried, and was dug back up to get them."

We laugh.

The captain takes Carra's hand and kisses it as her pale skin glows. It never occurred to me until then that this woman seems to find the captain handsome, and I guess he is, with his tall stature, dark looks, and bright smile. The rest of us bow to her in thanks, and her eyes seem to tear at our plight as she kisses her cross once again and holds it up to the sky.

The boy's running too far ahead, and the captain keeps throwing rocks in his direction, yelling, "Slower, by God!"

Suddenly, we turn the bend to see the boy sitting on a large rock. He points to a village in the distance down a knoll.

"Oh, that's where we should go?" the captain asks.

The boy points again and moves his head and hands back and forth in a negative way.

"Oh, we shouldn't go there?" The captain straightens.

The boy points at the path we are on and follows it all the way with his finger until it is close to the village and then shows us where the path splits and indicates we should take the one that avoids the huts.

The captain begins saying, "All right, so we just follow—" But before he can ask where the path leads, the boy disappears back up ahead.

"Well, that's it, then." The captain goes forth with his walking stick. "Let us keep moving. We'll need to find shelter before night falls."

It's a few hours before we come to the fork that leads to the village, and we go the way the boy showed us, which takes us again through a thick wood.

"Let's stop here and eat these berries," the captain says, pointing to the bushes lining the path.

"How do you know they're not poisonous?" Pepe asks, eyeing the little black berries suspiciously.

"I'm *mostly* sure these are the delicious bilberries. I had a most delicious jam from France that had a picture of these little beauties on them." He opens one between his thumbs, and red juice drips and stains his skin. "Yes, these are most definitely the little black hearts!" He pops it in his mouth with a sucking sound. "Um-um-ummm."

We grab for as many berries as we can pop in our mouths. They're the most wonderful things I've ever tasted. We take the time to fill our bellies and our pockets with as many as we can find, when something hits me in the back of the head and throws me to the ground. In seconds, a thin man, much older than me, is pulling off my trousers and tunic. I look to my side and see a man on every one of my companions plus two pulling off the captain's clothes. The man on me pulls off my dirty linen shirt and pants, then pushes me back down again. I watch as they're unhappy to see the captain's seams have already been torn and in anger take the captain's walking stick and hit him across his back with it. The savages laugh and spit and go back from where they came with the walking stick, and leave us naked and shivering as a cold wind picks up.

"I just got those pants!" Pepe throws a rock after them.

We all sit there, almost waiting for them to bring them back to us, but the captain pulls himself up with a grunt and wince, then hobbles over to the brush. He begins pulling the ferns out with his hands and throwing them all in a pile. We wonder if he's going mad, but we watch as he strips the largest fern and ties it tightly around his thin middle. He then starts tying fern after fern onto the stringlike plaits.

Halfway done, he looks up with a smile and says, "My Irish kilt!"

We all laugh and get up to copy what he's doing.

After the last fern is on, we look like a band of native warriors. We're still shivering but feel a little more pride walking again on the trail. Pitch dark sets in, but we have to continue.

"What's shimmering over there?" Andres points through the trees.

We step off the path to go toward it and come out by a large lake. To our right, we see the moon illuminating the thatched huts.

"I think we should stay away from villages," Carlos says to the captain.

But the captain squints his eyes and says, "No smoke means no fires, and no fires means no villagers." He starts walking toward the village.

Chapter 13

He's right; the village is deserted. The fires haven't been lit for some time, and no personal articles can be found. We check in each hut quietly to be sure and are startled by movement within the largest one. Three men jump up off the straw floor, and a small dog begins barking. Before we can turn and flee, we hear one exclaim, "Run!" in Spanish.

Immediately, the captain exclaims, "Brothers!"

They lunge toward us in the darkness of the hut, slapping us all on our backs. We're relieved we've found more countrymen.

"My name is Captain Francisco de Cuellar from—"

"Captain!" The tallest man jumps out and hugs him so hard the captain loses his balance.

"Alvaro?" the captain says, completely shocked.

Their dog's jumping up on my leg repeatedly, and it dawns on me as I bend down to feel the familiar wet nose all over my face. "Bella!" I scream, and suddenly, both Andres and Pepe embrace her.

After the excitement of the unexpected reunion dies down, we sit with Alvaro and his companions.

"You all look very lovely in your skirts." Alvaro smirks as he playfully tousles our hair.

The captain smirks. "I think we'll get another day out of them before they shrivel up and I get to show off!"

"Hah! Now I feel overdressed for this party." Alvaro's smile reaches his eyes.

"That better not be Philippe with you." The captain squints into the dark, trying to see if he recognizes the others.

"No." Alvaro's eyes twinkle in the faint light coming through the window. "He had a terrible *accident* as soon as you were taken off the ship."

The captain chuckles proudly and then pauses. "So, tell me, what became of my beautiful ship?"

Bella comes and tries to nestle in the circle of Pepe's lap, scratching furiously at the ferns.

"Easy, there, that's a Pepe original you're shredding there."

Alvaro sits up to start his tale. "I became captain after you didn't return. Talk about trial by fire! First time captaining a sinking ship in enemy territory." He rubs his scruffy beard back and forth nervously. "The ship was falling apart, taking on water faster than we could pump. Half the ship was sick from reducing our rations and water. I knew we had to make for land, but none was in sight. We were forcing the ship to its breaking point, and everyone on board gave up all hope. In the slight glimmer of the northern lights, there was an eerie stillness as I realized the pumps stopped working for the first time in days. All men came on deck, prayed, and resolved to give up and let the water rise. As dawn broke, we saw land right before our eyes! I gave commands that we were making to crash on the sandy shore and for everyone get to the ready! I steered right for the beach, but the tide swept us and stuck us right between a narrow wedge in the cliffs."

The captain asks, "Are you the only survivors?"

He flips his head back with a weird laugh. "That's the strangest thing! Every man made it off the ship!"

We all shake our heads in disbelief.

He keeps laughing. "The yardarms hit just above a ledge in the side of the cliff, and we managed to get every man off! Even the wounded!"

"Why aren't all your men with you, then?" The captain's brow tenses.

Alvaro gives him a crazy glance. "That's the ironic part." He laughs strangely. "I get every man off, and as soon as we're making our way toward a village, the Lord Deputy FitzWilliam surrounds us with cavalry and savages with muskets and arquebuses."

"Did you fight?" Pepe asks impatiently.

Alvaro turns toward him. "We were ready to, but some of the noblemen talked to his men in Latin. FitzWilliam told us there were three thousand English right behind them. He asked us which noblemen were on our ship and had them and the priests brought to him. He convinced them to surrender and promised us all we would keep our clothes and would be returned to Spain. Once our weapons were laid down, they attacked with brutal force, shooting, clubbing, spearing, punching. I ran right for the bog behind us with about fifty or so other men, but as soon as I reached the other side of the bog, these two were the only men with me."

"What about Bella?" Andres asks.

Alvaro finally smiles. "Oh, well, she's smarter than any of us. As soon as she heard FitzWilliam and the cavalry coming, she ran for the bog. That's how I got the idea."

We're quiet for a bit, and the captain speaks. "How many days did it take you to find this place?"

"This all happened this morning," his companion says.

"So there might be three thousand English troops in this area?" The captain becomes rigid.

Alvaro nods. "And they'll shoot Spaniards in the streets like dogs."

"This FitzWilliam, is he a deputy?" the captain asks.

"That is what the nobleman translated. That's why we trusted him. I should have never trusted anyone with steel-grey eyes."

"Well, we should rest, because as soon as dawn breaks, we need to get away from this place."

The captain settles himself down, and we all say goodnight.

∞∞∞∞∞∞∞∞∞∞∞∞∞∞∞∞∞∞∞∞∞∞

The door slowly opens in the faint dawn, and Bella sounds the alarm. We quickly get to our feet, but the startled man closes the door at the sight of us. The captain puts his hand up for us to stay quiet, and he listens to the intruder walk away.

Alvaro runs to the window. "It's only one clergyman, no one else."

With this reassurance, the captain hobbles out, shouting, "Please! Help us!"

The monk pauses, unsure of us foreigners, and he says something to the captain I can't understand. Surprisingly, the captain speaks back in the same odd language.

"Latin," Alvaro explains to us.

The captain struggles with it, but the monk's pointing a lot, and the captain keeps nodding gratefully. The captain shakes the religious man's hand with both hands and returns happily to us.

"We are saved, men!" He waves for us halfway back. "God has intervened to save us once again! Follow me. I'll explain while we're walking."

"What did he say?" I ask, walking one stride to his two.

"I understood most of it. First, he told of great danger. He said the English had gone around to all the villagers and warned each one that harboring or aiding a Spaniard was punishable by death." The captain looks back toward the other villages we passed. "He said they were rounding them all up this very morning and walking them to the gallows."

"Shouldn't we try to help them?" Andres halts.

Alvaro scoffs and throws his hands up in the air. "Yeah, you go back there and rescue them all."

Andres looks hurt but starts walking again.

The captain keeps his gaze ahead but puts an arm around Andres and brings him up to pace. "We can't help anyone but ourselves right now."

"So that explains the Irish welcome," Alvaro says.

"Well, all is not lost. Thankfully, the queen has her enemies, and the monk gave me direction to friends of King Philip, Chieftains O'Rourke, and MacClancy, six leagues from here, north of the mountains."

Alvaro stops. "But we aren't going north of the mountains."

"I'm very well aware of that." He smirks. "I'm hurrying to the other fantastic news God's messenger told of."

We wait for a moment for him to continue.

Alvaro spits, "What is it?"

"A Spanish ship has been sighted off the coast. The ship is searching the shore for survivors, but we must hurry." He's straining greatly.

Hearing this news, Alvaro, Carlos, and the other men quicken their pace. At first, I can't go any faster than the captain, but after a few hours, he slows, and I try to reduce my pace but see the others disappearing ahead. Andres is the only one who slows down to walk with the captain and me. Not including Bella, of course, who playfully keeps running back to us and circles around us. Pepe never even glances back.

"You two run ahead too." He stops, panting heavily. "I just need to rest my leg a moment."

"No, we'll wait," I say, sitting as Andres follows me.

"You'd be crazy to stay with me!" He runs his hand through his thick hair. "I wouldn't do the same for you, you know. This may be your only chance to go home. Run, now!"

But I didn't go. Not only did I feel sorry leaving him alone, I had a strong feeling that staying with him was key for my survival—some vague remembrance from my dream.

He sighs. "And I thought you two had brains."

Every time we get back up, he walks more slowly. Finally, we reach the top of a large hill and see the ocean in front of us. There she is, a beautiful galleon shining in the diamond water. Andres and I start screaming with joy.

"We made it! Captain, we made it!"

Bella barks at our joy.

The captain hobbles up and sees the ship bobbing there, in disbelief. At first he looks happy, but then he squints.

"What do you see there in the water, boys?"

I squint. "A rowboat?"

"With people in it," Andres adds.

"The boat's heading for the ship, right?"

"Yes," we both answer at the same time.

He drops his shoulders and slumps against a large rock.

"What are you doing? We have to go down and wait for them to come back!" I say, waving toward the beach.

"Look!" He points. "They're already bringing the anchor in."

I put my hand up to shield the sun from my eyes and see he's right; they are pulling anchor. My heart sinks.

Chapter 14

"I told you boys not to wait for me," the captain says, rubbing his leg.

"Pepe..." Andres shakes his head sadly, looking at the figures on the small boat getting pulled up.

"He didn't even say good-bye to us." I wonder if I can pick out his shape from here.

Andres bends down and pats Bella. "Well, at least we still have you."

But something makes her freeze, and she turns one ear toward the beach and stops breathing so she can hear better. I don't hear a thing, but she takes off running toward the beach. We watch from above as she makes her way through the reeds and rushes, and both of us gasp as she runs to a dark shape on the beach. Andres and I take off running too, and our hearts leap to see Alvaro sitting there on the sand, watching the ship set sail.

Another familiar voice comes out from the underbrush behind us as Pepe walks out, batting away the branches from his face, spitting out the imaginary leaves from his paranoid mouth.

"Those berries pretty much come out the same way they looked when they went in," he says, walking toward us.

"We thought you left!" I say, trying to catch my breath.

"Almost did," Alvaro says flatly without looking at us, eyes fixed on the ship.

"We thought we could tell them to wait for you, but they said they risked their lives every hour they waited." Pepe ties up his pants.

"Carlos and the others?" Andres asks.

"Yeah," Pepe answers.

I realize Pepe has pants. "Where did you get pants!"

He laughs. "They gave me some when they saw my skirt."

"You couldn't have asked for some extra pairs!" Andres yells.

Pepe laughs harder. "Alvaro remembered. He got a pair for each of you."

Alvaro throws two pairs at us without speaking and walks past us, back up the ridge. Andres and I quickly rip off our ferns, throw on the stiff pants, and follow, hoping Alvaro wasn't going to make the captain feel like this is his fault.

As soon as the captain sees him, he says, "You're a fool, Alvaro."

However, Alvaro throws him a pair of pants. "What kind of a first mate would I be if I left my captain behind?"

Pepe, Andres, and I all smile like three children relieved that their parents quit quarreling.

We walk north of the mountains for as long as the light lasts, and we have to sleep in the moss under some giant rocks overnight. We sleep much closer to each other than normal that night due to the cold and strange surroundings. In the darkest part of night, we hear howling and yelps somewhere very near.

The captain rubs his eyes quickly. "I think it's best we sleep in shifts. Make sure those wolves find something else to eat tonight."

He never wakes anyone else up, though; he takes the whole watch.

∞∞∞∞∞∞∞∞∞∞∞∞∞∞∞∞∞∞

In the morning, we start up the side of the mountain through the cotton fog that creeps up and over the peaks along with us. Many hours pass as we make our way over. Once at the top, we look down the beautiful valley that rolls to a shiny lake and then keeps rolling out to the blue-blue of the sea on the horizon. In the middle of the lake stands a mythical castle with five towers making up a circle. It's majestic and appears to grow right out of the water.

The captain puts his arms out wide, with his head up to the heavens, and says, "The Castle of Rossclogher!"

As we make our way down, I keep wondering how it is possible that anyone could have built anything in the middle of a lake, and come to the conclusion that these people must be magical.

"How are we going to get to the castle?" Andres asks as he slips on a rock and slides a bit down the dirt path. Pepe scoffs.

"Will they send a boat for us?" Alvaro asks, uncertain.

"We better not be swimming out there," Andres worries.

The captain squints and scans the surroundings. "I'm sure once we get there, we'll find a way."

Which only worries us more.

All except Pepe, who rubs his stomach. "I'm starving."

"We're out of the oaten bread Carra gave us, so you'll have to wait." The captain pushes him ahead.

We reach a wider path of small stones that leads to different pastures of grazing cattle.

"These must belong to the castle. There should be a herder or milk maiden nearby." The captain slowly turns around, searching for signs of life.

Andres screams, "I see a girl—there!"

We all turn, but the volume of Andres's sighting sends the girl running, and she disappears behind the hill.

"Good job, Andres," Alvaro says low.

The captain sighs. "Well, it's a good time to rest, then, and we'll wait for someone to see us."

"I just hope it's not the English that do." Alvaro lies down on a grassy spot and closes his eyes. We decide to do the same.

I don't know how much time passes, but I open my eyes to six shadows looming over us, and we jump at the stealthy intrusion. Alvaro gets to his feet, but one of them lays a spear right next to his neck. The captain immediately speaks in Latin. The largest man replies in the same language and only after a few exchanges, the man slaps the back of the captain as he helps him up, knocking him off balance on his good leg.

The captain turns to us as the savages walk away. "That's MacClancy, the large one. He's O'Rourke's subject and immediately welcomed us to his castle, where he says other Spaniards are presently harbored."

We all smile at the idea of a safe haven, such as this well-fortified castle in front of us. But we start walking away from the lake and back up one of the hills.

"Why are we walking *away* from the castle?" I ask.

"He said to follow him," the captain replies.

We pass a few small, thatched houses and come to a cove of heavy brush and boulders beside the hill. The men trek right through the brush, snapping it back on us, and disappear into the darkness of some sort of cave.

Alvaro pauses. "Is this a trap, Captain?"

"Why would they kill us in this cave when they could have killed us right there by the lake?" He continues limping over the rocks on the path.

The light vanishes quickly once we're in the cave, and all I can do is put my hands on either side of the narrow cavern and follow the noise of those ahead of me. About the time I start feeling like there's little air left and the walls are closing in, I see some light flash as a door opens to a room ahead. I step out after Alvaro into the small, rock-walled room and suddenly realize we must be *inside* the castle.

Pepe squeals in delight, runs to the small high window. "We went through a secret tunnel!"

Andres and I both pull at him so we can see too. Through the window, the dark lake glistens, and the spring green hills roll with the mountain in the background.

"I can't believe it!" I shout and turn to look at the captain's face. Even he's impressed.

We follow the men out to a court that is an open circle in the center of the fortress. By the way everyone's standing around, I realize it must be a communal area.

MacClancy talks to the captain, who in turn translates for us.

"They're getting ready for an attack. They've sighted the English on horseback in these areas, and most of their people have been brought into the castle."

"Hello, my brothers!" a Spaniard still wearing his doublet and pants exclaims as he comes and kisses the captain on both cheeks. Five other Spaniards stand behind.

With the approach of the Spaniards, MacClancy bows and walks away to his people.

"What great ship split apart and spewed you out onto this foul shore?" The Spaniard laughs.

"We come from the *San Pedro*. I was her captain." He decides to exclude the Judge Magistrate's ship for a reason.

"Oh, Captain." He and the others all bow slightly. "We wrecked on the *Juliana*. All of us that have survived stand before you." He seems sadder at this.

"How have these savages treated you?" the captain enquires.

"Much better than others in this wretched place. This Mac-Clancy is a very important savage. He and O'Rourke's clan are giving England hell over in Sligo, holding on to their lands the best they can."

"Can we get them to fetch us something to eat? We haven't eaten or drank for days."

"Well, you might have a problem there. These strange folk only eat once a day and at night, but I can get a maiden to fetch you all some sour milk."

"Sour milk?" Andres asks with a sneer.

"Yes, it's all they drink here, even though I've tasted the water and it is the sweetest I have ever tasted. So suit yourself."

"Please have them fetch the sour milk. We'll need something, however putrid, in our stomachs before suppertime."

We head to the fire, where a few small boys are sitting but get up and move to their fathers at our approach. Sitting, I have the chance to take in everything around me and see these people are very different from those at home. They wear similar dismal-colored short coats of goat hair over tight trousers and wrap blankets around themselves. The women have very long hair, and the men wear their hair past their eyes. The women wear linen headdresses tied in the front of their foreheads, and although most of them are very fair, they appear old and frumpy the way they're dressed. Nothing like the way Spanish women dressed back home. I thought of my mother, suddenly, and how pretty she always looked, and a pang punishes me for not thinking of her for so long.

Before I can think if she misses me by now, a young maiden returns with some wooden bowls and a pitcher. She's dressed like the others but is not as fair. Her face is pinched in the middle, with thick round lips that give her a fish-like look. Her dirty blonde hair is tied back with her headdress, and she stares at Pepe as she puts the bowls down to pour. Pepe watches her pour them. When all are poured, she passes them out, waiting to give Pepe the last one. She hands him his but is sure to make eye contact as she places it in his hands. Andres shot me a look, and I know he notices the strange behavior as well. I'm relieved to see her leave and go back into another area.

"What an ugly girl that is," Andres jabs.

"I don't think she's ugly," replies Pepe, searching back to where she disappeared.

I want to change the subject. I take a sip of the milk. "Ugh!" I let out after I swallow the warm and slightly chunky liquid.

Pepe and Andres both follow with similar looks of disgust.

The captain holds his bowl up to us like a toast. "When in Rome—" And he swallows the whole bowl down with a few gulps. He lets out an "Ahh" when he finishes.

The rest of us finish slowly. I save some for Bella to have, and I call her over. She eagerly comes to inspect my bowl, but after one lap, she sneezes and runs off. We all laugh that even a dog wouldn't drink the sour milk. I wonder if I'll be here long enough to grow accustomed to it.

Andres bends in close, as if any of the savages could understand us, and says, "You notice how much stockier these men are. They're built so thickly and look very strong."

"Yeah, I noticed too," I say, eyeing them.

Overhearing us, the Spaniard who welcomed us says, "Yes, they're very powerful and hardy fellows. They leave almost every night after supper and go out on raids on their rival clans, stealing everything they can get their hands on."

"It's the reason why they'll never defeat the English—they keep fighting each other," the captain says as the Spaniard nods in agreement. Hours fly by with us observing the strange habits of the savages, and a simple dinner of oaten bread and butter is served.

"This is all they eat?" the captain asks the Spaniard in surprise.

"Yes, except on their feasting nights, where they'll eat some meat, which we haven't had the pleasure of partaking in yet."

Chieftain MacClancy comes and sits next to the captain, and I'm waiting for the translation. I then notice Pepe's unusually quiet on my right, and I turn to see he's staring at something. I follow his gaze and sneer upon seeing the fish-faced girl across the fire looking back at him, smiling. I nudge Andres on my left, and he sneers also. Suddenly, I realize the captain's translating to us, and I nudge both sides to pay attention.

"It seems MacClancy has received word that the ship we had the lucky misfortune of missing, split apart and sank only hours after weighing anchor. They think all two hundred or more aboard were lost."

"Oh, no," Andres says, and we all think of Carlos and the others who were with us.

Alvaro looks amazed but remains quiet. I'm sure he must have been glad his conscience kept him with the captain now.

"So, the bright side is, you're all very lucky to have such an invalid in your company!" the captain says with a joyful smile.

The fish-faced girl takes us to a room that night and brings woolen blankets to lie upon the cut rushes piled on the floor. Pepe lingers at the door, probably hoping she'll return bringing something else, but Andres and I slump to the ground with Bella and fall asleep in minutes. We haven't had a bed like this for a very long time.

In the morning, we stumble out to the circle, and all of the savages are leaving through the tunnel to the fields. Pepe starts following them out, and Andres and I roll our eyes at each other and go with him. He doesn't take his eyes off her. I can't see what he likes so much about her except for the fact she's always smiling so stupidly at him. The girl wanders off behind the hill, and Pepe gets up to go in her direction. When we start to follow him, he actually turns to us. "You mind if I go alone?"

I scoff and sit right back down, not even wanting to look at him, and Andres says, "You don't want us with you?"

"I just want a little time alone." He doesn't even wait for a reply but runs off after her.

Andres slumps down angrily next to me, and we sit there, watching cows for an hour. Alvaro has walked off with the new Spaniards who are around his age. A rustle of woolen blanket makes us turn, and the most beautiful woman we've ever seen sits down next to us with a smile. The captain sits down with us too, and he's giddy for some reason, which I'm sure has to do with the beautiful creature beside us.

She reaches out a fragile, graceful hand and places it on my lap. I look to the captain, not understanding what it is she wants, and he chuckles. "I told her you were a gypsy and read fortunes!"

"What! I don't read fortunes." I try to push away her hand, but she only smiles more sweetly and holds it up to me.

"This beautiful doe, Nora"—she looks at him and smiles when he says her name—"came up to me in Latin and asked for a fortune telling. She must be confused between Spaniards and gypsies, and I couldn't disappoint such charm."

I take a deep and angry breath but see such happiness in her big, light brown eyes. Her freckles are all in the right spots and make her face look healthy and exciting. I pick up her weightless hand and turn it over, wondering if I can think of something that will fool her. When I stare into the delicate open hand, a vision of a similar graceful hand appears out of a torch lit temple room while wafts of spicy, exotic smells assault my nose. Dark lined eyes blink softly at the end of the arm I hold. Full, red lips part into a secret smile. *So tangible. So real.* A rush of sudden understanding of life, heart, head, and fate lines remerge along with planetary mounds and mystical symbols. *Memories?* I shake my head and come back to see Nora staring at me expectantly.

"Umm, I see here that you will find a great man, a man that is very powerful." I think since she's so beautiful it would make sense she would find a good man. She seems confused at my strange words and looks up to the captain, who translates. She nods happily, and the captain says, "She's MacClancy's wife." I worry then at the captain's interest in her.

I search her many faint lines for anything that comes to mind. "You worry too much and don't feel safe." The captain appears nervous at me saying this, but the beauty nods again in sad agreement. "You have no children yet from this worry. You have had two losses but no children." The captain gives me a look of warning, and I shrug my shoulders. He translates, and the poor woman grabs my hand and seems to be saying, "Yes," in her language. She sits back, waiting for more eagerly.

I continue, "You'll have a child and very soon. She will come by next spring."

The captain translates this, and she reaches for me, knocking me over, and kisses my hands. She runs off to her friends at the straw hut nearby.

"What did you do?" The captain looks confused. "I only wanted you to say some fluff about living a long happy life, and maybe a chance romance with a dark Spaniard would've been a nice touch." He winks at me.

But the woman drags three other young women to me. There are two pretty young maidens, with a giant of a girl in the middle of them. The tall one sits down for the first reading, her giant man-like hand outstretched. She takes her other hand to her flat unfeminine chest and says in a low voice, "Urard."

As I tell her of her health and hopeful future, she stares at me with her round olive green eyes. Her face seems half-female and half-male—as if it couldn't decide what sex it was. I'm very uncomfortable in her awkward presence and make up niceties that will please her so I can move on.

Ending the reading, I say, "A stranger from afar will see your... unusual... beauty." After the captain translates, she throws her head back strangely and brays like a mule. When she finishes, she points to the captain, then smiles as the other maidens giggle and pat her back in agreement.

"Oh, no no no!" He shakes his head, but Urard blushes and gazes at him strangely. "Move on to the next girl." The captain wants to be done with this so he can get some distance from the large woman. After I finish the third girl, I look up to see the fish-faced girl has returned with Pepe way too close at her side. She bends down for me to do hers, and I feel sick being so close to her. Andres, who has been quite bored with this attention I'm getting, suddenly is interested with her there.

"Maybe you'll see that fish-face really came from the sea. And she misses her fish mother and father," Andres says with the girl smiling stupidly, not knowing he's insulting her.

Pepe shoots Andres a glare. "Knock it off, Andres. Her name is Nessa."

I hate that he's defending her, and Andres is quiet after being disgusted by the same thing.

So I pick up her hand, look into her dull, empty eyes and tell her, "You'll fall in love with a young man, but you have a curse that will kill anyone who would try to love you. After the death of this first young suitor, none will have you in fear they will perish too. Because of this curse, you will end up sad, childless, and alone."

Pepe jumps in. "Don't translate, Captain, he's making this all up."

The captain looks at me. "Why would you want to say that to this young girl?"

"I swear I see that. I'm not making it up. You asked me to read her hand, and that's what I saw." I push her hand away and walk off.

The captain tells Nora in Latin, and after she informs Nessa, I hear the girl sob. I march back through the tunnel with Andres and Bella trailing behind.

Andres says as we come out into the castle, "No one will ever want to be with her once they hear that. She'll end up alone, I bet. Good job, Luis! Maybe even Pepe will be scared."

Chapter 15

Days later, a constant flow of women and men search me out to tell their fortunes. I flee through the tunnel and into the cow pastures to avoid them. Andres always comes with me, but Pepe's spending all his hours awake with Nessa.

Lying in a field, avoiding the cow piles, Andres says to me, "Do you think he's going to stay here and marry Nessa if we find a ship home?"

It's the question I have been asking since I saw how he looked at her.

"I don't know."

"Would you still go if he stayed?"

"Yes, Spain is our home. Our home is not with these people." But the truth is I have no home anywhere. Pepe and Andres and even the captain and Alvaro are all my home; the ship that broke to pieces felt like my home; even the rush bed on the floor in the castle feels like my home. The thought of us breaking apart here or in Spain is too much to bear.

A warning horn blows from the top of the castle, and everyone who's still outside rushes to the tunnel to see what the danger is. Andres and I reach the cave at the same time as Pepe and Nessa. He puts out his hands to help her down to the entrance, and I can't believe the change that's come over him—growing up overnight. We let them go ahead of us, and Andres puckers his lips up like a fish at them as they pass, making me laugh through my sadness.

As soon as we get through the tunnel, two strong men slam the thick and heavy door shut, then fix two large pieces of wood in the slats to lock it. All of the savages gather in the court, with MacClancy in the center. MacClancy's an unusually tall man with black wavy hair. He's powerful-looking, but whenever he smiles, you see the strong dimple on his cheek that makes him less fearsome. He seems stressed and unsure. He speaks almost directly to Captain de Cuellar. After they talk some, he translates to those who don't know Latin.

"MacClancy is saying he's received word that there're seventeen hundred English soldiers heading this way. They're on a direct path to the castle and surely have heard there are Spaniards harbored here. MacClancy feels like they should head for safety into the mountains where the English troops don't dare to venture on horses. He's asking what we want to do."

Alvaro speaks. "What does he have here to fight with?"

We watch as MacClancy starts speaking and gesturing excitedly, counting on his thick fingers and pointing to all areas around the castle.

The captain translates. "He says there are six crossbows, ten muskets, and eight arquebuses with plenty of ammo."

Alvaro considers this and asks, "Cannons?"

MacClancy shakes his head so we all understand and then speaks.

The captain says, "He says this castle is impregnable. The bog surrounds the whole lake, making it hard for artillery or horses to be used. No one can swim the great distance of the lake on every side and when the current strengthens from the sea in the spring no one can maneuver a boat. He says he has about a six-month supply of provisions we can have if we stay and defend it."

"Another situation where we can last as long as our supplies last?" Alvaro seems hesitant.

"What choice do we have? Go with the savages? Barefoot and freezing like we have all done on our miserable journey here? So then move on to find shelter elsewhere? When all of Ireland is either trying to kill us or afraid someone will kill them for helping us?" The captain shakes his head. "No, this is where we're staying, and our only option is to win."

Alvaro says nothing back, but the captain looks over his Spanish comrades. "Who is going to stay here and fight with me?"

The six unknown Spaniards step next to him, and Alvaro smiles a crooked smile and joins. Andres and I jump forward and turn as we realize Pepe hesitates.

Was he actually pondering leaving with Nessa instead of fighting with us for our lives?

Nessa looks at him and sees he might choose to stay. She runs off crying, and Pepe hurries to console her.

MacClancy speaks, and when he does, his brown-greenish eyes look sternly at the captain. He even takes his shoulders and seems to make the captain slightly uncomfortable.

The captain turns to us after speaking with him. "Mac-Clancy's asking us to hold his castle with our lives. He's telling me that we can't surrender for anything. Even if we will starve, we must hold the castle to the very end, and we must not let in any Irishman, Spaniard, or anyone else until his return."

The captain speaks to MacClancy and then repeats it for us. "I'm sure we can hold this castle. Even eleven Spanish soldiers are worth more than seventeen hundred Englishmen!"

They cheer, and maidens circle around de Cuellar, enamored with his bravery. Urard comes looming over him in her gangly awkward manner and pushes them all out of her way. A high-pitched wooden flute plays joyous music, and they dance in a lively light manner I've never seen before. She practically picks the captain up as he protests, and she spins with him around the room all out of step and time with the music. Alvaro's especially enthralled with their way of dancing and quickly picks it up and does it better than any savage. Bella barks and runs in circles, excited by the music, and tries to get Andres's attention. Their music is happy and wonderful and makes one's heart glad even if it's heavy. I sit and watch from a stool beside the wall of the castle, where the light of the fire and shadows of gay people dancing keep flickering across the walls and me.

There she is, Nora, beautiful as an angel wearing wool. She gathers the blanket around her on this cold night and sits next to me.

"Hello, Spain." She labors through the unusual sounds she has to make and then smiles.

She seems to be picking up some Spanish.

I smile and say, "Hello," back.

Upon seeing us talking, the captain shows up after escaping Urard and seeking refuge, pulls over a stool. She speaks to him.

"She said she came over here to warn you of the faerie folk," he says, laughing greatly at the end.

Nora seems confused why he's laughing so.

She repeats, "Fear-gortha, fear-gortha."

The captain takes a deep breath. "Oh, now she's telling me she needs to warn you when we travel later about something called the hungry grass. She says you have to make offerings while traveling, offerings to these here fairie folk..." He gives me a crazy look and circles his hand around his ear. "So she says if you don't, then these nasty buggers will make patches of 'hungry grass' that can trap and swallow men whole."

She has such a serious and worried face, I get slightly scared it could be true.

She puts an oatcake in my hand, and the captain says, "She says to carry that in your pocket at all times to use as a charm of protection against them."

Nora rests her hand on my shoulder, gives me a look of warning, and speaks again. As she talks, she uses her slender hands in a mesmerizing way to tell the story. I almost wonder if I hold her hands if she could still tell the story. Suddenly, the captain roars in laughter and breaks my eyes away from her hypnotic movements and enchanting words.

"These people are insane! She's now warning you about the 'little people' who come up from the ground and play tricks and the 'banshee' that foretells your death if you hear her, all in white with glowing, red eyes! Woo-woooh!" he finishes in a high-pitched voice, making his eyes roll in his head.

Nora stares at him suspiciously and walks back to her people.

"Where are you going?" He turns to me. "The prettiest ones are always crazy."

I leave the captain and decide to retire before Andres or Pepe. Pepe's nowhere to be found, and Andres is holding Alvaro's hands, spinning and jumping with the savages in merriment. I fall asleep quickly in the quiet of our room.

I'm walking up the crude stone steps of all different heights up to the turret. I look out across the dark night with hundreds upon hundreds of clear stars, when a wind blows across the hills and over the lake, causing the shining reflections of the moon to stir. It makes a whistling, eerie sound. The sound turns from a whistle and spins into a loud and mournful lament, and I look toward the sound. I turn around to the sea and see a glowing white woman with red-hot coals for eyes, glowing hotter and hotter as her moan rises to a horrible shriek that flashes out and hits me with great force.

I wake up with a shiver and see only Andres in the room, sleeping beside me. In the morning, he notices Pepe's absent also.

"I wonder if he left us for good," Andres says.

We walk out to the open circle and see there aren't any savages anywhere.

Alvaro rests against the courtyard wall, picking his teeth with a straw and I ask, "Have they all left so soon?"

"Yep, they're pretty quick. They're off before I got up." He reaches back with a yawn. "But it's pretty nice to have this whole castle to ourselves."

I realize Pepe must have gone with them after all. He must have woken up early and gone without saying good-bye.

"Let's go up to the turret to look at them going up the mountain." Andres heads up the stairs as I follow. We're startled to see someone already up there. His back's turned, but we know who it is.

"Pepe, you didn't go with her?" Andres asks.

Pepe doesn't turn, only shakes his head. He's watching them make their way over the mountains with all their flocks, and we decide to leave him alone.

Andres fumes on the way down. "I'm glad he stayed, but he's still not himself. I can't wait for us to leave this place."

Chapter 16

Everything's quiet for a few days, when suddenly Bella alerts us. We run to the turrets to see men on horseback trotting calmly in a single line down the narrow path through the bog, with English banners and flags waving. Great disarray ensues once they realize they can't go farther since the pathway ceased purposefully. Trying to turn, the horses are forced to step off the stones and into the bog. They all get stuck and whinny frantically, causing their embarrassed passengers to dismount and pull them out of the stubborn mud, many dropping their esteemed flags in the mud while doing so. We can still see them as they slink back a half mile on land to where more stable pasture fields lay, and they dismount to discuss their unusual situation.

Later that night, a band of brave men try to pull a cannon out to the shore of the lake, but it's so wide it keeps falling off the path and gets stuck as the exhausted men have to keep prying it up with crowbars and pieces of wood. These mud-men give up halfway there and abandon the cannon. The next day, trumpets sound by the shore, and all rush to see what's happening.

Two men stand on the hill. One shouts through a long voice trumpet that carries remarkably well over the lake up to us. He shouts a long monologue in what sounds like the tongue of the savages.

No one within the castle understands what he says, so the captain shouts in Spanish through his voice trumpet, "I can't hear you from there! Come closer!"

We snicker at his attempt to get them within range. The captain shouts, "Speak in Spanish so we can understand the terms of your surrender!"

Every Spaniard snickers at his cheeky presumption. The trumpet's passed to another man beside him, and then he speaks in English-accented Spanish.

"I am a messenger for our Lord Deputy, William FitzWilliam, ordained by Her Majesty the Queen." He keeps pausing to take another large breath to yell out sentence by sentence. "We are under orders that all Spaniards who have crashed upon our shores, after assaulting England, are to be detained and tried. The traitorous MacClancy clan is harboring these enemies to the crown within these castle walls, and if they are not surrendered to us, we will attack without mercy or regard for Spaniard, Irishman, woman, or child."

The captain yells, "Sounds like how you conduct business wherever you fight!"

Laughter erupts from the turret and carries across the lake without the aid of the trumpet.

This man then translates to a regal-looking man sitting straight on his white horse with a full body of armor, a short distance up the path. This must be FitzWilliam. He snaps something back angrily and kicks his horse to turn back, and the horse stumbles a bit on the high rocks on the side of the path, humiliating the rider in his haughty exit.

The man speaks again across the lake. "You leave us no choice than to vanquish you!"

"Good luck to you in your vanquishing, Deputy!" the captain yells out, and laughter again carries over the lake, and the man turns to walk back stiffly in his armor with the other man carrying flags.

The soldiers' numbers accumulate in the fields; the news of seventeen hundred may have been an understatement. Alvaro busies us by having us bring up stone after stone up to the turrets from the stockpile in the circle. It's backbreaking work, but they say that this can be as important as having a cannon if the English make their way to the castle by boat. We feel important, then, dragging each one up, and if they are especially heavy, we take them together. I'm holding a heavy one with Pepe, and we can hardy talk with the strain, but I try. "Are you feeling better?"

"I realized if we keep the castle that Nessa would come back, so it's made me stronger."

I can't believe it; he's still thinking of her, even when we faced death together. As soon as I get Andres alone, I tell him what he said.

Andres only looks sad. "He's changed. He's not the Pepe we knew."

Trumpets ring out with Bella barking at the unusual sound, and we return to the turrets again to see archers lined up with flaming crossbows. The order is called, and they all let loose. We duck at the whipping sound that carries across when they release, but are relieved as most fall in the lake as others hit weakly against the lower, rough castle walls. We all cheer at the failed assault, giving us confidence in MacClancy's claims.

Hours later, another attempt is made. Three longboats are brought forward, carried over the heads of the soldiers. They put them in the lake and half take out their oars while the other half holds muskets pointed at the castle. A knot rises in my throat as they start right for the castle, but midway a strong current hits them that spins the boat and makes it impossible to stay still, let alone move toward the castle. All three boats end up on the far shore. We all cheer again, invincible now.

We celebrate that night with double rations of oaten bread and butter. The captain says a prayer, and we listen and dance to Alvaro's new Irish music he's picked up. We awake to more trumpeting and hear in Spanish, "Traitors to the crown, we give you one more chance to surrender."

The captain and company laugh heartily at this. "Only if you promise to treat us under the same 'fair' terms of surrender and promise of 'safe' passage as those Spaniards you promised before! No! We know you, and you're a traitor to man and God! We would rather die with bullets or starve slowly before we die in your whore of a queen's noose!"

The men standing behind the trumpeters get so angry at the captain's words that they let loose their muskets without command. Some musket balls make it across the lake but again hit the wall without damage. The Spaniards laugh again as Pepe fills with courage and pulls his pants down, mooning the shore, causing even more laughter to erupt. The man speaking to us motions angrily back up the hill, and we all gasp as we see two half-naked men with arms and legs tied being dragged by four men down the path.

One Englishman shouts, "If you surrender now, we will pardon these fellow fish-eaters."

The captain says nothing but looks on with great concern.

"No response?" The Englishman pulls one man forward and holds him up in front of him and rips off the gag.

The prisoner screams out in a raspy, tortured Spanish voice, "Go Santiago!"

Furious at his defiance when he hoped for a plea, the man holding him cuts with his saber clear across his throat. We see the blood spray from our great distance as the Spanish man slumps to the rocks, and the Englishman gives him a kick into the bog. The captain almost leaps off the tower toward him. "Go Santiago" is our war cry. My eyes fill with tears at the bravery of that man. They choose not to take off the other prisoner's gag and casually slice his throat from behind also. He joins his countryman in the bog.

The Englishman shouts, "We will save all of our executions from now on for your enjoyment until you agree to our terms of surrender!" and they walk off and over the hill.

The captain gathers all of the religious relics, Spanish and savage alike, and passes them around to each of us. He lifts the largest wooden cross and holds it above his head. "We offer up prayer to you for those Spanish sacrificed upon this shore. We pray for their souls to go directly to heaven and hope you assist us in our plight so that their sacrifices are not in vain."

"Amen," we follow somberly.

There's no merriment that night. Before the purple light of dawn has faded, we're startled awake by screaming from our lookout. Again we rush to the turret facing their shore, all groggy with our blankets draped over us. Expecting to see something terrible, I'm surprised to see the sky filled with fat snowflakes.

"How long has this been falling?' The captain asks, bewildered.

"Only started twenty minutes ago. When it started covering everything, I thought I should get you!"

"Only twenty minutes and it's coating the ground already!" He gives a cheer and says, "What luck, what luck!"

We stay up there under our blankets wrapped around our heads. The wind's blowing fiercely, and the snowflakes fall, crisscrossing one another, causing our eyes to go in and out of focus. Andres keeps sticking his little tongue out, trying to get the large flakes that would drift near him, tempting him. The snow is knee-deep within hours, with no sign of relenting. Bella disappears in the snow and begins tunneling through, popping up here and there with her head covered in snow.

Alvaro perks up at something. "Captain, there's definite movement."

We all stand and watch. The English have packed up their tents, and every man is on his horse. The men farthest away from us leave first, and we watch as they all ready to retreat, ending the siege.

The captain, seeing the Lord Deputy leave his warm tent and getting help on his horse, screams out, "*Go Santiago!*"

All of us jump up and scream it with him again. "*Go Santiago!*"

The Lord Deputy looks our way but, just as quickly and pompously, kicks his horse to follow the procession off Mac-Clancy's land. We throw off our blankets and embrace in clumsy groups, jumping and still yelling, "*Go Santiago!*" while tears stream down our faces.

The captain then turns to us and says, "Eight fire ships may have scattered one hundred thirty ships, but eleven Spanish soldiers scattered seventeen hundred Englishmen!"

We cheer and put our arms around each other, amazed we're all still alive.

∞∞∞∞∞∞∞∞∞∞∞∞∞∞∞∞∞∞∞∞∞∞

When Andres and I see the parade trailing back down the mountain two weeks later, we know our threesome's going to be divided once again. Part of me wishes some harm has befallen Nessa so that the thing I feared would not come to pass. I'd imagined her tripping on the snow-covered mountainside and falling off, never to be seen again. But there she is, leading them through the snow with her ugly pinched face smiling, and Andres and I turn away as Pepe runs to her and hugs her.

MacClancy's hairy face is beaming. He looks upon us with greater respect and even shakes all of our hands with as much esteem. All of the women wrap new blankets around our backs and gift us with raw steaks they'd prepared for our celebration of winning the siege. Though half-cooked and unsalted, it's the most delicious thing I've ever tasted. The juices drip down my face, and everyone's filled with such joy. MacClancy asks the captain to tell the story over and over and each time yells, "Go Santiago!" with him at the end. Alvaro dances after finishing two steaks and actually takes a fair maiden to jig with him. Andres looks on, slightly jealous, since he usually jigs with him, but we clap to the beat everyone's fast feet are keeping. Even the captain asks Urard to dance, and she brays in surprise then sweeps the captain off his feet. At the end of the song, MacClancy gets everyone's attention with the horn. He gestures for the captain to come stand by him, and the captain translates.

"He says he can't thank his brave Spaniards enough for holding his castle—the castle his ancestors held for hundreds of years."

MacClancy puts his hand on the captain's shoulder, and by his serious gaze, speaks words to him of great importance. After he finishes, he embraces the captain tightly and pounds his back with his fists. The savages, hearing what he says, cheer and put their hands high in the air in celebration.

He turns with a not so joyous look to us and says, "He wants us to stay here and fight the English with him, unite, and marry into his clan."

This makes the Spaniards nervous and uneasy, all except Pepe who says, "It might not be such a bad idea, Captain. This may be our only chance for a life. There may be no safe passage back to Spain."

If anyone else had said that, it might have made sense, but since it was him, I retaliated immediately. "We are Spaniards, and our home is Spain!"

The Spaniards cheer at this, and one says, "Live Spanish or die Spanish, there is no other way!"

MacClancy misinterprets our cheers to mean agreement, and Nessa runs from the crowd and jumps into Pepe's arms.

MacClancy speaks again. His voice is deep and full of happy emotion as he pulls the captain back against his powerful frame and then with the other hand reaches out for one of the tallest figures in the room and brings her in front of him. Everyone cheers again, and the music starts up, and they pass the couple all around the crowd with everyone touching the pair with a blessing.

The captain has no time to translate, and after the commotion is over, he bows to the chief and then grabs Alvaro to huddle up with Andres, Pepe, and me. "We're leaving tonight, boys. Go fill your pockets with bread, return to your rooms, and pretend to sleep until no one is stirring. Then meet me by the tunnel." He checks over his shoulder to be sure no one is within earshot.

"Where will we go?" Andres asks.

"Anywhere closer to home. If we stay here, I worry we'll never set foot on Spanish soil again." He starts to laugh. "Urard is MacClancy's sister, for Christ's sake. He offered that she-man up to me!" His eyes widen and his volume rises. "There is such a thing as too much friendship!"

"I'm done with this place too, Captain. Time to move on," Alvaro says as he walks away toward the breadbaskets.

"Good boys," he says, slapping our backs, and walks off pretending to be happy about the chief's blessing to unite.

Andres and I start to fill our pockets too. Pepe floats near us but doesn't grab at any bread. Andres grabs some and stuffs it in his pockets for him. As soon as we fill every possible pocket and spot in our tight pants, we find our way to our small, dark room.

Trying to stay awake, we reminisce about watching the captain betrothed to Urard in front of everyone. We're laughing so hard someone shushes us from the room across from ours. Quieting down, Andres ventures where I didn't have the courage.

"So, are you going to come with us, Pepe?" His eyes already guess the answer.

Pepe stalls. "I don't know."

He becomes quiet again, forcing me to say something. "Well, do you want to stay here forever?"

He simply gives us a pained look and stares down at his feet.

"Do you want to learn her strange language? Her savage customs? Live in the foreign land for the rest of your life? Drinking sour milk and oaten bread? Letting your hair grow past your eyes?"

Andres snickers at the last line I threw in.

This hits a nerve. His head darts up, and his green eyes blaze. "And what do I have back in Spain? Huh? My mother left me! I have no family! No home! No..."

"What? No friends? Really? Because I thought we were best friends! I thought we were family! We all have been left, but we'll always have each other, forever!" I'm crying so hard by the end of this, I can't finish, but Andres does for me.

"Pepe, you're like our brother. We didn't have anyone else, but together we can be strong. Together we can get through anything. You leave us now, and you lose that—*we* lose that!"

He stays quiet and gazes up at us with a look I can't figure out. It could be a look of guilt, a look of anger, or a look of love. Whatever it is, it was the last I saw his face. He walks out of the room without glancing back.

We wait until the music ceases and the footsteps die away, scattering off to sleeping quarters. Even after the last sound we hear, we wait ten minutes more, although we're worried if we wait too long the captain will think we wanted to stay. We get up in the pitch dark and try to make as little noise as possible, but Bella begins doing circles ahead of us, making scratching sounds with her claws in excitement. Andres bumps into something in the hall and yelps, but a quick hand stifles his noise.

"Shhh," Alvaro says.

Andres holds on to his shirt as he walks on in front of us and I grab onto Andres, since there's no moon out to shed light.

"Alvaro, help me with this. Quietly!" the captain hisses as he strains to slide the weight of the planks across the door. They make a slight thud on the stone floor, but it's the gentlest they could be.

Alvaro pulls the heavy door open, and it makes an eerie squeak that seems to amplify in the silence and ricochet off the walls of the castle into every room. We hold our breath and wait for him to come. The captain exhales and puts his hand on each one of us, and I realize he's counting when he asks, "Where's Pepe?"

I turn around, hoping to hear him coming, but Andres says, "He's staying here."

"I knew that boy had no brain," the captain says as he steps over the threshold into the even darker cave, and Alvaro follows.

"He's not coming, Luis." Andres leaves the castle.

I turn again, straining my ears to hear someone running to catch us, but no sound stirs. I can't believe he's actually picking her over us. Bella waits for me and watches the emptiness I'm searching in.

I turn and move on too.

Chapter 17

We trudge over the windy mountains and follow the soggy road beside the sea north for three days, resting only when the captain has to sit and put his bad leg up. At night, when we're especially tired after walking what must have been fifteen miles, we talk for the first time all day.

"It's a good thing we have Bella here with us." Alvaro scratches her behind her ears, making her put her nose in the air and lick.

"I hate when she does that," Andres says with a disgusted look.

The captain lies back with his leg in the air, rubbing down the leg. "She has a wonderful talent for smelling English military scouts. As soon as those pointed ears perk up, we should all hide."

"Well, I'm down to my last loaf of bread," I say.

Alvaro speaks. "You better make that last. You've been eating far too much. I've two loaves left, and that'll last me four more days at least."

"But we've been sharing ours with Bella!" Andres protests, but Alvaro bends over and shakes Andres's rapidly growing belly. "Oh, you poor, poor thing."

Andres pulls away from his grasp. "I'm proud of my little belly. It's been sunken for months!"

Alvaro snickers but then turns serious again. "Captain, how long are we to keep going? We can't make a fire without drawing attention and if another cold front hits us, we'll have to find shelter."

The captain puts his leg back down and rolls up to a stand. "Well, then, we better keep moving."

Alvaro, Andres, and I stay on the ground, wrapped in our blankets. We hate how the captain never needs to sleep. We're only lucky that he did have a sore leg because he might never have stopped.

"Come on, now!" Bella runs to him. "You'll have plenty of time to rest when you're dead. Which you'll be closer to every moment we waste." He starts hobbling back off north.

Alvaro gets up too. "He's right. We better keep moving until we can't move anymore."

"That might be pretty soon," Andres complains as he stumbles on his blanket getting up.

We walk most of the night and stop only once for a short nap. By morning, we see a large village settlement right on the coast.

The captain turns to us. "Boys, you wait here, since I'm the only one that speaks Latin. I'll sneak in and try to find a holy man for aid."

Alvaro starts walking. "I'll go with you."

"No, Alvaro, no use in risking both our necks. Besides, you should stay with the little ones."

Andres gives a look mirroring my feeling of inferiority the captain just labeled us with.

He hands his blanket and his over shirt to Alvaro. "No need to have these stolen from me." Bella follows as he walks off, but he says, "No, Bella." She runs back to us but watches intently as he slowly follows the road into the village.

It seems like a very long time before we sight him again, but in reality it was probably only a few hours. He comes back with a nice thick woolen cloak, and Bella sprints to him, doing circles of joy upon his return.

"Well..." He lets out his breath but unveils a large wooden jug and two large fresh loaves.

Alvaro holds the jug immediately up to his mouth. "Wine!"

The captain pulls it away eagerly from him and gulps. "We haven't had wine for four months now, I think."

Then he hands it to us and breaks the bread in four sections. "We'll each give Bella a piece so Andres won't suffer more."

We laugh, and the bread's still warm when he hands it to me.

The captain gazes out on the damp and windy coast, chewing loudly. "Ireland's a miserable place."

"I would face hanging to reach sunny Spain again," Alvaro agrees as we eat and drink.

After his last bite, the captain takes the last drop of wine from the jug. "So, I found a small chapel in the center of the village. I slipped in unobserved. A priest was lighting the candles of the saints when I walked in. As soon as I asked for assistance, he took his own cloak and gave it to me and disappeared only to bring me back this bread and wine. He offered shelter for the night but warned that the deputy's men made unannounced visits to the village, searching for Spaniards. I said I wanted to keep moving, but asked where should I go. He said he knew of a"— but he spontaneously sucks in a quick inhale and as quickly burps it back out and continues like nothing had happened—"bishop in the village Derry, about three days' hard travel on foot from here if the weather complies. He said this good bishop was harboring Spaniards in a large castle on a hill and was trying to get them a ship to Scotland." He stands up, puts the cloak around Andres, whose teeth are chattering, and ties a rope around his waist to hold the hem up.

"Thank you," Andres says, finally getting warm again.

"Off again, boys!" He takes the jug with him. "We'll use this for saving water if we find a nice well or creek."

We make such good time that we reach Derry in two and half days. Just in time for a storm to blow in across the sea. We see the only castle at the top of the hill beside a cemetery and run in for shelter before we're soaked to the bone. A young monk sees us and hears our unfamiliar tongue, and immediately goes to get the Bishop.

The short but pleasant-looking man walks to us with his arms outstretched in welcome. He doesn't at all dress like the bishops I'd seen going in Corunna, adorned with gilded robes and tall silk hats. He looks like all of the other savages we've seen. The captain tears up at the sight of him regardless of dress, seeks out his hand, and kisses his ring. The bishop quickly brings him back up, embraces him warmly, and speaks to the captain. He waves back to the young monk who brought us dry blankets and takes our wet ones away. He holds them out far from him like he's worried about vermin hopping off.

He turns, and the captain translates, "The Bishop O'Gallagher wants us to follow him."

"Why is he dressed like a savage?" Andres asks under his breath.

"Because the English are searching for a bishop," the captain says with a smirk.

The bishop takes us to a room up the narrow dark stairs, where a dozen more Spaniards sit in front of the fireplace, eating their supper. They jump to their feet at the sight of us, and one says, "Friends!"

But the bishop steps in and, with great emphasis says, "*Captain!*"

The men seem ecstatic at this and one says, "We've been waiting for a captain to get us off this cursed island."

The captain appears both flattered and confused by this welcome.

"You see," the leader of the group starts, "the bishop has acquired a pinnace to get to the safety of Scotland, but none of us are sailors, all worthless soldiers." They all laugh at this.

The captain puts his hands on Alvaro. "Not only am I a captain, but I have here my commander and two brave sailors." I almost tear at his compliments to us; I forgive him completely for his "little ones" comment before.

The men clap, and the bishop says, "If you ask, then you shall receive," and he looks up with his hands clasped toward the ceiling.

"Which ship did you captain?" the leader asks.

"The beautiful *San Pedro*," the captain says, sitting by the fire, and some of the men rush to get him bread, butter, and wine. "And all of you?"

"We came from the *Trinidad Valancera*." He looks at his companions.

"Only twelve survive?" Alvaro asks.

He pauses a moment. "Our ship started to sink when we rounded Scotland, but we made it to the Irish shore before she finally sank. Three hundred men made it to the shore alive, and we were immediately helped by the kind Chieftain O'Doherty, who took us all to Bishop O'Gallagher, who harbored us in his castle." He takes another moment. "English troops came on horseback, came with muskets pointed at the surrounded castle. They promised fair treatment if we would surrender. So we trusted this deputy's promise and came out with our hands up. They marched us up to a field and stripped us of our clothing, then herded us in the center and began shooting us!"

His voice rises and his face turns red. The other men look either to their feet or to the fire. The speaker takes a breath to calm himself and his voice lowers. "In the bloody confusion, some of us managed to escape, and we ran back to the bishop for help. He took us all in again at the risk of his own safety, and we've been waiting for someone who can take us across the channel." He spreads his hands out to the twelve of them. "This is all that is left of three hundred."

"The same thing happened to me, friend," Alvaro says.

The captain says sternly, "We must gather supplies and leave as soon as we can, then. The deputy will come here again and we'll all be damned."

Andres and I, tired after our long journey and full belly, curl up with Bella and fall asleep to the sounds of the men planning the escape to Derry. Although it seems much colder without Pepe coiled up with us.

Chapter 18

The next morning, the bishop comes to take the captain to survey the pinnace. Alvaro's allowed to come, but both of them have to dress in savage clothing. They're gone for two hours, and when they return, the captain has his brows pinched together in what I've learned to be a look of great concern.

"So tell us of the pinnace?" a Spaniard asks.

The captain looks up to choose his words wisely, another bad sign. He begins slowly, "Well… I think she could get us to Scotland."

"Could?" the leader asks.

Alvaro jumps in. "She's in bad shape."

The bishop says, "I asked some of the lords in the area, and this is all that was offered."

"No, bishop, this is more than we could hope for." The captain is quick to say. "Once Alvaro and I do some work on her, we'll be sitting pretty, sailing off to salvation. We couldn't have asked for more."

The bishop blows out a relieved breath. "I have no doubt you can repair her, Captain. Let me start collecting your supplies."

The captain makes sure he leaves before he whispers, "Men, I'll do all I can, but we might be better off floating in a barrel to Scotland."

Alvaro chimes in, "The caulking's spewed, the mast has rot, and the main sail's threadbare in places."

"Well, can we repair it like you said?" the leader asks.

"We can do our best, but we have no caulk and no replacement sail. I might be able to get some timber and try to reinforce the masts, and Alvaro can fix the riggings. But if we hit any unhappy weather, we could be sunk," he says, looking at Andres's worried face, which makes him finish far too happily, "but it's all we've got, so we have to make it work. God has been in our favor this whole time, and I have no doubt He'll bring us through this too!"

∞∞∞∞∞∞∞∞∞∞∞∞∞∞∞∞∞∞∞∞∞∞

We stay in the dark room in the castle for another five days. Andres and I grow itchy from confinement, but we're also wary of what is coming. Alvaro and the captain are gone most of the five days, and at the end, the captain comes in and claps his large padded hands together. "To Scotland's shining shore!"

All of us gather our things, and the bishop holds mass for us with a blessing that we shall escape our enemies. We follow him down to the pinnace in one long chain, and he lets us kiss his ring, saying, "And the Lord be with you."

The ship is fatigued and broken like an old nag left to die in a green pasture. When I leap on, I can hear her moan, saying, "Leave me be!" The wood is dark with age and the floor's slippery from rot. I notice all of the captain's improvements but wonder if you built strong on top of weak, isn't it still weak?

Everyone appears weary. Even the soldiers notice a sea-tired ship when they see one. Even Bella, once we put her on the ship, goes scratching at the railing feeling safer on the dock. But when we look back at the bishop and see his hopeful, chubby, saintly face—we feel the power of his blessing.

The captain yells out, "Thanks be to God for Saint Redmund O'Gallagher!" and we all repeat, "Saint Redmund O'Gallagher!" and make the sign of the cross.

The captain hollers to Alvaro to untie the rope and push off, and we wave good-bye to the bishop and the hostile, mysterious island we thought we'd die on. Andres gives me a look, and we both remain quiet thinking the same thing, I'm sure—*we won't ever see him again now.*

As dusk draws near and the misty land is completely out of sight, Alvaro, after checking the riggings once again, sits down, leaning his back against the mast, and starts an Irish song on his flute. We all lie back and watch each star appear.

The captain breaks our moment of relaxation by saying after coming up from below, "Everyone up except Alvaro, and get a bucket. We're taking on water far too fast, and we have to bail out the bilge."

"Is that why we're not making good time?" Alvaro asks as he studies the old compass. "We should be a quarter of the way there by now, but since we're taking on water and the winds blowing against us, we're half that."

The captain squints up to measure our distance by the stars and nods in agreement to Alvaro. "Well, as long as we get there, don't matter how many days it takes." With that, he grabs a bucket and goes down to start bailing.

We bail all night until we have blisters, but there's no reprieve. Even though we formed a chain and didn't go five seconds before emptying a bucket over the side, the water's gaining. Alvaro yells down to us, "The winds picking up and dark clouds are blowing toward us."

The captain heads up to check as we keep passing buckets. We start losing our footing as the boat tosses around, and we realize there's a big difference being on a galleon in rough weather and being on a pinnace.

Andres hollers up after a rather serious crash into the hull and splashes into the water. "Captain, can we quit and come up? We're getting thrown around down here!"

But the captain doesn't come, which means things must not have been good above.

One of the men yells back, "We must keep bailing!"

Andres, miserable and wet, fishes his bucket that went floating away and gets back into his place in the chain. We try to balance each other during violent rolls, but all of us end up floundering in the bilge at different points. I feel queasy from the rocking and turn to see Andres bent over, getting sick in his bucket. After he's done, he just passes it up, palely, in the chain, and the men turn their heads at its passing. It becomes routine after every few buckets to get some of Andres's breakfast passed up, and he gets so used to throwing up that he merely takes a bucket, spits up, and keeps passing. We all tiredly laugh in the way you do in strange, stressful circumstances—a brainless laugh that your worn body can't control.

Suddenly, we hear a terrible tearing sound and the thunderous flapping of a loose sail. It's a sound we dreaded, since we know we have no replacement sail. We yell up the chain, "What happened?" and receive back down the chain, "The main sail's torn."

"Great, another thing to slow us down," the dark-haired Spaniard beside me says, and I decide to make another sign of the cross before getting my next bucket.

Andres got the next break, and when he comes back, he ceases getting sick. The winds die down overnight, and our two other smaller sails survive the storm, to our relief.

On my break, I go up to sleep on the damp deck and hear the captain say, "We'll make it there, boys! Keep the buckets coming!"

When I open my eyes again, everyone's on deck celebrating.

Andres, seeing me awake, runs to me. "We see Scotland!"

I run over to what looks like the Irish coast we just left. I jump and hug Andres, and his eyes are full of tears. Alvaro, in one swoop, picks up Andres and me and spins around on the deck. *Can we really have gone through all of this and see Spain again?* I look at the misty shore with wonderment. *How could Pepe have had such doubt?*

A bucket's handed to me, and I turn to see the captain. "We're not there yet. We still need to keep this barrel afloat."

When I go back down, I have to roll my wool pants up above my knee, for the water has risen so since my break. We float into the bay half-submerged, and some kind fisherman, seeing our distress, comes out to the boat to aid us.

The captain anchors the pinnace and, being the last to leave her, says as he hits a jug of wine on her porous hull, "I christen thee *Pinnace O'Gallagher* in the name of our patron saint." Then he kisses the mainmast and the boards of the small fishing ship that takes us into shore, where we get off and embrace the glorious rocky sand.

∞∞∞∞∞∞∞∞∞∞∞∞∞∞∞∞∞∞∞∞∞

Many days later, I'm watching the majestic sight of Edinburgh castle come into view. It looms there, almost a league above the village, a massive and imposing stronghold at the top of a giant rock. Two sides are built straight up from steep, deadly cliffs and the other slightly less steep side, with a winding and perilous path. Our horses, pulling us up the mountain, are already straining a quarter of the way up, and I wonder what will happen should the harness or hinge to the carriage break. Andres, already sick from the bumpy and long carriage ride, has to put his head between his knees at the sight of the incline. I can breathe again once we're within the fortified wall surrounding the castle. The captain gets excited. "The good bishop told me that King James has aided, clothed, and delivered passage to all Spaniards that have sought his help."

Alvaro speaks. "King James is no Catholic, though. Why would he assist us?"

The captain quickly explains, "Scotland is mostly Lutheran, but there are a few Catholic lords and counts that will sway the king for our last leg home, boys!"

I look up the high expanse of the steel-colored walls of the castle and feel uneasy.

It's hours before we're brought into a small room within the castle with no furniture and only one window. The captain paces while he waits for someone to bring us to the king. Finally, an attendant appears, and immediately the captain fumes. "There must be some mistake. The last attendant must have forgotten about us, since we've been standing here for hours waiting to see His Majesty."

The aged and bored-looking attendant barely bats an eye and says, "There has been no mistake. His majesty is very busy today and will have no time to meet with you. He asked us to bring you to your room, which we have. I've come to bring you your blankets and supper."

The captain appears shocked and watches dumbfounded as the attendant brings in a stack of blankets, pillows, a basket full of bread and butter, and a jug. The captain tries to move past his anger and asks, "We've had our clothing stolen from us and have been forced to wear the poor clothes of Irish savages. Could you please ask the king to bestow us with some civilized clothes?"

The Spanish-speaking attendant acts as though he hasn't heard what he said and coldly replies as he walks out the door, "I will make your request known."

The door slams, and we hear a slat swipe behind the door.

Alvaro runs to the door and tries to push it open. "They've locked us in!"

The captain's taking it all in. "We're prisoners."

Andres and I lay the blankets down on the stone floor and sit, eating the bread and butter we were given.

Alvaro takes a drink of the water and makes a sour face. "Stale water."

"Even the savages treated us better," the captain says as he stuffs a roll in his mouth.

Two months inch by confined in the small room. No clothing is brought for us, and our diet's poor. Andres loses all of his plumpness he acquired in Ireland, and we look like two street beggars once again. We can never get warm, even with two blankets laid upon the stone, the cold from the stones seeps through.

One day there's a knock on the door, and a well-dressed lord walks in, in clothing much like the captain and Alvaro had only months ago worn.

He speaks in Spanish. "I am Lord MacDonald and a fellow Catholic. I heard you have been kept here, and I've done my best along with some others to have you meet with the king. I brought some clothes for you to wear to approach the king in court today." He claps, and a servant carries in a pile of new clothes for us to wear.

"Thank you, Lord MacDonald." The captain bows slightly to him. "Your assistance is much appreciated."

The lord leaves, and we put on our clothes. The clothes are probably lesser quality than the clothes the captain had been used to, but for Andres and me they're luxurious. The silk hose and the linen-and-velvet tunics were the softest things we've had against our skins, thickened from all of the rough linen and wool we'd worn before.

Andres spins around in front of me when he's dressed. "Good evening, Lord Alba. Ready to meet with the King?"

We laugh and I say, "Would you ever have guessed we'd be meeting with a king?"

Bella jumps up on his silk hose, and Andres pushes her off. "Bella, that's silk!"

There's a knock at the door, and the sullen-faced attendant comes and says, "The king will see you now."

I pick up Bella to carry her with us, and Andres says, "Why are you bringing her?"

"I'm afraid to leave her behind. You never know what they'll do with us."

That makes Andres quiet. We walk behind Alvaro, who walks behind the captain, who leads the way aristocratically. Where he goes or whatever obstacles he faces, he always maintains an air of respect and confidence. When most would crumble, he grows stronger and makes us all stronger standing with him. The other Spaniards trail behind as we hurry to keep up with our pack. We're led down a torch-lit and carpeted path that empties into a large and beautifully adorned room. The way the portraits all hang and the velvet curtains drape, I have a strange feeling of remembrance—like I had been in such a palace before. Visions of endless glimmering banquet tables, silk dresses swishing at the end of jeweled fingers, and courtly music filling a candle-lit ballroom flash before my eyes. I shake the foreign images from my mind, and I'm shocked when guards open two huge doors that lead to court.

A dozen or so lords have gathered for our cause, and we see the Lord MacDonald standing in front of them. There are many plain-clothed attendants and members of the court, and in the center, on a massive throne draped in velvet and silks, sits King James. Beneath the golden crown, silks, and velvets perches a weak and disappointing man. He's plain and feminine-looking, and his legs barely fill out his hose. Above his chicken legs puff the pants that made his rear appear round. His doublet also seems inflated, twice the size it should've been with how small his legs, hands, and head are.

We follow behind the captain, who stands in front and speaks for us. James studies our movements with obvious lack of feeling. A courtly man stands beside the king on his right, all puffed out like the king but with peacock feathers sticking out at every possible place. He whispers something in the king's ear that makes him smile.

The captain bows and says something in what sounds like Latin.

The king clears his throat. "I grow tired of your church's outdated Latin." He says this rather flatly in good Spanish. Then turns to the man at his right and says something in some other language, and his court laughs.

The captain stays quiet and waits for a question. The room's hushed, all except for Bella's panting.

"The Duke of Parma is buzzing in my ear about sending you a ship." He strokes the pointed goatee on his chin that was the same yellow-gold of his amber eyes.

The captain nods graciously at this and still waits for more from the king.

James sighs dramatically and flips his hand. "So, I don't know what to do. Half of the world will be displeased with me if I give you safe passage, and half of the world will be vengeful if I decide otherwise."

The captain chances, "Maybe it would be wise to think of what God would have you do."

The king spurts out in laughter, and all those under him feel they have permission to laugh also.

"You sound like my dear departed mother, Captain, really, it's very sweet." His voice is bitter as he plays.

"I take that as the highest compliment, Your Majesty." The captain bows again.

The room starts to feel hot.

James pulls back and raises his weak neck out of his giant ruff, showing that the captain's starting to annoy him.

"Talking for less than a minute and you speak of mothers and God. How truly Spanish of you." He laughs, trying to regain his composure, and is satisfied with his people laughing with him.

The captain smiles with equal composure. "I wanted to thank Your Majesty for making us feel so at home here. I will make sure everyone knows of your graciousness as soon as I reach Spain."

"That is *if* you reach home, Captain. I haven't yet decided."

Lord MacDonald steps forward at this moment. "A merchant from Flanders has written to me that he will provide six vessels, supplies, and offers five ducats for every Spaniard that arrives safely on Flanders' shore."

The captain's happy to hear this and quickly says, "Your Majesty, what is your dilemma, then? You have no hand in our delivery other than making a profit off our ransom? Even *Her Majesty* would understand that."

He gives a look of warning to the captain under a down-turned brow, but the captain continues, "That is *if* it is truly a decision you have the power to make—"

The king jolts forward in his throne and spits, "Of course I have the power to make this decision. I am king!"

The captain bows and feigns an apology by saying, "Forgive me, Your Majesty. I do not mean any disrespect; only I've heard rumors your reign is limited by Her Majesty's hand."

James draws back slightly and proclaims, "Of course, I have the power and will do so if I so desire."

He turns to the man on his right and speaks to him. The man then helps him up by wrapping his arms around the king in a strangely intimate way. I hold my breath when he stumbles feebly down the small steps. "I am going to think upon this in my chambers."

Everyone parts for him to pass by, but when he approaches the captain, he turns and says, "Captain, I greatly respect your strong will to live and the passion you exude while doing so."

And he surprises everyone by leaning forward, grabbing the captain's face, and kissing him on the lips.

The captain, the most taken off guard, pushes back too late and wipes his mouth as the king draws back and proclaims, "Just what I expected—tastes like fish!"

Those who understand Spanish in his court laugh heartily as others translate, and the laughter continues as the king slowly makes his way out of court with a sneer on his pale face.

We walk back to our prison in silence, but as soon as we're alone, the captain rages, "What kind of a king kisses a man? The world is coming to pieces!"

Alvaro starts to laugh, and so we all did. Even the captain joins in.

Alvaro says, "I think his boyfriend was jealous," and we all laugh again.

The slats lift, and the door swings open. Lord MacDonald enters with meats, cheeses, bread, and three jugs of wine.

We clap and take them from him with many thanks as the captain says, "You could have warned me about that."

The lord laughs. "We have been trying to get the queen's hand puppet removed to no avail." He takes off his cape. "He wears all that padding for a reason, you know." He gives us a wink.

Andres and I dive in immediately on the meats and cheeses while Alvaro and the men begin passing the wine around.

The captain says, "Anyone who signs their own mother's death warrant for a kingdom has sold his soul and has the devil to pay."

The lord agrees. "You did quite a job twisting his hand there, Captain. If he chooses against us, then people will think he's weak and has no power. Very clever."

"Thank you for your kind words and aid, Lord."

"The Duke of Parma is very diligent in sending letter after to letter to court, along with the Catholic lords, in hopes of obtaining your deliverance."

The captain turns to us. "Better late than never, I guess."

The lord, unsure of what this meant, lets it roll. "We will all be fighting for your cause, and I will have my attendant meet your needs and bring you news."

He opens the door to leave, and servants file in one after the other with feather mattresses for each of us to sleep on. Andres's eyes shine.

Chapter 19

MacDonald keeps his word, and we don't have a want for anything, besides freedom. We keep getting letters speaking of progress as days slip by. Finally, after six months in captivity, the door's opened and it's Lord MacDonald.

He proclaims, "The merchant from Flanders is here with your four ships and has paid James in full for everyone's transport. James has accepted and allowed passage through the queen's waters to Flanders!"

We all cheer, and the captain asks, "When do we leave?"

"Today." We cheer again in surprise, and he continues, "We think it best to leave before he changes his mind or decides to alert the queen or the Dutch of your passing through."

Andres and I bend to gather our blankets, and the lord says, "Don't bother bringing anything. The ship's fully outfitted."

The captain goes up and hugs the lord. He looks embarrassed and says, "Just don't kiss me, Captain."

We're escorted out the building without any message from King James and into three carriages MacDonald arranged. Arriving at the dock, we see four shining brand-new pinnaces that make the captain almost weep at the sight. He shakes the hand of the merchant from Flanders for over a minute in thanks. Andres and I fight to stay with the captain and Alvaro, and we carry Bella, not wanting to lose her so close to home. Each ship has a full crew, and the merchant tells the captain and Alvaro to simply relax. We each get a hammock and even the ship's lower deck smells fresh.

"I think we're going to make it, Luis!" Andres says, swinging in his hammock.

"We're not there yet," I say, sitting on mine.

"We can't have made it through all of this to not make it home now," Andres says, sure.

"I hope you're right." I try to feel as confident as Andres.

Later, Alvaro yells down, "Boys! We're passing the queen's ports!"

I push off my hammock while Andres gets his foot caught in one of the ropes and trips and falls. "Luis!"

I untangle him and help him up. We go to watch and hold our breath as we gain trespass.

"We did it, Luis! We've made it!" Andres spins happily on deck.

"Yeah, that's a good sign we got through." But Alvaro watches the Dutch coast warily, and I know we aren't safe yet.

That night, Alvaro shakes me awake. "Get up, you two! On deck now!"

We run up with Bella at our heels and see a whole fleet of ships attacking the two pinnaces ahead of us.

"Who is that?" Andres gasps with his hand over his mouth.

"The Dutch," Alvaro says, filling a shot bag and loading a musket. "Here. Andres, tie this to your waist and remember what I taught you at the castle."

"What's happening?" I ask, barely finding my voice.

"The Dutch have already broadsided and boarded the other two pinnaces. The captain was quick to turn away, and now we're on a chase, but we're out numbered and we're getting chased into shallow water."

He hands me a pouch and musket. I look to where the captain is and can hear him frantically calling out orders to dodge the larger ships behind us.

Alvaro grabs his musket last. "Remember, these are heavy and have a powerful kickback. You need to brace it and fire on the musket rests. Here are two sabers if they get onboard."

Alvaro goes to leave, but Andres squeaks out, "Don't leave us!"

Alvaro looks back. "I'll be right back."

Andres turns to me, and he seems so small next to the long musket.

"Come on, we better find a rest to put these in," I say.

The captain yells in such a high pitch I can't even hear what he's saying, and he's hitting his hat and grinding his teeth while he yells.

Alvaro runs across to us and screams, "Brace yourself! We're about to run aground!" And we grab on as tight as we can to the railing as everything under our feet shakes and the force sends all three of us flying.

Alvaro hits the mast and grabs at his side in great pain as Andres and I go rolling across to starboard. I reach for Andres right away. I'm relieved to see he's fine.

"Bella!" Andres screams. We both look around and see her run up from the hold.

The captain hurries to us. "Boys, jump right away and swim to shore! Before those ships catch up!" He pushes us back to the side closest to shore.

It looks so far away. Andres is petrified again, and he clings to Bella in his arms. Alvaro comes up holding his side, sucking in short quick breaths to avoid pain.

Seeing his wound, the captain asks, "Can you swim?"

"Do I have a choice?" Alvaro answers, annoyed.

The captain helps me up on the railing, and Andres backs away, but Alvaro takes Bella and, with great pain, throws her over the side.

We both gasp. "Bella!"

Alvaro says, "Now that will get you to jump."

Andres gets up immediately on the railing and we both look down at the black angry water and then glance back at each other.

"One! Two! Three!" we yell again, and I pull him off into the water with me.

This time I come up holding his hand, and he starts to flail in the water.

"Luis! Luis!" He panics.

"Right here, I've got you!" I say as I struggle to hold him.

"Bella! Where's Bella!" he sputters.

I turn and see the white face right behind me, paddling toward me.

"Good girl, Bella!" we both cry as we see the captain and Alvaro jump off. Alvaro swims slowly and grimaces with every movement to us. But the captain can't be found. Alvaro sights him first, way ahead of us, floating on a piece of wood.

"Lucky bastard!" he screams to him.

The captain screams back, "Find a piece of flotsam and swim like hell to shore!"

We search around for any wood and can't see any. I start going completely under, trying to keep Andres's head above water, when Alvaro takes him and puts him on his back, and judging by his sharp breaths, I guess it was no easy feat.

"Let's go," Alvaro says, and we try to fight the current.

Shots ring out, and I glance back to see the Dutch are right behind us.

"They're shooting at us!" Andres screams.

Alvaro says, "Keep swimming. Don't look back!"

Bella's ahead of all of us, completely focused on getting to shore. But the shots are hitting closer and closer to us as I hear the all too familiar groaning of our ship breaking to pieces.

Alvaro, seeing that the shots are getting closer and closer, making strange wet *thrwep* sounds in the water, takes Andres off his back and struggles to float him in front of him by holding him by his scruff.

He barks out to me, "Just try to get out of range"—and then *thrwep*! Alvaro reels in pain.

"Alvaro!" Andres screams.

"Alvaro!" I cry, slightly ahead of them. He drops Andres immediately and holds his side.

"Boys, keep going or you're dead!" he says, his face twisted in agony.

I swim back and see Andres is merely a head, treading water, and try to get my arm around him and pull him, but he screams, "No! We have to help Alvaro!"

But I look at Alvaro and see death in his normally brilliant indigo eyes. His mouth's full of blood, his breathing's getting shorter and shorter.

"Leave!" he screams out with all his energy.

I turn and start dragging Andres forward, but he keeps crying, "Alvaro! Alvaro!"

I try not to think about him and struggle to get out of range like Alvaro said. The bullets stop sounding so close, and when I have a moment to look back, I see Alvaro is not where we had left him. Andres begins sobbing, and I turn to see if I can see the captain. I can't see him anywhere. I spin around in a circle and can't see one survivor anywhere. Bella, not wanting to lose me, swims back and she makes me move forward again.

"Andres, can you kick at all and help me?" I say, feeling like I'm not going to keep us both afloat much longer.

"Yeah, I'll try," he says as he tries to kick his legs vigorously.

We swim and struggle through the choppy water, but the shore keeps staying far away. I can't understand why, since we'd been able to get away from the boat, but something was keeping us from the beach.

"Luis... I'm... freezing!" Andres chatters.

"Me too," I say as my teeth begin to chatter.

"I don't... think... we're getting... any closer, Luis."

"We have to keep going," I say as a wave comes over my head, making me cough.

"Luis... we're... not going... to make it."

"Come on," I say, trying to pull him with all the strength I have.

The waves start to get choppier the closer we get to the shelf of the shore, and my muscles begin atrophying from stress and cold. Every movement's stiff and painful.

"Andres?" I ask, not hearing his voice for a while.

Nothing.

"Andres!" I shake him, and he says, slow and weak, "Pepe?"

"Andres, wake up! We're almost there!"

His head flops forward in the water, making him suck in some and start choking, bringing him to.

"Luis!" he screams, startled.

"Andres I'm still here! We're going to make it! We're almost there!" But a terrible muscle cramp seizes up my whole right leg. I have to stop and scream.

Andres says, wide-eyed, "What's wrong?"

"I can't move my leg!" I have to let go of Andres, who flounders immediately, and I only have my arms to keep me up.

"Luis, I can't swim!" he sputters.

But the pain's so great in my leg and I can barely keep my mouth above water. Andres's head is bouncing under the surface and coming back up in coughs, so I try to hold on to him, but it brings us both under. I kick my good leg a bit and bring us back up for a breath.

Andres says, "I love you, Luis," with his honey eyes welled up and tired.

I cry, "I love you, Andres."

And we see Bella come and circle us worriedly, and we both say, "We love you, Bella," as we both drift under the swell.

I open my eyes underwater and see his open eyes staring back at me, smiling, as I panic and suck in a mouthful of briny water that burns my lungs and makes me cough, only to suck in more water. Andres takes his last sea breath too, and everything goes black.

Beacons	Life 1 Ancient Egypt	Life 2 Ancient Sparta	Life 3 Viking Denmark	Life 4 Medieval England	Life 5 Renaissance Italy	Life 6 Golden Age Spain
Mole on left hand—Prophetic dreams	Sokaris	Alcina	Liam	Elizabeth	Lucrezia	Luis
Scar on forehead—Large, honey-brown eyes—Magic	Bastet	Ophira	Erna	Rowan	Sancia	Andres
Space between teeth—Green sparkling eyes	Nun	Theodon	Thora	Simon	Alfonso of Aragon	Pepe
Mole by wide-set, dark eyes	Nebu	Mother	Ansgar	Malkyn	Adriana	Old Man
Freckles—Brown eyes	Khons	Arcen	Keelin-Mother	Emeline	Caterina	Nora
Birthmark above knee—Amber eyes	Edjo	Kali	Dalla	Lady Jacquelyn	Cesare	King James
Two moles on jaw—Black eyes	Apep	Leander	Ragnar	Brom—Children's Father	Rodrigio	Hector
Picks teeth—Steel-grey eyes	Vizier	Magistrate	Seamus-Father	Ulric	Michelotto	William Fitzwilliam
Golden eyes—Animal	Sehket-Cat	Proauga-Horse	Borga-Goose	Mousie-kitten	Fia-Falcon	Bella-Dog
Scar on forearm—Slate-blue eyes	*	Nereus	Chief Toke	Daniel	Pope Alexander VI	Captain de Cuellar
Big Smile—Grey-blue eyes	*	Demetrius	Una	*	Perotto	Bishop Derry
Dimpled cheek—Brown-green eyes	*	*	Rolf	Hadrian	Alfonso d'Este Duke of Ferrara	MacClancy
Indigo eyes—Musician / Dancer	*	*	Gunhilda	Oliver	Juan	Alvaro
Orange Hair—Hazel eyes	*	*	Inga	Maid Helena	Guilia	Carra
Widow's peak—Ice blue eyes	*	*	Konr	Fendel	Isabella	Judge Advocate
Bray laugh	*	*	Orm	Gussalen	*	Urard
Pointed ears	*	*	Hela	*	Niccolo	*

Scar above eye	*	*	*	*	Jofre	Celtic War-rior
Beady eyes—Cleft Chin	*	*	*	*	Sforza	Philippe
Breaks out in nervous hives	*	*	*	*	*	Frozen-traumatized man
Fish-lips—Empty, dull eyes	*	*	*	*	*	Nessa
Very rosy cheeks	*	*	*	*	*	Old Woman
* = Not present in that life						

Seventh Life
Irish Robin Hood

Chapter 1

"Redmond! Don't run so fast!" Art pants out way behind me.

The top of my body's shaking with the speed as I run up and down the knolls and hollows of the valley I know so well. The wind's coming down from the mountain ahead of me, making it hard to breathe. My eyes tear from the wet Irish air streaming past my face and through my shaggy hair, fanning the dark brown flames.

"We're almost there!" I reach the top of the peak to see the forested valley and the Cusher River below.

I wipe the tears from my eyes and look across to the most beautiful sight I've ever known—Tandragee Castle. A fortress carved of rock, as long as the biggest ship, and as jagged as Christ's wreath of thorns. A stone king looking out over the whole valley high on a mountain, as if only God could have placed it there.

Art comes up beside me and says as he's bent over to catch air, "The sun's just about disappeared. We'll both be given all sorts for missing supper."

"We've a bit of time to spare," I say, squinting toward the sliver of orange sun still visible on the horizon.

"We'd better be heading home." Art turns around and inches back down the slope.

Imagining the day when I can return where I belong, I say, "That is my home."

"Arthur! Redmond!" Ma calls.

Coming over the last glowing green knoll, I see her, waving her thick arms toward us in front of the little thatched house. The light's turning from the faintest bit of orange to purple, and I can tell Da has already shooed all the animals in the barn to bed.

"You two little scoundrels, you know your Da gets a sour stomach if his supper is late!" She hits me on the backside with her rag as I run through the door. "You going daft, child, you forgetting to wash?"

I sigh and walk back out to the washing trough by the side of the house. I plunge my brown hands into the cold water and rub them dry on the apron hanging on a nail.

Art's already sitting beside the fire with his plate, Da's resting in his rocking chair, and my plate's on the small table Ma uses to prepare our meals. I take mine and sit beside Art. Ma brings Da his plate as he takes his pipe out and places it on the warm hearthstone for later.

"Thank you, Mary, but no thanks to you boys for the awful ache I'll have tonight."

Ma finally sits in her chair, and after Da gives a hurried grace, Art and I shovel in our stew and bread. When I begin to lick my plate, Ma chides, "Redmond! You've worse manners than that fat sow outside."

Art and Da both laugh.

I put my plate down and lie back on the floor thinking of Tandragee. "Tell me the story of Lord O'Hanlon again."

Ma puts her fork down, brings both of her hands up to her always rosy cheeks, and says with a sigh, "Oh, you ask me this every fortnight, Redmond. I think Arthur could probably recite every word, and he's only been here for a month now."

"Please, I won't ask you to tell it for a while if you tell me tonight." I try to give her all the charms of my eight-year-old face.

"Oh, well, there's nothing else to speak of." She unties her linen headdress, lets her auburn hair flow over her shoulder, and she seems ten years younger. Da now looks ancient next to her; he's all bent in his chair from a lifetime of hard farm work. No one would guess he's only two years her senior. "The O'Hanlon name's as old as Ireland. Your great ancestors were the chieftains of a good bit of County Armagh. They ruled the largest and most fertile parts of these hills and valleys we see around us on our little farm now. Yes, sir, the very blood that runs in your veins is that of the mightiest of warriors and leaders—the Lords of Orior." She holds her chin high and gives me a proud smile. "Your people built the castle you see upon that far mountain and named it Tandragee." I love how she lengthens that word out dramatically, like some magic enchantment. "Then the English came with their guns and cannons and swept us from our castle, stole our lands, and polluted our culture."

"Vermin on their *own land!*" my Da huffs.

Art looks up squinting, scratching his leg right above the faint birthmark above his knee. "But didn't an O'Hanlon fight for the queen?"

"Oh, you do remember every word now, don't you, Artie?" She gives a sneer at the thought, though. "Unfortunately, that he did, poor misguided Oghie O'Hanlon, fought and even was *knighted* by her cursed and wicked Majesty for fighting the Earl of Tyrone. Queen Elizabeth promised him that his lands would pass to his sons. Promises, empty promises; what are they good for?"

"The O'Hanlon's got Tandragee back briefly under O'Neill though," Da says looking up. "We almost held it, we did."

Ma turns to me. "You were but a wee little baby."

"Twas a bless'd day, with the sun shining through the clouds, that I stepped foot within those castle walls, where I belonged," Da says, nodding as his face falls.

"I can't believe only forty years ago an O'Hanlon lived in that castle." I look at Da who sits staring at the fire now. I thought he didn't hear me, so I repeat it, but he stays quiet, sitting with his head in his hand. Whenever he's deep in thought he would put his index finger right beside the large mole by his eye and the other three fingers across his mouth. I try to imagine what he's seeing—climbing castle stairs, looking out upon the valley from the turrets, and running through fields upon fields of soft wheat and barley.

"Well, your Da's sure had his share of ups and downs. Let us give him his peace now."

But he comes to, and he looks in my eyes. "I left right about your age to go abroad for an education. Came back to nothing, absolutely nothing." He hits his fist on his other calloused and dry hand. "Left a lord and come back a beggar."

"We're hardly beggars, Hugh. We're better off than most of the peasants around here, God bless them. We've everything we need, and better not take that for granted."

"Mary, I've a finer military education than most of the red-coats running around with muskets and I'm not allowed to command them, or fight with them! Hell! I can only get their horses for them and lift their fat Protestant arses up into their saddles."

Ma turns away when he gets to the word fat, and she pretends not to hear his cursing. Da picks up his pipe and walks out the door, slamming the metal latch hard, shaking the white plaster walls of the cottage.

Art whispers to me in the deafening silence left by the discord, "You're still lucky to have such greatness behind you."

The next day, Da comes in all rosy-cheeked from running and says with a huge grin on his face, "Redmond, boy! You're off to the finest school in England!"

Ma drops the wooden bowl she's cleaning. "Have you gone mad, Hugh!"

"Simmer down, targe, the boy's the same age as I was."

"It's not his age, old man, it's the money! Education abroad costs a fortune!"

"I just went into town and sold a few things—gave away that fat sow you hated so much."

"The sow! She was due in a few weeks!"

"I know, she fetched a nice price for it too, Mary." He tries to calm down a bit. "I got enough to pay for his travel and admittance; if we're thrifty, we can get by just fine."

Ma takes a deep breath and braces herself on the table. "Hugh," she begins, "why would you send off Redmond when you yourself said last night that your education was worthless?"

He turns with a look of pride I haven't seen on him for years. "Why, then, I realized last night that Ireland needs an army. An army to rid our land of invaders, and that army will have to be led by someone." He holds my shoulder. "I'd sell a hundred sows and everything my family passed down to see the day where I could walk back into Tandragee Castle again."

Ma, seeing that look in Da's eyes, knows there's nothing she can do to change his mind, so she goes outside to fetch the leather bag she has in the shed and gives it to me. "Redmond, dear, gather up your things."

I kiss Ma good-bye. She cries and runs back into the house as soon as my lips touch her rosy cheek. Art gets on the front bench of the carriage with Da and me, and we make our way down the bumpy, dirt path to the ferry. The wheels screech like a neglected banshee.

"Cart wheel's cursing for grease," Da huffs.

As we stand by the boat Da looks at me and says, "Learn everything you can know, boy. Take everything in. Not only what you learn in books, but watch the English and learn the way they talk, walk, and take a piss. Ireland will need it when you come back." I nod, and he bumps his head against mine, holding the back of my thin neck.

"Take care of my folks like they're your own, Art."

Art nods. His amber eyes fill with tears and Da slaps him on the back. "He's our own now, he's an official O'Hanlon!"

The whistle blows, and the boat starts away. I watch as the land of my ancestors drifts farther and farther away.

Chapter 2

"Art? It can't be you?" I laugh when I see him standing by our old carriage at the ferry. He's grown so much in the eight years I've been away. He's filled out to a strong fellow with broad, powerful shoulders.

"Redmond, my little man!" He has some inches over me while we embrace in greeting and slap each other's backs.

"Let's go get a bite at the tavern. I'm starving." I throw my bag in the back of the cart.

"Oh, no, your Ma would have my hide if I didn't bring you home at once."

The farm looks exactly like I left it, but my smile falls a little when my Da limps out, his back bent as he walks, his face worn and tired. He smiles at the sight of me, and I try to hurry to him as fast as I can so he doesn't have to suffer another step.

"Redmond, my boy! Home now and ready to take on the Planters!" We all laugh.

Ma comes running from the barn, throws down her basket of seed, and rushes right into my arms. Her smell reminds me of childhood. She pulls back to look at me. "Oh, you left a boy and came back a man!" She squints to search in my eyes. "There's my wee boy."

She hugs me tight again and takes me inside. I wish I'd been able to afford coming back sooner. It felt so long. Ma pushes me to sit in Da's chair, and she hurries to get me something to eat.

Sitting, I say, "It's so good to be home."

Ma smiles wide and puts a plate and fork in my hand.

After taking a bite, Art asks, "So, tell us?"

"Tell you what, then?" I say, smiling, knowing it'll drive them crazy.

"About England, you fool." Art sits on the floor in his usual place, but now he looks too big to be sitting cross-legged.

"My studies kept me busy day and night. Most of the boys there were rich Protestants, but they kept their distance. There was one other Irish Catholic who was my only friend."

Art straightens up and says to Ma, "He even sounds different now."

Then, in my best English, I say, "What do you mean, I sound different?"

They laugh as they hear me speak, so I keep going.

"Is there something wrong with the way I sound?" I say with a Scottish accent.

"Do another one!" Ma squeals, enjoying the show.

"Or would you prefer French?"

Art's taken aback a bit. "Sure, but now you lost your Northern accent."

"Well, I'll have some time to work on that again," I say as Da sits down slowly in Ma's delicate chair.

"I hope my money went to much more than some fancy words," Da says.

"I learned everything I could learn, just like you said—even graduated with honors. I excelled in fencing, riding, languages, military tactics, and strategy."

He gives a proud look, and a sparkle glints in his eye. "Art, you should have him show you what he knows, 'twill serve you well too."

Art nods as his body stiffens.

"Speaking of work, Redmond, you'll be happy to know I've secured you a great position working for Sir George Acheson of Markethill," Da says.

"What position would that be?" I stuff some bread in my mouth.

"Footboy."

"Footboy?" I say with my mouth full.

"I had to pull some favors to get it there, sonny, so don't be looking a gift horse in the mouth."

"I'd give anything to be Acheson's footboy. It pays better than any of the farm jobs around here," says Art.

"No, footboy sounds like a fine job, Da, thank you for all you've done for me." I take the last piece of bread to sop up the gravy.

That night, I climb up the ladder to the loft that seemed so much higher when I was eight. Art's already under the covers on our small mattress. I laugh at the sight of him. "This is going to be much different now that you're taking up more than half the bed."

"Quit your chittering." He turns over with an exaggerated pucker. "Goodnight, sweetheart."

I laugh, crawl under, and turn just as he breaks wind. He waves the blanket and snickers. "Good to have you back, Redmond, or should I say it in French?"

We laugh, and I drift off to sleep quickly.

I'm high above the dark water, the white slaps of waves breaking the darkness. I plunge into the frigid waters, and everything around me feels tight and suffocating. No matter how I move my arms, no matter how I move my legs, I can't get back up to the surface. I open my eyes in the stinging, briny water and can see the surface. My lungs start burning as I run out of air. I look to see a young boy sinking down to the depths. I see his small face with his large brown eyes, yet no movement would propel me farther. I suck in the black water and choke.

"Andres!" I sit up, clutching my chest and gasping for air.

Art startles. "What's wrong, Redmond?"

Ma cries up from downstairs, "Redmond?"

I can breathe again by the time she reaches the side of my bed, and she takes her thin hand and wipes away my sweat. "Another one of those drowning dreams?"

I nod.

Art asks, "You still have those?"

"Haven't had one since I left here." I breathe normally now.

Ma holds my head to her shoulder and says, "Remember what I've always told you. You will live long enough for greatness. The soothsayers are never wrong or to be taken lightly. At your birth, the wise lady pulled you from my womb and saw that birthmark on your left hand. She held it up to me and said, ''Tis the mark for great things, both triumphant and tragic, but this boy will be remembered.'"

Ma takes my hand out, and even in the light of the moon, we can both see the brown dot under the bottom of the fifth finger. She touches it. "You can't do great things if you drown, now, can you?"

"I'm fine now; everyone go back to sleep."

"Here, here," Art says as he rolls over, and Ma heads back down the ladder.

I can't get back to sleep, though. I'm deciding which troubles me more, the tragedy that will befall me or that I'm expected to be great.

Chapter 3

The sting of his crop whips across my face. "I have told you, boy, not to look me in the eye when you address me!"

I fight the urge to hold my hand to my cheek to stop the bite. I clench my jaw and wring my fists behind my back.

"You ignorant Irish yeomen will never learn unless there's pain in it." He straightens himself on his saddle and kicks his stirrup. "When I get back, make sure to have all my messages. I want you waiting here at the stable for me to return."

As soon as he disappears down his hunting trail, I kick over the step he used to mount his horse.

"I'm no yeoman!" I scream.

After walking out of the stables, I spy Sir Acheson's prize horse, the beautiful white mare prancing around in the field. She dances for me, and I think about how fast I could go if I had a horse like that.

A voice rises from the corner of the stables. "Why don't you ride her, then? He'll be gone for a bit."

I turn quickly to see a young man not much older than me sitting on a hay bale beside the stall.

"Do you work for Sir Acheson?" I ask, seeing he's not in the stiff uniform he forces all his help to wear.

"Thank the good Lord, no." He points to my cheek. "Seeing how he treats them and all." A tall dark-haired youth with blazing eyes of indigo steps forward. His skin is dark as if he works outside, but he's not the stocky farm-help type, more lean and sinewy like a rider.

"You should take your leave, then, before there's trouble."

He shakes off my warning and leans on the window that frames the beautiful white creature speeding around its corral. "If you don't ride her, I will."

"If Acheson returns, he'll have both our necks."

He snickers and in one fluid movement hops over the corral fence and starts walking slowly toward the mare.

"She's green, won't let anyone ride her yet," I say, jealous he's brave enough to try.

He says nothing but keeps walking toward her, not looking at her but in her direction. The horse stops, noticing she has a visitor, and gives a few nervous whinnies and spins around in the back of her corral. He puts his arm up, very slowly, and comes within a few feet of her, chanting some strange song. She snorts and walks backwards a few steps, and he slows down his movements as she watches him closely. He makes shushing noises as he reaches out to her nose, and she lets him touch her. I let out a breath I was holding the whole time. He starts to run his hands through her mane, and without taking his hands off her skin, runs them all the way down her strong back.

With one quick movement, he hops up on her bareback, and she lunges forward, startled by the feeling, and starts kicking and rearing. He seems stuck on her somehow. No matter how the horse moves, he keeps a perfect seat. He stays calm and never yells out as she thrashes. I'm glad he's having some trouble, though it doesn't last long. Within a few minutes, she's prancing around the corral, obeying all his leanings and leg squeezes, and he brings her up to me at the window. He dismounts like he has wings and wears a broad smile. "So you see, easy as that."

"You charmed her." I'm glad someone was having fun.

"Naw, I had my eye on her and would have already spirited her off without casting a shadow, but I saw how he struck you and thought maybe you deserved this fine beast."

"Ah, so, it's a horse thief you are?"

"Only the best in the county." He bows proudly.

"But you're only my age?"

"Oh, don't start comparing me to you, now, or you might start to cry."

"They hang horse thieves in these parts."

"Only if you're stupid enough to get caught." He looks me up and down. "Oh, I see why you're worried, though. You look pretty stupid."

He starts throwing a tin of saddle wax up in the air and catching it.

"Well, bless me with your knowledge, then," I say half-sarcastically, half-curious.

"Don't you have to be checking on those messages?"

"How'd you know what he said? He was speaking English."

"Really, I didn't notice." He throws it up and spins once before catching it.

"Do you keep all the horses that you steal?"

"Hold on, I never said I *steal* anything"—he shakes the tin at me—"but if you're talking about if these horses *follow* me home, I make sure to trade them in real quick for either coin or a legitimate horse."

"Where do you take them, then?"

"To a fair in another county."

I look at the magnificent animal and say, "They don't let us Irish even ride a horse like that."

"That's even more of a reason to take her!" He winks and throws me the tin and starts walking away. "Be sure to dye her with brazilet with alum when you go to sell. A white horse like this will stand out like a whore in church," he says over his shoulder before he disappears.

The mare throws her head in the air, shaking her mane in the wind. He had tied her up for me. I look back over at the kicked mounting step and hear Acheson's voice again: *"Ignorant Irish Yeoman!"* Something comes over me, and I open the door to her corral. I slip a simple saddle on her carefully and slide a bridle on as I untie her ropes. "Easy, girl. Easy, girl." She snorts as I climb on her and takes off running through the open gate as I cling onto the reins and saddle for dear life. I swear someone laughs as we bolt from the stables.

She runs all the way around Sir Acheson's large fields as I'm trying everything I can to direct her toward town. When I finally reach the village of Markethill, there's a commotion stirring. I turn to go back through the woods again to another town, but three horsemen come up behind me and block my escape.

How could they have found me so fast?

I turn to try to gallop through the crowded town, but two more horsemen appear, blocking my way.

I try in English, "Gentlemen, is there something wrong?"

They seem surprised by my perfect English but continue as one officer takes the white horses bridle in hand. "You are under arrest for suspicion of horse thievery. Until we can sort matters out properly, we will detain you for trial."

I watch as they take the horse to the stable next to the court-house. Sitting in a small room with two other unfortunate men, I call for some water. A guard comes with a pint of water and says, "Don't drink too much, there's nowhere to piss."

"Wait." I try to get as close as I can to the guard through the bars. "I come from a wealthy English family. There has been some mistake, but you look like a man who could use some extra coin in your pocket, and my father would reward well."

He cocks his head to the side. "What would you ask of me?"

"To make sure this matter goes away fast. It would be good if that white mare in the stables next to us becomes a sorrel overnight."

"Well, how in the hell can I do that?" He seems like he's about to walk away.

"Mix brazilet with alum and coat every white hair on that horse." I slip him all of the money I have on me and say, "This is to get you started."

He takes the money and studies me up and down. "You don't look like any horse thief to me, and you certainly don't sound like these Irish lowlifes. I'll do your bidding but expect that reward."

The next morning, I'm called to stand trial. The white-wigged magistrate in heavy robes is sitting behind his desk in the small courtroom. I'm brought to stand to the left of the courtroom, and Sir Acheson walks in with his nose in the air. He stands to the right with his lawyer, also wearing a white wig. The judge begins the details of the case and says, "Redmond O'Hanlon, what say you in your defense?"

"Your Honor and Sirs of the court, I am not guilty of this crime." Acheson clears his throat at this loudly. "I did not steal a white mare, Your Honor."

The aged judge holds his paper afar so he can read the paper. "It does indeed say a white mare was seized in your possession."

"'Tis a mistake, Your Honor, I was riding a sorrel, sir."

"May I speak, Your Honor?" Acheson says in his high, annoying voice.

"You may, Sir."

"A white horse was in my stable, a white horse was seen riding off under this thief, and a white horse now kicks in your court's stable."

The judge pauses a moment and asks, "Are the officers that detained Mr. O'Hanlon here in court?"

An officer from the back of the room says, "None are present, sir. They have all gone back to the garrison."

He scratches his head tiredly. "Well, then, bring the beast in."

The officer marches out the door and returns within minutes with a fine sorrel prancing through the large courtroom doors.

Acheson slams his gloves on the table and yells, "That is not the horse, you idiot!"

"Officer, are you sure that is the horse that pertains to this case?" the judge asks.

"It is the only horse in the stables, Your Honor."

Acheson screams, "That is not my horse!"

The judge asks me, "Is this the horse you were riding yesterday?"

"Yes, Your Honor, 'tis the very one."

He turns to Acheson. "You said yourself this is not your horse, so I cannot charge this man for stealing a horse no one's missing. This case is therefore dismissed."

Acheson picks his glove up, takes a deep breath, and says to me, "This isn't over, yeoman," and walks out.

An officer comes to untie my hands, and I make my way to where they have the sorrel tied up. I'm about to get on when the guard grabs the horse's saddle and, with his hand on his pistol, demands, "So, where's that reward?"

I gather the reins up in my hand and put them in his. "She's all yours. She'll fetch a good price. Just be sure to sell her in the next county."

He seems pleased with this, and I kick up my heels as I walk down the dirt road toward my home. Once I tell Da the tale, he laughs louder than I've ever heard him laugh before. As soon as he gains his composure, he says, "You'll have to go away from here for a time. Acheson doesn't give up easy, and he'll try to make your life hell if he finds you here, indeed."

"Already made my choice. I'm going on exodus in France. I'm sure their military will accept me."

He shakes his head in deep thought. "It's the very best you could do, son, right now, with all this retribution going on around us." He reaches over and hugs me. "Give Cromwell a steel kiss for me if you see him."

I pack up and say my good-byes, with Ma in tears yet again.

"Wish I could go with you." Art kicks his worn dried leather boots in the dirt.

"Going to miss this farm. I only feel alive while I breathe this valley air." I take it in deep.

"Oh, go on now, dear, 'twill be here when you get back." Ma wipes her tears with the ties on her headdress.

Da stands straighter. "That's right, Redmond. I'll never let those confiscators get their bloody hands on it."

And I walk down the glens and roads I know so well, alone, into foreign arms.

Chapter 4

Years later, when I think it's safe that Acheson has searched high and low for me and given up, I return. It feels so good to be back on Irish sod again that I don't even bat an eye at the old nag I have to ride on. In France, I rode the finest horses in formation, and now I'm given a bag of bones worthy of an Irishman. But I set my sights for that little cottage on the knoll and can almost smell Ma's stew over the fire.

I can tell something's different from the view up the road. Where Da once had fences for the livestock, I see shining, waving golden tails. I kick the old thing to gallop, but all she does is trot faster, farther up the path. I can't breathe as I see that the fields reach up over the hills and cover the area where I perfectly recalled the farm should be. My blood thickens, and I turn the horse to head to the only place I think I can find someone to tell me where my family has gone.

I walk through the dark, wooden doorway of the tavern and immediately inhale the thick smell of cheap whiskey and home-grown poteen. Only three men are in the room. The one in the middle turns at my entrance, and he does a double take upon seeing me.

Art says, slurring slightly, "Count O'Hanlon!" He turns to the man next to him. "He got counted off in France, you know."

The other man turns slightly and takes a look. "Well la-de-da," he says and goes back to his drink.

"I've seen the farm. Where's Ma and Da?"

"St. John gave us the boot two years ago." He takes a swig of his drink. "You can find them at your Ma's sisters, in the work-house out back. Sky farmers, now."

"I was sure Da would've appealed and gotten all our lands back."

"Oh, sure, he did that settlement appeal, but nothing came of it. Throwing good money after bad, is all. That bastard Sir Henry St. John is still sitting in Tandragee, watching all his crops grow where we laid our heads."

Art doesn't look good. His clothes are dirty, and his color's poor. I think of Ma and Da and worry about how they fare. Without a word, I turn and run out the door.

Art comes hollering behind me, "Redmond, where you off to?"

"Going to look in on them."

I jump on my horse and go much slower than I want. It feels like years before I reach the old cottage at the edge of town. The cottage itself is half the size of ours and in great disrepair. Behind a heap of peat stacked for the fire sits a small workhouse that has plants growing from the thatch and smoke seeping out the cracks in the walls. Ma sits on a large stone by the well, plucking a chicken. She looks up at the sound of my horse's trot, and her haggard face brightens.

"Redmond! Hugh! It's Redmond!" she yells behind her to the workhouse. My Da comes coughing out of the smoky building.

"*Count* Redmond, Mary!" He comes up with a warm embrace. "Come have a seat inside and tell us all about what you've seen."

"Have you appealed?" I ask, too angry to sit.

His face drops. "Sure, I've spent the last four years fighting them in court. Nothing, we have nothing."

Ma twists her hands nervously, turning pinker with every word. "But we are getting along fine here, Redmond. It's not so bad. We've got everything we need, can't ask for more."

"Never dread the winter till the snow is on your blanket, right, Mary?" He gleams at her with such pride.

"I sent back all I could for you. Did you get it?" I glance around, wondering why they couldn't have afforded a better place with that money.

"Oh, thank you, dear. Bless your heart for taking such good care of us, Redmond. We got every guinea." Ma looks like this is killing her.

"It paid for all the court appeals and lawyers. Now it's all we have to get by," says Da.

"Come on inside, Redmond. I'll make you some nice tea." The lines crease deeper on Ma's forehead.

"I've got something to do." I turn my old horse and kick her as hard as I can. With a whinny, she bounces to life for the first time, and we make good speed through the village and back up the dirt path I know so well.

I come to the place where my horse's tracks are still warm. I tie her to a tree and see her nostrils flared, sucking in and out as much air as she can draw. I walk out into the golden field and rip the top of the wheat to see 'tis near time for harvesting. I throw it down and go to the place where I was born. Nothing, not even a stone or ditch, gave any signs of the place I held so dear. It has been erased—makes me even doubt it ever existed.

I search for turf, take a flint out of my pocket, and work to light the driest parts. It starts to glow and smoke, and soon I have a small flame. I light each large piece and throw them, with a guttural scream, into every corner of the field. Nothing seems to happen at first, and then the fires reach up from the ground, creeping up each piece of wheat. I run to my mare, untie her, and take off into the other fields. By the time the sun starts to go down, I manage to ignite all of Da's fields, and I stand on my horse, overlooking the blaze on the peak I watched Tandragee castle from only years ago. I stand in the shadows as the light of the day vanishes, only to be replaced by the glow of the enormous fire. Dogs begin to bark off near the castle, and guns fire.

I shout, "This is only the beginning!"

I direct my horse away from the fire and back to the tavern Art's languishing in. The taproom's much more crowded now that night has fallen, and Art doesn't notice me until I come up right behind him.

"Redmond, did you hear someone set fire to St. John's fields?" He slaps my back, but when he sees my face, he realizes I'd already known.

"Here, Redmond, buy us one more pint, and we'll get out of here."

He staggers a bit out the door and takes a look at my horse. "Well, you're going to have to walk, because I can't keep up with that in my condition."

"We going back to stay with Ma and Da?"

"Oh, no, they've a small mattress on the dirt, too small for even the both of them. Oh, no sir, I'll take you to a little place I've come across in my journeys."

Even though he's intoxicated, he makes his way stealthily through the woods outside of town and tiptoes across the stones in the bog without one slip.

"Go tie your mare up here. She'll be safe. The Tories don't bother to come this way lately." He pulls aside some brush and reveals a small entrance to a cave. "Room enough for two. But we better sit out here and chat about what you've been up to tonight. It's a little cozy in there." He smiles and sits.

"Just gave St. John a little housewarming present." I start my pipe up and take a long drag while Art laughs heartily.

"If I didn't know that all St. John's dragoons would be crawling all over those fields right now, I'd have a mind to go watch the show myself."

"Well, you'll get your chance next one." I pass my pipe.

"Next one?" He takes a drag. "What are you talking about, next one?"

"Oh, I'm going to light all of his fields, every workhouse, every barn, every manor until I get up to Tandragee myself to give Ole St. John a message. I'll make him scratch where he doesn't itch!"

"What did they do to you in France?" He laughs. "I'll start calling you Owen Roe!"

"This is no way to live, Art, no way at all." I shake my head.

Art sobers up for a moment. "No, you're right there, Redmond. This is no place for me."

"Better to hang from Downpatrick than kneel for St. John or any other planter."

"'Tis the truth." Art sits up and asks, "So where do we start?"

"Have any guns or weapons stashed away?"

"Naw, do you?" He looks around my waist.

"No, but I'm sure those planters' houses and stables are full of them." I start getting up.

"Where are you going now?" he says in a high voice.

"To go get some guns."

I pull Art up on the back of my mare that protests the great weight. She tries to move sideways to get one of us off, but I give her a swift kick, and she begins to move slowly. We make our way around the roads, and I pick a planters' house near St. John's.

"Why you stopping this close to the fire?"

"They're all probably off putting it out to save their own fields."

"Oh, clever," Art says with a wink.

We dismount and watch from behind a stone wall. There seems to be only women in the house. I point to the stables and say, "No doubt there's a musket or two kept by the horses. Looks like no one's there."

"Let's go, then." Art starts creeping along the wall down to the stable.

"No, you go and light that east field. They'll think the wind blew the fire over and 'twill distract them. Be quick about it, though. This'll draw more men over."

Art nods and smiles. "Meet you back here in two shakes of a lamb's tail."

I can tell he's enjoying this. I watch him disappear down the hill, and I've faith in minutes he'll be throwing the sod like I'd told him to. I run, hunched over, behind the stone wall and reach the barn as a servant cries out, "The east field's caught!"

I push back on the wall when a door flings open from the stables, and two men run out and up the field, luckily, without a glance back. I dart in the stables and search up and down until I see her—a beautiful thunder gun—the largest of blunderbusses, right over the tack room door. I grab it and the six boxes of shot on the shelf there and make my way back out without breathing.

Outside behind the stable, I strike my flint in a bale of hay, blowing on it to catch faster. As soon as it takes, I run for cover and just reach the wall before men dash down to the stables for the horses, screaming that the stables are on fire as I make my way up the wall. I'm relieved to see Art grinning away, already on the horse in the woods. I hold out the gun, and he kicks her into a canter to come back to get me. I throw the gun to him, ammo already in my pockets and vault on her rear. She lurches and makes off quickly through the dark trees.

We hit five more planters' houses that night, dodging behind rocks and throwing sod in the dry fields. Art picks up two pistols, and I get my hands on a pretty decent sword still strapped in its sheath on a chair on a porch. Before we lit one of the barns on fire, we took the three horses with us and made plans to head to Monaghan on the morrow to unload them. Midnight, we lay our heads down in Art's cave.

He keeps snickering and finally says, "What would poor Ma think of us tonight?"

I laugh. "She'd be wearing down the beads on her rosary for sure."

"True, very true, but your Da's eyes would be tearing something fierce."

"We better get some rest now. We should be up before dawn to move these horses."

"Right you are, Redmond." He turns over and sighs. "I never lived a better night than this."

Chapter 5

As the cold still hangs in the air, I shake Art awake, and we make our way through the woods, each pulling a horse behind us.

"You're a nervous woman, Redmond," he scoffs.

"Can't be too careful, Art."

The sound of a rider comes through the trees on the lonely road to our right.

I give the extra horse to Art and say, "Stay here with your pistol set on this rider."

I kick my horse to cut the rider off at the pass, pulling my loaded thunder gun up straight at the rider's head. The man sees me, pulls his horse to a stop, and tries to reach for his waistcoat. I shoot quickly at the ground and point back up at the well-dressed rider.

"Keep your hands in the air and I won't have to use these other two shots," I say in English.

The man holds his hands in the air but is distracted by the whinnies of the other horses in the woods. The man turns at the sound.

"Oh, don't you mind them, that's just my men. All with their muskets pointed straight at your noggin."

He looks worried and starts lowering a hand toward his pocket.

"Oh, no, take your coat and waistcoat off and throw the bags over. The hat too!"

He complies. I kick them over to the side of the road and grab the fine animal's reins and step on them.

"Dismount!"

He leaps off.

"Are you with the military?"

"No, I am a merchant on business in Poyntzpass." I detect a Scottish accent.

I bend down slowly to search the bag with one hand as I keep the gun fixed on him. I find a large bag of coin. I reach in, remove one, and throw it in the dirt in front of him.

"Since you're no military man, I'll leave you something to get home with."

The man says nothing.

"Oh, and make sure you tell them you've been robbed by Count Redmond O'Hanlon." I put his hat on, tip it to him, and I take the two horses and loot back into the woods to Art.

"One more horse to sell at the fair." I take the other horse back from him.

"Well, there's no turning back now," he says, following behind me.

I jingle the bag of coins in the air. "We're on the pig's back now!"

We arrive at the fair by midday, and I go right to where the horses are. I get off and leave Art to tie up the five horses and walk to a squat man leaning on the side of the stables.

"You the man I should talk with to sell my horses?"

"That all depends," he says in a gritty voice. "You got papers?"

I smile. "I forgot them back in Armagh."

"You better go inside and talk to the boss then."

I head inside where the man pointed, and I'm surprised to see a young man sitting at a desk with his wide-brimmed hat down.

Without glancing up, he says, "You want coin or trade?"

"All depends on what we can get for them."

He looks up, and I recognize the face instantly. 'Tis the horse thief from Acheson's!

At the same time, a smile breaks across his face, and his indigo eyes sparkle. "You're that footboy who tried to steal that white mare!" He laughs so hard he can't continue. "I watched you take her and heard you got caught in town right after." He keeps laughing as I switch the weight off one of my feet.

"So what about the horses?" I try.

"I have to hand it to you, quick thinking about bribing that guard." He puts his feet up on the desk. "You may not be as stupid as you look."

"How'd you know I bribed the guard?"

He pauses with a smile. "Who do you think sold him the brazilet with alum?" He laughs again. "Good price I got for it too! Plus I took the white mare off his hands and sold it for twice as much in Ulster."

I don't say anything.

He shakes his finger at me. "That was a good day for me, but I still have to give you some credit for getting out of Armagh gaol. I took note of that little trick you pulled for a rainy day."

"Well, glad to be of service to you, then. Can we discuss the horses, then?"

He pauses again with a grin on his face and then turns to look at the window to see the horses.

"Four nice ones and a nag." He shrugs. "You selling them all?"

"Was thinking of trading them all in for two legitimate horses with papers." He starts getting up while I'm talking. "Fast horses, that is."

"I think I have just the pair."

We pass the whole line of horses, some good, some have seen better days, when he points out two fine horses at the end, one grey, the other sorrel.

"I will give you an even trade, those five without papers for these two with papers."

I'm about to seal the deal when a shiny black shadow flies by in the corral outside the stables. I rush to the fence to watch the biggest horse I've ever seen gallop in regal circles.

"That's a Cashel, Ireland's tallest and quickest horse. He's three years old, got papers, and been broken and trained by yours truly."

"I'll take him and the grey."

He laughs. "Oh no no no, he's worth more than all five of your horses." He gives a sharp whistle, and the black creature spins around mid-gallop and heads directly toward us. He comes right up, with his long black mane lifting to be caressed by him and the horse turns his head to me. As soon as I see the stallion's golden eyes I know I'm going to hand over the whole bag of coin I recently acquired.

"So how much extra, then, for the grey and this Cashel?"

He knows I'm smitten, and I can see him upping the price in his head. "Two pounds more."

"Throw in a saddle and bridle for him and the grey, and it's a deal."

He nods and takes my handshake.

"I call him Ghost, since no other horse stands a ghost of a chance of outrunning him," he says as he pats the horse's thick hindquarters.

I walk out to Art while the horse thief's getting the paperwork and saddling up the horses.

"What's taking so long?"

"He's no other than that horse thief who got me to take Acheson's white mare."

He laughs. "No kidding?"

"I got us two fine horses for these five, plus two pounds."

"Did you buy every hair on their tails? Two pounds!"

"Plus saddles, bridles, and papers."

The horses are brought up behind us, and I take out the few shillings I have left of the two pounds and throw it to the man with the indigo eyes. He catches it with one hand and gives the reins to me as he opens the bag and counts. Nodding, he takes out the papers from his coat pocket and hands them to me.

"Pleasure doing business with you, O'Hanlon. Be sure to come back again."

I realize he must have learned my name back at the gaol.

"I never caught your name?"

"People round here call me Cahir of the Horses." He smiles and takes his bag into his office.

Art looks at my glimmering beauty standing hands above his grey. "I see why the extra pounds."

Chapter 6

About a month later, Art and I are regular highwaymen. We wait on the most remote spots for lone well-to-do riders and are careful to wear masks and keep moving. Each robbery goes as smoothly as the first, and we collect enough money the first week to get Ma and Da a nice little tenant farm near our old farm, and the next week we have enough to get them some livestock to get them started again. Ma never asks where it came from, and Da shakes our hands proudly. As soon as they're comfortable, we have to start hiding what we didn't drink or eat in a night. A hole here, a rock there, but it never stays for long because everywhere we go, we'd hear another desperate peasant story, and we'd make sure to put it in their hands.

The Cashel's worth every penny. Every day he surprises me with something else Cahir had taught him. Ma sees him gallop to me when I whistle, and he gets down in a bow for me, and she swears he's enchanted. Art walks straighter, and the color comes back to his face. He looks able and young again, and the two of us are a mighty good team.

Art and I collect so many guns and weapons that we don't know what to do with them. I decide 'twill serve us best if we stash them all over the woods in well-known places in case of emergencies. Our favorite places are in between little hills covered in dense, long grass where a grown man can disappear. On days where there's thick military presence in Armagh, Art and I walk through the woods, scouting good caves, tricky bog walks, and thick brackets of thorns that we can hide horses behind.

∞∞∞∞∞∞∞∞∞∞∞∞∞∞∞∞∞∞∞∞

Art and I lie down in the tall grass under the shade of a tree, letting our horses graze in a clearing in the woods. We both doze off only to be woken up by the feeling of cold steel to our heads.

"Get up, you ruffians!" the leader yells in our language. "On your feet!"

I slowly rise to my feet with my hands up and see there are four redcoats. I give a look to Art to let me speak, and he nods slightly, understanding.

"What's the problem, officer?" I say in English.

"We're clearing these woods of Tories." He takes the gun from my head, puts it behind my back, and nudges me to move. "Go get those horses," he says to his men.

"Oh, we're no Tories, sir." I cock my head over to Art. "Just closed our eyes and let our horses graze a bit."

"What are you doing out here in the thick of the wood, then?" He studies Art. "A little lover's tryst?" He laughs, and so does the soldier pointing his gun at Art.

"No, sir, we're in search of a good stash of mountain dew that a fellow in the tavern was too tipsy to keep quiet about."

"Poteen, you say?" He checks around. "A good stash around here?"

"Well, he said he picked a nice spot near a field and a grove of silver birches, ten paces from a rock in the shape of a man's head. Stuck down low between a grassy crevice. Two whole jugs of it, he says."

This gets the officer's attention, and he searches around and spies a rock just like a bald man's head.

"There, that's the very rock. The good man found it for us," I say to Art, who's wondering what I'm doing, since he doesn't speak but three words in English. "Ah, and look, there's grassy crevices all around there."

"Which way did he say to take the ten paces?" The officer starts pushing me over to the rock as the other two tie our horses and come over to see what we're doing.

"He didn't say, so we'd have to take a guess." I reach the rock and take ten paces with the officer behind me. I stop right in front of a large grassy hole. "Would you like me to reach in, officer?"

He pauses a moment. "No. Edmund, give Luke your gun and come over here to reach in for a jug."

The younger man steps forward, and I move out of his way as he reaches into the grass.

Snap!

"*Aaaahhhhhh!*" the man screams, and the soldiers all jump and drive the guns farther into our backs.

Edmund keeps screaming in agony as he pulls both arms up with a traquenard clenched deep into his forearms, making the already red sleeves dark with blood.

The officer barks, "Did you know that was there yeoman?"

I try to act surprised. "I heard nothing of the booby traps, sir."

"Luke! Take Edmund immediately back on your horse to the village before he bleeds through."

Luke takes the screaming man, puts him sidesaddle on his horse like a child, and takes off toward town.

Art gives me a look like he's figured out my plan.

The officer nudges me again. "Back to the rock with you, and try another direction."

I walk back and take my ten paces in the opposite direction, straight to another dark hole. I stop and say, "Do you want to do the honor, sir?"

"Oh, no, yeoman, I think this time I'll trust you to find out what's waiting in there."

I take a deep breath and slowly put my arms down through the sharp grass. I have to bend even deeper to reach the bottom of the hole.

"I got something, sir."

"What is it, then?" He moves the gun off my back in suspense, and the other officer moves in for a look.

I pull my arms out fast and spin around with a pistol in each hand—one pointed at each officer. "Now, drop your weapons, or both of you will find out if these are loaded."

They both throw down their guns, and Art quickly picks them both up.

"Now, take off your uniforms."

They begrudgingly begin to take off their shiny brass-buttoned coats, and when the leader goes to hand it to me, he drops it to the ground.

"Oops," he says with a sarcastic curl of his lip.

I keep quiet and slowly pick up the coats, hats, and pants. Art takes one of their horse's leads and I take the other. I get up on Ghost, turn, and point both pistols at their chests. One of the men gets down on his knees as the other watches the gun. I pull the triggers.

They both flinch at the clicks. The look on both their faces when they realize they aren't loaded sends us reeling as we turn to gallop away deeper into the woods.

After our laughter dies down, Art says, "Did you ever think of what would have happened if he let you reach in for that trap?"

I reply, smiling, "An Englishman thinks, seated; a Frenchman, standing; an Irishman, *afterward*."

Chapter 7

The cold mud from the river's edge seeps into my boots as I crouch in the reeds along the swollen Cusher River. I start to make my way, squatting up the bank, toward the man I've followed here. I don't like being so close to the water. Something about the sound of the rushing water makes my heart beat faster and my breath get tight. Put me on top of the highest peaks, scaling the cliff walls, climbing to the tops of the tallest Scots pine, in the muddiest bog, or the darkest forest, but any churning deep river gets me in a panic. But this is worth it today. I think of my ancestors fishing in this very river and imagine them all watching me, whispering, *"Tandragee Castle."*

I hear his voice. I'm getting closer. I hear the slosh of boots and the casting of a fishing line with a heavy hook. I raise the barrel of my blunderbuss out of the reeds and level it right at Henry St. John's back. I pull back the trigger ever so slowly, but suddenly a boy jumps in the water beside him, splashing St. John.

"Look what you did boy!" he fumes. "Not only did you drench me, you scared away every fish up to Newry Canal!"

"Sorry, Father," the boy says with his head down.

St. John takes a step away from the boy, turns his back to him, and casts out his line again. I push my gun down and back away, wishing St. John had come alone.

Needing something to brighten my day, I ride Ghost down to the ferry and watch from a safe distance. The boat pulls up, with a fine carriage waiting. Two rich-looking gentlemen are deep in conversation as they step off the ferry. One puts his gloved hand up for the footman to come for their chests. When one of the men sees a young lass struggling to get off, he runs to assist her. I can see even from this great distance that her chestnut hair shines copper in the small amount of light that peeks through the grey skies. She wears a pale blue dress with yellow ribbons and a lace-trimmed kerchief pinned at her neck. I want to see her closer so I can see the details of her face.

The men help her from the dock to the carriage and make sure her things are loaded. I reach for the officer's jacket I have laid across my knees and put it on with the hat. As soon as the carriage leaves the ferry depot, I kick Ghost to follow behind. I keep my distance until we're approaching a wooded and overgrown part of the path, and then I push Ghost into a blazing gallop. We catch up to the overburdened carriage quickly, and I get the attention of the driver, who studies my uniform carefully and decides to halt his carriage.

"What is it, Officer?" he asks as a gentleman from behind sticks his head out of the carriage window to listen.

"I am the surveyor general of all the high roads in Ireland," I say. "I have been sent here to warn all carriages and travelers of this stretch of road. A dangerous highwayman has been through here but an hour ago, and we're afraid he might strike again."

The driver looks up the desolate road warily.

"Does anyone here carry arms for protection?" I ask.

"I have this musket here up with me. Any of you gentlemen armed?" the driver asks to the men in the carriage.

The man checks within. "We have our swords."

"Good you have that." I nod to the gentlemen and ask the driver, "Do you mind if I take a look at your musket? She's a beauty."

He shrugs and hands the gun down to me. I run my hand over it, hold it up to my eye, pull back the hammer, and point it straight at the man hanging out of the carriage.

"Drop your swords out the window, quick!" I holler.

Two swords, still in sheaths, clunk out the window. The driver moves slightly, and I point my gun back at him and say, "Get in the carriage so I can keep an eye on all of you."

He moves carefully down into the small carriage door and squeezes in beside the terrified girl. I dismount, put the musket in my saddlebag, and pull out my two pistols. I smile at the lass. "Easier to chat holding these."

She's even prettier close up. She has light brown eyes, and her face is kissed with Irish freckles. The red in her cheeks shows through her pale skin from the thrill of the robbery.

"Nobody worry," I say as I try to give her a dashing smile. "I only shoot people I don't like."

I open the door and say, "This is the lord examiner of all passengers. Everyone empty their pockets."

The gentlemen reach in and hand me their coins and watches. The young lady speaks in a soft voice, "My father sent me over before him with £100, but 'tis all I have to live on until he comes back in six months."

"Where is it, darling?"

"In my chest," she says quietly.

I close the door and walk back to the stacked chests and pull one down with a pistol set on the door. The first chest I open contains some men's clothes and a bag of coin. The second I pull down is much heavier. Inside is a whole silver tea set, a large silver platter, and a complete set of cutlery still wrapped up in its case. I whistle for Ghost, and he comes right to me and stands as I stuff each item in his saddlebags. The last chest is the lightest, and upon opening it, I see an explosion of ruffles, bows, lace, and silks. I reach down through the heavenly scented items and set my hand on a hard bag of metal. Pulling it up, I see what looks indeed to be £100.

I walk back over to her and see her beautiful, worried face. I take a half crown out of the bag and hold it in front of her. "I will give you this if you tell me your name."

"Muirin," she says, her eyes too shy to make contact with mine.

I hand her the whole bag, to her surprise.

"Redmond O'Hanlon has not robbed you. Make sure to tell everyone that." I swing myself over the saddle and turn Ghost to get one last good look at Muirin. I tip my tricorn hat to her and say, "Welcome to bandit country," and take off in the other direction.

I meet Art at the tavern and order a pint.

"Where've you been all day?" Art asks.

"Oh, just came this close to taking out St. John, but the timing was off." I shake my head.

"You'll get your chance one day." He takes a drink.

"Well, it's no matter since I met a freckled angel today."

His eyes perk up. "Angel, you say? Where'd she come from?"

"Fresh from the ferry. I robbed her carriage on Newry Road."

"You robbed her!" He starts laughing. "Always a good way to make an impression on a woman!"

"Of course I didn't rob *her*. I only robbed the English gents she was with." I take a drink and wipe the foam from my mouth and finish, "Sweet, sweet Muirin."

"Muirin, you say?" Art looks up. "I know a Muirin. I worked their farms right after you left for France. I'd bring her pony out for her to ride. Think it's the very same one?"

"Has your Muirin got copper hair, brown eyes, and little sweet freckles?"

He nods. "That's her for sure. Pretty little thing, she is." He seems deep in thought. "She always thanked me and even knew my name."

"She knows your name! Well, let's go, then. Get your hat. You're taking me to speak to her."

"Redmond, she's from a wealthy old Irish family that still has all their lands. We'd never get past the door!"

"Well, then, we won't use the door."

I leave a whole guinea for the barkeep, and he says with a gentle nod, "Always good to see you, O'Hanlon."

I nod back, but then remember. "Oh, Sean, did I hear your Ma's sick?"

"Sure, she's been having a fever for more than a week."

I put two more guineas in his hand. "Take her to the good doctor for me, would you? She was so kind to my Ma when I was away."

He takes the guineas graciously. "Oh, she'll be stronger by supper now, Redmond. Many thanks."

We walk out, and I let Art's grey carry the way.

Even in the dying light, I can see her father's manor is a grand English-style stone mansion up on the knoll overlooking paddocks full of beautiful thoroughbreds of every color.

"So what's your plan?" Art asks at the edge of the woods.

"I don't have one," I say as I gallop around the edge of the woods behind the paddocks, causing the horses within to neigh and run with my Cashel.

I watch the house from behind the bushes and notice the candles lit in what looks to be the dining room. I see her pass the large window. "There she is!"

Art and I follow the glow as it lights up the small windows of the stairs, and the light reappears again in the window at the far right.

"There 'tis!" I say as I take off across the field.

I head to the ash tree that reaches toward her window and stand on Ghost's back to get into it to climb. I crawl as far as I can down the branch before it starts drooping dangerously with my weight. I look in the glowing window as she fills her washbowl from an ironstone pitcher. She ties her thick hair back with a pink silk ribbon and leans over to splash water on her face.

I fight a moment of wanting to see what she will do next, but the good Catholic in me wins over the urge. I take some shillings I have out of my pocket and throw them at her window. I notice Art's running around below, trying to pick up each one. Nothing happens until I throw the ninth one, and then she appears with her hands cupped around her face to see out in the faded twilight. When she catches a glimpse of me with my tricorn hat, she jumps back. I freeze for a moment, hoping she doesn't start hollering and running out the door for help, and to my happiness, she opens the window slowly.

"Highwayman, is that you?" she says in Gaelic with a smile on her face.

"Call me Redmond." I try to get closer on the branch, but it starts to bend, so I inch back.

"Decided to come back for the £100?" she jeers.

"Well, my brother Art, here, says he knew you. Brought you your pony, he did."

She looks down out the window, and Art waves awkwardly to her. She smiles and waves back. "Art, where did you go? You never returned."

"I found a more lucrative business." He laughs.

She glances over at me. "I see you have."

"So, I just wanted to come to be sure you arrived home safe. These roads can be mighty dangerous with all those rapperees around."

She laughs. "No, I only came across one ruffian on the journey home."

"You never can be too careful, then. Although you were traveling with two pretty valiant bodyguards, there."

Her laugh's melodious and light. "I noticed."

Art whispers as loud as he can, "Redmond, better not tarry!"

"I thank you for making sure I've arrived home in one piece, and I wish you both well in all of your adventures." Her white teeth glow in the purple light.

"Well, good-night and good morrow, sweetheart." I tip my hat. "But it may be I will see you again."

She smiles again, closes the windows, and draws the curtains, taking her glow with it.

"Come on down, cupid," Art says.

When I hang on the last branch, I drop squarely on my saddle, and Ghost takes off at a trot.

"That went rather well!" I say, smiling, but I notice Art is not.

Chapter 8

'Tis a full moon on a clear night, and we decide to go toward Markethill. We're taking a path beside the road when we hear gunshots up ahead. Ghost slows at once at the sound, and Art says, "We better head back to Newry."

But in the moonlight, I see the form of a tall man on a delicate but large thoroughbred galloping toward us on the road. "We better stay put. Whatever 'tis, it's coming fast."

Shots are fired, and at least three men are galloping after one, and by their hats, I guess they are militia. The chased man spins around, and without any gun or pistol in his hands, he turns and charges straight at the men with a guttural yell. 'Tis so unexpected that the men turn their horses around mid-gallop and spin in circles as the man comes with his sword up in the air. The three men try to flee in the other direction as the dark man rushes up behind one of them and hits the man on his back. The soldier screams in agony as he slumps over on his horse.

The dark man turns his horse fluidly and tries to escape again, but the two relentless soldiers take chase. Aggravated, the dark man's horse rears as the man pulls it back to charge once again. One of the brazen soldiers lifts his sword high and keeps charging. When they come to pass, the soldier swings to hit the dark man but misses, and the exceptional dark rider turns so quickly he's able to hit the soldier from behind, causing the man to fall from his horse at great speed. The man lies injured on the ground. The other soldier stays his distance, still shooting at him.

The dark man rears back and screams, "Fall back if you know what's good for you!"

The soldier puts his gun down and walks his horse backwards. The dark man kicks his horse to gallop back down the road.

"Come on, Art!" I say as I try to catch up with him.

The man hears my horse in the woods. He slows and gets his sword back out. "Who goes there?"

I don't say anything but decide to appear out of the woods with my hands up.

"Are you following me?"

"No sir, I just wanted to compliment you on your fine riding back there. Really something to see."

"And who might you be, out in the woods this late?"

"Redmond O'Hanlon."

"O'Hanlon, you say? I have heard some about you."

"What do you go by?"

"Some call me Galloping Hogan."

"Well, I can see why." I laugh and try to walk Ghost closer to see his face.

At the sound of a stick snapping in the woods, he asks, "Have you another with you?"

"My brother, Art. We were headed back to our campsite. The moon's too bright to sneak up on anyone tonight. Would you like to join us?"

He considers it for a moment. "No harm in it, I guess, seeing as I'm having an unlucky night and all."

Once I ride beside Art again, he asks, "Why for?"

"We're forming a gang." I wink.

Once Galloping Hogan's in league with us, we all go out separately for small robberies and meet back at a predetermined spot to regroup and hide our plunder. I recruit my old friends Brian Kelly, Shane Berragh, Paul Liddy, and "Strong" John MacPherson, but I'm always on the lookout for more men.

∞∞∞∞∞∞∞∞∞∞∞∞∞∞∞∞∞∞∞∞∞

I see his red hair from a quarter of a mile away. I walk Ghost back behind a bush before the man can see me. As he canters by, I rush out with Ghost at top speed and have my pistol at his head by the time he turns to see me.

"Stop your horse!" I say.

He pulls his horse back, and we both stand there in the road. He wears white silk from head to toe, and about as many ruffles as a woman would have. On top of his carrot-orange head rests a white tricorn hat with a large white plume sticking back.

I yell, "Keep your hands on your reins, and you won't get shot!"

As I put my hands in the deep bags thrown over his horse, I pull out one heavy bag of coins.

"Please, sir, I am but a peddler that has sold my master's fine goods at the fair. He has threatened my life if I return with one shilling missing."

He even sounds like a woman.

"Just tell him Redmond O'Hanlon has robbed you. I've got a reputation in these parts."

"Oh, no, sir, he won't believe I've been robbed. He'll think I took everything for myself," he says with his thin brows pinched together.

"That's not my problem." I put the money in my saddlebags and get back on.

"Please, I beg you, will you please make some sort of sign that I have been robbed?"

"A sign?" I pull one side of my lip up.

"I've got it." He starts unbuttoning his fine coat and holds one side out far from his body. "Shoot a hole through my coat, I beg you."

I let a quick breath out. "Fine."

I shoot clear through the middle, leaving a small tear. His horse jumps at the close sound.

"Please, sir, one more to show that I have really put up a fight." He holds out the other side of his coat.

I take out the other loaded pistol I have on my belt and shoot.

He laughs. "And one more for good measure!" He throws his fluffy hat high in the air. I pull out the last pistol I keep hidden in my pants and hit it just before it touches the ground. I laugh at the game, look back at him, and he has a pistol pointed straight at my head.

His voice suddenly drops much lower, and I realize it has been an act the whole time. I still have my gun on him, though, and I say, "Well, I guess we'll find out who is a better shot, then."

"Well, I think that 'twould be me, considering you didn't reload."

He dismounts and comes over. "I'm taking everything back and then some. Get down off your horse."

"You can take everything I have in the saddle bags, but leave me be."

"I don't want to bring you in. I just had to prove myself to you."

"What are you saying?"

"I'm done peddling goods. I want to join your gang. I knew if I got you at your own game, you'd take me along."

I laugh. "You planned this all, dandy?"

"Every bit. I even followed you down the woods there from town this morning, just to be sure you'd notice me."

"In that outfit, how could I miss you? I could have been miles away and seen you coming."

"True, true. I have come out in my finest." He straightens a lapel proudly.

"Well, shake my hand, then, and let me go introduce you to the men. What do you want to be called?"

"Pedlar Bawn," he says regally.

∞∞∞∞∞∞∞∞∞∞∞∞∞∞∞∞∞∞∞∞∞

I still need the help of one more bandit that I've heard is working in my woods. I ask around and get word that Ned of the Hill has robbed only a mile from the village. I get on Ghost and ride off to find him. We venture to the most remote part of the road and sure enough, a man cuts me off at the pass and tells me to, "Stand and deliver!" in very good English.

I can really use another man who speaks English on my team.

I put my hands up and say, "I've come looking for you."

"You've come looking for me?" He scoffs, rolls his ice-blue eyes, and says, "And how do you know who I am?"

"You're Ned of the Hill, and the name's O'Hanlon."

"You're a liar."

"Why for would I be lying?"

"I hear he's six feet tall, as able as an ox, and a grand athlete."

"I'm most definitely a grand athlete," I say with a smug grin.

He takes his flintlock down and dismounts. "All right, toe to toe, then."

I walk to the side of the road on nice, even ground. We stare at each other for a moment, and then he comes at me. I know right away he's scrappier than he looks. He has me on the defensive almost the entire time. He's quick. Anytime I start to get some good hits in, he knocks me hard and moves out of range. He dodges and comes back quick. We fight like this for a good twenty minutes until he gives me such a wallop under the chin that it knocks me to the ground.

"All right, you won, you won!" I say, panting a bit and wipe the bit of blood that came from biting my tongue.

He sits, panting also. "So, you're really O'Hanlon?"

"I don't know, you just hit me so hard I can't even remember what I am."

He laughs at this. "Why for did you come looking for me?"

"We've been robbing this whole area for some time. We've all heard about each other. More militia and bounty hunters have been pouring in. I think it's time we started teaming up together to do this job right."

He considers it a moment. "But I don't keep most of what I take. I give it away to those I see needs it."

"Well, we're all doing the same thing, sonny. I barely keep anything for ourselves besides what we need for supper and supplies. Everything else we find a good home for. I just don't want the damn planters and Protestants having it all."

He's nodding, and then he sticks his hand out. "Well, then, count me in."

Chapter 9

I sit watching from the woods at the time Art says Muirin always comes down for her ride. 'Twas an unusually sunny day, and I know she'll be coming for a ride. Every minute feels long, and even Ghost is fidgeting. Finally, I see her. She's wearing a brown velvet bodice over a cream petticoat. Her hair is tied in a long braid, and she seems to shine as she walks down with her substitute for Art. The man goes into the stables, brings out a white good-sized pony, and puts a step down for her to mount sidesaddle. She thanks the man and takes off at a trot down to the trail I wait by. As soon as I see the fellow go back into the house, I go after her. She sits well on her horse and takes a few jumps over some fallen trees smoothly. When she reaches a clearing, I kick into a gallop to go along side her. She almost falls off at the sight of me, but as soon as she regains composure, she's smiling. She pulls her horse to a stop.

"Hello, Muirin!" I beam.

"You're making me feel like you can sneak up on me anywhere I go," she says as I keep Ghost walking in slow circles around her.

"That's because I *can* sneak up on you wherever you go." I smile.

She slides off her horse and walks it over to a large rock she sits on. I jump off too and let go of Ghost to graze, and stand in front of her. I can tell my nearness makes her nervous since she picks a piece of fern beside her and focuses on tearing each leaf off.

"Would you like me to stop following you?"

She laughs slightly and shrugs. "Tell me about some of your adventures."

I sit on the ground in front of her and tell her the story about being tricked by Pedlar Bawn and what happened when I stole my first horse. She's laughing hard by the end.

After a pause, she glances up at the house on the hill. "I'm so bored here."

I stay quiet.

"Every day I do the same things. Every day I go to bed wondering where my day went. What made this day different from the rest." She looks away.

"Until I came robbing your carriage, throwing coins at your window, and interrupting your ride."

"Exactly, that's what I'm saying." She smiles at me and peers into my eyes for the first time. "You're so... alive."

"Well, maybe not for long." I try to lighten her mood.

"Oh, don't say such things." But she still laughs.

"I've a fantastic idea. We can meet out here every day this time to talk, and I can tell you stories about the crazy shenanigans I escaped the night before." I peer straight in her eyes and say, "This way you have something unexpected to look forward to, and I've something to stay alive for."

She smiles so sweetly, it makes my chest tight. "I would like nothing better."

She steps on the rock to get on her saddle, and I try to show off by whistling for Ghost and hop on at a canter. Muirin seems impressed, and I follow her all the way back to her stable before retreating through the woods.

∞∞∞∞∞∞∞∞∞∞∞∞∞∞∞∞∞∞∞∞∞∞

Over the next week, I have the men take a vacation from their looting and gather all of my gang at the largest cave we found at the bottom of a rocky cliff deep in the woods. The cave's extraordinary in that it leads down to a first chamber that appears like the end, where there's a small crevice in the rocks on the right under which a nimble man can squeeze. The only one who has trouble fitting through is "Strong John," who's a giant of a man—over six feet in height and weighing more than fifteen stones. Two men on either side of the crevice have to push and pull him through, John grunting the whole time with the squeeze. Once through, there's one high-ceilinged cavern that can sleep twenty average men comfortably. But when Strong John comes hunching in and sprawls his massive girth, it fits only him and fifteen others. The two spaces off that room are perfect for storing guns, ammo, swords, and all of the clothing we steal and use for disguise.

As soon as everyone's through, I pull out a crate of fine liquor I got from the last carriage I hit and say, "I gathered you all tonight to discuss the rules of our gang." I point down to Art. "Give them all their own bottles, since we're celebrating tonight."

Pedlar Bawn reads the label once he's handed his. "This bottle alone is a good reason to celebrate." He pulls the cork out and takes a long swig.

"First rule," I say. "No killing unless it's in self-defense. Not only would you be breaking one of the Ten Commandments, the more killing there is, the more militia they'll send here from Ulster."

The men nod in agreement.

"Second rule: No drinking to excess—"

"What the hell do you mean?" Art interrupts.

"Are we joining a convent here?" asks Paul Liddy with his olive green eyes opened wide.

"Listen to me first before you all get your knickers in a knot. We need to be on guard at all times. All times! There is no safe time to dull your senses. I make this rule for the safety of the individual as well as for the safety of the group."

"It makes good sense," Ned agrees.

"That's because you're dry as a nun's gusset!" Brian Kelly says to the amusement of everyone but Ned.

Ned retaliates, "It is sweet to drink but bitter to pay for. When the drop is inside the sense is outside."

"Look, I'm leading this flock, and I say three times I find you intoxicated, you're out. Not another word said about it."

Everyone's quiet, either in agreement or anger.

"Lastly, I speak of the fairer sex. I want no harm coming to them. You lay a finger on any of them, Protestant, planter, Scotch-English, Irish, old, young, ugly or comely, you're out. One time, you're out."

They seem to agree on this, at least.

"Oh, I forgot one other thing: we must be able to gather at a moment's notice. I'll use this flute here to blow a high-pitched whistle. If you're in range, you meet here at the main cave. If you know where another of your brothers is, you go get them too. We need to be able to assemble in emergencies."

I come and sit among them.

"Okay, now that the rules are laid out, the next thing to discuss is the business side.

Seeing as we've teamed up all the bandits a day's travel from here, we're in a nice position to start a whole new business." I pause for a minute for suspense. "I'm thinking we start charging for protection."

"Protection from what?" Bawn asks.

"From us." I laugh and so does everyone else.

"So we're going to charge people a monthly fee to keep us from stealing from them?" Strong John asks.

"Us and any other bandits that move in on our territory."

"And how are we going to go about collecting these fees without the law nabbing us?" Ned asks.

"We can hire collectors from our loyal townspeople. People we know we can trust. If someone doesn't pay, we steal their horses or cattle away until they pay us back. Each of you can be in charge of an area and report back to me. Easy as that."

"How much will we charge, and what area are we going to cover?" asks Hogan.

"Well, I was thinking two shillings and six pence a month, and stretching from North Tyrone to Monaghan."

Kelly gives a long whistle.

"The peasants aren't going to be able to pay that a month, Redmond," Berragh says.

"We're not going to be collecting from the natives, Berragh. They already have our protection," Art scoffs. "This one's fit to mind mice at a crossroads."

"Sure." I nod. "Rob the Brits, charge the Scots, and give to the peasants."

"So, we're going to hand it all over to the peasants?" Bawn asks.

"Well, no, we need to keep some for our expenses, and need a hefty amount to acquire the spies we're going to need. Plus the money for bribes. After all of that, we give it where we can."

I look around at their compliant faces. "So, if I have everyone in agreement here, I'd like to make a toast. Raise your bottle and stand if you are with me!" I stand up and hold my bottle almost to the top of the cave. "To Ireland—to all that we hold dear and will fight to the death to get back!"

They all say together, "Sláinte!"

"Now with all these new recruits and collectors we'll be adding, where are we going to go get so many horses and guns?" I say rhetorically.

"'Twould take us all weeks to get that many horses and weapons," Ned says.

"I know just where to get them in one night," I say as they appear doubtful. "Bawn, help me pick out something fancy."

Chapter 10

The guards stop me at the garrison gates. "What's your business here?" one asks, holding his musket at my chest.

I put my arms up and say, "I am a merchant and need safe passage with a fortune to the Newry ferry tonight."

He replies without inflection, "Dismount, then, so we can check you for arms."

I jump off and allow them to pat me down.

"All right, you can enter."

"Whom can I speak to for an escort?"

"Lieutenant William Lucas," he says, sitting back down on the wooden chair they left for the guards.

I leave Ghost with the guard at the door and bring my bag, heavy with coin, inside the large stone building.

"Direct me to Lieutenant William Lucas," I say to a guard in the hall.

"I'll take you to him, sir."

Hearing the coin jingle as I walk down to the fourth room off the hall, Lucas is already on his feet when I enter.

"Sir, how can I be of service to you?" He eyes my fine black velvet coat with gold buttons over my black silk gold embroidered waistcoat.

I tip my velvet hat to him and say, "My good man, I have passage back to London tonight, and with the fortune I'm carrying, I'm in dire need of a large and heavily armed military escort. Of course, I will make it worth your while."

His steel eyes flash at the promise. "Well, when you say it that way, how can I say no?"

I chuckle along. "This is but one of ten bags I have. I didn't trust these roads with it all, so I will need to meet you and your men at the inn I'm staying at, say within the hour?"

"I think that can be arranged. At which inn are you staying, sir?"

"Ballymore." I turn to leave. "Bring your best horses and weaponry."

Two hours later, I sit in the tavern with my bags, full of ha'pennies, of course. The sound of many hoof beats stops outside the tavern door.

"Seany, boy, here we go."

He smiles nervously with excitement.

A soldier opens the heavy wooden door for Lucas, and he steps into the low-ceilinged room with his high hat scraping the plaster. He stands in front of me with only one other man with him. "Sir, we are ready."

"Oh, I think we have some time before my ferry." I check my jeweled gold pocket watch. "Why don't I buy you and your troops a pint?"

He sees the bottle of fine liquor I'm drinking from and sits beside me, sweeping his long tails of his coat. He motions his man to go out to bring his men in.

I turn to Sean. "Barkeep, bring me a glass for the good lieutenant here and a round for every man in uniform." I notice Sean's beading with sweat, and his face is turning red.

The men file in and find seats at the tables around the bar, all pleased with the offering of a free drink. I stand and hold my glass up. "Here's to a long life and a merry one. A quick death and an easy one. A pretty girl and an honest one. A cold pint— and another one!"

"Cheers!" they all say and throw back their pints.

"Drink up, Lucas! We've got a while before we have to leave, and a bird with one wing can't fly," I say, refilling his up to the brim.

"As long as you'll have another with me," Lucas says.

"This bottle's dry." I motion for Sean. "Barkeep, bring me another one."

Sean comes and fills up my glass with a new bottle, and as soon as I take a swig, I turn to talk to Lucas, and Sean replaces my full glass with a less full glass. Lucas is already one glass in and hardly notices when I turn around with a much lower glass.

"Another round for the boys!" Which gets them to cheer, and Lucas seems in too good of a mood to object.

"Lucas, here I am refilling my fourth glass, and you haven't finished your second!" I go to refill his.

"I better not, considering I am on duty tonight." He puts his glass down and begins buttoning his coat.

"You look like a man who can hold his liquor. Come on, just one more." I refill it anyway.

"Well, it would be a shame to let fine scotch go to waste."

I order another round for the troops before Lucas lays down the line of no more drinking.

I say, "Right you are, we best be going. I'll have my man bring my monies out while you get your men in order."

I clap my hands, and Ned comes out to load my saddlebags. We all mount and start off toward Newry. I can tell the drinks have some effect on the men by their rowdy voices and the way they're riding rather slumped in their saddles. Even though Lucas had four, he seems relatively unaffected by it.

I fill the air between Lucas and me. "In the past, I have always made this journey with a few of my men and my flintlock, but with this O'Hanlon around, I couldn't risk it."

"O'Hanlon will be swinging at the end of my rope by the finish of the month."

"Oh, but I've heard he is very resourceful. Always one step ahead of the militia."

"O'Hanlon's a common thief, a lowlife Irish peasant. The smartest one couldn't even count your guineas. To say he can outsmart the militia is ridiculous." He spits. "Beyond the pale, my man, beyond the pale."

"What is your plan for catching the highwayman, then?"

"No plan. Put enough money on him, someone's bound to bring his head in."

"You really think the people will turn on him? I've heard his people are loyal in the extreme."

"The more he steals, the more his bounty will be. It's only a matter of time before one of his henchmen gets greedy, and I'll sit back and wait."

"You're not afraid of him at all?"

"What's there to be afraid of?" He laughs.

We come to the last stretch of road in the woods before the ferry. I pull Ghost to stop, and the men halt behind me. "Lieutenant Lucas and his troops! I thank you greatly for your escort, and we seem to have picked a good night. Will you all shoot a volley into the air for celebration of smooth passage?"

I shoot my musket off, and the men fire, hooting and hollering. This is the signal, and suddenly men on both sides of the woods come streaming out. The soldiers have fired and are drunkenly trying to reload when they all put their hands up, seeing the many muskets pointing at them. Lucas tries to pull his pistol out, but I have mine up behind his head and say, "Lucas, throw your pistol down."

He sneers and drops the pistol.

"Everyone else, drop your muskets and your pistols. Now! All of you, or you'll get a bullet!"

I bend my head to Ned and say, "Collect the guns and ammunition." I go around to face Lucas and see his ugly grin. "Allow me to introduce myself, Lieutenant. I'm the lowlife Irish peasant who has just ambushed you and your men without even one shot. Now everyone dismount with your hands in the air." I point to Hogan and Strong John and say, "You two get the horses." I look back at Lucas and say, "Now strip down."

Lucas stares. I bring the gun up to his forehead and hiss, "Just give me a reason, Sasanach."

He slowly begins unbuttoning his decorated coat, peels down his pants, and pulls off his boots, never taking his cold, steel-grey eyes away from mine. "Just a word of warning, Lucas. If you dig a grave for others you may fall into it yourself."

He cocks his head away from me and lets fly out his pursed lips, "Goddamn Paddy."

Berragh lunges toward him and I throw my arm up to stay him. "What would you expect out of a pig but a grunt?" I point to Berragh and Liddy. "Take their clothes and bind their hands behind their backs."

When all is done and my men are mounted again, I say to Lucas, "The smile on my face will linger the whole night, since I'll be imagining you walking your troops back to that garrison in your undergarments." My men start laughing. "But better yet"—my voice rises—"the part I look forward to most is when you get to tell them who did this to you!"

I give a kick to Ghost and lead the way back to our hideout. The excitement and pride we all feel puts a charge in the air, and none of us gets to sleep until dawn due to each man's retelling of the fantastic story.

∞∞∞∞∞∞∞∞∞∞∞∞∞∞∞∞∞∞∞∞

I go the next day to meet Muirin at our usual time. I can't wait to tell her what we did the night before. She's already sitting on her rock in the clearing. Every time I think I remember her well, but each time I see her again, she looks more beautiful. I trot up and say, "Still alive!"

She laughs, but I can tell something's on her mind.

"What is it?" I say, jumping from my horse and sitting next to her on the rock.

She draws her legs up under her long skirt and rests her arms on top of her knees. "My father sent a letter that he's returning early. His business affair fell through, and he'll be back by the end of the week."

"I don't understand, what does that change?"

She appears like she's about to cry. "I won't be able to meet you out here when he comes back. He always comes riding with me. If I tell him I want to go alone, he'll follow me for sure."

I can't believe this great day could've been destroyed so fast. I try to think quickly. "Well, so we can't meet here. We can meet other places. I can climb that tree, you can go into town on an errand, and I can send you letters. We will find a way." I try to bring my hand under her chin to lift it up, and she flinches at my first touch. But I keep my hand on her chin regardless, and as soon as she relaxes and looks into my eyes, I draw in for a kiss. 'Twas just as sweet as I imagined, all until her warm tears hit my cheek.

"Muirin, I'm blazing sorry. I shouldn't have—"

"No, it's not that," she interrupts. "You don't understand. I'm a prisoner once my father's home. I'm not allowed to leave unless he chaperones me. My tutors live in our house, there are servants to run errands, and he receives the messengers before anyone. None of those things will work."

"What about the tree?" I say, half-serious, but she laughs through her tears.

"Father will shoot you out like a pheasant." She wipes her tears away, pulling back the sides of her face.

I take a deep breath, and we sit there with the wind softly blowing. The grey sky only makes the hay turn gold in opposition.

"Muirin, then there is only one thing to do." I turn to her and look in her swollen reddened eyes. "You'll just have to marry me."

She laughs hard. "You have to be joking! I've known you all of two weeks!"

"Are you laughing at my proposal? And I thought you were a kind lass."

"You are serious?" She stops laughing.

"Of course, I'm serious. I've a ring back in a hole near Tandragee."

She laughs again and beams.

"Okay, then, listen." I take her hand and cover it with my other hand. "I know this is quick and unexpected, and I would have liked to keep courting you for months, but if it's true you won't be able to see me or write to me, and I *know* your father would never agree to you seeing me, then this is what we must do."

She's quiet, so I press further.

"I have plenty of money to get you a nice cottage with a farm near my folks, and I can be with you every day. You wouldn't need a thing. You'd be free to go wherever you want, when you wanted to. Instead of being in this stone cage."

She stares back up at the huge house, looking cold in its own shadow. "When would this happen?"

"Anytime—three days, two days, one day, or right this brave second."

"I'd need to get my things and write a letter explaining this to Father."

"Pick a day. I'll come for you with a cart, and I'll take you to your very own cottage."

She lifts her face up to the sun and smiles a crooked smile. "Tomorrow, then. Can you get a cottage by tomorrow?"

"I can get a castle by tomorrow if it's what you wanted," I say as I squeeze her hand.

"No, a cottage is more than enough." She gives me a kiss on my cheek and walks to her horse.

I watch her get on and lift up in her saddle as she rides away with a secret look back. I sit in the field for a moment and wonder what I've just done—if 'twas the right thing to do for her—but then I think of the alternative and, honestly, it isn't even an option. I whistle and jump on Ghost and race toward town to find a place as bless'd as she.

Chapter 11

That night, I put three months' rent down on a tenant farm for Muirin, and I head to the tavern for supper. As soon as I sit, Sean comes over to me. "I heard all about what you and your boys pulled off." He shakes his head. "You guys are something else!" He slides me a mug.

"Couldn't have done it without you, Sean."

He laughs. "I can't believe Lucas didn't notice your drink disappearing! 'Twas some trick! I could hardly keep from laughing. Had to lower my head under the bar, I did, so no one would notice."

"Can you get me a plate of whatever your Ma made?"

"Sure thing, Redmond, on the house."

"Oh, no, I haven't given you your cut yet." I slide a small pouch over to him.

"I'd have done it without this, but 'twill go to some use." He starts to go for the food but turns. "Nearly forgot, you have a gentleman who's waiting for you in the snug."

I turn and look into the small room off the bar and see a man with his back to everyone in a red uniform. I pick up my mug, walk over, and sit with my back to the bar also. The man turns, gives a faint smile, and says with a thick Scottish brogue, "Heard about your exploits last night."

"Oh, news travels fast within the garrison." I grin.

"No, was there to see Lucas limp in half-dressed with all his sorry men lagging behind him."

I laugh heartily. "Alister, what I would have paid to see that."

"Not a good move, Redmond. Lucas wanted you before, but now he's waged war." He shakes his head. "He had a whole list of bandits prior, but after yesterday, he's set his sights on you."

I shrug my shoulders. "I'll take my chances. The man didn't impress me."

"Well, I've come here to warn you. Lucas has gotten Ormonde to pay for thirty of the best mercenaries to come Tory hunting for the next three months."

I whistle. "Good to know, thanks for telling me."

"Let it be said by me, lay low the next three months and go bury your money somewhere deep."

"But I bank my treasure in the hearts of my people. No safer place, I tell you. I see with many eyes and hear with many ears."

"Well, still, lay low. Be careful not to bolt your door with a boiled carrot. And stay away from the garrison for damn sure."

Sean brings over my plate with warm bread in a basket and fills up Alister's drink.

"I'd like to give a toast!" I hand the bottle over to Sean to drink from. "A toast to faithful arms, clever companions, and discreet spies."

Sean takes a sip. "Don't know if I fit into any of that, but I'm honored, truly honored." Then he walks back to the bar.

I push a three-pound bag of shillings under the table to Alister. He takes it and puts it inside his coat covertly. "I'll be sure to share this with the clerk."

"You're one of my best intelligencers. Whatever you need, I can get you."

"This is fine." He gets up to leave. "You know they've paid almost as much for hunting Tories as they have for killing wolves!"

"Oh, no, now you got me sympathetic for the wolves."

He smiles wide, showing his deep dimple, walks out, and puts his hat on after he gets out the door.

∞∞∞∞∞∞∞∞∞∞∞∞∞∞∞∞∞∞∞∞∞

I wait early morn outside Muirin's house. I see she's arguing with a few women inside. I'm about to open the door to see what they're doing to her, but she opens the door with tears streaming down her face. When she sees me with the cart, she smiles and runs into my arms.

I hug her tight and say, "You sit right here while I go inside and get your things."

"They're all right there by the door." She fumbles for something to grab as she climbs up to the seat.

I open the beautifully carved door, that I have no doubt some poor miserable Irishman got paid nothing for, and see a stack of chests, crates, and bags. As soon as I bend down for a chest, someone grabs my arm hard by the elbow. I turn around, ready to punch the guy who put his hands on me, but see 'tis a large woman in plainclothes with a dirty work apron on.

She speaks in Gaelic, "You're making a big mistake, outlaw. She's not your kind. She's used to all of this." She puts her hands up to point out the high ceiling and wood carvings of the fine house. "No matter how much you steal, you're going to end up with a noose around your neck, and she'll be left with nothing but a bad reputation."

Her words hit me hard, and instead of realizing she's only speaking the truth, I yank my arm from her grasp and bend down again for the chest. I walk out and stack it on the cart. Every time I go back in, she says something else to me, but I pretend not to hear her and keep filling up the cart until the last chest. She gets in front of me and blocks the door this time.

"You're taking her away from her family, and once you're gone, she'll have nobody, and her father won't ever take her back."

"Get out of our way," is all I can think to say.

She huffs and moves away toward the fireplace. "I've said my piece."

I open the door and throw the last chest in. Once on the seat, I give Muirin another big hug, but I don't talk the whole way to our cottage. My mind can't block those words out.

The cottage is only three farms away from my Ma's and 'tis the last house on the path. There's a slight incline up, and once we're on the top of the little hill, Muirin brings her breath in quick. "Oh, it's perfect, absolutely perfect."

She clasps her hands together, jumps out, and I watch her run down the hill toward the little thatched cottage nestled against another hill. I drive the cart down to the house as she reaches the door. She screams once she's inside, and I'd hoped 'twas because she liked all the furniture I'd stocked it with. I appear at the door, and she's rocking back and forth quickly in the pine rocking chair.

"I thought I was supposed to carry you over the threshold?" I smile, leaning against the frame.

"We're not married yet." She laughs as she looks around, studying every corner, every beam, and every catin-clayed wall.

"Have I done this all going after my back?" I scratch my head jokingly.

"No, I wanted to see the house before I married you."

"Oh, then the truth comes out. You're after me for my money."

She laughs, gets up, and throws her arms around my neck. "Let's go."

ᴏᴏᴏᴏᴏᴏᴏᴏᴏᴏᴏᴏᴏᴏᴏᴏᴏᴏᴏᴏᴏᴏ

We drive all the way to the church in Newry her parents were married in. As I come up the narrow dirt lane and see the small stone church, a strange feeling washes over me. I search my memory, trying to figure out if I'd ever been here before.

"There 'tis! Oh, isn't it beautiful," Muirin coos.

"Grand," I answer, but I don't really know quite how I feel about it. We pull up in front of the sleepy church, quiet now in the late afternoon. I lift her down from the carriage, and she goes inside where a church lady welcomes her to change. I look out from the top of the hill down into the lough valley. The hillside is lined with small fisherman's houses, and boats dry upside down on the thin, rocky beach. A shiver runs through me, yet the wind off the ocean is warm. What is it about this place? Newry is both welcoming and foreboding all at once. I feel like staying here and running at the same time.

Nevertheless, this is where Muirin has her heart set on being married, and I'll have to put my superstitious feelings right where they belong—far from my matrimonial thoughts. I check back to the church to see if Muirin is ready yet, but the door's still closed. I follow the worn grass path back behind the church, and I'm surprised to be comforted by the ancient graveyard sinking into knobby ground. Most of the stones are so old and worn by wind there is little left of them, and the moss obscures any carvings on some of the less ancient ones. One grave draws me from the path, and I place my hand to trace the faint Celtic symbol.

A strong breeze whistles from behind suddenly and lifts the cap clear off my head. I lunge to hold on to it, but it rolls along the uneven grass with the spirited wind. It settles at the far side of the graveyard against a tall stone. I cram it back on and almost turn back to the church, but I catch the odd carved bird in the corner of my eye. I wipe some of the dirt away, and there perches an ominous crow staring back at me. Rubbing away more sediment, I expose elaborate scrolls that trail all the way down to the dark soil. I place my hands on the cool ground and feel something, something resonant. Is this some ancestor of mine, pulling me to where his bones are buried?

"Ahem." I turn to the priest standing halfway into the graveyard with his Bible in his hands. I hurry from my crouched position and almost stumble among the graves. He nods and starts back to the church, and blood rises to my cheeks that he should spot me in his graveyard on my wedding day.

I catch up beside him and try to explain my strange behavior. "That is a beautiful grave, that one with the crow on it."

"That's no Christian grave. It's a rune left by the Norsemen that invaded this area hundreds of years ago."

"You don't say," is all I can think to say as I scratch my head, wondering why I was so drawn to it.

The priest opens the heavy worm-holed door, and the setting sun shines through the high windows down on Muirin waiting at the front of the church for me. She looks so pretty standing there in her blue dress, the one I robbed her in. The priest begins our prayers, and it all blurs into a distant song as I watch her blush when she senses me staring at her. The priest's words echo in the small church, since I'd decided not to scare Muirin away with meeting my acquaintances all at once. When 'tis time for the ring, I slide a well-worn gold band with a crowned-heart clasped between two hands down her dainty finger. She sees it and smiles, thinking most likely of where I got it from. I hold her gaze and the words barely come out, "Let friendship and love reign."

Tears well up in her sparkling eyes as the priest wraps our wrists together with rope in the sacred handfasting. When we reach our cottage, I pick her up and carry her light body in through the door, then place her on the small roped bed. I couldn't have asked for more.

∞∞∞∞∞∞∞∞∞∞∞∞∞∞∞∞∞∞∞

In the morning, we awake to a loud knocking on the door. I put my hand up to my lips to make sure Muirin stays quiet and go to grab for my gun.

"If you're grabbing for your gun, don't bother, it's just me, Art!"

I walk to the door and open it halfway. "What're you doing here?"

"Funny thing, I was talking to Sean last night, and he asked me how you like your new place. I said, 'Redmond got a place?' And he tells me where he heard 'twas. So I had to see for myself."

"I bought it two days ago, Art. I haven't seen you since then."

"Right, but here's the other funny thing. You told all us outlaws not to rent a house but to stay in a different spot each night. So why would you go and buy a place if you tell us that?"

"I'll explain all of this to you later tonight, okay?"

He raises his eyebrows at this and nods, but then quickly pushes me into the house and breaks through inside. He sees her right away.

"Redmond, what are you doing?" He puts his hands out, baffled.

"It's not what you think, Art. We've been married."

He hits his hand up to his forehead. "Why were you keeping this from me? Aren't I your best friend?"

"You are my best friend, Art, but this is between me and Muirin."

He glares at me and then gives a quick look to Muirin, who huddles under her blankets, and flies back out the door.

Chapter 12

The rest of the week, I stay home with Muirin. I check in occasionally to our meeting spot and the tavern, but it seems like they're off taking care of business, and I'm enjoying my time with her. But after eight days goes by, I feel like I have to go back on the road for a few days to contribute. Muirin walks out to see me get on Ghost. "I'm going to worry every minute you're away."

I kiss her head. "I'll be back soon."

I ride Ghost far out by Monaghan, trying to stay away from the mercenaries. 'Tis past noon when I hear someone coming. I get on the road before the rider appears, and I start trotting. The person takes an unusually long time to catch up, and I practically have Ghost at a walk. I almost fall off my horse when I see her. She has thick raven hair down to her seat, and it shines like a brand new shilling. She's petite but has a beautiful form, and even though she sits on a nag, she sits like a seasoned rider.

"Good day, miss," I say in English.

But she replies in Gaelic, "I don't speak English."

"Well, lucky for me I speak some Irish as well!"

She studies me as we trot side by side, and it makes me uneasy.

"What's a young lass like you doing out on these dangerous roads alone?"

"Well, I'm not alone now, am I?" She gives a small smile.

"Would you like me to accompany you, then? Two shorten the road."

She just nods.

"Where are you headed?"

"To Newry. I have to fetch £100 from a merchant man there by nightfall."

"That is a small fortune. You best keep such things to yourself, since there are those that'll take advantage of your trust. Some say *Redmond O'Hanlon* frequents these very roads."

She laughs roughly. "Well, I've heard he's a blazing handsome man, so I think I'll know him when I see him."

I grin at the assault she dealt unknowingly. I steal some glances at her here and there, and I'm captivated by the wildness she seems to exude—like some unbreakable horse or earthly sprite. We ride down the road for a few miles until she comes to a turnoff.

"Here is where we part ways. Good luck on your mission, lass. Remember, tell no one of your errand."

"Good luck to you too, and if you see O'Hanlon first, tell him to go to hell for me!"

Again I laugh and couldn't wait to reveal myself to her. I wait by that pass for hours, listening for the slow sound of her nag. Finally, I hear her coming. This time I wait for her to pass.

Then I quickly dash out after her, saying, "Did you get back safe?"

She keeps moving her horse forward. "Sure enough."

I pull my gun out. "Well, then, hand it over."

She simply laughs and keeps going. "You wouldn't rob a lady. I've heard about your three rules."

"With respect to you, I said I'd never *harm* a lady, but I don't have any problem *robbing* one."

She laughs again witchy-like. "So why for, are you pointing that gun at me if you're not even going to use it?"

She really begins to frustrate me. I pick up speed, grab the bridle of her horse, and pull her awkwardly to a stop. But her horse is not only old but has a nasty temperament. It starts kicking and rears away from my grasp. The girl laughs all the while, but I go and block her.

She continues, *"With respect to you,* I can't give you this money. I promised my master I would bring it all back, and he threatened to cut an ear off if I handed it over to you."

I try to read her large honey-brown eyes to see if she's telling the truth or not. "A shame, you have such pretty ears too."

I try to get hold of her horse again. She takes off one of the two bags she has tied to her saddle, and she throws it into the bog on the right of the road.

"Why for did you do that?" I try to control my anger.

"Well, I promised him I would never *hand* it over, so if I throw it, then I can say I still didn't *hand* it to you."

"You couldn't have just dropped it at my feet?"

What a strange girl this is. I'm beginning to wonder if she's normal at all. But I smile and dismount with pistol needlessly pointed in her direction as I slowly inch into the mud backwards. Halfway in, I hear a commotion and watch as the imp stands on her nag's saddle with her other heavy bag in hand and jumps over to Ghost's. She digs her heels in and takes off. I grab the bag and run to jump on her nag, but the nag bucks when I come near. I go after the horse on the road as she goes in circles, and I finally grab her reins dragging on the ground and bring her near. I jump on the short and plump pony and dig my heels in but only get a slow trot out of her. I scream to the sky as I realize she's tricked me.

After the sick feeling comes over me that I've lost Ghost, I try to cheer myself up by opening the bag on my tired ride and scream again when I see they are just coppers! I think about the day over and over again and by the end of the night, I begin to see the humor and laugh out loud to myself. My only thought is to get Ghost back, and since she was headed toward Monaghan, my only hope is to try to go back to where Cahir's dealing. I dig out a stash I have off Monaghan road, since I know 'tis going to cost a fortune to get Ghost back, especially once Cahir realizes how much I care about him.

I haven't seen Cahir since I acquired Ghost. I usually send Liddy or Berragh to sell the horses we get our hands on. The fat, gruff man's still in the place I saw him previously, and before he can ask my business, I say, "I'm looking for Cahir," and keep walking.

He pulls a gun on me immediately. "Not until I remove your weapons, boy."

I let him remove my pistol, and he nods that I can go in. Cahir's facing the wall in his chair, and as soon as I walk in, he says, "Good to see you, O'Hanlon" and he spins around "It's been too long."

"You know why I'm here."

He smiles a knowing smile. "I hate to tell you this, but he's already been sold."

"She only nabbed him yesterday! How could you have sold him so fast?"

He keeps his cool. "I had a man come last night looking for the finest horse we had, and you know there's nothing better than him."

I wonder if he's lying to get me to pay more, so I turn and go to the corral I bought him from. Instead of seeing Ghost there, I see another familiar figure leaning against the stall, cleaning her fingernails. Cahir comes up behind me. "Oh, I see now, she's working for you." I lean against the side of the wall. "Oh, she's good, Cahir. I never saw it coming. Had the plan right from the beginning, she did."

She looks up, slightly interested.

"You've got to tell me your name. I need to know the name of a girl so clever and daring, who can pull one over on me."

"Síofra," Cahir says.

"Well, Síofra, I'd pay you handsomely if you hand my stallion back over."

"He's sold." She swipes her hair away from her forehead, revealing a white scar.

Cahir says quickly, "But Síofra, you delivered him to the gent and know where he is, don't you?"

She glances up, suddenly very interested. "You give me ten pounds, and I'll go get him back for you."

"Ten pounds! You're already making his sale three times over!" I walk around in frustration. "I'll give you five pounds if you tell me where he is, and I'll go get him."

"No sell," Cahir says, "Ten or nothing."

I kick the wall behind me. "Fine, ten, but I want him tonight, and I'm not paying until he's back."

Cahir and Síofra both agree, and Cahir goes to get Síofra's horse, a beautiful, shining thoroughbred. She doesn't need any assistance mounting and throws her dainty leg over to ride astride. I look away at her lower legs showing obscenely from under her skirt. She and Cahir laugh at seeing my modesty for her. She doesn't seem to care in the slightest and gallops right out of the stables.

After some time, just sitting in Cahir's office, I say, "You're not worried about her at all?"

"Worried?" he scoffs. "She's one of my best. She'll steal the sugar out of your punch, she will."

"Is she your sister?"

"No, not my sister."

"Your wife, then?"

He laughs. "No, not my wife." He changes the subject. "I've heard you're running a whole racket from here to Tyrone. That true?"

"Might be." I lean back in my chair.

"Well, I got a little problem with that, you see, since I work seven counties that include your three."

I pause a moment. "Well, I'm always looking for a good horse thief."

He laughs again. "I can see why too."

"Look, I've brought together all the best men to unite against the English. We can't make it on our own for long, but this way, the way I see it, we've got safety in numbers."

"How does it work, though? You sticking your nose in everybody's business? Dipping your hand in everyone's pockets?"

"My men listen to me, but I let each one govern their own area. If you joined us, you can keep doing what you're doing. We've just got each other's backs is all."

He thinks for a moment. "I might be interested."

Our negotiations are interrupted by the sound of someone galloping into the stables. I go out the door to see the bless'd sight of Ghost standing there. I whistle, and he comes right up to me, pushing his roman nose into my chest.

"Ten pounds, thank you." Síofra pants.

I walk back out and down the path a bit to where I left the money, since I don't trust a soul there. When I walk back in, Cahir and Síofra are discussing something.

"Here 'tis, all ten in guineas and shillings." I take Ghost's reins and say, "Pleasure doing business with you both," and lead Ghost toward the exit. "Oh, and as a reward for besting me, Síofra, I'm giving you back your noble steed."

She laughs.

"Hold up, O'Hanlon!" I turn slightly to see Cahir getting on his fine animal. "We're coming with you." On the way up the path, Cahir yells to his man, "Keep things going, Mickey, until I get back. And don't put a dirty finger on my liquor!"

Chapter 13

By nightfall, we reach the main cave, having picked up Berragh and Liddy along the way since we crossed their turf. Strong John and Kelly are sitting by a fire outside the cave when we approach. Strong John yells out, "Síofra!" and he comes running to her and picks her small frame up high in the air like a child. I don't understand until John puts her down. "'Tis my big sister."

The thought of her being big next to the giant is laughable. "You're related to her? I never knew you even had a sister, and a horse thief, at that. You never thought to mention that?"

"Well, Síofra told me not to, and what she says, I do." He smiles and lowers his voice. "She's in league with the fairies, you know."

Síofra gives a bewitching smile.

Cahir pushes through us all and sits by the fire. Kelly takes the cork out of the jug they're drinking from and pours him a cup, which he accepts with a nod of thanks. We all sit, and Cahir says, "So, let's get down to business. Where are we going to get our hands on some first-rate horses?"

I reply, "If it's horses you want, I have an idea."

∞∞∞∞∞∞∞∞∞∞∞∞∞∞∞∞∞∞∞∞∞

We blow the signal to gather, and everyone shows within thirty minutes with their recruits in tow. I give a count and whistle at the total of twenty-nine men, but realize I'm missing one of my leaders.

"Hogan, have you seen Art?" I ask.

"Nope, haven't seen him for a couple of days."

Would he actually disband because of our fight?

I try to shake it off so I can focus on the task at hand. "Everyone fill your pockets with shot, each take a musket, pistol, and sword. Remember all we've taught you and keep your ears perked for my commands."

They nod anxiously, and Kelly yells with his sword held high and grey-blue eyes sparkling, "Well, let's go, then!"

Cahir's riding next to me and asks, "Where we headed, then?"

"I got the hard word that there's a militia setting up their fortification in Banbridge. Their defenses are down, and it's a good time to take what we want."

"You're going after the militia?"

"I think I'm addicted to it," I reply with a grin.

I shush my men and have them walk their horses to keep the noise down. We come upon the half-built fort at the time of the changing of the guards. I get to see without even sneaking up how many sentries we have to worry about. One man guards each entrance to the stables. I go back to tell my men and pick twelve of my best to go gag and bind each man. "The trick here is to walk slowly and silently behind him while one man puts the muzzle to his head. The other silences him so as not to alert the others. Once you've got your man down, I want one man to make a single owl hoot. When I hear six hoots, I'll bring nineteen more men down to get the horses. The rest of you will stay and hold our horses and fire from here if we get any attention."

With the sound of a shadow, the twelve men move down upon the stables. I hear the first hoot, and the five follow closely. I motion for the next group to follow me down just as quietly, and we find eighteen horses within. They each take one while Cahir and I follow with our muskets raised behind them. When we reach the safety of the woods, I look at Kelly, who has blood streaming from his nose.

"What happened to you?"

"Our sentry put up a little fight, gave me a nasty wipe, and broke my nose, he did," Kelly says, trying to feel the bones.

We take to the main road, and our herd leaves a cloud of dust behind. Cahir rides up beside me and says as he takes the lead, "We're headed to the fair at Ballybay."

'Tis Strong John who notices the patrol gaining on us from behind, and I know they can overtake us since we're hampered by the extra horses.

I scream, "Halt!" They slide to an abrupt stop. "Form a semi-circle!" The men file into place with the quickness of trained militia. "Wait until my command to shoot!" I put my horse in the center and hold my breath as the patrol stops, aware of our unexpected formation.

"Surrender and no one will get hurt!" their commander yells.

"No! No surrender! We're all prepared to fight to the end!" I move Ghost forward a bit and say, "You're outmanned and outgunned two to one! Surrender to us!"

Their commander steps his horse over to another officer, and he comes forward under a white flag.

I turn to my men. "Be ready if this is a trap." Ghost prances out to meet him halfway.

"You have the upper hand here, there is no doubt. If you give every one of those stolen horses back, then we will have no bloodshed here tonight."

"I can agree to giving you back all the horses." His face widens in a smug grin as I say this. "At a guinea a piece, that is."

His face falls, and anger distorts his features. "You're selling the militia back its own horses?"

"Yes, and if that's not agreeable, I will shoot dead every member of your patrol." I keep my face still.

He looks at my well-disciplined men and juts his chin out. "A guinea per horse, agreed."

"And I want your patrol to retire a thousand yards with no threat of reprisal."

He takes in a deep breath, puffing out his chest. "You drive a hard bargain, outlaw, but agreed." He walks his horse over and counts out eighteen guineas from his purse. We have nine unarmed men bring the horses to my position, as he has nine come to take the horses.

"You'll hang someday, O'Hanlon, and you'll see my face in the crowd."

"Something to look forward to, then, Commander."

I canter back to my men. We wait until they fall back, and we take to the woods and celebrate into the night.

∞∞∞∞∞∞∞∞∞∞∞∞∞∞∞∞∞∞∞∞∞

The next morning, I go back to our farm, anticipating Muirin running out the door to see me as I come down the hill, only to be surprised to see Art's horse in one of the paddocks. When I open the door, they're laughing together as she's making supper and he's sitting by the fire.

"Good to see you, Redmond," he says.

Muirin comes running to me with her hands covered in flour and gives me a tight hug. "You were gone for three days! Thank God Art came to check in on me."

I glance over to him, and he gives me a little grin. "Art, so this is where you were last night. You mustn't have heard the call?"

"'Twas a call last night? No we didn't hear a thing, did we, Muirin?"

"Art came by yesterday looking for you, and I begged him to stay for supper since I didn't want to have another supper by myself."

"What about my Ma and Da? They're only three houses away."

"I went to them the first two nights, and I thought you were coming home anyway."

"Well, we could have used you, Art, but we managed all right." I go and sit in the smaller chair by the fire.

"Oh, tell us all about it, Redmond, while I finish this soup."

She's so rattled by my story, I forget all about the anger I feel for Art. After supper, I realize my worries are foolish, and I thank Art for looking after her for me. He leaves soon after.

It becomes a strange agreement, but whenever I have to go on the road or travel to talk to my spies, Art will come and stay with Muirin. It makes it easier for me to leave, and I do feel more comfortable knowing someone is there to protect her. I try not to think too hard about what *his* reasons are for doing it; I just push it from my mind.

I walk into the tavern and say, "Sean, how you been?"

"Where've you been, Redmond? Better than three months since I've last seen you. And what's this I hear about you being married?"

"Sure it's all true and 'tis the reason why I haven't been here for long."

He chuckles. "Well, good to see you back, but I have some good news and some bad news. Your man Alister came a week ago and wanted me to tell you that the mercenaries were being recalled."

"That's great news, Sean. Not one of my men was caught."

"Sure, but here's the bad news. St. John and three of the other bigwigs around Armagh are putting in their own money into tracking you down."

I scoff. "St. John can buy a whole army and they'll never get their hands on me."

"Alister says it like it's some kind of game to St. John, like you're one of his game animals. He's telling folks all around here how he and his son are going out every night searching these woods for you, and they won't stop until they smoke you out."

"Well, what can I do about that?"

He clears his throat and lowers his voice, even though we're alone at the bar. "Maybe you just might want to get the hunter before the hunter gets you."

I sigh. "I've had my chance before, but it might come down to that. Thanks for the information, Seany." I hand him two pouches.

"One's for you and the other's for Alister, if you see him first. Actually, I should give you another to have on hand so when he comes to you, you can give him something from me."

"Thank you, Redmond, but the other bad news I have to tell you is that they've put a bounty on your head: thirty pounds for you and twenty for each of your men."

"Well," I say as I walk out, "then I just have to be sure to give everyone I know more than that so there's no incentive."

∞∞∞∞∞∞∞∞∞∞∞∞∞∞∞∞∞∞∞∞∞∞

No one's in the main cave this time of the day. I blow the whistle ten long times and then again five minutes later. Strong John, Ned, and Liddy are there first, followed by Kelly, Cahir, and Síofra, and Galloping Hogan comes last.

"I guess this is our turnout." I look around. "I just got news that the mercenaries are gone."

Liddy gives a sharp-pitched whistle in celebration.

"But," I pause. "There's word St. John's wagging his new-citizen tongue all around Armagh that he and his son are going on the hunt for me and my followers."

"Let him come, then," Kelly retorts with his dazzling smile.

"Well, Sean had a pretty good idea. He thinks we should go after him first."

Everyone's waiting for me to continue.

"I've been thinking, it's never good to go shooting a well-to-do Englishman, unless you want the whole army of Ulster at your door. Then it came to me; we go ransom the boy. He can't be but nineteen or so now. How hard would it be for us eight to go nab him?"

Cahir says, "Strong John alone could go and pick him up over his head and carry him home."

"So we go watch the house. If he comes out to go anywhere, we get him. We bring him back here and send a message to St. John that he better leave us alone."

"It's worth a try, and there's no jug here anyway," Strong John says.

We ride to the base of Tandragee castle and wait for a rider to come down the path. We must've waited over an hour.

"I don't think he's coming," Ned says.

Suddenly we hear the cacophony of hounds being released. Panic sweeps all of our faces when we think they might be headed our way, so we take off deeper into the woods. We watch the hounds pass with three riders dressed up for a hunt behind them.

"Let's follow them. They're sure to break up in the fields, and that would be a perfect time to take him," I say.

We follow St. John and his group to a clearing as the two other riders go to their left with the hounds. "Where are you go-ing, William?" one of the riders calls over the noise.

"I'm after fowl today." He turns his horse away.

We have to stay deep in the cover of the brush to wait for the perfect time to pounce. We watch, as he doesn't seem to be hunting for anything. As soon as his father's out of sight, he puts away his gun and just rides around the perimeter of the field. He then stands daydreaming, staring out on the field. I turn to Cahir, who looks impatient, and shrug. Finally, our chance comes when he decides to go for a jaunt in the woods. We all close in on every side. When he spies us, he screams, "Outlaws!" at the top of his lungs.

His horse is fast and sure-footed and keeps pushing into Ghost as I try to get hold of him or his reins. He fumbles to get his musket out from his saddlebag, but Strong John swats away with his long arm and flings it behind us.

"Outlaws!" he yells again.

Finally, Hogan races up on his dainty horse and does a quick spinning motion right in front of the boy's horse, forcing it to stop before colliding. He screams one last time before I can shove a rag in his mouth, but in the shuffle, a shot rings out, and we all look up to see two hunters. One's loading his gun again quickly, while the other keeps his muzzle directed at me.

"Release my son or I'll shoot, and be sure, I won't miss." St. John's dull, empty eyes are set on me above his musket. I see his face for the first time in my life, and 'tis all pinched together in the center with fish-like thick lips.

"If you fire a shot off, I'll still have time to send this bullet into his head." I show St. John the pistol held against William's temple.

"Let go of my son, and I will bring you set in, unharmed."

"What, so we can hang in good health?" I shout.

"Hang the harpers wherever found." He sneers.

The insulting dig enrages Strong John, and in one quick action, he unloads his musket and hits St. John's companion in the chest.

Síofra shrieks, "No, John!"

John draws his sword and yells, "Pog me thoin!" and runs at St. John, who shoots him in the center of his forehead. St. John immediately turns his horse to flee. Everyone but me takes their weapons out and releases a volley after him. One bullet hits St. John in the arm, but he keeps riding.

Síofra rushes to John, but we all know what a shot to the forehead does. His massive form's spread out in the leaves; his sword lays by his side. Fallen Goliath under a river of Síofra's tears.

She touches a scar over his eye and says through her pain, "He got this saving me." She sucks in her sniffles to continue, "I was just a girl when I tried to take my first horse. I snuck into a planter's stables and was almost home free when I heard a hammer click. Before I could turn around, something hit me as I heard a shot go out. Whatever hit me took the blunderbuss from the man and hit him hard over the head with it. I heard John's voice, *still hear it*, 'Síofra, are you hurt?' So full of worry. He put me on the horse and rode us away back to the woods. 'Twas not until we stopped and he turned that I saw he was holding his head. The blood was pouring down his left side. Never once complained or held it against me." She broke into tears again. "He loved me that much."

I hear some of the men tearing up too and decide not to embarrass them by looking at them.

"God be with him," I say, and they all echo the sacred prayer.

I bind William's hands behind his back and tie his waist to his saddle. After securing him, all seven of us lift John up over his saddle. Síofra insists she lead his horse home. We follow behind her, in somber procession, as the light leaves the sky.

Chapter 14

Although we wanted to mourn Strong John's loss, we're left with a hostage to deal with. Cahir takes Síofra and John's body home. The rest of the men come along with me. We blindfold William and take him back to the main cave. I tell the hostage to sit, and he tries awkwardly to get to the ground with his hands tied behind his back. He sits there, against the wall of the cave, slumped over, blind and gagged—truly a pathetic sight.

I turn to Ned. "Go find someone you trust to send a message to St. John. We want £100 for safe delivery of his son, or we shoot him by the end of the week."

The prisoner overhears me, and as soon as I remove his gag, he says, "He'll never pay that, you know."

"Quiet now or I'll be forced to plug you back up."

I walk out the cave to clear my head, but I feel guilty to leave the boy in such a painful position, no matter how angry I am at how the day turned out. I go in, untie his hands, and retie them in front of him loosely so the ropes don't chafe, and I remove his blindfold.

"Now don't be getting any grand ideas of escape. I have a man at this cave entrance at all times. If he sees so much as the tip of your shoe, he'll shoot."

I purposely avoid looking into his eyes, since I know what might befall him. I try to imagine him like some animal slated for slaughter. I walk back out and tell Kelly to take the first shift as guard. I want Bawn to sit with the prisoner and make sure he doesn't go into the other weapon rooms. I rest with my men at the fire, and we cook supper in silence in respect for Strong John.

Seeing there's some stew left, I bring a plate of it in to the hostage with a bowl of water. He takes the fork hungrily, tries to scoop up some on the plate, and brings it up to his mouth, but since his hands are tied, it ends up falling off the fork and spilling down his chest.

"I can't watch this. You're like a baby." I take the fork from his hands, scoop up a full fork, and go to stuff it into his mouth. He doesn't open at first. So I say, "Fine by me if you starve."

Then I put the fork and plate down to see him open his mouth wide like a wee bird. I shovel the food in quickly so I won't have to do the silly thing much longer. I bring a bowl up after for him to get a drink, but it ends up spilling out the side of his mouth and down his shirt.

"Thank you," he says softly.

"No thanks needed. I have to make sure you don't die before I hand you over."

"I tell you, he won't be paying your ransom."

"Well, we'll wait and see, won't we?" I turn to Bawn. "Can you take the night shift as well?"

"Sure thing, but what'll I do when he has to make water or the other?" Bawn's eyes flip up immaturely.

"You'll have to bring him outside, then."

"But I'll have to untie him so he can, you know, use his hands."

"Right, I see, so untie him and keep a gun at his head."

"I'll have to stand right there and watch him?"

"Jesus, Bawn! No, you can let him go shite all over the countryside, and we'll see if he comes back! Of course, you'll have to watch him! I don't know, sing a song or something to keep your mind away from it."

Bawn wrinkles his nose.

"Did ya see what I just had to do, feed him like a baby magpie? You think that was fun? Now do as I say and be happy about it. We'll all have a turn at it so it won't only be you."

He seems to feel better thinking everyone will have to do it and goes back to his spot across from the prisoner.

I walk back out and wish I could go home to Muirin. I decide taking hostages is a bad business. Last time we'll ever do this.

In the morning, Cahir and Síofra return. Síofra looks like she'd been crying all night and not slept a wink. She takes one look at Kelly leaning beside the entrance and charges into the cave. Cahir and I follow after her. The prisoner's sitting up against the wall with his head up to the ceiling and his eyes closed. When he sees Síofra coming, her wild Medusa hair hissing, he instinctively rolls into a fetal position.

She kicks him and screams, "He'd still be here if 'twas not for you!"

I pull her off him before she can do any damage, and she wriggles like a cat being caught. "Let me off, O'Hanlon, this is my fight!"

I try to whisper in her ear, "'Tis not the one you should seek vengeance on."

She laughs, sounding a bit cracked. "I'll seek vengeance on them both!"

Cahir looks her in the eyes. "Vixen, we'll punish St. John best by holding his son and making him pay."

She stops wriggling for a moment. "Can you promise me, then, that if St. John fails to pay, I get the pleasure of shooting this cat of a kind?"

I think about it for a moment. "That sounds fair."

The prisoner looks up. "You'll get your way; he'll never pay."

She screams and flies into another fit. "Don't you talk to me, Sasanach! You're not one of us! I'll send you back to Hell where you and your kind belong!"

She squirms out of my grip, pulls a hair off his head, and marches out of the cave.

Cahir whistles. "I wouldn't want to be him right now. That whipster's going to do all sorts of magic."

"You mean the fairies?" I ask, unsure what he's talking about. The prisoner looks concerned.

"Sure, that, and she's a bit of a witch. When we were little, shorter than a goat we were, she gave me this." He pulls out a little wooden charm that's roughly carved into a horse-like shape. "She gave this to me saying 'twould let me talk to the horses." He laughs. "I thought she was cracked, but 'twas true. As soon I went to the horses, 'twas like they understood me. Even the feistiest stallion bucking for everyone else cooled and let me ride it. I swear that girl's powerful."

Síofra's gone for a day, I imagined off conjuring or dancing with fairies. The next night, Hogan comes to me in the middle of his night watch. "The prisoner's shaking something fierce."

I go in to see him on the ground with his legs tucked up and arms brought close to his chest. His forehead's wet with sweat, and his teeth are chattering uncontrollably. I put my hand to his head and feel he's burning up.

"Hogan, go get my blankets outside and some cold water."

I feel a twang of guilt that I hadn't given him blankets to sleep under. I peer into his light green eyes for the first time and see the faraway look of someone close to death. Hogan comes back in with a pile of blankets he collected, and I put them under and over him. I keep wetting a cloth, holding it to his head and neck the way Ma would do, making sure he keeps taking sips of water. All night I do this, and by morning, he sleeps soundly with only a slight fever. Feeling I did all that I could, I go out to see Síofra at the fire.

"He'll soon be a load for four," she says with her eyes on the fire.

Cahir asks, "Síofra, have you had him blinked?"

She looks up, smiling.

"You're taking this out on the wrong person. St. John's the one you want," I say.

"Oh, I have plans for him too."

"The whole point of this plan was to teach St. John a lesson. The boy is just our means of doing so. Leave him alone, and go after the one who deserves it."

She stands up, throws her drink in the fire, and takes a whole bunch of sticks we kept for the fire and throws them on the ground. She studies the way in which they fell and then jumps on her horse. "Fine, then, who's coming with me?"

Everyone stands still, unsure.

"Cahir, get your arse on your horse, or I'll rip that charm off your neck!"

Cahir takes one look at me and leaps on his horse.

"What are you doing, Síofra? We have to wait to see if St. John gives in. We need to get the upper hand with him. Make him pay."

"Oh, I'll make him pay." She glares at the whole group. "You saw what I did to the boy, and anyone who doesn't have my back will be shaking along with William there."

Liddy, Kelly, Bawn, and Berragh all head for their horses like scolded children. She gives me a triumphant look and kicks her horse to lead her charge. I go to sit with Hogan in the cave as he watches over William's recovery.

"I heard every word that went on outside," Hogan says. "She's going to get herself killed in that blind rage."

About an hour later, Ned comes back.

"I sent my messenger out, and he returned with this letter from St. John."

I take the letter, crack the seal, and read out loud: "I'd no sooner pay the devil than give you a half penny. Rot in hell, Roman."

I'm silent at his complete disregard for his son's welfare.

William clears his weak throat. "I told you he would never pay."

"We have a few more days still." I know I'm reaching.

"He's probably got his bodyguards around him. That woman is going to walk right into his trap."

"You think he's laying a trap, then?" Hogan asks.

"Of course, he is. He cares more about besting you than he cares about what happens to me."

"Hogan, you stay here with William, and I'm going to try to warn them." I take off on Ghost and try to follow their trail.

I get all the way up to the base of Tandragee, where we waited for William three days before. Many shots ring out, and horses whinny. I speed up to the noise, hoping I'm not too late to help. Before I reach the clearing at the top of the hill the castle sits upon, the sound of many horses comes my way. I take my pistols out and hold Ghost steady so I can get two good shots off well. But 'tis Síofra and Cahir thundering toward me.

I shout, "Where's Liddy, Bawn, Kelly, and Berragh?"

"Coming right behind us! Get moving, Redmond! They're hot on our tail!" yells Cahir.

I see Bawn, Kelly, Berragh, and Liddy coming with a dragoon, following with his sword raised. I take my musket out, level it, and shoot him right in the hip, causing him to drop his sword and pull his horse to a stop.

Kelly gives a cheer and shouts, "Get moving, O'Hanlon! There's more!"

I turn Ghost and gallop after them all the way back to the cave. I watch as Síofra, with pistol still in hand, swings her leg over, and slides down her horse. She walks into the cave as I run after her. She slips under the rock quickly, and by the time I'm under, I hear Hogan fighting with her. She pushes him away and puts the pistol right against William's temple. She says through her teeth, "This is the gun I killed your father with." Then pushes him over and spits, "Now we're even!"

By the time I get back out, she has vaulted onto her pony and taken off.

Kelly rushes to get on his horse to go after her, but Cahir says, "Let her cool in the skin that she heated in."

I look at Cahir and ask, "What in the world happened?"

"I told you not to bother her." He sighs and sits on a log.

Liddy chimes in. "You should have seen her, Redmond! Flew out of here like a banshee and rode all the way up to the castle!"

"St. John was out riding with a few of his men, and she started chanting something eerie at the top of her lungs, galloping right toward him with her pistol blazing!" Kelly says, all excited.

Liddy continues, "St. John went straight for her with the men in tow. As soon as he was in range, he pulled the trigger, but his pistol malfunctioned—"

"'Twas no malfunction, boys," Cahir says.

"Well, whatever 'twas, his pistol wouldn't fire. She shot him straight in the same spot he shot John, the very spot!" Liddy finishes.

"How did she escape the dragoons in one piece?" I ask.

"Cahir stayed with her all the way up and took one of them down when they tried to shoot Síofra."

Cahir is silent.

"Once Síofra took down St. John, she just turned to go back, with three other men chasing her with a vengeance." Berragh gives a panting laugh. "'Twas like she was in a trance, paid no mind to them coming after her!"

"Liddy, Berragh, Kelly, and I had to hold them off as she and Cahir got away." Bawn leans back and smiles. "'Twas rich madness."

"She's cracked, for sure," Liddy says.

Cahir laughs. "I bet your boy, William, in there, needs a change of pants after she was through with him."

This makes us all laugh and gets rid of the anxiety this all caused. Liddy, laughing louder than all the rest, sounds like a mule braying as he throws his head back.

Berragh asks, thumbing the cleft of his chin, "What are we going to do with him now?"

"I can take him out in the woods if you want," Kelly offers.

"I can't believe this has gotten away from us like this. A terrible plan I had." I get up to go talk to William. "I need some time to think."

Hogan gives me a look of disbelief, and he goes back outside to hear the story himself. William tries to sit up but starts to cough thickly. I kneel down on the cold stone ground and realize he needs some warmth. "Come on, William, you can sleep by the fire tonight."

When the men see me come out with William, Cahir asks, "What's this?"

"Cool it, boys. He's got a bad cough, and until we figure out what we're going to do, letting him sleep by the fire is the Christian thing to do."

I throw the blankets on the ground near the fire, and William tries his best to lay them out with his tied hands, coughing the whole time. The pathetic display seems to soften the men's hearts, and they drop their edge against him for now.

"Sounds like a bit of the chin cough to me," Liddy says, covering his mouth with his shirt. We hear the sound of a horse rushing toward us, and we all stand up with our pistols out.

"Boys, put your pistols away. It's me, Síofra."

She comes and sits near William, which makes him shift away slightly.

"You only left but an hour ago?" I ask.

"You timing me now?" She laughs, much lighter than we'd seen her before. Her brown eyes are happy again and her smile's wide. "I've seen the most wonderful sign, is all."

"What kind of sign you see?" Kelly's eyebrows rise with interest.

"When I rode out to the clearing across the woods, a warm fairy breeze kissed me and stilled my horse. I knew a message was coming, and I waited for it. Suddenly the largest flock of wrens I'd ever seen came across the sky. They did three large circles around the clearing and then flew off in the sacred direction."

Cahir, who must have been used to her talking like this, asks, "What does it mean?"

"The wren is our sacred bird, and three is our magical number. I have balanced nature by taking a life after a life was taken. Nature was showing me that John's spirit is with truth now and awaiting rebirth."

We're all quiet around the fire, not wanting to anger her, but also not comfortable with how different this is from our faith.

She notices the reaction. "Well, some of you might know." She looks at Cahir. "Long ago, the druids were the sacred teachers of wisdom and magic in our ancient culture. The Celtic kings of Ireland used to rely on druids for every decision. They were highly learned people who were in touch directly with the gods and goddesses. When the Sasanaigh came"—she gives a glance to William—"they killed any of the druids that didn't adopt or convert to Christianity, forcing many to feign Christianity and go underground to pass our ancient religion down through their children." She looks at us proudly. "I am one of those children, and I won't stop fighting for our culture that is being washed away."

"You say this is the religion that's sacred to Ireland?" I ask.

"Sacred as the green grass, sacred as the rocky coast, and sacred as these woods that shelter us."

I nod. "Anything Irish I take to heart."

William speaks up. "My mother used to tell me stories of the druids. She'd always say 'Truth in heart, strength in arm, and honesty in speech.'"

Síofra's mouth falls agape. "How is it your mother knew anything about us? That's our sacred saying."

"My mother wasn't English, or Protestant. She came from the O'Sheil clan and told me the stories of her people so I wouldn't forget where I came from."

"What the hell's happening here?" Kelly laughs. "We've got the queen of the fairies telling us about some forgotten Irish religion, and now the Protestant tells us he's an O'Sheil!"

"If your mother is an Irish Catholic, why is she letting your father kick the Irish families off their own lands?"

"She tried to fight him. They fought all the time. He treated her terribly and ridiculed her beliefs. He grew more and more violent. Even locked her in a tower and kept me away from her." He's quiet for a moment and puts his thumb in the space in his front teeth. "She died when I was twelve, and I didn't learn until three years ago that she threw herself out the window." He finishes in a coughing fit.

It lasts for almost a minute, and Bawn passes him his bottle, saying, "Sounds like you need this more than me."

"Thank you very much," he says after he wets his throat.

"Well, I never thought to ask everyone their story. I guess we all have one. Hogan, what's yours?"

He takes a swig and starts, "I was a son of a blacksmith and was just a boy, maybe around nine or so. Well, my father followed the rebellion and helped them by fixing their horses and such. So he brought me along with him to assist him, but Cromwell's cavalry took us captive. My father stood up to one soldier who beat him unconscious. The same soldier grabbed me and went to go hang me from the oak tree." He pauses here and smiles. "All to a divine interference, the captain's horse threw a shoe, and the captain told the soldier to bring me over first to fix the shoe, and then he could hang me." He laughs. "So under that pressure I gave off some anxiety that the horse felt, and she wouldn't let me lift her leg. The captain got so frustrated at me that he got off to hold the animal, and seeing 'twas my only chance, I turned and clobbered him over the head with the hammer." He does the motion for us and sent us all into spits and laughs. "Then I jumped on the captain's horse so fast that all the soldiers just watched as I galloped away. And that's why they call me Galloping Hogan."

"What a grand story, Hogan. You swear it's the truth?" I ask.

"True as a druid." And we all laugh at his quick wit.

"Now, Kelly, I'm sure you got a good story. All the Irish rage in you had to come from somewhere."

"I'll pass, not in the storytelling mood." He drinks some more.

"Okay, I'll go, then," Berragh says. "I do have one interesting story my Ma always tells. When I was four, I begged and begged my Da to let me ride a young colt that he knew not to try me on. But as wee folk do, I wore him down until he gave in and put me on saddleless. So I grabbed the colt tight by wrapping my strong arms round the poor thing's neck. Sure thing, the animal bolted and headed right for the flooded Barrow River." He sits up and takes a drink. "I clung to the horse's mane like a tic on a dog's tail, and the beast plunged under the water. The animal surfaced and attempted to get back out, but the water swept us away nearly fifty yards down river. The colt emerged sputtering, found its footing, and dragged itself out with me still clinging on. My da said I was as blue as a bilberry and knocked out. I was put in my Ma's arms, and they thought me dead until I came to."

Cahir chimes in, "Berragh, don't you know the saying, 'He that is born to hang will never be drowned.'"

"I'll drink to that, then!" Berragh smiles and raises his glass.

"Liddy, what's your story?" Hogan asks.

"I hate to say it, but I had a pretty grand childhood."

"Ugh... go on now. You going to tell us you're really a Protestant, then?" Kelly jokes.

"No, wasn't that. Just lucky to come from a nice-sized tenant farm that my folks held on to. They were hard workers, though, never rested more than they had to. Right up and down with the sun, they were."

"So how'd they get such a scandalous outlaw for a son?"

"When Art and Redmond asked me to fight for our lands and to help the people the only way we could, I couldn't say no."

"Ah, we got here a regular altar boy!" Kelly slaps his leg.

"Speaking about altar boys," Ned begins, "you boys might be surprised to hear that I was on my way to the priesthood."

There's an uproar of hoots and whistles, and men leaning back and kicking their legs in the air laughing.

"Ah, go have your fun, everyone, have a good laugh on me now!" Ned's grinning.

As soon as Cahir can stop laughing, he asks, "So, tell us when you sold your soul, then?"

"Blazing funny you are there." He takes a deep breath and laughs. "Okay, okay. I came from a privileged Irish family and was fortunate enough to be sent for an education abroad in the great aspiration of my mam to become a priest. On a break from my studies and home from the continent, I heard a terrible moaning and crying coming from the cottage of a kind old widow who was always nice to me as a child. Well, I knocked on her door, and she tells me how the tax collector was on their way to collect taxes she didn't have. I waited for the man to come and said I'd talk to him, but the bailiff was set on taking her last cow in repayment. The bailiff and I had words and both drew pistols, and before I could think, I shot the man dead and took off for the hills."

"Well, the good Lord had another calling for you," I say.

Liddy asks, "Bawn, what about you?"

"Oh, I was a peddler for a rich merchant and made a pretty fair living but lacked the thrill of adventure. So I tricked O'Hanlon and made him take me on."

I say quickly, "No need to go down that road again."

Everyone laughs who knows the story.

"Cahir Dempsey, your turn," Síofra says.

"Oh, well, my story, hmmm… I think I forgot my story."

"I can remind you." Síofra grins playfully.

"No need for that now." He stares right in her eyes. "Melodious is the closed mouth." Síofra laughs as he says with a nervous look I've never seen before, "I feel like I'm in confession." He stretches his back. "Well then, instead of my life story, I'll tell you one of my most dangerous moments. I'd just stolen a prize horse. A real beauty she was. Six men were chasing me on horseback, and they were closing in on me, I tried to lose them in the woods. I climbed up to the Dempsey castle ruins and hoped they'd lost their way, but I saw them coming up, and there was no way back down. I rode the horse into the ruins and up the crumbling stairs. The men dismounted and charged up with their guns and swords. I only had one choice, and I kicked the sweet thing to go right out the empty window. The poor beast broke my fall and was gone instantly. I hurt my leg terribly in the fall, so I limped through gunfire toward the river. Once I reached the river, I floated to safety."

"Okay, O'Hanlon, let's hear yours," Hogan says.

"Well, you know, it's like all the other poor miserable natives' story. I won't bore you all, the story's been well-worn."

"You really have the gift of storytelling, Redmond," Cahir says, and we all laugh.

"Well, then, I'll finish up this storytelling session with a toast," I say as everyone with a bottle raises it. "May we all be alive at this time next year."

William looks surprised at this, and Cahir says, "To another year!"

Chapter 15

I stand on an island in the middle of the lake, holding a scian to a lamb's neck. The lamb's bleating, but I slice its neck. I watch as the blood runs down onto the ground, forms a red river that slithers its way to the water, turning the lake red. I'm entranced by the red lake, when someone comes from behind and stabs a knife in my back. I fall to the ground and feel my soul leave my body like a last breath. Hovering above me, I see Lucas take a sword and cleave my head off. He picks up my head and holds it in the air in triumph, then brings it down, impaling it on a stake.

My eyes flash open in hopes of escaping the nightmare. I wake up before everyone else and feel the wet mist of the early morning on my face and blanket. I notice with all the festivities the night before that even our hostage guard fell asleep. I see William lying there and decide 'tis time. I shake him awake, and he startles, seeing me over him. He gets up clumsily, his balance thrown off by his tied hands.

I put my arm straight out behind his shoulder and say, "Let's go for a walk in the woods, boy." He swallows hard, begins walking, and even the snapping of the branches under our feet doesn't wake anyone else up. Ghost, seeing me walk away, trots up behind me and nickers. I give him a pat on his shoulder and he keeps walking with us.

"Is that my horse over there?" William asks, seeing the sorrel tied up in the distance to a tree.

I stop. "Do I have your word if I let you go that you will tell no one about what happened here?"

"If you give me my life, I will take this secret to my grave."

I see truth in his green eyes. I bring up a blindfold to tie, and he says, "How will I get home if I'm blind?"

"I'll take you to the village and let you ride home from there."

I reach up to tie it, and he pushes it away slowly. "What if I didn't want to go back but wanted to join you?"

I laugh. "You're not serious, are you, now?"

"No, I'm serious. I want to do this for my mother and her people." He coughs a little, but it sounds like he's improving.

I stare at him for a moment and go against what every fiber was telling me about double agents and enemies that can sell you out, and say, "You can stay, William O'Sheil, but if I catch you selling secrets or trying to bring me in, I'll cut your heart out myself."

"I'll prove myself to you."

∞∞∞∞∞∞∞∞∞∞∞∞∞∞∞∞∞∞∞∞

The only way Kelly will let William in is if he passes his test. We meet at the bog, and instead of looking nervous, William looks suddenly alive. We wait until his cough's gone and begin things under the full moon. Everyone except William, skips along the bog stones carefully placed just for fast feet. William falls three times into the mud even before we get to the place where Kelly initiates all his recruits.

Kelly says, "Okay, then, get in this here wax sack."

William steps in quickly, trying not to seem at all afraid. Liddy starts stuffing the sack full of straw around him. William looks confused by this.

"It's to keep the mud from getting in," Liddy explains.

Kelly brings the sack up over his head. "Don't worry now, O'Sheil, you'll have space enough to breathe. I left a wee hole here for you."

Hogan ties a thick rope around the sack under where his arms are, and Berragh and Bawn heave the sack into the air. Liddy and Kelly move the sack into place in a marked space and start lowering him down slowly.

William cries out, "Yeeow!" when his chest starts going under. "How far down are you going?" He tries not to sound panicked.

"Until your feet rest on the plank we put down there."

A little more down. "Okay, I'm on it!"

Kelly gives the sign to tie it up, and we all go and sit on the large rocks near William. I light my pipe, share it, and say, "Tell me why you do this again?"

"This is how I get some of my information. I have my men lie in the bog here sometimes up to three hours next to this bridge to hear what the soldiers' movements are and what they're planning." He takes a drag. "Plus it's fun." Smoke blows out through an evil grin.

Art walks into the group. "Fancy seeing you here, Art, how long's it been? Two weeks or so?" Cahir asks.

Art gives him a look. "Missed you too, sweetheart." He grabs the pipe from Bawn and takes a puff. "Who's the poor slob in the sack?"

"Oh, just St. John's son." Kelly laughs.

"Very funny," Art scoffs. All of our reactions make him freeze. "That's really him?"

We all laugh. Cahir says, "See what you miss playing house?"

"Hey, there, now." I jump in. "Art's making sure Muirin's safe, no cracks about that, then."

I don't like the way everyone looks at each other.

Art asks, "So this is what you've been up to the last few days?" He takes a breath in. "Why didn't anyone think of coming and getting me? This is some serious shite."

"Well, after St. John was off the walk," I start, "the boy wanted to join us, so Kelly here wants to test him first."

"Join us?" His mouth curls in disgust. "St. John's brat?"

"Look, you missed a lot here, Art, so with respect, let us handle this," Cahir says.

Art blows a puff of smoke out the side of his mouth slowly. "Right, then."

We sit for two more hours until we bring William out. He's shaking from the cold but has a big smile on his face when we cheer as they peel away the bag.

"Wasn't that bad," he says as Síofra wraps a wool blanket around him.

Everyone gets in line to hop the stones, and Art stays behind to speak to me. "Redmond, you haven't been to see Muirin in a week."

I put my hand up to my head. "I know, Art, it's been a crazy week."

"I understand, but she's been in tears whenever I see her. She has nothing but you."

"And you," I retort.

"You and I both know she'd rather see you."

"Well, we're going to take William out for his first job, and then I'll go home tonight."

"You two coming?" Hogan calls back.

"Yeah, keep your knickers on!" Art yells.

∞∞∞∞∞∞∞∞∞∞∞∞∞∞∞∞∞∞∞∞∞

"Run!" Hogan screams.

"Follow me, boys!" I yell back, taking the lead.

We gallop our horses at top speed down the dirt road. As soon as I see the path I know so well in the woods, I take a quick right, and all my men follow. Not stopping to see if they followed, I keep riding in the darkness of the wood. Even on a full moon, the dense trees leave us blind. I have to trust the horse's better sight, and Ghost knows this pathway best.

"They found the path, Redmond!" Bawn yells from the back of the pack.

"Head for the east cave!" I turn hard again and cross a small creek, the splashing of the enemies' horses close behind us.

I grab the two heavy bags of coins we just acquired and jump off at a run. I slap Ghost's rear end to tell him to keep running, and the other men's horses follow his lead.

"The militia are still coming!" Berragh whispers loudly.

"Everyone in quick!" I say as I pull the large furze bush away from the entrance, getting pricked deep by the thick thorns. When the last man is in, I dive into the cramped space also. This cave's deep but narrow. Each of us has to slide down on our backsides into a pitch-dark tunnel. Having no candles or torches, 'tis a frightening experience. We reach the larger space at the bottom, and each of us pants and tries to slow our breathing to listen.

"I hear something at the entrance," Síofra whispers.

Sure enough, the thorn bush rustles, and a voice echoes down, "Lower him in, boys! Slowly, we don't know what's down there."

The man's flailing kicks scrape the sides of the tunnel on his way down.

"Lieutenant Lucas!" the hanging man says in a high-pitched, nervous voice. "This cave is very tight, and I can't see the nose in front of my face." We hear him coming down to the large cavern. "I think I can hear something down here!" he yells back.

"Well, light your damn torch and see what it is!" Lucas shouts down, echoing.

We hear the flint hit and see the tiny sparks fly, extinguishing before they hit the ground. Finally, a spark takes, and the torch ignites. The soldier, happy to have light, goes to pick up his pistol he laid down on the ground and inhales in shock to see my brown boot standing on top of it and eleven pistols leveled at his head. William jumps forward and covers his mouth so he can't scream while I take the torch from him.

"What do you see down there, private?" Lucas calls.

I hold my finger up to my lips and whisper, "Shhhh."

We all hear water and look around to see a large puddle appear at the officer's feet. Cahir points to it, and everyone grabs their mouths to keep from laughing.

I whisper in the officer's ear, "If you want to live, I want you to tug back on your rope and holler to your lieutenant that you want them to pull you back up. Say 'twas nothing but some lizards down here, and you'll live to see another day—"

"Private? Can you hear me? Respond or I'll send someone else in!"

"If, when we remove your gag, you try to be heroic and say anything other than what we said to say, then we'll shoot you full of holes. Sure, they'll probably kill us too, but then what does it matter if you're dead? And you might be thinking you're smarter than me and once you get up there safe and sound you'll tell them. But ah, not so clever now, I have very loyal and high-up men that will find out which soldier had that honor of catching O'Hanlon, and he will search you out. If you somehow disappear, then my men will find your old mam, or your sweet wife or your wee children, I can promise you that."

I give a quick nod to William, who pulls out the gag on the man.

"Officer? Respond!"

The man seems too scared to form words but then sputters, "I'm fine... Just some lizards down here... is all. Pull me up, boys!"

We watch him hoist the whole way up and wait to hear what he says.

"Where's your torch?"

"Dropped it when I hit the side of the cave."

"Well, let's keep looking. They have to be around here some-where."

We all sit in silence for a good thirty minutes, until we hear Ghost's friendly nicker down the cave.

"Let's go, boys! Ghost wouldn't come back unless they were long gone."

After the last person's pulled out, I say, "Back to the main cave." I glance to Art, who gives me a reproachful look, and I add, "See you tomorrow, boys, have to get back to Muirin. Glad to have you, O'Sheil!"

William gives a proud smile and jumps on his horse.

"Wait, this is your winnings from tonight. I want you to get to hand it out to whoever you think needs it."

He nods and leaves to follow Cahir out.

∞∞∞∞∞∞∞∞∞∞∞∞∞∞∞∞∞∞∞∞∞

William and I are sitting in the tavern snug after a rich job. "In the three years it's been since you joined, we've increased our take threefold."

Síofra comes to bring us our drinks. "With William telling you the goings on at the la-dee-dah parties, and with me working these taverns where the militia gather to talk, you've got every-thing covered."

"True, I'm sitting in a nice spot between you and William whispering in my ear." I give William a strong pat on the shoul-der.

"Well, I best be parting ways here before someone catches me with you."

"Good-night, then. I'll be along in a bit."

He leaves the tavern.

"You going back to Muirin tonight?" Síofra asks.

"Oh, yeah, I want to wrap all this business up here before I head home."

She gives me a reproachful look only women can make. "You can count your coin at home too, you know."

"Don't you be starting too, now. I get enough from Muirin."

She leaves to see to a man who enters, and she sits him at a table across from the snug. I have my back turned but hear the man order sup and drink. When Síofra brings him what he asks, he whispers something to her. Shortly after, she brings me a drink I hadn't ordered and whispers in my ear, "This well-dressed gentleman come in here just now has slipped me some money to ask you which road you're taking tonight."

I smile, enjoying the challenge, and reply, "Why, then, I'll take the dark and quiet road to Markethill."

I wait until the man leaves and say on my way out, "Didn't know I'd still have some fun tonight."

"Careful there, Redmond, he looks like a clever fellow," Síofra says.

I tuck my money in one of my hiding places in the woods and make my way to Markethill. When the road gets real dark, I expect him to pounce, and he does.

"Stand and deliver!" the now-masked man says.

Pretending to shake, I say, "Sir, I have nothing."

He laughs from the bottom of his thick belly. "Ah, but I just watched you count every bit of a small fortune, so hand it over!"

"Oh, you got me there, then. Alright, then, let me get it from my saddlebag." But I pull out my pistol quickly and say, "I won't hand it over without a good fight."

We fire at the same time, but since we're some distance away, both of us miss our mark. With no time to reload, we draw swords and charge each other. The sound of steel goes clashing like the titans through the woods. After some time of skilled fighting and no bloodshed, the man pants, "Okay, then, let's draw a truce!"

He backs his horse away and draws off his mask, revealing a sweaty, round face, and even in the darkness, can tell his eyes are a slate blue.

Intrigued now with this skilled fighter, I ask, "How about joining me for a nice gill of poteen?"

He watches me dismount, and I head over behind some rocks to pull out two gills of poteen. He smiles widely. "I have been known to be fond of a drop."

Chapter 16

The man sits behind a tree beside me with a great grunt and asks, "I must know the name of such a staunch adversary."

"'Tis Redmond O'Hanlon, my good sir."

"Redmond O'Hanlon!" He puts his face to the night sky, smiling. "The main purpose of my travel to Armagh was to meet the famed O'Hanlon, and here I tried to rob him." He laughs for a bit and takes a swig of poteen. "It feels like a torchlight procession going down my throat."

"Well, here I am, your dreams come true. So you must tell me yours now."

"Richard Power," he says, rolling up his sleeves, revealing a long scar on his forearm.

"Oh, that's not a name." I look him up and down. "No, you seem more like a Captain Power to me."

"Captain Power," he repeats. "Sure, I like that."

"Well, seeing I've never reached a truce before with sword, I'll have to ask you to join my crew."

He thinks for a little and takes a long drink. "As long as I'm in Armagh, I'll join you, but I was headed here to make a gentlemen's oath."

"Out with it, then." I take a drink.

"If I was to be captured or imprisoned, that you would do everything in your clever power to free me, and I would return the same oath to you."

"Sure thing to have more behind me, and no doubt I'll stand black for you."

We sit in the woods together that night, drinking and telling stories. I know Muirin will have my skin, but Captain was far too interesting to cut short.

Captain asks, "So where do you recline?"

"Oh, we sleep in the woods or in a nice warm cave."

"A cave?" His voice goes up. "Oh, no, it won't do. Follow me; we'll find a nice farmer to take us in."

We get on our horses and ride out through the commons. He picks a nice little cottage that still has smoke from their chimney. "Smoke means someone's still awake."

I stand behind Captain as he knocks on the small wooden door. A young man pulls the door open a crack and asks, "Who comes calling at this dark hour?"

"Only two weary travelers far from an inn."

He stares Captain and me up and down with the one eye in the crack of the door and opens it for us. "Céad míle fáilte. A weary stranger is always welcomed into our house."

We walk in and remove our muddy boots as a young, pretty woman comes and takes our coats to hang. The man says, "Come and rest yourself at our fire. Can we offer you a drink of milk?"

"No, sir, the fire will be more than fine," I reply.

But Captain says jovially, "Sure, some milk will be grand."

The woman goes and pours out the last of the jug into Captain's wooden bowl, filling it only halfway.

The man says, "It's all we have left, I'm afraid."

Captain bellows, "More than enough, my good man, more than enough."

The woman's eyes dart up to the loft and the man whispers, "We have three babes asleep in the loft, so we must keep our voices low." The woman sits on the floor beside him and leaves the chairs for us.

"You have a right cozy house here," Captain flatters, but it makes the young woman gush in tears.

"What did I say?" Captain opens his eyes wide.

"We're facing eviction first thing tomorrow."

"Can't you borrow from a good neighbor to help?" I ask.

"That's the thing, we're owing fifty pounds to pay off the mortgage, and he's threatened to evict anyone who helps us," she says.

The man quickly follows, "You see, our black-hearted landlord wants this property cleared so he can plant it for himself. 'Tis the only way the rack renter can get us off."

Captain speaks, "I might be able to assist you here. If I were to loan you the money, would you promise to pay it back?"

The man looks surprised. "If I had to work day and night and die trying, I would."

"I thank you greatly for offering the loan, good sir, but the landlord says we can't have borrowed a shilling," his wife says.

"Oh, don't worry your pretty head about that. I'll think of a good plan by morning," Captain says.

The young woman drops all the worry from her face and runs around happily, making two beds for us on the floor by the fire.

In the morning, with all the wee children tottering around, it makes me have a pang of sadness that Muirin and I hadn't had any of our own yet. Captain makes up a promissory note for the farmer to sign, takes fifty pounds from his purse on his belt, and puts it in the farmer's hand.

"Now here's the plan, listen well. 'Tis important to wait for the landlord to have the sheriff and all the bank's people in his presence when you give over this payment, or else he might take it and say you never paid. Make sure you get a *written* copy of payment for your proof, and when he asks if you borrowed it, you say a relative of yours gave you this money to hold for him, and seeing that you're in such need, have had to use it."

The farmer takes a deep breath for strength, and Captain and I get on our horses to leave. The young lady tears while holding her smallest baby. "You have no idea how much this kindness means to us and you can only have been sent from the good Lord."

Captain leads the way up on a hill overlooking the farm by the road down to cottage.

"Why are we stopping?" I ask.

"So we can see the landlord coming and watch how he fares."

Within twenty minutes, the pompous gent rides his sleek horse down to the cottage, and he tries to bully them of the property, but the farmer seems to stall him well. The bank's people come along, led by the sheriff, and we see the farmer hand over the money like Captain instructed. We hear the landlord curse all the way up to where we are, and it brings a smile to Captain's face. The bank's people and the sheriff depart, seeing that the mortgage is paid, and the landlord stays cursing and swatting his hat at the farmer. The farmer closes his door, and the landlord gets on his horse and speeds out in fury.

"Watch and learn, boy!" Captain rides to the curve of the road up ahead. The landlord stops his horse, and a masked gunman points his pistol at his head. Captain says, "Stand and deliver!"

The landlord says, "I have nothing on me."

Captain laughs. "I just saw the sheriff and the bank meet you out there at that farmer's house. Empty your pockets now, or I'll shoot and empty them for you!"

The man hesitantly hands over the fifty pounds, and Captain says, "Any other valuables?"

The man says, "No, nothing else."

Captain packs his sack and says quickly, "Oh, do you happen to have the time?"

The man instinctively reaches for his watch but freezes halfway, realizing the trap.

"Hand it over now! The fob too!"

He reaches in a secret pocket and begrudgingly pulls his gold articles out. Captain snatches them up and warns, "If you don't change your ways and treat your tenants, better I'll follow you and take everything you ever get your hands on. Now ride off and don't look back."

The landlord kicks his horse and runs. Captain trots back to me with an impish grin and says, "Enjoy the show, now?"

"Quite a plan." I smile. This is going to be interesting.

I take Captain back to my men by the main cave, and some have already heard of his accomplishments elsewhere. I tell them all the story of the farmer, and Captain stands up. "Come, Redmond, I almost forgot the ending to the story!"

We ride back to the farmer's cottage, and the couple runs out with the children in tow and welcomes us like royalty.

"Won't you please come in and have some bread I've baked?" the woman asks.

Captain replies, "Thank you, dear, but I have but a moment and came to look in on you."

The farmer speaks, "Your bless'd plan worked and we kept the farm!"

"And to make the story even sweeter, as soon as the landlord left, a masked highwayman robbed him!" His wife nearly shakes with happiness.

"Well, along those lines—" He pauses and takes out their promissory note, and with a dramatic flair rips the note in little pieces and throws them up in the air to fall around the couple like thick snow. They smile with the joy of children on Christmas, and Captain tips his hat and says with a tight smile, "Captain Power took care of you."

We ride off to the tavern to celebrate.

Chapter 17

We walk in to see the whole gang already partaking in spirits. The leaders, with most of their recruits, fill the large room. Even Art has showed. They all cheer, seeing us come in, and Captain seems to gain admiration very quickly wherever he goes. He puts his hands up to quiet everyone, and he picks up a glass on the bar, saying, "I'm sure dry for thirsty!" and yells out to Sean, "Give everyone a round and steaks for every fellow!"

They all cheer even louder, and he toasts with his glass in the air, "'Tis better to spend money like there's no tomorrow, than to spend tonight like there's no money!"

The walls are shaking with the volume of their thanks. The mood in the tavern's joyous, and we all drink up and finish our sups. I stand up, wait until the room quiets down somewhat, and say, "Thank you to Captain for his generosity!"

"Oh, I never said I was paying!" he pretends, and everyone laughs.

"Well, then, I don't thank Captain, I thank myself!"

"Toast!" Liddy yells.

I clear my throat, giving me time to come up with a proper one. "'God made the Italians for their beauty. The French for fine food. The Swedes for intelligence. The Jews for religion. And on and on until he looked at what he had created and said, 'This is all very fine, but no one is having fun. I guess I'll have to make me an Irishman!'"

They erupt with laughter, and I sit. Cahir stands up, swaying slightly with drink. "Well, then, I'll give a toast too!" He holds up his glass and slurs, "'I have known many, and liked not a few'"—he turns to look at Síofra across the room—"'but loved only one, and this toast is to you.'" Everyone's quiet in the awkward moment as he raises his glass to her.

Kelly yells out, "Just kiss her and get it done with, Dempsey!" and the room rocks again with laughter.

Cahir smiles, taking the jest in stride, and points to the fiddler. "Play my song, and I'll bless everyone with a little song and dance!"

The happy music starts, and he yells to the center of the room, "Clear the floor, make room!"

The men push the tables to the side and get up on them, clapping. 'Tis an old favorite of the rebels, "Follow me up to Carlow." He stands in the middle, still as an oak until he springs to life at the first word:

"Lift MacCahir Og your face
Brooding o'er the old disgrace
That black FitzWilliam stormed your place,
Drove you to the Fern
Grey said victory was sure
Soon the firebrand he'd secure;
Until he met at Glenmalure

With Feach MacHugh O'Byrne."

At the chorus, the whole room joins in. Cahir stops singing, runs over to grab Síofra, and the two of them spin around the floor together.

"Curse and swear Lord Kildare,
Feach will do what Feach will dare
Now FitzWilliam, have a care
Fallen is your star, low.
Up with halberd out with sword
On we'll go for by the Lord
Feach MacHugh has given the word,
Follow me up to Carlow."

Cahir handles his feet well, and Síofra seems to be floating on air. She's beaming as they dance, and I wonder why I never noticed before that they were so obviously sweet on each other. The chorus stops, and he lets go of Síofra to sing as she continues to jig around him, kicking high and springing up unnatural-like.

"See the swords of Glen Imayle,
Flashing o'er the English pale
See all the children of the Gael,
Beneath O'Byrne's banners
Rooster of the fighting stock,
Would you let a Saxon cock
Crow out upon an Irish rock,
Fly up and teach him manners."

Again the chorus comes in, and the boys are now jumping from table to table all singing at the tops of their lungs. The excitement's so thick in the room it makes my eyes tear—not wanting this great moment to end.

"From Tassagart to Clonmore,
There flows a stream of Saxon gore

Oh, great is Rory Oge O'More,
At sending loons to Hades.
White is sick and Lane is fled,
Now for black FitzWilliam's head
We'll send it over, dripping red,
To Liza and her ladies."

Yips peal out, and the boys jump into the circle for dancing the last chorus. 'Tis a sea of bobbing heads, all shouting and pushing each other off them for room to dance, all the while smiling, though. All hold the last note for as long as they can, and when, done cheer so loudly I have to hold my ears to keep them from ringing. Cahir's up on the table, and he jumps onto the boys in the circle, who catch him and spin him high in the air. I look to Síofra, who is glowing from Cahir's performance.

Suddenly, a man I'm unfamiliar with reaches over, grabs Síofra, and holds her face against his in a rough kiss. Cahir seeing this from above, jumps from the boys' hands, and vaults across the bar onto the man, pulling him down to the floor without harming Síofra. He gets up on top of the man quickly and gives him a puck of his fist hard on the side of his head, causing the man's head to whip and knocks his two eyes into one. Cahir gets up and spits on his shirt. "You're out of the gang. Get out of here fast before I lose my temper!"

The man gets up, unsteady, and makes his way out the door quickly. Síofra's still glowing. Cahir turns to check on Síofra but takes a step and falls on the ground.

William says, "Fell over his shadow, he did!" and everyone laughs as Liddy and William carry him to a room with Síofra tending to him.

Art and Kelly head to my table and sit. Art says, "I think that's Cahir's first infraction."

"Oh, shut your gob, Art," Kelly says.

"'Tis a good man's case, though." Captain hits me on the back.

"No, Art's right, 'tis one of our rules. This is the first warning. I'll give it to him when he's feeling grand in the morning." They laugh.

"I'm going to get another drink." Captain pulls his chair out.

Kelly says, getting up to go with him, "Watch it, Captain, Art's counting drinks!"

Art moves over to Captain's seat, and I know what's coming. "So, you went right home, huh?"

"Art, you have no call in telling me when I should go home."

A chair pulls out on the other side of me, and I see 'tis Alister in plain clothes.

"You have just saved your distance, Alister!"

"For what?" he asks.

"Oh, nothing, came at the right moment, is all."

Art takes the hint and carries his pint over to the bar.

"How about a steak, you greedy-gut?" I call Sean over.

"Just a pint, Sean."

Sean nods, and I ask, "So what's the hard word, then?"

Captain comes back and sits to listen. I nod to Alister and say, "Captain's one of us now."

He gives a nod to Captain. "Sorry to dampen your celebrating, but there's a lot going round in the garrison." He sits back as Sean brings back a pint. "A proclamation's gone out, Redmond, that if the local people don't give you up within twenty-eight days, then four men will be shipped to the plantations in America."

"They can't be serious, Alister, can they really do that?" I ask.

"Can't tell if they're serious or not, but they're making the threat tomorrow. Picking the four men at random and taking them in to make the locals talk."

I can't say anything.

"Hate to tell you at the same time, they've raised your bounty to £100 and £50 for each of your men."

Captain laughs. "I could retire on the fortune this room would bring in!"

Alister gives me an unsure look at my new friend's black humor.

"The last thing is they're going to start felling trees in glen woods, trying to find your hide-outs."

"Well, many thanks to you, can't say my night's not ruined, but thanks all the same. Sean's got something for you." He nods and goes over to the bar.

Captain asks, "You think the locals will trade you in?"

I blow out some hot air. "Can't be sure, but they've said to me before they'd rather live in extreme poverty with dignity than to inform."

"Let's hope that's true." He takes another swig.

"The key to keeping your own from betraying you is to imagine your men like a pack of wolves. Keep feeding them the best cuts of steak, even if you get left with scraps. Just make sure they don't want for anything, and they'll never bite the hand that feeds them."

Captain pushes back stiffly in his chair. "Never forget, though, that a *caged* wolf will pass up a steak for the want of freedom. A pardon is a mighty tempting thing."

"Not to my men." I take a drink, but the worry fills my head.

By the time I reach home, the house is dark. I open the door quietly, take my shoes and outer clothes off, and crawl into bed.

Muirin wakes up, though, and turns over. "Oh, you're finally showing up, then?"

"Sorry, we had an outlaw come from far away to join us, and tonight we celebrated."

"I don't even understand why you got married, if all you want to do is run around the woods with these vagabonds."

She turns back over to face the wall.

I sit there in the dark thinking about how I'll wake up before she does and slip out the door again.

I'm on the island again, and this time there's no lamb but a large fish in the lake that flops out on the dirt and is running out of air. I move to put the fish back in the lake, but I hear a growl behind me. 'Tis a large grey wolf baring his teeth at me. I pick up the dying fish and throw it to the wolf, but the wolf has no interest and pounces in the air at me.

The nightmare wakes me up, and I decide there's no better time to disappear than now. The purple light of early dawn is coming through the window, and the morning chill is in the air. I turn to look at Muirin's beautiful face as she's sleeping. She has her pillow scrunched up in a tight ball, and her brown hair spills off the pillow onto the bed around her. I feel sick at what I've done to her, but I can't make myself stay home when there's so much to do. I throw on my clothes and boots and open the door inch by inch.

Twenty-eight days come and go, and the good people of our village keep their mouths tight, even at the risk of the four men awaiting deportation. Frustrated by their loyalty to me, Lucas realizes the threat doesn't work and releases the men back to their families. A month later they try a new tactic: if the villagers won't point out outlaws, then make the outlaws turn themselves in. A proclamation's made that any blood relative or wife can be taken and brought to the gaol and released only when the outlaw turns himself in. As soon as Alister informs me, I head straight to our house and get Art to bring Ma and Da to form a plan. Muirin's giving me the cold shoulder, but as soon as she hears about the proclamation, she speaks to me. "We have to leave Armagh?"

Art replies, "They'll be coming for you all first. Best be leaving this very day."

Muirin glares at me. "Well, you're coming too, right, Redmond?"

I pause for a moment, and she breaks down in tears, throwing herself on the bed.

Right away, Ma tries to pacify the situation by going over to her. "We won't go far, sweetheart, maybe a day's travel or so. Redmond can come whenever he pleases."

"He already comes whenever he pleases." She keeps sobbing.

Art gives me a reproachful look and goes to sit at her foot, while Da shrugs.

"I have to stay here, Muirin. If I go there, the proclamation has gone out to all counties. You all are at risk wherever I go with you."

Da chimes in gruffly, "This is a fight he must finish, dear."

She sits up and wipes her tears. "I'll only go if Art can go with us."

Art looks a little too satisfied with that comment, and I reply, "Of course, he'll be the one who is taking you to Donegal."

"No, I mean I want him to live with us. I'll feel safer with him around."

"He's an outlaw too, Muirin, the same danger lies there!"

But Muirin's far too clever. "He's not my husband or your blood relative. He's much less known than you, and you can't think I'll go a day away without him. He's the only person who looks in on me."

This is a dig at me, and I know she's only doing this to hurt me. I look at Art and ask, "Would you want to go with them?"

He sees Muirin's pleading eyes and turns back. "If Muirin will only go if I go, then of course I'll go for her safety."

She throws her arms around his neck, and I feel like walking out. Ma walks over, trying to assuage the situation. "You can come visit us whenever you like Redmond. We'll get along fine."

I busy myself with packing up both cottages in the two carts they're taking with them. Everything that doesn't fit, we leave behind. I kiss Ma and Da good-bye, and Muirin gives me a weak hug. I nod to Art in thanks and watch the two carts bob and buck up the hill. I take one last look at the cottage that had once been so happy and has now turned into some sort of cage to me. Now 'tis empty and free for some happy family to fill.

Chapter 18

The next night, an old outlaw friend of Captain's invites him to a rich dinner party. He asks me, William, Ned, and Cahir to come along since we all speak English. He has a big stone manor the size of Muirin's father's on an old Irish estate on the edge of north Armagh.

Cahir whistles at the grand house. "He stole enough to buy this?" Then he looks at me with his dark eyebrows raised. "Maybe we ought to reconsider keeping all our takings for ourselves."

Captain replies, "Well, he's about retired now, I think. He was a highwayman before most of you were even a glimmer in your father's eye."

The door opens, and a rosy-cheeked old fellow grabs Captain Power with both arms in a long embrace. "Good to see you again, my boy!"

"Pleasures all mine, Harry. Thanks for having us. These here are my business partners, Redmond, William, Ned, and Cahir."

The man's eyes sparkle while he looks us over. "It's like I'm seeing a legend come to life."

He welcomes us into his dining room, and already at the table sits an older man and woman.

"Let me introduce you all to Patrick and Kate Mulligan. This here is the famed Richard Power and his men."

Captain shakes and kisses hands. "So nice to hear such an old Irish name."

We all sit, and the food and drink keep coming. Every once in a while, I notice Harry will get up and pace in front of his large window. I wonder if he's always this anxious, or if he has some sort of troubles. I look to Captain, and by the way he's shoveling his face, I guess 'tis some strange quirk of Harry's. Toward the end of dinner, Patrick Mulligan, who's been pretty quiet the whole dinner, says to us in Gaelic, "Beware, fellow countrymen, he's pacing at that window because he's watching for troops to come. Once they arrive, he has to give a signal, and you'll all be trapped."

We're all silent, but Captain has the wherewithal to say, "Thank you for that charity," in a happy unsuspecting tone.

Harry turns quickly with a fake smile. "Oh, come now, don't all start speaking Gaelic when you know I can't understand a word of it."

Captain laughs, and we pretend to also. Captain picks up his glass and stands. "I'd like to make a toast in thanks to our generous host, one of the best and most trusted friends I ever had." He holds up his glass, and all of us do as well. "Better fifty enemies outside the house than one within."

Harry hesitates a moment, swallows hard, and nervously glances out the window, and replies, "My turn to toast." He stands and starts, "To one of my oldest friends. 'May you be poor in misfortune, rich in blessings, slow to make enemies, and quick to make friends. And may you know nothing but happiness from this day forward.'"

Instead of drinking from his glass, Captain throws his drink right in Harry's face. Once the man wipes the stinging alcohol from his eyes, he sees Captain with his pistol pointed at his face. The Mulligans run from the room.

Harry speaks with great effort, "'Tis better to be a coward for a minute than dead for the rest of your life."

Captain replies, "Well, now you're both."

He shoots him right between the eyes. Harry falls back to the floor, and Captain stands over him and curses, "May the cat eat you and the devil eat the cat."

He sees a large red-jeweled golden cross on top of his velvet coat. "I always wanted this," he says as he rips it off in one pull. Captain goes to the window to see if the troops are there yet. "All looks clear, boys. Let's go before the redcoats arrive."

∞∞∞∞∞∞∞∞∞∞∞∞∞∞∞∞∞∞∞∞

Days later, I walk into the tavern, and Sean immediately goes under the counter for something. "This came here for you, I think. It has my name on it, but it's from Donegal."

"Thank you, Sean."

I open up the letter and have to sit by the window to read.

> *Redmond,*
> *We got here just fine, and Donegal is a bless'd place. Every bit as pretty as Tandragee but with far more land to go around. I've tried my hand at being a merchant and doing quite well, if I do say so myself. I'm not only writing to tell you of our settling in but to give you some troubling news. Muirin seems to have come down with a blast. She's one day rosy-cheeked and smiling and now is down with a nasty fever and cough. Your Ma and Art don't leave her bedside, but she's been asking for you*

whenever she wakes. I think you should come, son, the doctor says it's looking grim. She might never comb a grey hair.

Godspeed,
Da

I stand up to pay some to Sean and leave for the road, when the door opens and Alister enters.

"Redmond, they've got one of your men down at Downpatrick."

"What, which man?"

"Your man Dempsey. They brought his mother in last night, and since she was ill to start, he turned himself in this very morning."

I put my hand up to my head. "What terrible timing."

"Rumors have been swirling that they're going to try to get him to talk in exchange for a pardon."

"Cahir would never talk."

"I wouldn't be too sure, I'd heard he was already meeting with Lucas and turning crown's evidence."

I sit to think. "I was going to leave to go to see my sick wife in Donegal."

"Not a good idea. If Cahir's talking, you better go to the woods and sit tight. Plus Lucas has brought in more troops from Ulster. They're all over the main roads, searching for Tories."

I take out what I have left in my pocket and go to hand it to Alister, who grabs it up quickly. "Redmond, you better go disappear somewhere fast." He walks out.

I turn to Sean, who heard the whole thing and becomes pale.

I ask, "Might you have a piece of paper somewhere so I can write to Muirin why I can't come."

Sean gives me a pained look. "Sure thing, and I'll even post it for you too."

After the letter's written, I head back to the main cave to tell the men.

"We already knew he went in for his mother, but do you really think he'd turn evidence on us all?" Bawn asks.

"He'll lead them right to this spot," Kelly says, "and we'll all be swinging by the morrow."

Síofra chides, "Cahir would never turn on us, you fools. He'd go down by himself if he had to. He had to free his sick ma. Stop speaking ill of him now."

Everyone's quiet after that, poking sticks in the fire and holding their pistols in the other hand.

Suddenly there's noise of a horse coming. Everyone tenses and watches. I give the owl hoot to hear one right back. "Relax, it's one of us."

Cahir appears through the bushes. "Why's everyone so quiet?"

Síofra goes running to him and jumps into his arms.

"Dempsey's back!" Liddy yells.

He puts her back down after the embrace, and we all notice his blooded lip and black eye.

Kelly whistles. "They sure did a number on you."

William stands rigid, though, and says through his teeth, "You're all fools. Don't any of you realize that the very fact that Dempsey's out and not staked on a spike is because he's turned evidence?"

"Glad to see you too, William," Cahir says with a smile as he sits by the fire.

"Is that true, Cahir? Did you turn evidence?" I demand.

"Sure 'tis true."

William moves to go at him, but Liddy and Kelly hold him back.

Cahir laughs, though. "Wait, now, let me explain."

William, keeps fighting to be freed to charge him.

"Will you control your man, Redmond?"

"William, sit down. We've got to hear him out."

Cahir begins, "I turned evidence, sure, but all against my enemies: outlaws and shady characters around the county. This way I got to get out *and* put away our competition. Didn't betray any of my confidences, which is why Lucas gave me these pucks."

I smile, relieved at his loyalty and good wit. "How many did you impeach?"

"Seven of the worst, but I've heard they all got word anyway and blew out."

William relaxes and sits again, but Cahir glares at him. "Where's my apology?"

William smiles, bends over, and drops his pants. "Right here." Pointing to his left cheek.

Everyone laughs, and all is right again. I avoid the tavern for a few days, afraid of a response to my letter. But Art comes walking into our camp, with a stone scowl upon his face.

"Art, how's Muirin?" I ask.

He flies into a rage and shouts, "Like you really care! She's been tortured with fever the last two weeks, crying your name, asking when you'll come, and you just sit here with your boys like a child dodging chores!"

Cahir and Kelly get up to keep him back from me, but I wave them away.

I try, "Art, I got the letter last week, and then Cahir went to the gaol, and Alister warned me that the troops were all over the main roads and that I better stay here."

"How's it that I got here, then, huh?" he yells. "I didn't see one redcoat the whole way!"

I'm quiet with guilt and say, "Can you just tell me how's she's faring?"

"She's dead, Redmond! Died two days ago!" He turns to walk away but drops something in his wake. "Here's her last letter to you. I'm going back to bury her."

He disappears through the brush.

William and Berragh are sitting with me at the fire and both get up to leave me to read the letter. Seeing her elegant penmanship makes my eyes tear, and it takes quite a bit to even begin to read. I know that whatever is written on the page would make my heart ache for the rest of my life.

> *My Dearest Redmond,*
> *'Remembered Joy*
> *Don't grieve for me, for now I'm free!*
> *I follow the plan God laid for me.*
> *I saw His face, I heard His call,*
> *I took His hand and left it all...*
> *I could not stay another day,*
> *To love, to laugh, to work or play;*
> *Tasks left undone must stay that way.*
> *And if my parting has left a void,*
> *Then fill it with remembered joy.*
> *A friendship shared, a laugh, a kiss...*
> *Ah yes, these things I, too, shall miss.*
> *My life's been full, I've savoured much:*
> *Good times, good friends, a loved-one's touch.*
> *Perhaps my time seemed all too brief—*
> *Don't shorten yours with undue grief.*
> *Be not burdened with tears of sorrow,*
> *Enjoy the sunshine of the morrow.'*
>
> *No matter how sad I seemed at the end, I would spend a hundred sad days for the happy days of the beginning. You were the song in my life, and I will love you always.*
>
> *Until we meet again in a better place,*
> *Your Muirin*

William pats me on the back and says quietly, "The earth has no sorrows that heaven cannot heal."

I tuck the letter into my coat pocket and go off alone in the woods.

Chapter 19

Berragh and I are up all night waiting for a merchant carriage due in off the ferry. After taking the money and goods and hiding them at various locations in the woods, we decide to catch a nap before heading back to the main cave to report. Exhausted, we lie down in bushes to sleep. I'm so tired that the first time something crawls across my face, I barely even wake up, but the second time the thing comes back, I grab it by the tail and see 'tis a lizard. As I lower the tiny thing into the grass, I look up to see a tusked wild boar staring right at me. As I move, the thing charges, and I grab at Berragh, waking him, and we run off toward the road. The thing's catching up to me something quick, so I go back through the other way, heading for a large tree that's near where we were resting before. I jump for the lower limb right as the thing reaches me, and swing my legs around the branch to pull myself up. The beast stays on the ground, rubbing its tusks back and forth on the trunk. I decide to see where Berragh has gone and climb to the top of the tree. I see him swimming across the violent river. He reaches the opposite bank and stands up, searching for me.

I scream from the treetop, "The beast's still under me!"

Berragh, finding me in the tree, smiles and puts his wet arms up and screams triumphantly, "He who is meant to hang can never drown!"

As I'm laughing, something catches my eye about halfway up the very same road we would be returning on. It's a large militia ambush. If the boar hadn't run me up the tree to see that, I would've been caught for sure.

I whistle to Berragh and motion in the direction and call out, "Ambush!"

He calls back, not too loud, "Main cave!" and points in the direction of the other road. I nod and watch him whistle for his horse to cross the river and leave. As soon as I see the boar leave, I crawl back down, and the whole way home I think about all the people who knew I was taking that road home today.

I need some time to think about the ambush, so I head to the tavern. Sitting alone in the snug, I go over and over what I said to which person. I jump to my pistol under my coat when someone lays a hand on my shoulder.

Alister throws his hands back. "Don't shoot!"

I relax. "Sorry, I'm a little jumpy."

"Perfectly understandable for a man with £100 on his head."

"Someone set me up for an ambush yesterday, and I'm trying to figure out who 'twas." I know 'tis safe to talk to him about it, since I haven't talked to him in a week.

"I'll be on the lookout for a spy for you. I'll watch everyone coming and going from Lucas's office. Follow him out when I can to see where he goes."

"You're a true friend, Alister, many thanks for that."

"Well, I have some more news having to do with the good Archbishop Plunkett."

"Oh, is he saying more sermons against me, telling the locals to turn against the Tories?"

"No, he's been arrested, accused of conspiring for the Catholics abroad."

"They're starting a holy war here, if they don't release him."

"Problem is they keep searching for those to testify against him, but they can't get a soul to."

"Rightly so, I hope he's freed in a week. But what's this have to do with me, then?"

He takes a deep breath. "Word is that if you were to offer up your testimony against him, you and all your men would be *unconditionally* pardoned for your crimes."

I push back in my chair from the shock. "You've got to be kidding me? They're that desperate! A full pardon for me and my men!" I whistle long.

"It's something you might want to think about. Redmond, the noose is getting tight for you now. This may be your only chance at a long life."

"Oh, it might be nice to think about, but no sooner would I curse in church than I would perjure an innocent man. Nope, not on my soul."

"Well, I knew you'd probably say that, but I thought I should tell you." He gets up to go, and I push him a pouch I had in my pocket.

"Will they let him go if no one testifies?"

"No, I heard they'll take him to the tower."

"May the Lord be with him, then, and many thanks for your loyalty."

"I'll be on the lookout for you." He gives me a strong nod.

"I know you will, Alister. God bless you."

Chapter 20

Captain arranges for us to have a whole house and three jugs of poteen to ourselves, since a nephew of his is away. We thought it best that we take turns in the house since 'tis good to have someone at the main cave at all times. If anyone gets close, they'll be able to get our weapons to safety. So Berragh, Kelly, Liddy, Hogan, Ned, and a new young recruit who has taken a liking to William, all volunteer to stay at camp.

"We'll switch camps at nine. See you all along the path later," I say.

Kelly shouts, "Leave some poteen for us, would you!"

Cahir says, "Let's see if I'm in a charitable mood!"

A stick comes flying toward us on our way out the path. The house is close, maybe a half mile from the main camp. On the way, Art comes up right next to me, and I can hardly make out his face.

"I can't see a stim in this darkness," Art says as he knocks his boot's toe on a rock and nearly falls. I laugh, and I'm glad to have broken the silence between us since Muirin's passed. "Listen, Redmond, I'm sorry to have talked to you that way—"

"No need to apologize. You were right. I should've gone and will think about it for some time."

"I should've known you would've gone if you could've, and I'm sorry for taking it all out on you. 'Twas just so terrible having her ask for you 'til—"

"So we're good now, then?" *Will he just stop talking about her!*

"Always have been." He puts his arm behind my back for the rest of the way there.

There's a small clearing with very little farmland; just a space cleared for the house, and the woods surround it. It has a small bedroom and a large keeping room with a huge stone hearth. We start a fire, and the room heats up nicely. We all get our own seat, and Captain goes right to getting a jug open and hands mugs out. Bawn grabs up Cahir's flute and attempts to screech out an unrecognizable tune that burns our ears.

"Aw, that's the tune the old cow died of." Cahir snatches back his flute to all of our relief and begins to play some happy music as we pass the pipe around, listening to Captain tell story after story.

Art interrupts, "Did anyone hear that?"

"Not with Cahir tootin' away," William says.

Cahir stops, and we freeze to listen. We all pull out our rich gold watches—quite a humorous sight—and I say, "Too early for the switch. It's only 8:30."

"I bet they've crawled in early." Cahir picks back up his song.

"Keep a calm sough, boys," I say, stopping Cahir again. "I definitely heard voices near the front door."

The front door is off a long hallway leading to the bedroom first and then out into the keeping room. As we all have our ears perked, we jump at the violent sound of the door being kicked in.

"Quick, the candles!" I say, grabbing for my pistols. "Art, shovel ash on the fire!"

As I make my way to the doorframe they're about to come through, Cahir opens a window and tells Síofra to go get help. She drops out the sill. Art turns a table over, and he takes cover behind it with Captain, William, and Bawn. Cahir's busy at the window covering Síofra's escape in case we're surrounded.

They kick in the bedroom door and one of the intruders whispers, "Layout?"

Dempsey now is on the other side of the doorframe, and when we hear them coming, I shoot both pistols and reload as Cahir shoots both of his. Whenever we hear movement, we send another volley down, but we have to be careful since we've a small supply of ammunition. From the sharp cries, we figure we've wounded at least five men and have managed to slow them down a bit.

They yell, "Charge!" and ten at once rush down the hall together, and Cahir and I can only get two shots off.

As soon as the mass comes near, Cahir ducks behind the door and slams it with all his might while they're running in the darkness. Cahir manages to catch someone's hand in the process, causing that person to scream in great agony. Cahir opens the door slightly for the miserable fellow to remove his crushed hand and then slams it again. As we brace the door, William and Art move a tall dresser in front. After 'tis in place, they all get behind the large oak table as I scatter the chairs around for the intruders to trip over in the dark.

The soldier keeps shooting at the door, and splinters of wood come flinging through the air.

Cahir turns to me. "If Síofra doesn't fly there, we're fish in a barrel once they're through."

"Once they're through, we keep firing one at a time so we can reload. If you run out of ammunition, then throw anything you can."

There's a gaping hole blown in the door that a man tries to dive through. I send a shot out and hear it hit him somewhere. Seeing the hole's a bad idea, someone cries, "Push!"

With a loud rumbling, the dresser moves halfway, and Cahir shoots out through the crack. A blast from a musket comes toward us and hits the leg of the table, busting it to pieces. Bawn fires a shot off, followed by Captain, and then another huge blast from them that shakes the table. The room flashes like a terrible thunderstorm. Each time a shot rings out, we can see where a soldier is, and we shoot. It makes the soldiers shoot less, since we all fire right after the musket shot, making it a dangerous task. Glass, splinters, and blood flies everywhere. The bodies on the floor are piling up, but they keep coming down the hall. Must be a whole patrol out there. This isn't just some random Tory hunting.

Luckily, as I'm reloading my last round, we hear someone cry, "Retreat!"

I turn to check if anyone's hurt and see William's holding his arm. He grits his teeth and says, "I think it missed the bone, though."

"Give me your ammunition, then. You stay behind the table."

I turn to my other side to see Dempsey pulling out a large splinter from his head. "Ugh! Mother of all splinters!"

"This beautiful, gorgeous table," Bawn says as he kisses it. "I'm keeping her."

Captain has crouched to the window that's shot open. "Shhhh! It's not over yet. Boys, be at the ready!"

Glass bottles hit the roof, and we hear the horrible whoosh of fire catching.

William gasps. "They're smoking us out!"

Cahir quickly crawls to the back window and pokes his head up, but a musket fires and shatters the glass above his head. He comes back over. "We can't get out; they've got us surrounded now."

We look up and see thick smoke coming down from the roof, made all the worse by the dampness of the thatch. We're getting steamed within minutes, and the rafters catch fire.

Captain smirks at the impossible situation. "Got a plan for this too, O'Hanlon?"

"Sure, pray!" I say as a large beam collapses.

"Here, put the table back up so we can get under it!" William commands. The smoke's so low, we all start trying to breathe through our coats.

Captain locks eyes with me. "Pleasure working with you, O'Hanlon."

"There's nothing so bad that it couldn't be worse," I say, coughing. "'Tis not over yet."

"Oh, I think 'tis," Cahir says as another beam falls right next to the table, totally engulfed in flames.

Art says, "This is it, Redmond. I'd rather hang than burn in a fire." He starts crawling out from under the table and looks back to us. "Come with me! I don't want to watch you all burn here."

Bawn begins to move out. "Hanging's my choice too. Good luck!"

We watch as they crawl down the hallway.

"I never thought I'd die like this." Captain watches a badly burned beam above us.

There's a commotion around the house—muskets firing suddenly from the woods. We crawl to the window and see the redcoats running from a surprise assault from behind. We immediately drop out the window and flee to the woods to save our bacon. Ned and Hogan gallop up.

Ned cries, "Run to the woods! We'll cover you."

"Where's Bawn and Art?" Hogan asks, looking back at the burning structure once we reach the woods.

"They might be at the door or may have turned themselves in by now."

My eyes well up, watching Síofra, Ned, Hogan, Berragh, Kelly, and Liddy all riding around chasing down the redcoats and making them turn and run. They come trotting proudly back, and to my great joy I see Bawn and Art there with them, still coughing.

"By the time we found the door with all the smoke, we heard the ambush, so we waited until 'twas safe to come out," Bawn says with a ring of soot around his thin mouth.

Cahir gasps at Síofra. "How on earth did you get there so blazing fast?"

"You still doubt my powers, even now?" she says with a charming grin.

"You sent your fairies out?" he asks in awe.

She laughs hard. "No, you fool, I nabbed your flute from you when you were opening the window." He feels his pockets for the flute. "So then I only walked in the woods a little and blew to kingdom come for them to hear me."

Cahir just stares at her in amazement, and I say, "That's why we keep you around, cleverer than all of us combined I think."

"And maybe a bit of help from the fairies." She gives Cahir a wink.

We turn to walk back to our rock home, and hearing the crashing sound of the house caving in, Captain says, "We all better chip in for some repairs."

Our laughter could've been heard for miles.

Chapter 21

In the morning, after our thrill from cheating death has faded, I decide to go talk with Alister about what he might've learned about last night. When I walk into the tavern, he's there in the snug as I expected. I wave to Sean and walk over to my spy right away.

He looks me up and down. "Not a scratch or burn! I'm beginning to doubt you're human."

"Oh, I almost found out."

"Well, you've got a wolf in sheep's clothing I think there, Redmond."

"I know, Alister, I know." I lean back. "So, what have you heard?"

"I found out only an hour before they left that Lucas was going after you at that house. I couldn't do nothing for you then."

"So that means they probably didn't know much ahead, then, right? Which makes sense, since Captain didn't invite us but around noon."

"Can you remember who was with you from that time forward?"

"Yeah, I was at camp and Captain, Art, William, Cahir, Síofra, and Ned never left to go anywhere."

"So, then, who was there at noon that left and came back?"

"Berragh, Liddy, Hogan, Bawn, and Kelly, they all went for lunch after."

"And who was not there at the house at the time of the ambush?"

"Berragh, Liddy, Hogan, and Kelly."

"Well, this morning I asked around and heard that they had inside information from within your camp. And seeing the ambush failed, I was expecting someone to come and talk with Lucas—"

"Did you see something?" I say, losing patience.

"I saw a young boy come in but an hour ago and stayed for a bit and left. I followed him back to the woods where he disappeared."

I felt the heat of my anger surface. "I know who 'tis Alister." I rush to get up.

"Well, tell me, then?"

"It's a young new recruit that's been hanging around our camp the last few weeks—" I pause and throw my head back. "Of course! He started coming around right when I realized someone was leaking."

"I'll let you go deal with him, then."

I take out a pouch, give it under the table, and nod good-bye to Sean. I reach the campfire in a complete rage. I pull Art, Cahir, and Captain aside and tell them of what I learned from my source.

Art says, "The little snitch has gone to the river fishing. Let's go."

We see his skinny form at the banks, bent over, taking a fish off his hook. He gets up nervously, and seeing Art's fierce look, he tries to turn and run. I jump off my horse to chase and leap on him to bring him down. He tries to kick and punch me off, but Cahir's quickly over me, tying his hands and feet. He's about to gag him, but I say, "No, I need to ask him some questions."

I stand him up, tie him to a tree, and stare into his black eyes. His face's so narrow and thin he could kiss a goat between the horns. "What's your name, boy?" I say in a low, slow voice, trying to keep my head.

"Rory."

"Rory, sir!" Art demands. "This one suffers from a double dose of original sin."

Rory stares up, confused by our assault, and says meekly, "Rory, sir."

"Did you go talk to Lieutenant Lucas yesterday?" I ask.

He looks nervously at Art, who's brimming over with anger.

"Tell him where you went boy!" Art yells.

His eyes dart around and he starts shaking. Art slams the trunk above his head and causes the boy to duck.

Rory immediately cries, "Yes, I met with Lucas yesterday."

"Have you gone there before?" Captain asks with a serious glare with one eye closed tighter.

"Yes, twice before, sir," the boy mutters.

"Are you responsible for telling Lucas where to find me?" I ask, beginning to shake.

He pauses a moment. "Yes, but—"

Art flies into a rage and takes something from his pocket, and what happens next happens so fast I couldn't have stopped it. Art shoves the knife into the boy's mouth, and in one sweep, removes a large part of his tongue. Horrified, Cahir and I take a few steps back as the boy gurgles and screams.

I look at Art and say, "Why did you do that?"

"I lost it, Redmond! We all almost died last night because of this rat!"

Captain defends him with, "It is said that he who keeps his tongue keeps his friends, so it should also stand that he who loses his friends loses his tongue."

Cahir and Captain untie the traumatized boy.

"I'm not saying he didn't deserve it, but I would have liked to have gotten more out of him, like if Lucas knows our main site or if he's working with anyone else!"

"Sorry, Redmond, I just lost it." He cleans his knife with his shirt.

Cahir says, "Well, you can nod, can't you? Did you talk of our main camp?"

The boy nods. Art fumes, "I'm going to kill this little traitor!" I have to hold Art back.

"I've an idea." Captain goes to his saddlebag and brings back a quill, ink, and paper. He wets the point and puts the quill in the boy's hand. "What have you told Lucas of our camp?"

The boy stands there crying with his coat sleeve in his mouth. I say, "If you answer this, we'll take you to a doctor."

The boy made an x on the paper—a sign of illiteracy.

I ask him as Art stares him down, "Are you working with anyone else?"

He stares back for a moment but shakes his bloody face back and forth.

Cahir looks to me. "What'll we do with him now?"

"Take him to the doctor, say he got in a fight with an outlaw. Here." I hand him a pouch from Ghost's saddlebag. "Pay the doctor and give the rest to the boy."

Captain says, "We better find a new main camp, though, since we can't be sure what he's told."

"Right, Cahir, meet us all back at the south camp. Rory's never been there." I watch as Cahir lifts him up and holds him still tied on his lap as he rides out.

We all gather at the south camp, and I explain what happened with the boy.

"I can't believe he was giving Lucas movements. I thought he was a good kid," William says, shaking his head.

Kelly nods in approval to Art. "Well, having your tongue cut out for snitching seems justified. I would have done the same."

Liddy and Berragh nod as well.

"It's all over and done with now. But I've learned a good lesson now. With the stakes getting higher, we need to stop bringing in recruits of any kind. We can only trust those that have earned our trust."

Everyone nods in agreement.

"Let's quit talking about this boy now, and talk about where we're headed tonight," Cahir says.

William sits up. "Two days ago, I got wind of a wealthy merchant due on the five o'clock ferry. Pockets and chests full of coin from selling an estate in London."

Captain perks up at this. "Sounds like a job for me. Redmond, why don't you take this one with me?"

"Sure would be nice to have a distraction. I'll meet you at the dark bend on Newry at half past four. I want to check in at the tavern to see if Sean has any messages. William, come with me, and you rest go out and see to your business."

"I can't, Redmond. I have a dinner party to throw, inviting all of the wealthiest of Armagh. After tonight, I'll have some good information to share."

"Fine work, William. So, Liddy, you come along then."

∞∞∞∞∞∞∞∞∞∞∞∞∞∞∞∞∞∞∞∞∞∞

I walk inside the tavern, but I'm surprised to see someone I don't know at the bar. "Where's Sean?"

"You O'Hanlon?" the man asks.

"That depends, who's asking?"

"I'm Sean's cousin. He told me to say his ma's in trouble. She's facing eviction in an hour, and he's gone to try to stave it off. He said to ask you to go help him."

"Do you know how much she owes?"

"£40, or else their taking all her furniture in repayment and putting her out on the streets."

I turned to Liddy. "What time is it now?"

He looks at his watch. "Ten minutes to four."

I sigh. "Okay, Liddy go back to camp and tell Cahir to go in my place. I won't be able to get there in time if I go to help Sean."

"Sure thing, Redmond, if it's a stash you'll be needing, I left £50 in a hole behind the church."

"Thanks for that. Now get going; you'll just have time if you leave now." I watch his tall form walk away with his shoulders hunched, his lanky arms swinging and his feet flopping out like he was wearing shoes three sizes too big.

I get to Sean with the monies right before the bank shows up and meet back at south camp at 5:30. We all sit around waiting to see how much Captain and Cahir pull in. We hear someone run up, and I call and hear one hoot back. Cahir runs through the bushes, out of breath.

"What's wrong, Cahir?" Síofra leaps to her feet.

"It's Captain! He was taken. 'Twas a setup! It wasn't a gent with his pockets full. The carriage was full of soldiers. All undercover! Captain had me stand cover in the woods, and he went up to take the gent, but as soon as he stopped the carriage, he had seven muskets pointed at him."

"How come you didn't help him? How is it you got away?" Art asks.

Cahir smolders. "If I shot at any of them, they would have filled Captain with bullets. I knew the only thing I could do is run and get you all."

I say, "Well, it's not Cahir's fault. It's not the time to bicker. Hogan, you're our fastest rider, you go and try to follow them and see where they take him. Come back and we'll have a plan by then."

"Isn't this Blind Billy's bargain, Redmond?" Art asks. "Don't you think sneaking into the gaol when they'll be expecting us is the nail in your coffin?"

"I made a promise to Captain, and I've got to uphold it."

Cahir turns to me. "There's still a rat among us, though. The boy couldn't have known, since William told us only last night."

"We don't have time for that now. We have to get Captain out. They'll be time for finger pointing after," I say.

"But how can we be sure that someone here's not going to snitch this plan?" Síofra asks.

I look around at everyone at the campfire and say, "Because I'm not letting anyone out of my sight until we've got him back."

Chapter 22

We wait up all night discussing our options based on the gaol he's in. Hogan comes back at four in the morning.

"Where've you been?" Síofra asks.

He sits down. "They took him to Armagh."

"That's good news for us. I know that gaol well," I say.

Cahir smirks. "Redmond, once—"

"Don't you start with that now, Cahir."

"Any other news?" Art asks.

"They've got him in Armagh until tomorrow night. They're going to take him to Downpatrick."

"What?" Berragh asks.

Ned follows with, "Why Downpatrick? That's a day's ride from Armagh!"

"Apparently Captain's charge is that of a murdered merchant. He shot and killed a man in Downpatrick and his relatives want to see him hanged on the spot he killed him."

"Well, we've got to set a plan now and get in to speak to him by tonight, then," I say.

At dawn, William shows up at the fire and asks, "What's going on this early in the morning?"

Cahir stands up and tries to read his face. "You really don't know?"

"Know what? What's happened?" He looks legitimately worried.

I say, "Your tip went wrong. 'Twas a trap, and Captain's been taken to Armagh."

His mouth drops open. "I got that tip from a good source, though. Rory must have told Lucas I'm in league with you."

"Let's not go over this now; we don't have time. Sit down, William, and hear your part."

I make them pledge to stay at the campsite while I leave with William to go to Armagh.

There are sentries all over the place. William and I are dressed in our finest clothes and head to the door with only one guard. When the guard looks up at me, I see 'tis the very same guard I bribed years ago.

"I was hoping you could assist us, guard," I say in my haughtiest English. "I am looking to speak to your notorious prisoner, Richard Power."

"Go around to the front speak to the lieutenant. He's put out orders to let no one visit the prisoner."

"Even if there's money in it for you?" He glances up but stays quiet. I take a step closer and say, "Power robbed my merchant carriage only last week. I knew he and his ruffians hid the large amount of coin I was delivering." I take out a pouch. "All shillings, and if he talks, then I will give you £10 of it."

He opens the pouch to check the amount, then whispers, "I'll have to wait until the lieutenant leaves, and then when I wave you over, go right into the room on your left. Tell the guard there that Percy says he'll give you a cut."

William and I wait for about an hour, and we see Lucas leave with two men, and Percy waves for us. When we walk by him, he says, "Now be quick about it, the lieutenant will be right back."

Once through the next guard, we open the door to see Captain lying on his cot, whistling. He smiles upon seeing us. "Sweet is your hand in a pitcher of honey! Good to see you're a man of your word, Redmond."

"Well, we're not here to bust you out just yet. The building's surrounded with guards, but I came to tell you my plan. Before you're set to leave tonight, me and my men will come and light every building in the town on fire. All the troops will be scattered and busy putting out fires, and in that chaos we can break in to rescue you." I smile, proud of the plan we came up with, but Captain shakes his head.

"No, that won't do. It's not just the guards you see around the building here. Lucas, expecting you might come, has brought most of his troops from Ulster in while I'm here."

"Well, you got a better plan, then?" William asks.

"Actually, I do." He gives a smug smile. "They're transporting me to Downpatrick tonight, but since we're traveling at night, midway they're going to stop for lodging. And guess which inn they're planning on lodging at?"

"Sean's?" I can't believe the luck.

"Sure thing. I bribed my guard for the details. It's a better time to free me, since there's only a small troop of infantrymen under Lucas."

There's a tap on the door. "Times up!" the guard says.

"Fine, we'll have a plan ready for the inn." I get ready to go.

William nods. "Sit tight, Captain. The Lord will open a gap for you."

"Wait." Captain puts out his hand. "I need some coin to pay my bribe."

I hand him a pouch and leave with William. On our way out, the guard asks if we got the location of his stash.

"No, the thief didn't open his mouth." I take out another small pouch for him and say, "Thank you for your troubles."

William and I race back to camp to pull together a new plan. By nightfall, we all mount with our saddlebags full of ammunition and loaded guns and head to the tavern.

"They're staying here? Are you sure, Redmond?" Sean asks.

I reply, "'Tis the word. They're coming right through here, and they're planning to stop for the night, with Captain."

"Oh, Redmond, you know I'd want to help you and Captain, but if we do what you say, someone's going to come back and suspect me as an insider." He starts panicking.

"Sean, we can't do this without your help."

Sean bends over and tries to breathe in and out to calm himself. "You've been so good to me and my ma, how can I say no? But," he emphasizes, breathing quicker again, "you'll have to wound me in some safe way to cast suspicion off me."

"If that's what you want, I'm sure we can think of something," I say. "We better get in position. They'll be here shortly."

I wait in the woods, and in my position, I can see when they arrive. I hear the troop coming and let a breath out in relief when it pulls to a stop at the tavern. Lucas gets out of the carriage first, and he gives the order for all men to stand guard as they secure the inn and bring the prisoner out. Lucas goes in for some moments; then one of his men gives a whistle, and they bring out Captain heavily manacled. After ten minutes, all the men are allowed in.

When I open the ancient door, I pretend to be caught off guard by the full room of soldiers.

The men turn to stare at me, in one of Bawn's most ruffly and lacy pale blue outfits.

"Little Bo Peep has come for a drink!" Lucas exclaims to the enjoyment of everyone.

I wear a long, curly haired wig under my plumed hat and hope I look different enough to fool Lucas.

Síofra heads my way with her tray. "You pay them no mind, sir. What will you have to drink, then?"

I look to see where Sean is, and I see him bent over behind the bar.

I put on a thick French accent and say, "I'll have some cognac." I walk over to Lucas and ask, "What is all this?"

Lucas appears impressed by my worldly accent and changes his tone.

"We're here transporting one of Armagh's most infamous characters, Richard Power."

I feign a touch of fear. "Is this not safe here?"

"Oh, no, it's safe. We have him manacled up there with four armed guards on watch. There's probably no safer inn tonight."

Síofra brings my glass and I turn to Lucas. "Will you share one of France's best cognac with me?"

Lucas's eyes flash, and he replies with a smarmy smile, "I think I could manage that."

I turn to Síofra. "Bring us the whole bottle and a glass for my friend here."

As she walks away, I whistle at her swaying backside. "These Irish women are beautiful in the extreme!"

Lucas studies Síofra intently. "This one is rather unusual."

Síofra comes quickly back and smiles seductively at Lucas as she's placing the bottle and glass down.

I stand up. "Pints for all the guards keeping me safe tonight!"

They cheer, and Sean, finally pulling his nerves together, gets to work filling the pints. I turn back to Lucas, who is still set on Síofra while he sips his cognac. I throw back mine and ask her to fill my glass back up for me.

She says as she's pouring, "I love a man who can throw back his liquor."

I say, "Well, then, come and sit on my lap as I drink it."

Síofra comes over with a wide smile and sits on the edge of my lap. I wink at Lucas, who immediately throws back his glass too.

Lucas catches up quickly, and Síofra says, "You sure can handle your liquor too, Lieutenant."

I push her off my lap. "I am a generous man, go on."

Síofra spins between us and lands on the lieutenant's lap, and seeing the troops have finished their pints, I say, "Another two rounds of pints on me!"

Lucas is too enamored with Síofra tickling his chin to have heard it. I lean over to Lucas, annoying him slightly since it distracted Síofra away from him, and say, "Lieutenant, I would give anything to see a swarthy fellow like Power. Is there any way I can get a little peek?"

He says, "Go, it's the second room on the right of the stairs." He turns back to Síofra, who is giggling and leaning into him.

I walk upstairs and wave to the four guards, who stand at my appearance. "The good lieutenant has allowed me to get a little peek at your prisoner. I've heard much of your outlaws and wanted to see one for myself."

They look at each other. One nods and opens the door a crack. I already know which room Sean was going to get the lieutenant to pick, but I have to check if there are any guards within the room. I peek in, and Captain, seeing me in my ridiculous disguise, beams and gives a girlish wave. I nearly laugh and pull my head back quickly to compose myself.

"Oh, he is a shady fellow. To show my thanks, I will send you up a couple of rounds."

They give me a quick bow of thanks, and I walk down and nod to Sean, who brings strong drinks up.

Síofra's now holding the lieutenant's cognac up to his lips and giggling away as he drinks. I walk over to Lucas and say, "I'll be right back. I have to go make my water."

But Lucas sweeps his hand for me to go, too engaged in Síofra to care. I pretend to be looking for a place to go and dart around back to the window I know Captain to be at, and check that Lucas didn't put any guards back there. Seeing 'tis all clear, I whistle three times for the all-clear signal, and eight of my men come out of the trees.

"William, Art, Cahir, Kelly, Ned, Liddy, and Hogan go in the secret chamber to the upstairs hall and tie and gag the four guards. Captain is alone and manacled, so you will have to break the shackles with the butt of a musket—"

"That will make a terrible noise, though. What will we do about that?" Ned interrupts.

"I was about to say there, when you jumped in, that I will get Sean to play his fiddle, and Síofra and I will get everyone dancing and singing to an old English song. We'll cause such a ruckus, they won't hear a thing." They all nod. "Cahir whistle for Ghost and get him to put his legs up like you trained him and you all can slide down his back. The rest of the plan still stands, and Bawn, you stay to hold the horses."

I head back in, and the room's swaying with drink. I look to Sean to bring out his fiddle, and he starts playing. I start to sing at the top of my lungs, and some of the more intoxicated fellows join in. Síofra bounces off Lucas's lap and begins to dance around the floor like a pixie. She keeps her eyes fixed on Lucas as she spins around, and it appears that she's dancing just for him. I glance up, seeing the boys struggling in the hall, and even see Cahir turn to look at Síofra wide-eyed in jealousy, but a hand pulls him back. Since the whole room's singing the chorus, nothing's heard from the landing.

I yell at the end of the chorus, "One more time!" and Sean keeps playing while the men keep singing. I hear one slight bang and know they're breaking the manacles, and I start to stamp around on the floor at every beat. Síofra throws her weight down to do the same, and it catches on, and all the men are stamping. The old tavern seems to rock with vibrations as the plaster starts crumbling in places on the ceiling, and at the last note, I stamp wildly, ending with one loud jump.

Everyone cheers, and Lucas immediately brings Síofra back to his lap. I sit back down with them out of breath and I say, "I forgot to send the guards upstairs a round of drinks." I turn to Sean. "Go bring them two bottles."

Lucas hardly notices. After five minutes, I say, "Where has the barkeep gone to?"

Lucas turns slightly. "Upstairs."

I go back upstairs and to my dismay see the guards all lying in blood on the floor. I check each one for breath—all dead. Sean comes limping in from the other room with a knife stuck in his leg.

He whispers, mighty proud of himself, "What do you think, Redmond, look good?"

I say, "Lie down, then, so you appear badly injured, and put some of their blood on you so you look like you've got more stabs."

I take a moment to check out the back window to be sure they all got away, and once I see no one, I run to the landing and yell, "Lieutenant, come quick!"

He sobers up immediately and pushes Síofra off his lap so fast she falls to the floor with a yelp. Lucas and four men run up the stairs with arms, see the dead men with bloody Sean moaning on top of them, and search the room for Power and the intruders. Lucas picks up the broken manacles and swings them at the window, breaking the glass.

He screams, "Check all the rooms to be sure, and everyone to their horses!"

They file out of the tavern, and each man— so clearly drunk— has difficultly mounting his horse. Lucas throws his hat down and yells, "Pull yourselves together, men!"

He kicks his horse and speeds down the path. I whistle for my horse and catch up quickly. He gives me a glance. "Glad to have you with us."

"Let's catch the scoundrel! Where do you think they're headed?"

He squints at the road. "They look like they're headed away from the mountains. We'll just keep following them."

I smile, knowing Hogan has reversed all of their horses' shoes. I check behind and see that the troops are in terrible formation, some lagging way behind. After following the tracks back to the woods, he looks back at his men and curses. The woods are pitch black, and the tracks are lost. Lucas spits, and rears his horse. "Men, go back to the tavern. We've lost the trail. We'll have to begin again in the morning. And don't mention to any superiors about any liquor!"

He charges down toward the tavern and I slowly drift off to follow the path to where they're really headed. By the time I reach them, they've started a fire in the middle of the bog and are laughing about the events of the night.

Once they see me, Captain stands up. "Three cheers for O'Hanlon!"

They give three cheers for me, and I take a bow. We laugh and toast into the night, even in the midst of treachery.

∞∞∞∞∞∞∞∞∞∞∞∞∞∞∞∞∞∞∞∞

In the morning, Captain pulls me aside. "I'd love nothing better than to tarry and fight alongside you, Redmond, but it looks like you have a caged wolf here."

I nod. "Sorry 'bout that."

"No worries. It is a long road that has no turning." He breathes out. "I'm going back on my own again, and I suggest it might be the best thing for you to do too."

I shake my head. "I will find out who did this."

"That's what I'm afraid of." He smiles and gives me a pat on my back. "I'll never forget you, though, O'Hanlon, and my promise still holds that I'll come back to help you if you ever need it."

"I know you will, Captain."

"Say good-bye to everyone for me. I think it's best they don't see which direction I'm headed in." He laughs heartily as he gets on his horse.

"Captain!" He turns. "May you die in bed at ninety-five, shot by a jealous spouse!"

He laughs. "May the road rise up to meet you.
May the wind always be at your back.
May the sun shine warm upon your face,
And rains fall soft upon your fields.
And until we meet again,
May God hold you in the palm of His hand."

I watch him saunter off with his face to the sun.

Chapter 23

Alister sits beside me in the snug. He has a worried look on his face. "What is it now?" I sigh, getting used to bad news.

"Where's Sean?"

"Oh, he stabbed himself in the leg to cast suspicion away during the breakout. He's mending at his ma's."

"You've got some pretty loyal members there, O'Hanlon. Don't know if I'd stab myself in the leg for you."

"I hate to tell you now, but you're putting your life on the line for me just meeting like this." He smiles. "So what's the word now?"

"My troop was invited to guard William St. John's party two nights back. I was trying to keep my eyes and ears open, when none other than Lieutenant Lucas walked in. St. John went to greet him like an old friend, and the two of them had a long discussion out of earshot."

I'm quiet.

"It all makes sense. He's paying you back for what you did to his father. He hired that boy to be his go-between, and now he's forced to meet with him in person."

"But he was there with us in the house when we were ambushed. He got shot."

Alister sits back. "He probably thought they would've killed you all quickly, and what better cover than to be there too?"

"I don't know; it doesn't sit right."

"You're not seeing what's right in front of you. Here, was William close to this boy?"

I nod.

"And did William know you'd be on that road the day of the roadblock?"

I nod.

"Did William know about meeting at the house?"

"Yeah, but—"

"But nothing, he knew. And didn't he tell you to take that carriage from the ferry? Plus he met with Lucas that blazing night to confirm that you were after it? This William's a blue lookout."

I take it all in. "I better go have a talk with him, then." I go to slide a pouch over, and he pushes it back toward me.

"No, I did this as your friend, Redmond."

"I'll have none of your slack-jaw, soldier. Take this money."

But he just smiles and walks out.

∞∞∞∞∞∞∞∞∞∞∞∞∞∞∞∞∞∞∞∞∞∞∞∞

I gather everyone back at camp that night. I start, "What I am afraid to hear I'd better say first myself. We all know there's a bad member here among us." Everyone looks around at each other. "I hate to think it, but it's plain to see." I take a breath and stare at William. "I hear Lucas attended your party."

Everyone makes some sort of noise at the surprise, but William keeps his eyes on mine. "He did come to my party, but I didn't invite him."

Cahir speaks. "Did you talk to him?"

He glares at Cahir. "Why, then, I did talk to him."

Everyone's in an uproar I put my hands down to quiet them. William starts to speak,

"When I saw him come through the door, I decided it might be a good idea to talk to him, try to find out who might be meeting with him."

Art shrieks, "Likely story, St. John!"

That's the first time anyone called him that for a while, and it seems like it struck a nerve.

William turns back to me. "Do you think me a stag? That I'd inform on you?" He looks deep in my eyes. "Why would I be the snitch when I got myself shot and almost killed in that house?" He holds up his tied-up arm.

"I don't know, maybe you had some kind of deal or something?" I give away my uncertainness by making it a question.

"Look." William's getting upset now. "I didn't need to stay with you all. I could've gone back right after you released me to go to Lucas, but I didn't. I fought with you all. I gave you the best tips for the fattest purses. I've risked my life along with you all for years! If I wanted to get some kind of revenge, why would I wait this long?" After he speaks, he puts his thumbnail in between the space in his teeth, deeply anxious.

He's right; he wouldn't have waited this long if 'twas revenge from the kidnapping.

William keeps going. "So you all figured out a way that makes this sound like me, but every one of you knew Rory, and many of you had the opportunity to go meet with Lucas after I told you all about the carriage that night."

He's right again; they all had access to the boy, and all went out in the day that Captain was taken.

"Redmond, you're not actually listening to this Gobshite!" says Art. "What would the cat's son do but kill a mouse?"

"Well, then, if you did talk to Lucas, how come you never told any of us about it?" Ned asks.

"Because I didn't get anything out of him! He talked incessantly about being brought up in rank and could I put a good word in for him. I said, 'Not until you've caught O'Hanlon,' and he laughed and said, 'All in good time, all in good time.' Do any of you think that's newsworthy? I forgot all about it when I heard that Captain was taken."

I can tell the others don't trust him anymore, and I realize I shouldn't have done this in front of everyone. I look in his green eyes, and I don't see a touch of guilt or deceit. I know I have to prove to everyone that he can be trusted again.

"If it's true, why would William have waited so long for revenge? Doesn't make a bit of sense, not one bit. I believe him when he says he didn't give information to Lucas, and I trust William."

Some nod, and some look away.

"Well, on a whole other subject, there's the fair in Banbridge tomorrow, and we all know the gents and ladies that come back are loaded with money and prize animals." I give a stern look around and say, "And I won't be telling anyone which road I'm going to wait on for my health!"

Cahir looks up. "You want me and Art to come, then?"

I almost agree but see William sitting there, deflated. "No, Cahir, I think I'll bring William to help me, to show good faith."

William glances up. "I'll be glad to come help you, Redmond."

Cahir lets the air whoosh from his mouth in an exaggerated way, causing his whole body to blow back. "You've got a death wish, Redmond. We might as well be whistling jigs to a milestone."

"Don't take me up till I fall, Cahir."

"Oh, very well, let you take what you'll get. Let's go, then Síofra. It's like my ma always said, 'Don't give cherries to pigs or advice to fools.'"

Síofra gets up to go with him. "God be with you, O'Hanlon." Then she gives a curious look to William. "Take care of him, William."

They leave, and Art leans in. "I'll come with you and keep an eye on things." He glances at William.

"Fine, then, you and William, come with me, and we'll leave at dawn."

∞∞∞∞∞∞∞∞∞∞∞∞∞∞∞∞∞∞∞∞∞

'Tis a beautiful spring morning. The dew's thick, and the birds are already out singing. I lead them to the spot I want in Hilltown, right on the other side of the mountain so we can surprise those coming over. We make such good time even going uphill that we have half a day before the fair's even finished.

"William, go check to see if that cottage is occupied."

William hops off and walks down the hill to knock on the door. After a moment, he kicks the door in and yells, "All clear!"

Art and I take our horses down slowly, and William says, "It looks like someone hasn't been here in a while. The cot's full of dust and dirt, and there's no food to be found anywhere."

"Well, I didn't get much sleep last night, so I could pass the time with a nice nap."

Art says, "It's too dangerous for us all to nap at the same time in these parts, so we should stand guard for each other."

"True. We'll go hide our horses behind the house, and we'll let William take the first watch."

William agrees, heads outside to hide the horses, and I hear him sit outside with his back to the door. I search around, see a pile of wool blankets, and hand two to Art. I get between the blankets and close my eyes. Something moves, and I open my eyes to see Art staring at me.

"I just can't close my eyes with him out there."

"If I can trust him, then so should you." I roll over and close my eyes again.

I don't know how long I'd been asleep, but footsteps behind me cause me to wake up. I start to slowly grab for my pistol under the blanket, and once I have it in my hand, I spin around with my pistol up but take a blast to my gut. I look back up in shock and see Art at the end of the carbine.

I can barely breathe, and my whole stomach's on fire. "Art, *you* sold me?"

Hearing the gunshot, William bounds through the door and fires but misses. Art runs at William, hitting him in the head with the butt of the gun, knocking William to the ground. Art escapes out the door.

William moves toward me, and his green eyes connect with mine as I try to catch my breath. I laugh and say, "See... I knew it wasn't you."

William laughs slightly and tries to look at my wound. His face tells me I have only moments left. He picks my head up and puts it in his lap, and I try to talk through my shallow breaths and pain.

"An oak is often split... by a wedge from its own... branch."

"I shouldn't have left you. I should've known."

"Never mind that all." I wave a hand feebly in the air. "Promise me one thing, William."

"Anything."

"As soon as I take... my last breath... I want you to take my head—"

"Take your head?"

"Listen. I'm sure Art's... on his way right now to Lucas somewhere... close by. Once he... gives him this location... they'll swarm the place. I don't want them to get... my head. I don't want it put... on a spike for my ma... to see."

He starts crying without noise, just quick tears streaming down his face. "Why don't I put you over Ghost and bring all of you back?"

"Because... you're going to have... to fly from here. They might be waiting... all over these roads."

I have a terrible sharp pain, and my head's getting dizzy. "Promise me, William...! Take my head... and hide it somewhere... Lucas can't find it!"

"All right, All right, I'll hide it."

"Good, then... as soon as I'm gone... wrap and run... and be sure to... take Ghost with you." I relax a bit and I seem to be going numb. "You know... I almost shot you... and your father... fishing in the Cusher?"

"What do you mean?"

"You must've been... only eight or nine but... I snuck up to shoot... your dad and out... you splashed and... I just didn't feel like... taking two lives that day."

"Should I thank you for not murdering me?" He laughs through his tears.

"I... want to say..." I start losing my vision and my voice slows, "Sorry... I... ever... doubted... you... O'Sheil."

His tears hit my face, and I feel myself fading. My breathing slows and then stops. The world goes dark.

Beacons	Life 1 Ancient Egypt	Life 2 Ancient Sparta	Life 3 Viking Denmark	Life 4 Medieval England	Life 5 Renaissance Italy	Life 6 Golden Age Spain	Life 7 Cromwellian Ireland
Mole on left hand—Prophetic dreams	Sokaris	Alcina	Liam	Elizabeth	Lucrezia	Luis	Redmond O'Hanlon
Scar on forehead—Large, honey- brown eyes—Magic	Bastet	Ophira	Erna	Rowan	Sancia	Andres	Síofra
Space between teeth—Green sparkling eyes	Nun	Theodon	Thora	Simon	Alfonso of Aragon	Pepe	William St. John
Mole by wide-set, dark eyes	Nebu	Mother	Ansgar	Malkyn	Adriana	Old Man	Father
Freckles—Brown eyes	Khons	Arcen	Keelin-Mother	Emeline	Caterina	Nora	Muirin O'Hanlon
Birthmark above knee—Amber eyes	Edjo	Kali	Dalla	Lady Jacquelyn	Cesare	King James	Art O'Hanlon
Two moles on jaw—Black eyes	Apep	Leander	Ragnar	Brom—Children's Father	Rodrigio	Hector	Rory
Picks teeth—Steel-grey eyes	Vizier	Magistrate	Seamus-Father	Ulric	Michelotto	William Fitzwilliam	Lt. Lucas
Golden eyes—Animal	Sehket-Cat	Proauga-Horse	Borga-Goose	Mousie-kitten	Fia-Falcon	Bella-Dog	Ghost-Horse
Scar on forearm—Slate-blue eyes	*	Nereus	Chief Toke	Daniel	Pope Alexander VI	Captain de Cuellar	Captain Power
Big Smile—Grey-blue eyes	*	Demetrius	Una	*	Perotto	Bishop Derry	Brian Kelly
Dimpled cheek—Brown-green eyes	*	*	Rolf	Hadrian	Alfonso d'Este Duke of Ferrara	Mac-Clancy	Alister
Indigo eyes—Musician / Dancer	*	*	Gunhilda	Oliver	Juan	Alvaro	Cahir Dempsey
Orange Hair—Hazel eyes	*	*	Inga	Maid Helena	Guilia	Carra	Pedlar Bawn
Widow's peak—Ice blue eyes	*	*	Konr	Fendel	Isabella	Judge Advocate	Ned of the Hill
Bray laugh	*	*	Orm	Gussalen	*	Urard	Paul Liddy
Pointed ears	*	*	Hela	*	Niccolo	*	Galloping Hogan

Scar above eye	*	*	*	*	Jofre	Celtic Warrior	Strong John MacPher-son
Beady eyes— Cleft Chin	*	*	*	*	Sforza	Philippe	Shane Berrah
Breaks out in nervous hives	*	*	*	*	*	Frozen-traumatized man	Sean the Barkeep
Fish-lips—Empty, dull eyes	*	*	*	*	*	Nessa	Henry St. John
Very rosy cheeks	*	*	*	*	*	Old Woman	Mother

* = Not present in that life

Epilogue

I clutch for the hole in my stomach, and I'm happy to find it gone. I open my eyes to the glow of the same sunset, as whales breech on the shoreline and spew water spouts behind me. Flocks of small birds fly together and shape-shift like fish in the sea over the dunes. I close my eyes and listen to the soothing sounds of the ocean and the seabirds.

It could have been five minutes, or it could have been five years that I sat there. I understand now how Zachariah said time didn't exist here. I lie back on the worn vinyl seat. Zachariah waits a moment and then ventures, "Are you all right?"

I let out a long exhale. "This going back and forth is getting harder and harder."

He only nods.

"In the beginning, it was a shock to open my eyes and see another body, but when I come back into the body I know so well, know as me, it feels foreign, suddenly."

Who am I now?

He gazes out the window as if staring at something far off in the distance. Something I cannot see. I start to wonder if he has heard me at all, when he surprises me with an answer.

"It is important you *feel* your soul instead of *see* your soul."

When he speaks it's as if his words are thick and heavy—strung together with molasses. Every sentence, every word has to be digested slowly, for fear I might miss something profound. Something incredibly valuable. I swallow each word and try to absorb what he means.

How can you feel your soul?

"Before you touch my arm, I have no idea what I'll see next, and suddenly I wake up in another body—another world."

"Scary and intriguing at the same time," he remembers. A glimmer of wistfulness flashes in his eyes.

"I feel instantly attached and completely submerged, and then just as quickly, I'm pulled away. Like a whole world exploded and disappeared right before my eyes."

"Soul whiplash." He sums it all up in two words.

"That's exactly what it feels like."

Silence settles in around us and causes us both to shift in our seats. He points to the old beach house and opens his creaky car door. "Come on."

I grab the old car handle, which takes quite a bit of pressure to release. We walk together on the top of the dunes, following a narrow pathway, with the long grasses reaching out and tickling my arms. Summer seems to be ending here, the wind chases away all remnants of the hot sun.

I try to fill the space between us. "Does everyone have a famous life?" I think of Lucrezia and Redmond.

"The odds are that after a certain amount of lives, you're bound to have one or two. It is a whole other lesson when you choose to be someone in the spotlight. There are benefits to fame, but you have seen there are many pitfalls to it also."

We reach the beach house and walk up the sandy steps that lead to an extra wide wraparound porch littered with chipped white rocking chairs. Zachariah walks to the farthest end and chooses a chair overlooking the quiet bay.

"Did the captain ever make it to shore? What about Bella? Oh, please tell me that she made it."

He shakes his head, unyielding. "You will have plenty of time to find out those answers later. Right now we have to stay focused."

Focus. It's so hard with all the questions cropping up in my head.

"When I was inside Edinburg castle, I had an over whelming feeling of déjà vu, but I'd never been in that castle before?"

He pauses a moment to search his memory. "The rich, ornate furnishings reminded you of your previous life in Italy. You will find the more lives you live, the more moments you will feel that nostalgia."

"Is it possible to remember a past life while you're alive?"

"It is possible, and some people are very impressive with what detail they can recall, but for the most part, people remember little of the lives they led before. Although, many times, young children have been known to remember details of the last life they lived, but it usually disappears by the time they are four or five."

"I thought you said, though, that full consciousness is harmful if you access it within a life?"

"The small amount that people might remember doesn't cause any harm."

I raise my eyes to look at the sky-blue-painted bead-board ceiling to think. "So this is the life I learned devotion to a higher cause?"

"A larger cause. You can't really say thievery is a high cause." He laughs.

"William, or Pepe, picked us this time? Over St. John?"

"Yes, he chose you this time."

"Is that why I didn't completely trust him? Some leftover feeling from abandoning me in the last life?"

Zachariah moves his head in agreement. "It was residual."

"That was the first time he's left us... left me."

First, but not the last.

"We are all on our own path. This can bring people together as well as split them apart."

Thinking of splitting, I ask, "Who was Nessa? Was she new?"

"Yes, she was new in your life, but not to Pepe."

"Oh, so he knew her from before." I understand a little more.

"Although you have a group that incarnates with you, that doesn't mean those in your group don't have others as well." He emphasizes these last words with his brows raised in a Mister Rogers'-message-sort-of-way.

Nevertheless, that doesn't stop the jealousy from setting in. I don't like the idea of the people I've become attached to being attached to other people. I rock myself back and forth, and the sound of the swaying on the planked porch is soothing. He rocks his chair in time with mine.

"Those dreams I had about drowning and watching a boy drown with me. That was residual from the last life too?"

"Trauma tends to stay with you subconsciously."

"I even said Andres."

"You tap into your subconscious much better than some."

I start chuckling. "I even named the captain, Captain again."

"I couldn't believe it when you came up with that." He cracks a smile.

"That cross Captain ripped from Harry was the very same cross Carra stole from him in the previous life."

He nods. "You will see certain objects reappearing. With each life you lead, the more attached you'll get to objects, songs, people, and places."

"So was being devoted one of the big lessons?"

"That was the second big lesson. At first, you were devoted to the wrong people; then, you were devoted to the right people; and lastly, you were devoted to a larger cause. A cause that reached beyond your own selfish pursuits to try to bring change or ease the suffering of many people."

"So I've learned two big lessons now, sacrifice and devotion?"

"Right. Can you see any other smaller lessons you might have learned in this life?"

I think for a moment. "I learned to trust people, but I guess that got me in the end."

"Well, it's good to trust people, even if they let you down."

I let that sink in a bit, but something inside fights its absorption. All the faces of O'Hanlon's life flash through my mind's eye, until it stops on one picking his teeth. "I learned how to get my facilitator pretty good."

He laughs. "Yes, you might have gotten him good a few times, but he was behind Art murdering you."

He steals the breath from me. "*He* set Art up for that?"

"You never noticed it, but Art held great jealousy of you your whole life: his parents died; yours were relatives of lords; you were sent to school; you became a leader; you got Muirin. I think the last straw was that he held you responsible for her death. He felt if you had come, she would have recovered. Lucas approached him by chance right after."

"I never saw all that."

"Art brought Rory in to help him bring messages, and he paid him to befriend William to set him up for the fall."

It's all settling in. "He cut Rory's tongue out so he couldn't point fingers."

He nods. "Art kept setting you up, but you always outsmarted Lucas. Art decided he was going to have to do it himself."

"I never thought it could've been him."

"Well, water under the bridge now. It all was important for you."

"So, I guess Lucas did get me in the end, then."

"Yes, he did, but you sure gave him a good fight." Sea-glass eyes sparkle as he remembers something. "You brought up facilitators before, and I realized I forgot to tell you about another important person."

"Who?"

"We call them catalysts, or the person who assists you to reach a common objective."

"Who would that be in my lives?"

"In this last one, it was your da. He made sure you were educated, which was key to you being able to lead, fight, and disguise yourself. It came at great sacrifice to him, but if you had not done that, you would never have been a legend."

"Was he the old man in the armada life?"

"Right. It was important for you to be safe when you ran away, and he helped you feel like there was someone there for you when you had no one."

"I don't see what Adriana catalyzed, though?"

"If you had stayed with your mother, you wouldn't have had the interaction you had with Cesare or your father. Because you went to live with Adriana and she was your father's cousin, you were able to get close to them."

"Malkyn is obvious. Had she not opened her door to the sick, I wouldn't have had any place to go with Rowan and Oliver."

"Right, and Nebu was the one who brought you and Bastet together."

My rocking lulls me into a trance. "I never would've realized that soul was responsible for so much."

"It's usually hard to see, but it's extremely important."

The bay is so still it looks like a painting. "Is it time to go back again?"

"That is all I can think of." He sits, up getting ready to touch my arm. "The next one is one of your favorites." He shuts his mouth with a suspicious grin.

"Are you being sarcastic? Usually the first life of the next big lesson is miserable."

"What do you mean?" He laughs.

"I usually make the biggest mistakes in the beginning lives."

Zachariah appears to choose his words carefully. "That may be true, but I promise I'm not being sarcastic. This next life is one you hold very dear."

"That's a relief. Well, then." I take a few breaths. "Time to go back down the rabbit hole."

He gives a reassuring smile, places his hand on mine, and everything goes dark.

Acknowledgements

This book would never have existed without the help of the following people:

Patricia, my mother, for always being there and forever fueling my creativity.

Erin, my sister and writing buddy, the one I listen to for all my writing ideas and problems. (erinwaters.com)

EJ, my husband, for allowing me to go after my dream.

Scott, my son, for all your smiles and hugs.

Annabelle, my baby girl, the newest light of my life,

Edward, my father, for reading my first drafts—and never saying I'm wasting my time.

Jessica, my niece, for being my young-adult guinea pig and one of my fastest readers.

Richard Webb, my amazing history teacher, who wrote on one of my assignments that I would be a writer one day. Your contagious love of history and exuberant encouragement inspired me.

Bethany Yeager, writer & critique partner extraordinaire, my other go-to-girl for everything writing. (beyeager.blogspot.com)

Donna, for creating my fantastic covers & graphics. (digitaldonna.com)

Linda Ingmanson, my thorough and superb editor.

Bethany Beard, my super-quick and excellent copy editor. (lastdraftediting.com)

Guido Henkel, for formatting both my ebook and print book. (guidohenkel.com)

Absolute Write Forum Members & Kindle Boards Forum Members, for tons of writing, publishing, and promoting advice.

Bibliography

Bradford, Sarah. *Lucrezia Borgia*. New York: Penguin Books, 2004. Print.

Dunford, Stephen. *The Irish Highwaymen*. Dublin: Wolfhound Press, 2005. Print.

Francisco de Cuellar. *Captain Cuellar's Adventures in Connacht and Ulster*. Corpus of Electronic Texts Edition. Web.

Hanson, Neil. *The Confident Hope of a Miracle: The True Story of the Spanish Armada*. New York: Vintage Books, 2003. Print.

Howarth, David. *The Voyage of the Armada: The Spanish Story*. Connecticut: The Lyons Press, 2001. Print.

Island Ireland Documents. Island Ireland. Web. 12 Dec. 2011.

Kilfeather, T.P. *Ireland: Graveyard of the Spanish Armada*. Dublin: Anvil Books, 1967. Print.

McCallen, Jim. *Stand & Deliver: Stories of Irish Highwaymen*. Dublin: Mercier Press, 1993. Print.

Oggins, Robin S. *The Kings and Their Hawks: Falconry in Medieval England*. New Haven: Yale University Press, 2004. Print.

Made in the USA
Coppell, TX
22 June 2021